SIXTEEN
Summers

Diann—
Happy
reading!

Also by Caitlin Moss:
THE CRACKS BETWEEN US

SIXTEEN
Summers

CAITLIN MOSS

Cover design by Canva
Photography by Caitlin Moss

ISBN: 9798511321714

For my amazing children—

Isaiah, Maci, Emmie.

I love you so much.

Summer 16

BROKEN HEARTS AREN'T *supposed to hurt this bad.*
At least I never really thought they could. Tate wasn't supposed to die first. He promised me he wouldn't, anyway. I told him I never wanted to live a day without him, and he told me he'd never let me. It was a sentiment I took as gospel, not realizing how far beyond his control it was.

The last thing he said to me was he loved me, and he'd be back soon. His hands cradled my face and I smiled into a kiss as he pressed his lips against mine. They tasted like citrus—familiar and sweet.

We were out of butter. That was why he died.

After our first date sixteen summers ago, we started an end of summer tradition making berry cobbler and the crumble on top was never complete without the richness of butter melted with brown sugar. I asked him to run to the store for me—a simple, mundane errand that turned my life into a complete tragedy.

He never made it to the store.

For the first hour he was dead, I was mad at him. Charlie,

1

just six-months-old, was hoisted on my hip and I was irritated because Tate was late—it shouldn't have taken that long to run to the store for one thing. I assumed he started wandering the aisles, buying unnecessary snacks for the kids. Or maybe he dropped off in the book section and started reading. Words always distracted him. Sucked him in after the first sentence and he couldn't stop until he read the last whimsical and poetic line. It was an endearing quality, but I tolerated it more than I loved it. Especially in that moment, during Charlie's witching hour when I really needed Tate home to hold him so I could finish the dessert before bedtime.

An hour after he left there was a knock on the front door. I opened it in an irritated frenzy, swinging the door until it hit the wall in the entryway. Once then twice. I started to give an apology for my unintentionally aggressive welcoming, but the breath left my lungs as soon as I saw the police chaplain on my doorstep with a uniformed police officer. I was so confused I barely muttered a hello.

"Are you Tabitha Jones?" the chaplain asked.

I read his lips as he said my name, but I didn't hear the sound. My eyes narrowed on their solemn faces, and I glanced down at the chaplain's hands.

He was holding Tate's wallet.

My feet and hands went numb. Fear and shock drenched my entire being.

Not him. Not my Tate.

But I knew.

It didn't matter what the chaplain said because I knew Tate was gone.

At first there was silence. A quiet so loud it screamed in my ears as I tried to make sense of what was happening. I walked around hollow and numb, nodding at the news, letting it sink into my skin until I wore it inside every inch of my being. My chest was tight, and I didn't want it to release for I knew it was closely holding the most delicate and sacred part of me.

Then finally my throat hitched, my heart dropped, and a cry escaped my lungs. It sounded like my entire life shattering like glass.

I WOULD HAVE given anything to linger in that last kiss a moment longer. I wished I had run my hands over his shoulders and laced my fingers in his. I wished I brushed his brown hair away from his forehead and stared at his green eyes as long as I could. I wished I laid my head on his chest to hear his heart beating one last time. I wished I had told him, it was fine, and I'd make something else for dessert, even though cobbler was his favorite. I wished I said it was a stupid and unimportant tradition.

I wish. I wish. I wish.

Everything I had come to know crumbled the instant I knew Tate died.

The memory of him was still so fresh and vivid for me to believe he was really gone. I could still see his green eyes and his perfectly crooked smile. I could still hear him whisper good night in the dark even as his side of the bed lay empty. I could still see him dancing in the kitchen. I still knew exactly how it felt to be loved by him.

All of these things were still so real to the touch in my mind but now, they were just memories.

I wished I knew it was our last summer together, though, there wasn't anything I would have done differently. Our son, Toby, had turned ten and he reminded me more and more of Tate every day. He had his mannerisms and his eyes. He was still just a boy, but I often saw glimpses of him as a man. Charlie was only six months old and a spit fire of a baby. It didn't bother me though—we had waited so long to have him. I never expected it to be as hard and painful as it was to get pregnant a second time. I got pregnant with Toby unexpectedly and quickly, but it was nearly a decade of fertility drugs and completely giving up hope before two lines appeared on a pregnancy test again.

We were a complete family of four—just me and my three boys. Sixteen years of me and Tate and every memory making us more whole and complete.

People used to tell me marriage wasn't all hearts and

butterflies forever—that as time marched forward the attraction and lust would dull around the edges. But that was never true for us.

I should have known life had something else in store for us that would tear apart the perfection.

When we went to Bora Bora that same summer, I literally felt like I was living in a dream. We had walked along the dock barely floating above the aqua-colored water and made love at all hours of the day and night under white hotel sheets—the ocean whispering to us just outside the door.

"Happy anniversary, Tabitha," Tate said before tracing his lips along my jaw.

I hummed into his kisses. "I didn't know year thirteen was going to hold such luxury."

He laughed—my favorite sound, like a song written just for me.

Looking back, I'm not quite sure why we chose such an expensive vacation for our thirteenth wedding anniversary. Thirteen was a random number of years to celebrate so big and this year in particular was entirely inconvenient. I was still nursing Charlie and had to pump breast milk in our suite several times each day, and I was just barely out of my post-partum baby blues. But when the advertisement for Bora Bora flashed across the television and Tate asked if we should go, I said why not. We weren't both usually spontaneous in that way. Tate was. But not me. I sometimes think it must have been an act of God moving the chess pieces around in front of us so we would be able to have one last, sweet summer to top all of our other memories.

Tate loved Bora Bora. He told me we should go back every year. He wanted to take the boys snorkeling and hike the Valley of the Kings—the lush, tropical vegetation always tempted him that way. It was such a stark contrast to the old-growth forests and snow-capped mountains of the Pacific Northwest.

When the two of us arrived home, it wasn't long before we packed up a minivan full of camping gear and snacks and headed to the mountains with the kids.

"Don't you ever get tired?" I said, half-laughing but mostly out of breath as we hiked the steep trails on Mt. Rainier. The flowers were in full bloom and the sun beat down on our backs, making us all sweat. Toby kept up with Tate and Charlie slept in the carrier on Tate's back.

"Tired?" Tate replied, laughing and guzzling half a bottle of water. The summer sun glistened across his brow. "There is far too much life to live to be tired."

I paused, mid-stride, trying to catch my breath. "Your dad is a robot," I said to Toby who was throwing a handful of trail mix in his mouth. "And don't hog all the M&M's."

Toby smiled mischievously.

"You better start eating some then because between me and Dad, the chocolate is going to be gone." Toby laughed and it echoed through Tate.

"That's how y'all do it, isn't it? The sugar rush keeps your energy up."

Toby shrugged. "I don't know, Mom. You should try it."

"Nah, she'd rather eat kale chips," Tate snarked playfully.

My mouth fell open as they teased me for my healthy choices. If there was one thing it was easy to be in Washington, it was granola.

"It's probably because she's a vegetarian." Toby laughed and tried to catch his breath. "Somebody, get my mom a hamburger or she's going to pass out!" he continued to tease.

I shook my head and smiled as they roasted me halfway up the mountainside. "Hey, I'm a *pescatarian*. If you're going to make fun of my eating habits, be accurate."

"What does that even mean?" Toby's brow crumpled in confusion.

"I still eat fish," I answered with a breathless shrug.

"That seems so unnecessary to have a label," Toby said with a straight face.

I laughed at my ten-year-old's choice of words.

"Go easy on her, Toby." Tate laughed and elbowed our son playfully as I trailed behind them. Even the back of their tan necks looked the same. Their hair was the exact same shade—even the hair line around their identical ears matched. They were best friends. Inseparable—an exclusive boys club I was only allowed admission to because I was the mom and the wife.

Charlie giggled in his sleep, his chubby cheek pressed against Tate's back, and my heart surged. I loved them. I couldn't imagine life without a single one of them. I didn't—even for a moment—take them for granted. So many of my friends would complain about their husbands or their kids, and while I wasn't blind to the difficulties, I was completely shielded from their pessimism. Life wasn't perfect but it was everything I wanted it to be.

Back at the house, I poured a glass of crisp, white wine while I rinsed and coated blackberries with sugar. Toby was upstairs playing video games and Charlie sat in his highchair with Puffs littering the tray.

"End of summer cobbler time?" Tate asked, walking up behind me and placing a hand on my hip and his lips on my neck.

"Of course." I flashed a bashful smile at him. "Time to commemorate the best summer to date."

"It's definitely been my favorite." He smiled his perfectly crooked smile and eyed my glass of wine on the counter. "Did you pour me a glass?"

"I will after you run to the store—I don't want you drinking and driving." I raised my eyebrows at him. "Apparently we're out of butter."

"What a tragedy." He nuzzled his face in my hair and wrapped his hands around my waist. I leaned into him for a brief moment. A moment I now wish lasted much longer.

"Just butter?" he asked, grabbing his keys off the counter.

"Just butter." I smiled. "Thank you."

"Alright," he said, cradling my face and kissing me. "I love you."

"Always will." I smiled at him and he looked at me the same way he did when we first met in college, and it made me blush.

"I'll be back," he said, closing the door behind him.

But he never was.

At 5:23 p.m. Tate left this world.

It was my favorite summer of ours together. If only it hadn't ended with him getting t-boned by a semi-truck at the intersection five minutes from the house.

They didn't want me to identify him at the morgue. They worried the extent of his injuries were too gruesome for the young widow to remember. I went anyway. I needed to see it. Otherwise, I'd never believe it.

The images of his disfigured and bruised body are forever etched in the darkest places in my mind. His expression was vacant when it was always full of joy. His skin was almost gray when it was always tan, his cheeks flushed every time he smiled. They attempted to cover up which parts of him were no longer attached to his body, but I could tell.

It wasn't my Tate. My Tate was whole and complete—the rock keeping me steady. The love of my entire life.

AT TATE'S SERVICE, I stood there in a trance as they lowered his body into the ground. Music played and a hushed cry echoed through the crowd. Charlie was asleep on my shoulder and Toby, just ten-years-old, stood silent next to me. His green eyes were wet with tears and his hair dipped over his forehead, reminding me how much he looked like Tate.

It was a nightmare. An inexplicable nightmare.

A deep ache pulsed in my bones. A rawness I couldn't swallow was trapped in my throat. I felt gutted. Empty. Exhausted with grief. Completely broken and entirely incomplete.

This type of pain was unfathomable until I was living through it.

I squeezed Toby's hand and kissed Charlie's forehead—holding on to the two pieces of Tate left in this world. I knew I had to be strong for them, but I was completely lost as to how I could be. My heart was shattered. It felt like it was completely gone from my chest and replaced with a throbbing pain that made it hard to breathe.

I never knew pain until I knew this kind of loss. It didn't seem possible it could hurt this bad. A broken heart should be theoretical. Emotional. Not a physical pain cutting through every corner of my being.

Losing Tate was like losing oxygen.

But that wasn't even the most painful part. The most painful part was realizing I was still alive and somehow, I had to keep going.

One

10 Months Later

TIME MOVED PAINFULLY slow after Tate died. The beat of each second hung in the air and a fog filled my mind at all times. For weeks our house was full of well-meaning and intrusive people, and our fridge was overflowing with casseroles and leftover pizzas. I didn't have to buy milk or bread for months because it was constantly left on my doorstep with a note and bouquet of flowers that would soon be dead on my counter.

Charlie, being just a baby, knew nothing different except for the fact that he got to spend so much extra time with his Nana and Papa. He'd giggle and coo into their faces, filling the house with a melody of hope and life. Something that felt impossible for me to grasp.

Toby struggled. No one should have to lose their father and their best friend. Especially not at ten years old. We spent our time alone talking endlessly about his dad. Tate was the love of my life and he was Toby's hero. All we wanted to do was talk about him. We'd cry and hug and pray. Then we'd let the numbness roll over us and pretend we were okay for the outside world. A vicious and endless cycle for weeks that somehow turned into months.

Ten-year-old boys shouldn't have to be that strong. But Toby was and I always admired his bravery—took any piece of it I could and carried it onto the next day. Once school and therapy started, I began seeing glimpses of the boy he used to be before his dad died. It had only been ten months, but it felt like an entire lifetime ago.

When our fridge was no longer full of casseroles and the calls and texts rolled in less frequently, my mom and dad became my constant—a beautiful yet gut-wrenching distraction from our reality. Life tried to pick up where Tate left off. The world kept turning and I felt like I could barely keep up the pace.

I had to relearn how to be alone and after sixteen years with someone—nearly my entire adult life—it seemed impossible.

When my friend, Lydia, and her husband, Tim, came to town from Newport to stay for the first weekend after school was out in June, she brought their sons, Eli and Caden. They were practically cousins to Toby, and they offered a loud and rowdy sense of normalcy for him. Lydia had been my best friend since high school. She knew the intricacies of my life before and while I was with Tate. Now she was there to witness the ruin after he died.

She and Tim were one of our favorite couple friends up until they abandoned us to live on the coast of Oregon in Newport five years ago. Tim and Tate had been friends since college, and I knew losing one of his best friends was hard on him. It reminded me grief is experienced at different levels.

The four of us spent many summers together, except for that last one. I knew they felt guilty about not seeing Tate during his final summer. I also understood the guilt was as impossible to understand as it was to change the reality of the circumstances.

Relief lapped at my bones when I saw Lydia standing on the front porch after they arrived at the house. She wordlessly wrapped her arms around me as the boys tumbled through the front door to find Toby. Tim patted my shoulder and followed the boys upstairs to help get everyone settled. The tension in my chest released as soon as I was in her arms—my best friend was my safest place. At least now that Tate was gone. Her arms held every pent-up emotion and buckets of tears. I cried into her shoulder for a long time before I pulled away, seeing the mascara I left on her white shirt.

"I'm so sorry, Lydia. I'm a mess." I wiped my eyes as she tossed her long brown hair over her shoulder.

She looked down at the mascara smudge and smiled with tears in her eyes. "Well, now so am I."

I laughed softly and took a deep breath, trying to regain my composure and led her inside. She immediately waltzed into the kitchen and poured glasses of wine before pulling ingredients out of the refrigerator and pantry to make dinner. Lydia always knew exactly how to step in and help when it was needed. She came for the funeral and a few times after, but I hadn't seen her in months. We still talked regularly. She was the first person I called after the chaplain showed up on my doorstep and quite often the last person I texted each night before I fell asleep.

I took a seat on the floor next to Charlie, now nearly a year and a half old, who was happily playing with wooden blocks. The way Lydia maneuvered around the kitchen reminded me of how precious our friendship was. The ease of how she knew where the pots and pans were and where I keep certain ingredients in the pantry, compounded with the way the boys fell back into their friendship within a moment of seeing each other, highlighted the relief and comfort I hadn't felt in almost a year. So much had changed but at least this friendship had not.

"Mom, can I go ride bikes with Caden and Eli?" Toby said, bursting into the kitchen. His cheeks were flushed with excitement.

I glanced at the clock. "You only have an hour before dinner but yes, go ahead." I pressed my fingers against my eyes and took another sip of wine as the boys escaped outside.

Lydia placed the seasoned salmon in the oven and stirred the risotto on the stove before lowering the heat and turning around to face me, leaning her elbows on the kitchen island.

I stared at her blankly, allowing my face to show how tired my soul was.

"You okay, Tabitha?" Lydia asked, each word lined with deep empathy.

I shook my head slowly. "I don't know what okay is anymore. I mean, I'm breathing. The kids are happy." I shrugged and Charlie giggled on cue, making me smile through my swollen and sad eyes.

Lydia walked out of the kitchen into the family room and sat next to me on the floor.

"You know it's okay to say you're not okay."

I nodded and swallowed.

"No one is expecting you to be."

"Yeah, but my boys. They need me."

Lydia nodded. "They do. But they need to know it's okay to feel everything too. Even when it hurts." She tucked a loose strand of my blonde hair behind my ear. "How's Toby?"

"Better than me, I think." I shrugged, swallowing tears. "Kids are resilient that way, I guess. He's sad though. Getting back into the normalcy of school, sports, and going to therapy was good for him. Routine helps."

Lydia nodded thoughtfully. "How's your routine?"

I dragged my eyes from Charlie to her. "My routine differs based on a toddler's schedule." I turned to a giggling Charlie, my voice changing an octave as I tickled his chin. "Isn't that, right? Who's the boss now?"

"That must be so hard. I don't know how you're standing on two feet. Babies are already exhausting and to add that Tate di…" Her voice trailed off.

"It's okay. You can say it. Not saying it doesn't make it any less true or any less hard."

Lydia swallowed and her eyes filled with tears. "Is there something I can do? Or is that a terrible and redundant question without an answer?"

I smiled weakly. "Just be here. That's enough for now."

She gave my leg a squeeze before standing and walking to the kitchen to grab plates for dinner. When she closed the cupboard, the door bounced open, so she closed it again. It bounced open again. And again. And again. The sound of the wood bouncing against each other sent a shooting pain across my chest.

"Don't bother. Tate had planned to fix that. He never got around to it."

Lydia's fingers lingered on the edge of the door as her empathetic gaze found me sitting cross-legged on the living room floor. Her eyes were filled with so much pity that I immediately burst into tears. Tears spilled from my eyes uncontrollably for several minutes before I could finally manage to formulate words.

"Those are things that kill me, you know?" I said, finally. "There's just so much history in these walls. So many memories. So many reminders that he's gone." My face crumbled again and I sobbed into her shoulder as Charlie squealed after knocking his block tower down, completely unaware of the father he would never come to know.

Lydia held me as I cried, her own tears falling into my hair. I felt like a child. I was supposed to be strong. To stand up on my own two feet and raise my boys. I was supposed to heal. I was supposed to move forward and create another happy life separate from the beautiful one Tate and I built.

Everything told me I could, that I was capable. But every part of me was too angry and sad and lost to actually make it happen. I began to believe people didn't move on from this type of tragedy. And they didn't move through it either. They just moved with it. Carrying it from place to place while it ate away at their insides. It had been nearly a year, and I was still just as sad.

I missed Tate more than I ever imagined anyone could miss someone. It was like missing a part of myself in a world that constantly reminded me it was gone and I needed it to function properly.

"Will I ever stop crying?" I asked, pulling away and wiping my puffy, wet cheeks.

"No," Lydia said calmly, placing a hand on my cheek. "Probably not. But the tears will fall differently as time goes on.

They might be slower or sometimes silent; they might just kiss the corners of your eyes or pour down when you least expect it. But no, Tabitha, you probably won't stop crying, and you sure as hell don't need to apologize for it."

I let out an emotional sigh. "I miss him so bad."

"You should," she said, squeezing my hands tightly in hers. "You loved him. A part of you always will."

"It feels like a dream—a nightmare really. I just want him back." My voice broke into another sob. "I don't know how to still be in this life—the life we created together. It's too hard."

He was everywhere, even when he was nowhere to be found.

"Do you think you want to move out of this house?" Lydia looked at me so intently, it felt like she wanted to absorb as much of my pain as she could.

"Sometimes. I don't know." I shook my head, numbly.

"I wish we lived closer. I hate that I can't just pop in whenever. I want to be here for you as much as I can." She glanced around the room searching for a solution. "Do you need me to move in for a while? Being five hours away just doesn't feel close enough right now."

"Oh, Lydia. You don't have to say that. You're still just a phone call away. And I've got to figure out my life with or without you." I shrugged. "But I appreciate you for offering. Ten months ago, I would have said yes, but I really feel like I need to figure out what I'm going to do next on my own. Time is moving faster than I'm ready for and you never know when you're going to run out." I smiled at her, but it was weak and forced. My eyes drifted to the last family portrait we took hanging on the living room wall. I narrowed my eyes slightly. "I still can't believe I'm a widow."

"Doesn't even sound possible," she agreed. The silence fell over us for a moment as the reality continued to soak in. "Hey, whatever happened with that condo Tate bought? It's only ten minutes from my place in Newport, isn't it?"

A flash of surprise washed over my mind. I had completely forgotten.

"Gosh, I haven't even thought about that place. What was

it? Two years ago since he bought it?" I looked at Lydia for confirmation, but she shrugged as I continued. "He wanted to fix it up and rent it out, but he never got around to finishing it. I think the resort has just been renting it out for us in its dilapidated state." I tossed my head back on the couch and pressed my eyes closed—almost embarrassed at the detail I had missed. "I signed so many things after his death, I didn't really even pay attention. I've been so focused on putting one foot in front of the other, I just haven't thought much beyond that. But I guess I can't wallow in my grief forever, can I?"

"Wallow all you need." Lydia smiled and took a sip of her wine. "Hell, come wallow in Newport if that's what you need."

I let out a soft laugh through my exhausted tears and paused to absorb her words—hearing the echo of the boys laughing while they walked through the front door and Charlie giggling at his Aunt Lydia.

Maybe I did need a change. Maybe it was time to start planning for what came next.

Summer 15

W HAT DO YOU think?" Tate asked, peeling his hands
from my eyes as he walked me into the condo he
purchased—without telling me—in Newport. My
feet hesitantly stepped on the worn-out navy
carpeting as the stale smell mixed with the salty breeze drifted to
my nose.

"Tate, honey. It looks like a *lot* of work," I said scanning the
narrow hallway that led to the great room, clad with more old
navy carpet, dingy cream paint, and cabinets from the 1970's. I
didn't want to hurt his feelings, but I was also irritated he went
ahead with the purchase before telling me it was a done deal. We
had been looking for an investment property for years but could
never decide on a location. When Lydia and Tim moved to
Newport four years earlier, we decided it was the perfect place.
We missed our friends and visited them often. In return, we fell
in love with Newport's quaint atmosphere, sleepy beaches, and
close proximity to civilization.

Toby was at their house playing with their boys while Tate
stole me away to show me the condo he purchased without my

consent. I wasn't angry but I was always hesitant when it came to real estate. I trusted his judgment and expertise, but I worked in accounting—I cared about numbers.

"But the potential? I mean…can't you see it? Look at the view?" Tate said as he strode to the back of the condo.

The back wall of the family room was all windows framing a beautiful picture of Yaquina Bay and the lit-up arches of the Yaquina Bay Bridge. I followed him to the balcony. The door was the same royal blue color as the front door. The air smelled like salt and I could hear sea lions barking along the shore of the bay. A foghorn went off in the distance, making me smile knowing how much Toby would love it. The exterior of the building was covered in faded cedar shingles washed out to a muted shade of gray from decades and decades in the salty sea air.

"The view is exquisite," I agreed, smiling at him and kissing his cheek as I tucked myself under his arm.

He gave me a breathtaking smile that made me agree with whatever he wanted, even if I was still torn in my gut. We'd been together a decade and a half, and his touch and his stare always did me in. But especially his smile—I could never say no when he smiled at me that way.

"And the condo?" His smoldering green eyes were hopeful.

"Is old," I said definitively, letting out a laugh.

"Come on, babe. You've got to see the potential." Every word he said and move he made pleaded with me to fall in love with the musty, old condo.

"The countertops are orange." I plastered a smile on my face and raised my eyebrows.

"We'll get new countertops and new cabinets too," he dropped his arm from my shoulders and walked back into the condo, gesturing around. "And floors. Paint. Furniture. Easy fixes. It's just outdated but that view—" he pointed out the window, "—that view is never going to be outdated. This is a great piece of real estate. And we get to reap the benefits. Want to hear the best part?"

"Tim and Lydia are ten minutes away?" I suggested smugly.

He laughed. "Okay, second best part."

"What is it?" My voice stayed even.

"The resort handles all the bookings *and* the cleaning." He leaned against the wobbly table in the great room. "We won't have to worry about setting it up as a vacation rental or worry about security—it's all inclusive."

I gave him a petulant look, trying not to smile. "So fancy," I teased.

He grinned and pulled me closer to him, his hands resting on the small of my back. "All we have to do is call and say when we're coming, and we get first dibs on the room for however long we want."

I twisted my lips as I looked up at him and placed my hands on my small, growing baby bump. "But with the baby coming in six months do you really think this was the right time? I mean, how are you even going to get down here to do the renovations? It's a five-hour drive. I know it's only August, but February isn't that far away. The baby will be here before we know it."

He smiled and nodded.

"I'll tell you what. I'll hire someone to do the cabinets and counters right away. We'll tackle the rest after the baby is born." He kissed my forehead and it smoothed out the worries formulating in my head. "There are so many memories to be made here, Tabitha. I just know it. Oh, and I almost forgot: they have an indoor pool and jacuzzi right next to the crabbing dock. I know how much you love crabbing."

I bit my lip to contain my excitement. I did love crabbing— I grew up on boats and docks with my dad, stuffing bait traps with raw chicken and chatting for hours until we pulled up dozens of Dungeness crabs.

"That *is* pretty amazing." I smiled, rocking on my toes so I could reach his lips. I kissed him softly. "Are you sure this won't be an added stress for you, Tate? Because we can't deal with more stress. Not after how long it took us to get pregnant this time." I tried not to bring it up. But when we tried and failed to get pregnant for nine years to the point we literally gave up, it's hard not to mention how precious the baby growing inside me was.

"I promise. I will not let this stress me out." He ran his

thumb across my cheek. "I already talked to Tim and he knows a guy that does cabinetry, so I'll get him out here next month and we'll find a countertop guy too. With the price tag of this condo, we can spare a few thousand to get those fixes done."

"Few thousand? Babe, counters and cabinets for this place will be at least ten." I walked around to the kitchen and surveyed the space again.

"Right. A few thousand." He flashed a wry smile, and I shook my head. He was always so convincing. The perfect salesman. No wonder he was so successful in real estate.

I took in a sharp breath and walked back over to him, letting his arms wrap around me.

"Okay," I said, simply.

"Okay?" he asked expectantly.

"Okay," I repeated. "You already bought the place, Tate. What else can I say?"

"That you're excited. That you see it the way I do." He grabbed my hand and pulled me back down the hallway. "Look. Here's the kids' bedroom. Bathroom. And here's our bedroom."

The existing furniture was still in the room. A king-sized bed with a headboard from the seventies and vertical blinds decorated the single window—the perfect accent to the faded cream-colored walls.

"Charming," I said, sarcastically. "Two bedrooms, one bath, and a spectacular view. I don't know how you did it, Mr. Jones, but you found the most perfect vacation slash investment property for my family and me."

I was teasing him and he knew it.

A smile spread across his face as he ran his fingers through my hair, gently gripping the back of my neck and pulling me closer. He kissed me softly and pulled away.

"You're going to be very happy here, Mrs. Jones. Think of all the summer cobblers we'll make."

I smiled as he pulled me in again and kissed me harder until we fell to the empty mattress. A frenzy of passion ensued. It was everything we had always been—everything I would always remember us to be.

Two

S O, IT SEEMS like you and Lydia had a nice time last month?" my mother, Jenny, asked.

"We did." I eyed her curiously. "What made you bring that up?" I asked, washing the heads of romaine lettuce in the sink and placing them on a paper towel. My parents were over for dinner for the second time that week—a year ago it would have been excessive but these days it was necessary.

"You just seem different, I guess." She shrugged. "You said it was a nice time but now that it's nearly August, I just *feel* like you're different."

I narrowed my eyes on my mother. She was very intuitive. She had me very young and my dad—while not my biological father—raised me as his own because he loved my mom so much. I think because she went through so much at a young age, she could identify the hurts in others easily. She could also recognize the healing.

"I'm just trying to find a way out of all this…grief, I guess," I said plainly.

"You don't need to find a way out, Tabitha. Just a—"

"Way through," I said simultaneously. "I know, Mom. You've always said that. Dad has always said that. But you are fifty-seven and married to the same person from thirty-seven years ago. I am thirty-seven and still in love with my dead husband." My voice broke and I cleared it away. "Sometimes we can't just *get through* things, Mom. Sometimes we have to pave a whole different life."

My mother smiled at me gently as tears rimmed her eyes and she nodded. She was good at that: understanding unexplainable pain. I didn't even entirely understand the waves of emotions I was continuing to process. It took months before I had a day that almost felt normal. Then the grief returned for weeks. Then I had a couple days in a row that felt normal. Then grief consumed me yet again. It wasn't until I realized my normal days weren't that at all; they were just me adjusting to a different life. The one I had to live without Tate.

She squeezed my hand as I ripped the lettuce and placed it in a bowl.

"Do you know what you'll do?"

"What do you mean?" I asked, blinking away the last of my emotions.

She shrugged but I could sense the sadness on her shoulders. "With life? What's next?"

"Well, that's actually something I've wanted to talk to you and Dad about." I bit my lip and drew in a deep breath.

"What is it?" My mother could never wait for a solution or answer to a question. I knew I was like her in that way.

"Later, Mom. I'll tell you just…later." I looked at her with my eyebrows raised and she nodded in agreement.

A SMATTERING OF chatter, laughter, and mouths full of spaghetti filled the dinner table.

"Oh, he likes his spaghetti, doesn't he?" my father, Carlisle, said. He was smiling at Charlie with a tomato-sauce-stained face as his chubby toddler fingers tried to use a fork. "Just like your dad, isn't that right?"

I swallowed an unexpected lump in my throat and met eyes with Toby. His face was washed with grief and longing for someone he missed terribly. I winked at him and cleared my throat—we would cry about it later but for now we would save face.

"We all really like spaghetti, don't we?" I said, brushing a finger against Charlie's chubby cheek.

"Now, Toby," my mother said. "Tell me how was school this last year? Every time I see you, we talk about all your baseball games, but not school."

It was July so I wasn't exactly sure why she was bringing up a school year that ended a month earlier, but I had a sneaking suspicion it had to do with changing the subject.

Toby shrugged. "It was okay."

My mother looked at me expectantly and I shrugged too. Toby was more athletic than he was into academics. He did fine in school but didn't care to chat about the details.

"What's your favorite subject?" my mother asked.

"Recess, so I can play soccer," he answered as he swirled spaghetti on his fork.

My parents laughed.

"And what's your second favorite?" my father asked.

"I don't know. Probably math." Toby nodded at his own answer. "Dad was good at math."

I cleared my throat. "That he was."

My parents nodded and smiled; I saw glimmers of tears in the corners of their eyes.

"Your dad would be very proud of you, I'm sure." My father said it quickly and cleared his throat. I could feel the rise of my own emotion in my chest, and I shoveled it down.

God, we missed Tate.

It was terrible to not have him sitting there at the table and eating with us, but at least I knew pieces of him still lived in each of my boys. I'd gotten really good at blinking away my tears at this point. But as soon as the curtain closed on the day, I'd curl on Tate's side of the bed, and cry until my tears ran out.

Life was so unfair. So incredibly unfair. I missed him. I longed for him. I didn't understand how I was living without him. It was irrational and implausible but there I was, every day, breathing and living with him buried in the soil, marked by a polished block of cement.

Beloved husband, father, and friend, his headstone read but he was more than that. So much more. Anyone who knew him knew Tate was the life of every party. The heart of his home. The soul of his family. There wasn't a headstone big enough to capture who the man lying in the ground was when he walked the Earth.

"I'm excited to see what my new school will be like next month though," Toby said, interrupting my thoughts. His tone showed a hint of excitement and I smiled softly at him.

My parents' eyes snapped toward me then back to Toby. "What do you mean 'new school'?" my mother said.

"We're moving," Toby said, his forehead furrowed in confusion. "Didn't Mom tell you?"

My dad stayed quiet, mindlessly taking another bite of food, but my mother's eyes fell on me. "No, she didn't yet."

I sighed and looked at her intently. "That's what I was going to tell you tonight."

My mother nodded and I let out a sharp breath. I knew this would upset them, my mom especially. They were very involved grandparents and I needed every ounce of help I could get. I also knew I couldn't rely on them forever. I'd have to find my own way to stay afloat.

As we carried on with our dinner, a sadness lingered between us. For once, in a long time, it wasn't because of Tate.

When the meal was eaten and the boys were tucked safely in their beds upstairs, I walked back down the staircase and into the kitchen to find my father handwashing dishes and putting them in the cupboard.

When he attempted to close the cupboard, it popped open.

And again.

And again.

And again.

My heart ached watching the cupboard refuse to close, wishing Tate had just fixed it when I asked him to. As if that would help me not be reminded of him every time I roamed the house. Tears stung my eyes and I blinked them away.

I was so tired of crying. I wanted to scream.

"Your cupboard just won't close," my dad said on his fifth attempt, a chuckle escaping his throat.

I let out a sharp breath, my chest deflating. "Yes, I really need to schedule to get that fixed. Tate really wanted to do it, but..." I shrugged and looked at my dad. His eyes were deep and full of sorrow he didn't want to express.

"Oh, I can fix it, Tabitha, don't worry—" he began.

My face crumpled and I began to cry as I clung to his arm—anything to keep me stable. The shock of emotion wrecked through me more quickly than I ever imagined.

"This isn't going to go away, is it, Dad? With anything. I'm always going to expect him to put the dishes away and complain about that damn cupboard bouncing open. I still expect him to walk through the door and tell me he's going to fix it." My voice rose and I could barely breathe through my tears as my dad held me close. I pulled away and wiped at my cheeks, pausing to catch my breath. I held my shaking hand to my mouth. "I can still smell him, you know? Like I know he's gone but it just feels like he's on vacation or a business trip. Dead just doesn't sound right."

My mother was in the room now, anxiously waiting to pull me in for a hug as her eyes spilled over with tears.

"He's not coming home though, is he?" I let out another cry as my parents held me. "He isn't coming home."

"Oh, honey. He is home," my mom said as our tears spilled onto each other.

This made me sob. I believed in heaven. I believed Tate was there. But it was just so far away.

"Mom, I am only thirty-seven. Heaven still just feels like an idea. I'm not even close to meeting him there. I have a whole lifetime before I ever expect to see him fact-to-face again. Do you even understand that?'

I was livid. Angry. Sad. Heartbroken over a life I chose but would never get. My husband was dead. Gone. Forever. His absence shattered the world we created, and I was left to pick up the pieces.

"It's so unfair, Mom," I shouted through tears. "It is so fucking unfair!"

She pulled me in her arms and I could sense both my parents looking at each other over my shoulder. I knew they didn't know what to say. There weren't words *to* say.

"You're right, honey," my dad said. "Life is unfair."

I cried even harder until I couldn't catch my breath. I was nearly hyperventilating and tried to focus on taking deep breaths. When I finally was able to draw in a deep breath and gain some semblance of composure, I pulled away and wiped my cheeks with the palms of my hands.

"I know it may not feel like it right now, honey, but God does—"

"Please don't tell me God has a plan for me," I interrupted and shook my head. "I cannot always try to find the good in my husband dying."

My mother drew in a breath and nodded like she understood.

"Every time someone tells me to be strong, to be thankful for my boys, it could be worse, or look how God is providing for us makes me feel like I'm not allowed to still be sad and angry that Tate's dead. It's unfair. Silver linings are bullshit right now. If God loves me then He knows I'm sad. He knows we're devastated, and it doesn't mean this was His plan for me and my boys."

"You're right. I'm sorry. I didn't mean to minimize what you're feeling." She pressed her lips in a straight line and glanced at my father, his eyes were glistening and heavy with concern. "I think God probably is very sad too. For you and the boys. He knows exactly what you're feeling. I do believe God loves you and will guide you through all this grief even if I don't know what that looks like."

"I believe that too." I let out a deep breath, exhausted from trying to balance my faith against my circumstances. I turned to face them, ready to change the subject. "So, I bet you two want to hear about Newport, then."

"Newport? What do you mean?" my mom asked, her voice concerned and eager.

"Me and the boys are moving to Newport next month just in time for school to start again in September."

My parents' eyes widened as they looked at me and then each other.

"Why?" my father asked.

"Well, Tate had purchased that condo as an investment property almost two years ago now, so I'm going to move there with the kids. Change of scenery." I let out a deep breath.

"But didn't he want to sell it? Said it was just sucking up money." My mother's forehead was creased with worry.

"No, Mom, he wanted to remodel it and use it as a vacation rental when we visited Tim and Lydia. He just never got around to it. So that's what I'm going to do. It doesn't need much."

Tate had done as he promised and had the cabinets and countertops replaced, but he never got around to replacing the floors or painting. This was something I knew I could handle—we had done enough remodeling projects in our home together I at least felt like a confident amateur.

"But you'll be so far away? You can't have the kids living in Newport," my father said, clearly trying to wrap his brain around how this would work.

"Why not? It's a real town. People live there. There's a school and everything," I said defensively. "And besides, I'll be near Lydia and Tim so Toby will be near their kids. They really are his best friends. They'll be at the same school and he will even be in class with Caden."

"You've already enrolled him?" my father asked, slightly aghast.

I nodded. He drew in a sharp breath, realizing the extent of my plan.

"What about the house? And your job?" my mother asked.

I had spent eleven months knowing I needed to pave a new path and spent the last month panning out the details.

"Cecilia said I could work from home. And I have renters lined up in September."

My parents' eyes were glossed with confusion and concern.

I shrugged. "Accountants can work from anywhere—we're not exactly considered the heartbeat of the office. Plus, you'd be surprised by how many meetings can just be emails."

My father gave a small shake of his head. "I don't think anyone would be surprised by that."

I smiled at him and my mother ignored us and continued to press.

"But Newport is just one of those places people visit in the summer and is totally dead in the winter. You don't want that, do you?" She was almost pleading. I knew she meant well, but I knew her desire to have us close didn't align with what was best for us right now.

"Well, maybe I need a little quiet. Something different. A new place to heal."

"Aren't you worried it will be too much for the boys?" my father interjected.

"No." I shook my head in exhaustion, tears stinging my eyes. "All I'm concerned about is the fact my boys will walk into every day for the rest of their lives without their father. So, I kindly ask you to just love us and support us as I try to make our life okay again."

"But, Tabitha, you don't have to run from this life." My mother reached out and held my arm like it was a precious jewel.

"I'm not running, Mom. I just need to start over. A clean slate." I wiped my final tears of the night from my face. "How things are going here isn't working. I need to find a different way to move on. Tate always told me it's okay to let things go. Sometimes it hurts less than trying to hold onto a life that's no longer here. Maybe it will be a disaster and I'll come back. But maybe…hopefully, it's where I need to be."

Summer 14

I STARED AT THE white and blue plastic stick sitting on the counter. A tremble rose in my chest.

Not pregnant.

Again.

I didn't know why this kept happening. Why did we even bother trying anymore? I got pregnant with Toby so quickly—too quickly. We weren't even ready to have a baby. Now after six years of trying, two rounds of IVF, four rounds of clomiphene, and dozens of negative pregnancy tests, I was done. *Done.* It was too emotionally taxing to continue to try and fail. Over and over again. I felt stripped and broken. We already had Toby. Why did we feel entitled to have one more child?

I stared at the test another few moments before wrapping it in tissue paper and tossing it in the trash.

As I walked out of the bathroom and entered the long hallway from our bedroom, I stopped and stared at the long white wall clad with dozens of picture frames. Each picture a memory: a highlight of our life together, gingerly balanced on single nails piercing through the drywall. A picture of Tate and I at college graduation, our hats flying in the air. One from our wedding, our faces frozen in laughter holding half empty glasses of champagne. Another with Tate holding me from behind, our hands gently curved into a heart shape around my round and swollen belly. We were so excited to be parents. I stopped at the black and white photo from Toby's newborn photoshoot. He was so small—his nose a perfect shiny button between two plump cheeks as he slept in Tate's arms and I gazed at them both.

The picture was beautiful. But it wasn't real. It was the most staged picture we'd ever taken. It appeared as if I was looking at Toby but I was really looking at Tate. I wanted Tate back. I remembered feeling exhausted and angry and sad this new member of our family tore him away from me.

I struggled after we had Toby. *Really* struggled. It wasn't until I was diagnosed with post-partum depression a few weeks after the photo was taken, that I realized depression had stolen my first month as a mother. I had completely warped expectations leading up to his birth. After he was born, I felt like a complete failure. I hated the baby stage. It was so hard. Hard on me. Hard on Tate. Hard on our marriage.

I remembered screaming at Tate to *just be helpful!* And he'd take several deep breaths trying not to raise his voice at me, but he would anyway and shout, *I am trying to be!*

The shouting would continue until we were slamming doors and retreating to our respective corners of the house until we calmed down enough to apologize to each other.

He'd always say sorry first and I'd always start crying.

It was a terrible year in so many ways even though it was also wonderful.

Tate carried me those first few months of motherhood. He was so patient—quick to apologize and always willing to forgive me. He was the reason we made it to the next picture: Toby covered in blue frosting from his first birthday cake smash with both of us smiling on either side of him. Tate had blue frosting on his nose and his smile was rooted in joy. Mine was rooted in relief. Being a mom of a baby proved to be more challenging than I had anticipated.

It was a year of tears, fighting, and never ever sleeping. I stared at the two pictures that flanked the beginning and end of my first year as a mom.

It's funny what pictures capture. It's funny what they don't.

Maybe God was saving us from another terrible year. Maybe that's why I couldn't get pregnant. How would I get through a year like that with an eight-year-old boy relying on me?

I let out a sigh and continued my way through the house, letting my mind absorb the good memories made there. Because there were so many more good ones than there were bad. I needed to stop being ungrateful. I had a beautiful son and a husband that loved me dearly. I had it all. Even though I couldn't get pregnant again.

Four was always our number.

It's perfect for the buddy system, Tate would say. *Everyone has a ride partner for the state fair and Disneyland rides.*

I swallowed hard at the memory, praying Tate would be okay being a family of three.

I couldn't do it again.

As I made my way out to the back patio, I sat in an Adirondack chair as the setting sun began to turn the summer sky into a light shade of lavender while Tate and Toby played catch in the grass. The warmth of the August air kissed my cheeks and the laughter from Toby made my chest tighten.

I pressed my lips tightly together as I watched Toby chase a grounder that rolled past him.

Tate turned and looked at me with hopeful eyes, a smile dancing across his happy face. I just stared at him. He knew why I had gone upstairs. Now he knew why I came back quiet and unsmiling while my hands trembled in my lap.

He cocked his head to the side in concern.

I shook my head slightly and his face fell. Every emotion crumbled in my chest. I desperately wanted to give him another baby. I knew that was what he wanted. It was what I wanted too. But I had given up. Six years of disappointment was too many. My hope had run too thin.

I cleared my throat and stood before Tate could approach me, grabbing the spare baseball glove off the picnic table.

"Alright, put 'er there, Toby." I held out my glove, pounding my fist into the palm of the leather once. Then twice.

Tate watched me shake off the disappointment and continued to play catch with Toby and me. I knew we would talk about it later, even though a part of me didn't want to. I wanted to pretend we didn't just spend thirty grand to have Tate inject me with all kinds of hormones, only to extract five eggs and fertilize two and have none of them make it. I wanted to pretend this wasn't the second try. I wanted to pretend I wasn't on fertility drugs for the years prior. I wanted to pretend I didn't want another baby.

I also wanted to pretend I was strong enough to keep trying.

After Toby went to sleep that night, I found Tate in bed with my phone open to my search history. He stared sadly at the phone while his thumb pushed through page after page of useless information. I knew what he was reading. I was reading it just hours prior.

Why can't I get pregnant? I had typed angrily.

Was it me? Was it Tate? Was it the fertilizer we used on our lawn? Did I not eat enough meat? Did I eat too much? Was it the bubble bath I used or the chemicals in the lotion I smothered over my body for decades? Did I work too much? Was I too stressed? Did we have sex at the right time? Did we have sex too often? Should I try this tea or that supplement?

All stupid questions with no definitive answer as to why my body didn't want to get pregnant.

His eyes drifted toward me as he set the phone down. He clasped his hands while his elbows rested on his knees. I held his gaze for a moment before I shrugged and walked to my side of the bed and curled under the covers. Tate's eyes watched me—they were heavy with sorrow not only directed at me but belonging to him as well.

"I don't want to do this anymore," I said finally, holding his stare with the duvet pulled up to my chin.

He nodded and drew in a breath. "Let's just take some time. Relax. Let your body recover and get back to normal and then we can talk to Dr. Henderson about our next steps."

"Let it go, Tate," I snapped more angrily than I anticipated.

He looked at me slowly, a question glimmering across his eyes. "Tabitha, it will be okay. It will happen."

"No, Tate, you're not hearing me. I don't want to. I *cannot* do this again. I'm done trying to have another baby." I pressed the palms of my hands on my eyes. "I don't want another baby. I just want to enjoy the life we have." I swallowed hard as tears slipped from under my palms out of the corners of my eyes and down to my pillowcase.

Tate reached over and pulled me into the curve of his body, wordlessly tucking me under his chin.

"Please don't be mad at me," I whispered through my tears of shame.

"For not wanting another baby?" he asked, confused.

"For not being able to *have* another baby." I sniffed and turned my face from under his chin.

He placed a gentle finger on my jaw and tilted my face in his direction.

"Hey, I would never be mad at you for this. This isn't your fault. This isn't something we can control." He pulled me closer and kissed my angry forehead as tears spilled from my eyes. "When I said yes to a lifetime with you, it wasn't conditional. We have a good life, and we have a wonderful son. At the end of the day, you are all I care about. You've already given me the life I want to live."

"I just feel like I let us down." Every confession that left my mouth felt like a release as it hit Tate in the chest for him to carry for me. "We've always said we wanted two kids. Ever since we first met and now it just isn't going to happen."

"You didn't let me down, Tabitha," Tate said, brushing my hair away from face and wiping my tears with his gentle fingers. "If it's too much to try to make this work then it's probably time to move on."

"I'm so sorry," I whispered as I buried my face in his chest.

"Don't apologize. I hate seeing you hurting. And a plan that isn't working out should never be what hurts you." He drew in a breath and pulled me closer, his arms a comfort wrapped around my body and my soul. "Sometimes holding on to things we thought we'd have hurts us more than letting them go."

Three

I T WAS RAINING when I pulled into the parking lot of our condo. The sound of the rain against the metal roof of my minivan reminded me of how Tate would drum his fingers along the dashboard rhythmically to the sound of the music. It was a welcomed reminder. I hated road trips alone with the kids. Not because they were unruly, but I always worried about the logistics if something were to go wrong. A flat tire. A blown alternator. I never wanted to be stranded on the side of the freeway alone with my children. It seemed daunting. The sound of the rain made me feel like Tate had arrived at our new life with us, even if it was just so he could ensure we arrived safely.

It was the day after the one-year anniversary of Tate's death. I didn't know how we made it a year already. I also couldn't believe I decided to move myself and the boys to a condo five hours away from home.

With my car idling at the curb (and Toby and Charlie both fast asleep inside it), I walked into the lobby of the resort's office with a pounding heart and tired eyes to check in as a permanent resident.

As the receptionist's fingers pecked at the keyboard in front of her, my eyes scanned the room. It was exactly the same as the day Tate brought me, and I was fairly certain it had been the same twenty years before that. Old, lacquered wood covered the walls and ceiling, bringing out the rich cedar color and highlighting the deep, dark knots in the grain. A mounted fish hung over the Bait Shop sign posted in the corner next to the reception desk; a fan whirred, quietly creating a light breeze in the office, and the vending machines hummed from inside the doorway. Two computers rested on a desk in the small nook in the opposite corner with laminated Wi-Fi passwords taped to the screens which was right next to a small staircase leading to the restaurant where Tate and I ate crab cakes and watched the sun go down. It was taped off with plastic and had a rope at the bottom of the stairs with a sign that read: DO NOT ENTER.

I furrowed my eyebrows.

"What happened to the restaurant?" I asked, feeling slightly disappointed I wouldn't get to eat there again.

"Oh, it closed down a year ago and hasn't been leased again," the receptionist with a long blonde ponytail and black-collared shirt said with a shrug.

"Oh." My eyes lingered in the space where Tate and I sat with a glowing votive candle between us. We had only eaten there once after he showed me the condo, but I was excited to have a restaurant at the same resort we lived. I let out a deep breath, letting go of the memory and turned back to the receptionist as she handed me the key cards programmed to our condo.

It felt odd when I realized the keys to our home were cards. Almost luxurious.

That is, until I opened our new front door.

The carpet was the same faded navy color as two years before and it stretched from the back door to the front and grew dingier at each exit. The cabinets Tate had picked looked good—a crisp white, accented by the gray quartz I told him to go ahead and purchase. I had forgotten how tiny the kitchen actually was; a small galley turned peninsula with all the necessities and none of the luxury. It was a mesh of today and the seventies with appliances from the nineties. It still smelled old—damp almost—and I knew replacing the floors and painting the walls would make all the difference.

Easy fixes. Doable.

Even for me.

"What do you think, Toby?" I said, hoisting Charlie on my hip, even though he squirmed to get down.

Toby wordlessly plopped his bag on the floor and diligently looked in each bedroom, examining the old furniture and the layout until he made his way to the balcony overlooking the bay.

"Dad picked this place?" he asked, looking at me and his brother.

I nodded. "We never got to stay here last summer but he thought we'd love it. He told me we'd make a lot of memories here." I offered a small smile, hoping Toby was still excited about the transition I decided for us.

Toby nodded as he peered out at the water and then turned back to the condo. "He said that?"

"He did." I smiled, remembering Tate's excitement when he first showed me the place. At the time it was the promise of many memories, but today it was the promise of a new beginning.

Toby chewed the side of his cheek and examined the old furniture. "And there's a pool?"

My face spread into a smile as I nodded. "And a crab dock. Do you think you're finally ready to learn?"

He nodded enthusiastically. "Yeah, can we go tonight?"

I smiled at him, feeling more content than I had in a year. "How about tomorrow?"

HERE, BUDDY, PUT this on," I said, holding out an orange life jacket as we passed the pool access door the next morning.

"But I know how to swim," Toby retorted.

"But the rule is under thirteen years old," I said, pointing at the blue and white sign above the life jackets, stating life

35

preservers were required on the dock for those under the age of thirteen.

Toby let out a sigh and shrugged into the life jacket as I pushed Charlie in his stroller, carrying two crab traps folded under my arm. The bait was in the basket under the stroller.

"What is that smell?" Toby said, holding his hand to his nose in disgust as the reek of fish washed through the air. It was strong and lingered until the breeze pushed it past us only for it to return in waves.

"The smell of a crab dinner coming soon." I smiled at him wryly. I knew he'd get used to it. Even if the smell was disgusting. I nodded toward the wooden countertop inserted directly into the side of the building. "And that's where people gut their fish."

He pretended to gag, and I laughed, another sweet release reminding me we were going to be okay.

Eventually.

The crab dock jutted out into Yaquina Bay and sat directly next to the harbor that housed dozens and dozens of boats varying in shape, size, and name—a yacht named Lucille and a fishing boat named Glenda. Even a Steamboat named Tommy Boy. There were a few dozen hooks ten feet apart for crabbers to hook their traps to along the dock. It was empty and only a few hooks were wrapped in rope, hopefully promising crab later that night.

"Where do we go?" Toby asked, his eyes moving down the dock.

"Whichever hook you want. You pick," I said, smiling while Charlie clapped to the sound of the sea lions barking in the distance.

Toby picked two hooks near the end of the dock and I parked the stroller, pushing down the breaks and setting down the traps. As I locked the metal latches so the trap would take shape, I pulled the bait from under the stroller and heard a splash behind me.

I turned around to see another crabber had joined us as he tossed his own net out into the icy water. He was tall and wore a rain jacket with the hood up so it covered his face. He seemed to be minding his own business, and I felt slightly relieved. I wasn't in the mood for small talk. I turned my attention back to Toby.

"What is that?" Toby asked, his face scrunched.

"Bait," I said, plainly, picking up the raw meat. "This will lure the crabs in the cage through these doors. You see?" I moved the doors open and showed him how they didn't swing both ways. "But they can't get out."

He smiled, understanding washing over his face. "Which is why it's called it a trap!"

I let out a soft laugh. "Exactly." I winked and began showing him how to place the raw chicken breasts in the bait trap.

"You know, the best bait is raw chicken meat," a deep voice said behind me. The sound was smooth and pleasant, but his words seemed to be laced in arrogance, and it irritated me. He was interrupting a moment where I was teaching my son to crab for the first time. I fell short in so many ways, especially in the last year, but with crabbing, I was entirely competent and excited to create this memory with Toby.

I glanced at Toby, who was looking at the man behind me. I cleared my throat as I heard the man's footsteps draw closer.

"Thank you," I said politely, my voice even in the salty air. "I am using chicken meat."

I met his eyes, and he held my gaze. His eyes were a beautiful shade of brown, dripping in both arrogance and charm. His face was sharp along the edges but soft around his mouth and eyes.

I blinked away, focusing back on the traps I was filling. I didn't care what he looked like. I wanted him to go back to minding his business so Toby and I could carry on with our morning.

"White or dark meat?" he asked, showing no understanding he was intruding

I drew in a breath and stood, both traps filled to the brim.

"Both," I said with a smile plastered on my face.

He nodded at me in approval, which irritated me even more. I wasn't seeking his approval. I didn't need it, and, quite frankly, didn't want it. I turned back to Toby who was mesmerized by this man saying nothing more than I was already teaching. I studied Toby's face for a moment hoping he'd break the trance he was in and turn his attention back to me, but he didn't.

"Why do they like the chicken meat? In the lobby they sell worms. What's the difference?" Toby asked the man, eager for an answer.

I opened my mouth to answer but the man was faster than me.

"Well, what would you rather eat?" he answered with a smile that broke through his serious and sharp façade. I looked from Toby to the stranger with dark eyes and watched him curiously.

Toby laughed. "Good point."

I drew in a breath. "It's because there's better meat for the crabs to eat with chicken," I said looking at Toby and the stranger nodded behind me. I didn't see it. But I could sense it. Like his eyes were watching me and making sure I knew how to crab. My fingers brushed the permit I just printed out in my pocket just in case he was going to ask for it. I turned to face him, prepared to end the conversation but he continued to speak.

"Sounds like your mom knows a thing or two," he said, his hands in his pockets as he rocked back on his heels and looked out at the water. He was completely comfortable on the dock taking up space in his perfectly olive skin. I was waiting for him to tell me he owned the place.

"My papa taught her how to crab. She's been dying to take me and now we live here so I guess I'm going to get really good." Toby was smiling as he told the stranger more than I wanted him to hear. He turned to me. "Huh, Mom?"

"Yeah, you are," I confirmed, my face twitching into a half-smile as I grabbed a wipe from the stroller to clean the chicken off my hands.

"You live here? Well, welcome then," he reached out his hand to Toby. "My name is Dylan Thompson. Nice to meet you."

"Toby Jones," my son said as he proudly shook his hand.

Dylan's eyes examined the stroller and me, waiting patiently for me to join in on the introductions.

"Tabitha," I said, shaking his hand. It was warm and firm as it encased mine. I could feel a callous across his palm, but his fingers were soft as they reached my wrist. I pulled my hand away almost nervously and turned to the stroller. "This is Charlie."

He bent down to the stroller and let Charlie give him a high-five. I drew in a sharp breath through my teeth, a wave of uncertainty hitting me, and I felt overly protective.

"What a cutie," he said, standing again and looking me in the eye. "So, you live here now?"

I nodded, giving him a pleasant but hesitant smile, not wanting to reveal too much about my living arrangements to a stranger. This wasn't like meeting a typical neighbor. There were hundreds of units at the resort and very few were permanent residents.

"Yep, and my mom's best friend lives ten minutes away now so I get to play with Caden and Eli whenever I want." Toby smiled, excited to be meeting new people and enjoying the adventure I promised our life in Newport would be. I felt a small pang of guilt for wanting to reel him in, as if my hesitance was holding him back from loving his new home.

"That so?" Dylan smiled at me, but his eyes landed on Toby. "Where are you guys from?"

"Tacoma, Washington. My mom said it was time for a fresh start." Toby was triumphant and eager to regurgitate the speech I had prepared with him, though I had hoped he would have saved it for his teacher, not some random man on the crab dock.

Dylan smiled. "Welcome. If there's anything you need, let me know."

"That's very friendly of you," I said. My words were polite, but my tone had an edge.

I worried he was being far too forward with my children. It didn't matter he was polite and kind of attractive—I could tell even though his hood was up and his hat was low. He seemed like the kind of guy that knew how good looking he was and used it as a weapon to get his way.

Tate was always my common sense and voice of reason. I desperately wanted to call him and tell him about this man named Dylan on the crabbing dock, but the knowledge that I couldn't hit me like a punch to the gut. I felt an emotional ball of frustration lodge in my throat, and I swallowed it down to force another polite smile at this stranger that now knew where I came from and where I was living.

"Well, the Welcome to Newport sign does say 'the friendliest.'" He continued to smile, still observing me and my family.

Creep.

There was a line between small town manners and overbearing confidence. In my mind, he was edging over it a little too quickly.

"Do you live here too?" I asked, clearing my throat with a nod at the complex behind us that had access to this dock, trying to get as much information from him as he got from Toby.

He shook his head. "I don't."

"Oh, on vacation then?" I asked, assuming he was here for Labor Day weekend.

"Nah," he said, shaking his head and giving me a small smile. "Local but I don't live here."

I felt a rush of relief, knowing this man wasn't going to be staying too close to my family, and also a surge of panic wondering what he was doing on a private dock that required a key card to access it. He seemed nice enough, but he was a bit of a know-it-all and suddenly knew far more about me and my boys than I wanted him to know.

Kids certainly have big mouths that can complicate things.

"But if you ever need help or would like someone to show you around, let me know," he continued, a smile pulling at the edges of his lips.

Was he hitting on me? In front of my two kids? I couldn't believe his nerve. His forwardness. His irritating confidence.

"Thank you but my best friend has lived here for five years so we're a bit more familiar than we may seem." I was polite, but I was direct. I still wore my wedding ring and used my left hand to tuck a loose strand of hair behind my ear. His eyes caught on it, and I saw his body freeze for a subtle moment, and he nodded in understanding.

"But we live right up there!" Toby pointed his finger to the direction of our condo perched on the hillside next to the water's edge. I pressed my eyes closed as Toby continued to reveal more of our life to this stranger. My mind began running through all the small-town serial killer and kidnapper documentaries I watched late at night when the kids had gone to bed. I tilted my head from side to side, cracking my neck and hoping to shake out every worst-case scenario coursing through my brain. "Mom's going to fix up the condo real nice—it'll be practically brand new."

"Is that right?" His face broke into a smile and his eyes twinkled in the gray daylight over the glassy water. His entire expression was slightly unnerving. "Sounds like your mom is pretty talented. You're a lucky kid."

My eyes narrowed on him again. He seemed genuine but there was an aura dancing around him that was a bit too direct and a bit too friendly. It struck me as pompous, and I was ready for him to leave. I drew in a sharp breath and distracted myself with getting Charlie a toy as he squirmed in the stroller.

"Yeah, she's pretty cool," Toby said, offering a small smile before turning around and watching a large, commercial fishing boat glide across the bay. He swallowed visibly hard. I knew he meant what he said. I also knew my ten-year-old son lost his father only a year ago and didn't feel very lucky.

"Well, you guys let me know if you need any crabbing pointers, okay?" He said it to Toby's back, but he glanced at me briefly and I felt my eyes narrow on him.

"I think we got it, thanks," I said, tossing the trap out into the sea water.

He watched me for a second longer, and his lips curled into a grin before he walked away.

I knew how to crab. I had been doing it for years. There were things in life I needed to be saved from. This was not one of them.

Four

A FTER WE WALKED back into the condo, Toby started playing a game on his tablet while I laid Charlie down for a nap. When I returned to the living room, Toby was engrossed in a game, his gangly, preteen body strewn across the couch.

"That Dylan guy was cool," he said, glancing up at me.

My eyes narrowed on my son. "Was he?"

"Yeah, he seemed really nice. Knew a lot about crabbing." Toby shrugged, not even looking at me.

"It wasn't anything I didn't know," I said, feeling defensive and realizing Toby didn't see the same arrogance I saw.

Toby shrugged again and kept playing his game, tapping at the screen in his hands.

I didn't know if I'd see this Dylan guy again, but I knew I'd need to keep my eye on him if I did, seeing that he made such an immediate impression on Toby. I didn't mind if Toby had male role models—I knew that was best for him—I just didn't envision them being someone we knew nothing about, gently and pompously gaining the admiration of my son. My guard had been on high alert since Tate died. It had to be. Life didn't give me any other choice.

That evening we returned to the dock to check our traps; the sea lions still barked in the distance and the water was calm and glassy until we started pulling on the ropes. My eyes kept darting around the dock and up at the breezeway connecting the dock to the pool access building, watching and waiting for Dylan to show up again.

It wasn't until we were back in the condo with a bucket of fresh crab ready for dinner that I finally let out a sigh of relief. And then nearly a laugh. I realized I was freaking out for nothing. He wasn't a serial killer. He was just forward…and irritating. We'd probably never run into him again.

I showed Toby how to pick the crabs up by their backsides so they wouldn't pinch him, and I let him gently slip them into the giant pot of boiling water. He laughed each time their legs tickled and poked his fingers. Charlie waddled around the condo with a piece of French bread, leaving butter smears on all the furniture as I finished setting the table.

The smell of crab and melted butter mixed with the sound of laughter and determination as Toby perfected his method for cracking the shell delighted my senses. I smiled and licked the butter dripping from my fingers as I took in the scene before me.

Toby looked up at me with a grin as he dunked a piece of crab meat in melted butter. "Aren't you glad you're a pescatarian and not a vegetarian, Mom?"

I let out a small laugh, surprised he remembered the word from a short, yet long year ago.

"Of course."

He winced as he squeezed the metal plated seafood cracker against a crab leg and crab juice squirted out of the shell, splashing his nose. He and Charlie let out roaring laughs I felt in my soul. I didn't know what life was going to look like for us anymore but if my boys were happy, I knew we were headed in the right direction.

I SPENT THE next day ripping out the old, musty carpet and hauling it to the dumpster before painting the walls in the family room and kitchen my favorite shade of white: Alabaster. We had also used it at the Tacoma house. Tate laughed when I called it the perfect shade of white.

White is white, he had said. *That's like having different shades of black.*

There are different shades of black, I had answered him plainly. *Haven't you ever been to a paint store?*

He had laughed so hard at the absurdity I could still hear it in my mind.

Every stroke of paint on the dingy cream walls made me smile as I remembered the conversation while also sending a dull ache across my chest.

I mostly let Toby play video games as I worked feverishly during Charlie's nap, doing my best to keep him contained in the boys' bedroom when he was awake. He didn't sleep well, like one-year-olds normally don't when you have important things to accomplish. But I still managed to get all the old carpet out, exposing the decades-old plywood beneath that smelled of ancient dust and saltwater. I completed nearly all the painting in the main room, which, in turn, masked the smell.

The condo was a disaster, and so was I. My clothes and fingers were covered in paint. I sweat through my shirt and had remnants of dust and dirt on my arms from hauling out the old carpet. The outdated furniture was pushed to the center of the room and paint cans littered the small countertops. I had already decided we'd be ordering in rather than making a delicious homecooked crab feast like the night before.

Living in eleven hundred square feet of a construction zone with two kids, I realized as I stood in the middle of the mess, was insane. I felt so thankful Tate had already taken care of the cabinets and countertops. I couldn't even imagine living there without a functioning kitchen.

When Charlie woke up from his nap, I decided that was enough home improvement for the day. I fed him a quick snack and packed a few towels and an extra swim diaper before donning my own swimsuit and taking the boys down to the pool.

After hours of swimming, Toby was finally worn out enough to return to the condo without complaint for a dinner of delivered pizza.

Charlie fussed through the evening after swimming; I worried he was possibly getting an ear infection. He hadn't slept well during his nap, but it didn't necessarily surprise me. He was in a new environment, and I was rushing around, removing the old carpet and painting walls, not being the nurturing, attentive, and sad mother he was used to.

By nightfall, I was exhausted. And for once in the last year, it wasn't from grief, but from manual labor and swimming with children. My bones begged for sleep, my eyelids were heavy and drooped lower each time I blinked. Toby fell asleep quickly, but Charlie fussed and cried out every time I tried to lay him down. It was a song and dance—back and forth—that went on for hours but when he finally fell asleep, he laid like a rock in my arms.

Once I laid him down in his crib next to Toby's bed, my body ached for sleep. I wasn't used to manual labor; even my fingers were sore. As I finally curled into bed, I knew I'd have no trouble sleeping at all even though I was in a strange place with a different mattress and the wrong kind of pillow.

My neck seized up.

Nope. The pillow mattered.

I sat up and pounded my fist into the lumps of the pillow, not understanding why it didn't feel right. I realized quickly it was Tate's pillow; a firm, foam rectangle he swore molded to the shape of his head. Apparently, it didn't ever take the correct shape of mine and would leave me with a stiff neck anytime I slept on it. I had never gotten rid of it because it still smelled like him. Or at least I pretended like it did. I let out an exhausted sigh and tossed it to the other side of the bed and pulled my pillow toward me.

My head fell to my own pillow in elated anticipation. I sunk into the crisp sheets and let out a sigh that relaxed my entire body onto the mattress.

It was my turn to sleep. Finally.

As soon as I closed my eyes, my mind began to drift to a deep, dreamless state until I was abruptly jerked out of the trance I was falling into.

Thump, thump, clank, thump...thump, thump. Clank.

My eyes shot open.

"What the hell?" I muttered into the night as I glanced at the clock. It was nearing midnight. Surely, it was just someone getting home from a late night of clam chowder and drinks stumbling through the door and dropping their keys a few times. The building was old, and the walls were thinner than anyone would like, but the footsteps were so loud it seemed they were purposefully slamming their feet against the floor. I prayed they would walk softly as the night continued.

Silence lingered for several minutes. Almost long enough for me to fall asleep until the pounding of steps echoed on the ceiling again.

Thump...thump, thump. Clank.

It had seemed they decided to start running up and down the hallway. The pattern continued for nearly forty-five minutes before I ran out of patience and lost my temper, fueled by deep exhaustion.

"I swear to God if they wake up Charlie..." I said to myself as I threw off my covers, shoving my feet into slippers and wrapping my body in my fluffy, pink robe before heading out the front door and up the stairs to the condo above me.

I knocked on the door, taking in a deep breath trying to muster up at least an ounce of manners for when I tell the vacationers renting above me to please keep it down. The door opened immediately after I knocked, like my presence was expected all along.

Dylan.

His eyes flashed in surprise before he smiled at me. He pulled the door open wide, his arm bracing the top. I glanced at his bicep filling out his black t-shirt and blinked away, pulling my robe tighter and shaking my head slightly.

"Of course." I rolled my eyes. "What are *you* doing up here?" I hadn't meant to say it like that—I didn't mean to sound rude at all. I was just so tired that the words tumbled out of my mouth before I could stop them.

Dylan glanced behind him and back at me—his face smug, a grin spreading across his lips. "I probably should ask you the same thing, considering you're the one knocking."

I shook my head slightly again, remembering why I stomped up there in first place. "Right. Sorry. Well, no, I'm not *sorry*. Do you mind keeping it down? It is nearly twelve-thirty and all I can hear is you stomping up and down the hallway. And I swear, if you wake up my toddler, you will see the wrath of a mother you cannot even imagine."

Dylan raised his eyebrows, his dark eyes sparkling with charm and arrogance. He watched me for a moment.

"My apologies." He pressed his lips together, withholding a smile. "There was a leak in the sink, and someone has a reservation starting tomorrow and this is the only time I could get to it."

"Why are you fixing it? They have maintenance here." My brow furrowed in confusion.

"I own the unit so..." His voice trailed off, explaining his inherent responsibility to maintain the unit himself. My mouth fell open and I closed it.

Of course, the pompous, irritating, invasive crabbing expert owned the unit above me. And even less surprising, he was stomping across the floor during the midnight hours without any regard for anyone else.

"Can you just keep it down?" I crossed my arms and drew in a breath. "Please."

"Will do." He smiled again, looking at me like he was amused by me, then leaned in slightly. "I'll tip-toe."

I gave a curt nod and turned to walk down the stairwell.

"I like your robe," he called from the doorway, still smiling and watching me in amusement.

My eyes drifted to my fluffy, pink robe and I knew I resembled a cloud of cotton candy. A rush of embarrassment laced with irritation crept up my neck as I turned back to face him.

"Thanks," I said sarcastically. "People wear them over their pajamas…you know, when they're trying to *sleep*."

He laughed, leaning against the doorway.

"Please just keep it down, Derek," I said turning back down the stairs.

"Dylan," he corrected me.

"Whatever," I responded without looking back, though I smiled to myself. Whether I was charmed or triumphant, I wasn't sure.

Summer 13

"WAKE UP," TATE whispered in my ear.

My senses began to wake before I even opened my eyes. The sound of Tate's voice in the calm of night. The touch of his skin. His breath on my ear. But my eyes refused to open. I didn't want them to. It was the dead of night. A fact I knew because it was still pitch-black outside. In the middle of August, the sun rose before six.

"No," I mumbled into my pillow.

"Yes," he whispered, shaking my shoulder gently.

I opened one eye and glanced at my phone screen, then turned to him sharply. "Tate, it's four o'clock in the morning."

"It is," he said, kissing my shoulder and running his fingers up my back under my tank top. My skin was warm with sleep and his touch made me shiver.

"Tate," I said seriously, my voice raspy from the early wake up. "I am not in the mood to have sex right now."

He laughed against the skin on my shoulder, and it made me smile. His laugh always made me smile. It was a breath of fresh air. Like a song I never grew tired of—the very heartbeat of my soul.

"But are you in the mood to catch a plane?" he whispered.

I sat up immediately and stared at him in disbelief. "Excuse me?"

He smiled wide and crooked and perfect. "Get dressed."

He rose from the bed, already dressed in airport attire—joggers and a zip-up hoodie—and grabbed the two rolling suitcases from the corner.

"Where are we going?" I couldn't believe it—couldn't even process it, really. Tate had tried for years to surprise me. It was always a struggle for him because I could read him like a book. I even guessed his proposal, and he had to improvise the next day.

But this. This was shocking and I in no way saw it coming.

It had been a stressful year for us. I still couldn't get pregnant even after a trying IVF. The process was long, painful, exhausting, and really expensive. The aftermath was almost harder. The negative pregnancy test result was adhered in my brain in a way I couldn't shake. Telling our family, our friends—every single person crossing their fingers and praying for us—was far worse. It was like reliving it over and over.

I hated it. Getting pregnant with Toby was an easy little accident followed with joy and congratulations. Well-meaning people always asked if we were having more kids. Little did they know those words felt like small daggers as they punctured my heart. I vowed to never be that person again. The one who asks women if they were trying to get pregnant—the insensitivity and weight of the question varies too vastly for it to even be acceptable.

But I was still hopeful and so was Tate. If it bothered him, he never let it show, even though I knew we both wanted another child. In between negative pregnancy tests, we distracted ourselves with raising Toby and furthering our careers.

Which wasn't hard to do, considering work was constantly busy for me and Tate's business was growing faster than expected. I could barely keep up with him. It fit his personality though. There weren't many breaks in real estate and Tate hated to rest. Even on vacation.

"Seriously, where are we going?" I repeated, expectantly.

"I think you should just wait and see," he said, exiting our bedroom. "Meet me downstairs in twenty minutes."

"But Tate, I didn't pack anything."

"I know. I did." He barely looked at me—nonchalantly meandering out of the room.

"You're a terrible packer," I called out to him.

"Have a little faith." He laughed, continuing down the hallway.

"Tate..." I called again.

"Twenty minutes, Tabitha. You don't want to be late."

"Where are we going?" I hollered, playfully desperate, but he didn't answer. I was amused. Of all the romantic things Tate did over the years—this was making it to the top of the list.

I hopped out of the bed and entered the bathroom to find leggings, a t-shirt, and a sweatshirt neatly folded on the ottoman in the center of the bathroom with a note telling me to get dressed, my parents and coffee were downstairs, and an Uber was waiting outside.

My mouth fell open and I couldn't pick it up off the floor. I literally dragged my chin all the way to the airport until I read our departure at the check-in kiosk.

"Hawaii?" I exclaimed as he completed our check-in and turned to face me. A small, sheepish smile laced with smug satisfaction spread on his face. "Tate. How did you?—"

"You've underestimated me, my dear. Being married to me for ten years is no simple feat."

I blinked heavy with an astonished smile on my face. "I mean, it is if you wake me up at four in the morning to whisk me off to Hawaii."

He let out a laugh and pulled out his ID as we walked to the TSA security line. "Good choice then?"

I opened my mouth but nothing came out. I smiled so wide I laughed. I was giddy and nervous. There were checklists to go through before a vacation. None of which I was able to do. I wondered if he packed the right bathing suit or bought the appropriate toiletries or if he even remembered sunscreen. I worried whether or not he left enough instructions for my parents with Toby. I felt terrible for not saying a proper goodbye the night before. But I was also thrilled to escape to tropical waters and white, sandy beaches.

He grabbed my hand and spun me gently into his arms as he nuzzled his face in my hair and brushed his lips against my ear as he whispered, "It may have taken me over ten years to finally surprise you, but the look on your face alone right now is worth the wait."

I leaned back into him, biting my bottom lip to give my cheeks a break from the atrocious amount of smiling happening far too early in the morning. I handed my ID to the TSA agent.

"Destination?" she asked as she examined my boarding pass.

"Hawaii!" I shrieked out of joy and excitement making the agent take a half step back and laugh. I jumped twice and clapped my hands together. "I'm sorry, I had no idea where he was taking me until fifteen minutes ago."

She nodded with a playful roll of her eyes. "Have a good time," she said plainly before moving on to the next people in line.

Once we were through security, I practically bounced across the beige stone floors of the airport. We had been to Hawaii before but never on a day I was expecting to be a regular Monday where I dropped Toby off at daycare and headed into work. This was different. A surprise tropical vacation killed any Monday blues that had crept in my mind the night before. I didn't even care I was running on four hours of sleep. I was headed to Hawaii—*on a whim*—with the love of my entire life standing next to me looking both satisfied and thrilled for the same reasons.

WHEN WE WALKED out of the Kahului Airport, the immediate scent of tropical flowers and white sandy beaches washed over me as quickly as the salty, warm air. Maui was always such a dream, but I still didn't feel like I had woken up yet, so I wondered if it actually was.

The entire morning was a blur. A magical, surreal, perfect blur that led me to laying in Tate's arms on the beaches of Maui celebrating ten years of marriage with drinks in our hands.

"Where do you see us in five years?" Tate asked, as the salty breeze whipped through my hair, the setting sun still warm on my face. I sat between his legs, my back against his chest and our toes tickling the sand as we gazed out at the turquoise water.

I contemplated for a moment. "I would really like to either move up as the lead accountant at work or move to a different company entirely."

"Really?" Tate was clearly taken aback by this. "I thought you liked working for Cecilia."

"I do," I said slowly. "But I've been there for over ten years now and not much has changed. It's a solid place to work— great benefits, stable income." I shrugged. "I don't know, change might be nice in five years."

"Why wait? Quit when we get back. You can find something else, no problem." This was typical Tate: always impulsive, believing the pursuit of dreams would always fold out into success.

"Tate…" I began.

"Why not?" he asked, sweeping my hair off my shoulder. "If you aren't entirely happy at work, don't waste another minute there."

"I'm not unhappy, Tate. I love my job. I don't *want* to quit. I just might want something else in five years. Toby will be much older so I could work somewhere without needing a schedule that aligns with the daycare's schedule. I'll also have enough saved in my 401k that I could work somewhere and take a small dip in my retirement—I mean, if it would pay off in the long run." I picked at my nails and then looked back up at him. His eyes were as hopeful as they were excited. He was always encouraging me to take chances. He had the ability to love my smallest most realistic dreams and make them sound like lifetime achievements. I let out a laugh. "I mean, it's a maybe. We'll see how the next few years play out."

"Alright. New job. What else?" he asked eagerly.

"We're not moving to San Diego with Justin." I eyed him knowingly.

Tate laughed. I knew how much he missed his brother, but San Diego was just not feasible on our income. We weren't hurting by any means, but a penny didn't stretch as far there as it did in Washington, no matter how quickly the housing market was rising.

"I wasn't going to suggest that." He threw up his hands. "But maybe a vacation rental somewhere?"

I smiled. "As an investment?"

"Of course." He smiled, his mind clearly wandering through the possibilities. "Where do you think? San Diego?" he asked hopefully. I rolled my eyes and laughed. "Seriously," he said.

I shook my head and let my laugh turn into a breath. "*Seriously*, I don't know that we'd get a good enough return on that or be able to visit often enough to make it worth it for us." Hopping on a plane with a child was not simple. Airport mornings rarely went the same way that morning had gone when just the two of us flew over the Pacific to be there on the beach with the ice from our Mai Thai's melting into the white sand.

"You're probably right." There was a beat of silence, both of us pondering the right place to invest in a vacation rental.

"Lake Chelan?" he asked finally.

"Too crowded."

"Suncadia?"

"Too ritzy."

"Ocean Shores?"

I twisted my lips and shook my head.

"Hey, Lydia and Tim are loving living in Newport." It was a loose suggestion and it made me laugh.

"Lydia would freak—she'd be so happy."

"Would you?"

I shrugged, not because I didn't know if I'd like it but because I hadn't thought about it yet. I hadn't even attempted to process it as a real suggestion. "Probably," I said, finally. "But would you?"

"Of course." He kissed the top of my head and ran his

hands down my arms until he laced his fingers in mine and held me closely to his chest. He drew in a sharp breath. "What about trying again?"

The air escaped my lungs quickly. Another baby was on every five-year plan we had discussed. For both of us. And yet, we were still hanging in the balance, teetering in the realm of uncertainty. Not knowing if we could, let alone if we really even wanted to. The disappointment of failure caused a ripple effect we couldn't stop.

"I don't want to count on it," I said into the wind, hoping he didn't hear my doubt but also hoping he understood if he did.

His arms tightened around me and it made my throat catch. "Whatever you want to do is okay."

I nodded, absorbing his words and the comfort it brought. And yet, a pang of desire shot across my chest. I leaned my head back and rested it against his shoulder and closed my eyes.

"I want to try IVF again," I said finally.

"You sure?"

"Yeah, I've been thinking a lot about it." It was true. I thought about it all the time. It wasn't on the forefront of my mind or the first thing I thought of in the morning, but it lingered in the back of my mind. It clawed at me gently yet constantly until it became painful. "I don't want to tell anyone about it though. Not this time. If it doesn't work again, I don't want to have to call anyone."

"Okay," he said softly, kissing the side of my head. His lips were an ointment for my wounds. His arms were a safety I couldn't imagine being without. His heart beating against my back felt like the rhythm to the life I always wanted to live.

"What about you?" I said, pulling out of my thoughts. "Where do you want to be in five years?"

He turned me around with one swift and gentle movement, so I was facing him and gingerly tilted my chin toward his face with a finger.

"With you."

His sincerity made me laugh and blush. Even after ten years, Tate always looked at me like I was his entire world. I'm not sure he ever realized he was also mine.

"It can't be about me forever," I replied, making sure our goals and dreams were staying on track.

"Oh, but it can be all about you for *my* forever."

I shook my head as I intertwined my fingers behind his neck. "Well, then I guess you will never get to find love after me because I'm dying first." I let out a laugh. "You promised."

Tate was smiling at me, and it was wistful and dreamy, like he was perfectly content and entirely in love. His eyes reflected the ocean water, and the sun made his skin glow against his breathtaking smile. I froze the memory of his face in that moment and prayed it would never fade.

Five

"ARE YOU FREAKING kidding me?!" I screamed to no one but the damn miter saw that decided to go kaput when I was only a few square feet away from completing installation of the new floors in the condo after a month of living on plywood floors. "No, no, no," I pleaded with the saw to work for just a little bit longer.

Only four more cuts were left.

That was it. So close, yet so far.

Charlie was at his new daycare—which was my only reprieve from his busy toddler behavior while I worked remotely on my computer and laid down the new floors. At first, I tried to keep Charlie home with me, but I realized quickly I needed him to be in the safety of a daycare and not scraping his sweet toes on rusty nails protruding from the floor's surface.

As it turns out, I pulled the carpet and linoleum up a bit too prematurely; the delivery for the new vinyl plank flooring was delayed. I was completely frustrated with myself, wishing I had waited for the boxes of flooring to be sitting on the front patio before I tore up the old carpet. Even with the new carpet laid in the bedrooms, it still felt like our life was completely under construction.

On the bright side it did give us the month to finish painting. I took my time and let Toby help—every splatter simply fell on the plywood. The white paint made the condo look fresh and modern and accentuated the cedar tongue-and-groove vaulted ceiling flanking a skylight. I let Toby pick the color for their bedroom and he opted for a deep navy. I hung white curtains and tied them back with rope—it was nautical-themed and out of my character, but Toby loved it and it fit perfectly in our new abode.

I stared at the broken saw in a frustrated daze. I was so close to being done. It had taken days even though the room wasn't all that big. I forgot how hard it was to complete projects alone.

I unplugged the saw, plugged it back in, and turned it on.

Nothing.

Switched it off and on again.

Still nothing.

It was completely dead.

I balled my hands into fists and let out a frustrated groan that echoed in my soul. My fingers were raw, and my knees ached from days and days of laying the new floors. The microwave blew the week prior, and I had just replaced the leaky faucet in the bathroom. I couldn't handle another thing breaking.

I bit off more than I could chew. I wanted to go home. And I wanted Tate to be there when I arrived.

This isn't home. This can never be home, I thought painfully.

"Piece of shit!" I yelled as I angrily chucked the saw in the dumpster outside, unwilling to even see if it could be fixed. When I aggressively turned on my heel to march back to the condo, I saw Dylan standing just outside his condo's front door, leaning his elbows on the railing. He narrowed his eyes on my screams and the corner of his mouth twitched into an almost condescending smile—an expression I could feel in my stomach.

"What, *Derek*?" I yelled throwing my hands up while

walking into my condo and slamming the door.

I didn't even wait for him to answer. Didn't even care to see what his expression was. I leaned my back against the front door and started crying.

A stupid, pathetic, and frustrated cry.

What was I even doing here in this stupid little town in my tiny condo I didn't even want in the first place? Why had I moved? What was I trying to prove?

I couldn't do it. Not alone. Not without Tate.

As my back slid down the door, I sat, hunched over my knees, collecting my sobs with a few deep breaths until my emotions were steady enough to think logically.

"I can do this, calm down," I whispered to myself like a crazy person.

I pulled my phone out of my back pocket with shaky and calloused hands and started scrolling through miter saws online, checking prices and reviews. After thirty minutes, I had wasted far too much time, only to realized I didn't want to wait a few days for it to arrive by mail.

Instead, I wiped the mascara from under my eyes and drove straight to the local hardware store to buy a new one.

I stared at the aisle lined with every type of saw for a painfully long time, wanting the cheapest option that wouldn't malfunction and cause me to chop my hand off. The flooring was already taking far longer than I wanted it to, and I had to finish in one hour before it was time to pick up the boys. I was in a hurried race for time and my sanity. I grabbed a saw off the bottom shelf and turned around quickly, bumping into the man walking behind me with such force I bounced back and nearly fell over.

"Oh, my God, I'm so sorry. I wasn't paying attention," I said as my eyes adjusted on Dylan standing there with paint-splattered coveralls, a black ball cap, and a navy rain jacket. His face spread into a smile. Less condescending than it was just two hours ago, but heat rose to my cheeks and I let out a breath, hoping my embarrassment would go with it.

"No problem," he said, still looking at me like he was amused. "Tabitha, right?"

I nodded and decided to be nice. "Dylan?"

"You remembered this time," he said and my eyes drifted to his lips. His smile was disarming.

"My saw broke," I said with a shrug, explaining why I was there without him asking and feeling slightly mortified.

"I saw that," he said and I pressed my lips into a hard, embarrassed line. He gestured to his paint-covered attire I didn't notice earlier. "I need more paint."

"Did you follow me here?" I accused him. I knew he saw my temper tantrum in the parking lot. What were the chances we'd both end up at the hardware store two hours later?

He shook his head with a smile and I blinked away trying to ignore how perfect it was. "No, just out of paint. I promise. All that work you're doing on the condo below my unit is inspiring me to make a few changes myself. I've heard you working hard every time I swing by."

I gave him one solemn nod. I always heard when he was 'swinging by.' His truck roared obnoxiously from a mile away. I could hear him coming as soon as he turned into the parking lot.

I didn't talk to him much after the night I told him to keep the noise down, just more or less a hello or curt nod in passing, and it felt odd he was aware of what I was up to in the privacy of my own home.

"Well, at least I'm not causing a raucous in the middle of the night," I said sarcastically with a smile.

He held up his hands. "Hey, I apologize. I wasn't used to having someone live below the unit. It didn't get rented out much after the previous owner sold it."

I nodded. "I see. Well, hopefully I'll be done soon. I just have the rest of the floor in the hallway and then it will be nothing but laying rugs and furniture deliveries." I gave him a small smile and turned to walk away, unsure of why I was rambling and offering him more information when I was still slightly irritated by the little information he already had.

"You could borrow my saw if you want," he called, making me turn to face him. "It's just collecting dust when I'm not using it."

I almost said yes. His smugness had somehow evaporated

and transformed into a charming indifference. But I didn't want his help. I wanted to do this on my own. For myself. For my boys. For Tate.

"Thank you for the offer. But I never know when I might need a saw again," I said, my tone softening as I gestured to the box in my hands.

He smiled, revealing a dimple on his cheek I hadn't noticed before, and shrugged. "My saw is all yours anytime you want."

"I'll remember that." I turned to the checkout stand and bought my own saw, ignoring his politeness and attempts at chivalry. I glanced up at him again before taking my receipt from the cashier. He was engrossed in paint chips, holding up three different shades of white in his hand.

It was brief, but it made me smile.

WHAT DO YOU think?" I said to Toby when he walked in the condo.

The new furniture was delivered just days after I finished the floors while Toby was at school. A new, overstuffed sectional and rustic dining table were welcomed replacements for the old rickety leftover furniture from the eighties. It already felt a million more times like home.

Toby threw down his backpack and flopped on the couch.

"This is awesome!" he said, grabbing the remote and flipping on the TV.

I walked over to him and took the remote, turning it back off as Charlie waddled up to the new coffee table, slapping it repeatedly and giggling.

"Come on. TV later. Let's go grab some dinner before Lydia and the boys come over," I suggested.

I was so happy to have my best friend close. We met for coffee or lunch most days, and Tim helped haul away the old furniture the day before. They were the constant familiarity I needed while learning to live in a brand-new place. Tim and Lydia made the transition almost seamless.

Almost.

As Toby and I walked along the bay on the sidewalk, seagulls glided through the air and we stopped at the port dock where the sea lions congregated to bark and snuggle like sardines in a can. Toby laughed as a sea lion wouldn't let another back on the dock and Charlie squealed in my arms, completely mesmerized by such strange, loud, and majestic creatures.

The dock was empty except for us, a far contrast from the warm, summer weekends. A peaceful calm and quiet danced over the Wednesday autumn evening sky.

We grabbed fish and chips from a restaurant on the boardwalk and found a bench at the end of the strip of tourist shops, coffee shops, candy stores, and Ripley's Believe it Or Not!.

"We'll have to check that place out one day," I said, nodding toward the museum.

Toby nodded with a mouthful of French fries. "Dad told me about that place once."

"He did?" Tears stung the backs of my eyes. No matter where I went, I always found Tate in the details—like he was still living in the air I breathed.

Toby nodded. "Yeah, he said it's crazy—full of wax statues and weird stuff."

"Well, I'd love to take you soon." I smiled, pressing back my emotions. "How do you feel about Newport so far?"

He shrugged. "It's good. Kind of feels like we're on vacation. Dad would have loved it."

We talked about Tate all the time. He was embedded in the very fibers that made us a family. Toby and I had finally reached the point where we talked about him without crying—at least not every time—like he wasn't dead but just somewhere else for a little while.

"What about school? You doing okay there?"

"Yep. Caden's friends are nice. There's this kid, Zach, and he's really good at soccer. Like, *really* good. And he picks me every day at recess to be on his team." He leaned in playfully like he was about to tell a funny joke. Tate used to do the same thing. "So, I guess you could say I'm kind of a big deal at school now."

I laughed. "I'm glad you like it. I actually think I know who Zach's mom is."

"Really?"

I nodded. "I met her at pick-up. Maybe we could set up a time for you boys to play one day. Would that be fun?"

He nodded and took a bite of a French fry.

"You miss home much?" I asked, handing Charlie another piece of fish.

Toby swallowed hard as I dipped my fried fish in tartar sauce. I didn't want to bring it up. Home wasn't what it used to mean with Tate gone. But I needed to make sure my son was okay. His world was turned upside down in an instant—like mine but different for his tender ten-year-old heart.

"Not really. At least not what home was without Dad." He shrugged.

I reached out and brushed back his brown hair that had fallen over his forehead and my finger lingered down to the scar on his neck. He twitched his shoulder and gave me a timid smile. I stared at him a moment before Charlie squealed for another French fry.

"I know exactly what you mean." I smiled at him and pulled him in for a hug. An insufferable bond held us together. It was me and Toby against the world with our sidekick, Charlie.

After we tossed our garbage in the trash, we walked in the direction of the condo. The boardwalk remained mostly empty and quiet except for the sounds of the bay and a man playing guitar in the distance. We strolled slowly along the water, pointing out each boat to Charlie and searching for more seals in the distance.

"Hey there, Toby," the man playing guitar said, smooth and calm. It sounded familiar. For a moment I thought it was Tate and I was sure I was losing my mind.

"Dylan!" Toby said running toward the man with the guitar. He wasn't wearing a hat for the first time since I'd first met him, so I didn't recognize him right away. But Toby did and his instant familiarity with Dylan left an odd feeling in my chest.

"How's the new place been?" Dylan asked as if he was best

friends with my son.

"Good. Mom made it awesome." He smiled, and Dylan returned it.

"Like you said she would." His eyes flitted toward me as I made my way closer with Charlie in the stroller. "And school?"

"Good. I'm in Caden's class. Our teacher is Mrs. Sanderson."

"She was my teacher, too!" Dylan's face beamed with a genuine smile. "She's the best. I can't believe she's still teaching. Tell me, does she still have different colored reading glasses for each day of the week?"

Toby nodded and laughed.

My heart beat faster as Toby continued to give this stranger more and more personal information. Although, he owned the unit above us, and I kept running into him around town so I wondered how much longer I could refer to him as that.

"Well, aren't you just *everywhere*?" I asked, incredulously. I tried to sound playful, but it didn't come out that way and I immediately wished I didn't say anything at all.

"I live here," he said plainly, placing his guitar next to him on the bench. "It's a small town, Tabitha. You might need to start getting used to seeing the same folks over and over. You moved here too."

I couldn't be sure, but his face was washed with something that looked almost sad—like, maybe I offended him, and it made me swallow a surge of guilt. I was unintentionally rude to him once again.

And this time, he didn't deserve it.

Toby looked up at me, his eyes slightly narrowed.

"Right," I said, finally. "I'm sorry. I guess I'm just still getting used to it around here."

I swallowed hard and my hands began to sweat.

"I like your guitar," Toby said, running his hand over the strings.

"Toby, please don't touch it without asking." I looked at Dylan apologetically and he waved off the concern.

"Don't worry about it." He turned back to Toby. "Do you play an instrument?"

"No, just basketball and soccer."

Dylan laughed at Toby's response. "Well, maybe one day you can find time for a little music too."

"Yeah, maybe." Toby stared thoughtfully at the guitar. "Maybe you could teach me one day?"

"Toby, honey, I don't think—"

Dylan waved off my concern again and smiled at Toby. "Yeah, maybe." He turned and gave Charlie a playful pinch on his leg dangling out of the stroller, making him giggle and wave at Dylan. "And how's this guy sleeping now? Better I hope."

I felt taken aback, remembering how just a few weeks ago he was struggling to find a routine in the new condo, and I yelled at Dylan about it. An embarrassed flush rose in my cheeks.

"Better. Thank you." I offered a polite smile and shifted on my feet. I felt so out of place. I had somehow forgotten how to stand or what to do with my hands. Meanwhile, Dylan was completely chill, lounging on a bench, playing guitar, and making friendly conversation with my child.

"Will you be around tonight?" Toby asked Dylan. "My friends are coming over. Maybe you could teach us to play guitar tonight."

"Oh, Toby, I don't think Dylan can tonight," I answered for him.

Dylan met my eyes from his place on the bench—that same smug, amused, charming look causing uncomfortable irritation to creep through my pores.

"Maybe another time." He smiled and leaned back on the bench.

Don't count on it, I thought. I didn't know why he drove me crazy.

"Yeah, maybe." Toby turned to me. "Mom, can you get his number?"

I blushed in embarrassment and Dylan laughed. I looked at him apologetically again.

"Here," he said, holding out a large, calloused hand. "Give me your phone."

His demands were irritating yet gentle and convincing. I

placed my phone in his hands, our fingertips touching, and my hands began to shake. I felt like I was doing something wrong—like I was having an inappropriate conversation with a man that wasn't my husband and then giving him my number. Logically, I knew this was completely acceptable—meeting a sort-of neighbor and agreeing to him teaching my son to play guitar one day—but in my heart, it reminded me of how desperately I wished Tate was there.

Dylan punched in his number and sent a text to himself.

"Now, we'll always be able to get a hold of each other." He gave me a small, shy smile and his eyes lingered on my face, making my cheeks warm under his gaze.

I pressed my lips together nervously and nodded before we said goodbye and walked back to the condo.

WHEN LYDIA AND Tim arrived with Caden and Eli, the boys—including her husband, Tim—disappeared in the kids' room to play video games while I poured us each a glass of red wine. We sat on the couch, with the deck door open, letting the crisp, salty, autumn air flood the room.

"So, Toby told Caden you've made friends with a neighbor," Lydia asked, taking a sip of wine.

My eyes darted quickly to hers. I was surprised this was something Toby even talked about with his friends. I waved the comment off.

"Not really *friends*, but we met the guy that owns the unit above us. He doesn't live here though."

Lydia narrowed her eyes. "Old guy? This place is crawling with old people."

I laughed genuinely. "We did kind of move to a retirement community, didn't we?" I contemplated for a moment. "No. Our age probably. Maybe younger. I'm not really sure. Toby really likes him. I sometimes think he's just hungry for male attention. He and Tate were so close that it probably feels nice having that male presence around."

Lydia's eyes widened and dazzled. "So, a man our age that

Toby loves has a *presence* in your life right now?"

I looked at her in confusion and scoffed slightly. "Oh, no. Not like that. We've only run into him a handful of times. He's nice enough. Kind of annoying but he's good with Toby."

Her eyes narrowed on my mine.

"What, Lydia? My husband has only been gone a year. I'm not letting someone in that easy," I said exhaustedly.

"I'm not saying you are. I'm just saying—well, I don't know what I'm saying." She threw her head back and laughed. "Tell me more about him. Is he attractive? What does he do for a living?"

I sighed. "I don't even know. Like I said, we've only met a few times. He owns the unit above us, said he's local, a self-proclaimed expert crabber, offered to let me use his miter saw, and Toby wants him to teach him how to play guitar." I shrugged.

"Well, look at you: slipping right into the local scene and getting to know all the eligible bachelors," she teased.

"I don't even know if he is eligible. We've never even had a true conversation." My eyes narrowed. "And that's not really what I want or need right now, is it?"

Lydia smiled. "I suppose not. I just don't want you to shut yourself off from the world and the opportunities around you."

"Not this guy, Lydia." I laughed, shaking my head.

She shrugged. "You never know."

I raised my eyebrows at her. "He plays guitar, Lydia."

"Well, that's kind of adorable," she said before taking a sip of wine.

"It's not adorable. It's corny." I leaned back on the couch and shifted my wine glass between my fingers. "I'll bet he's one of those nomad musicians that breaks hearts and moves to the next town. Not my cup of tea and not what I need."

"Says the lady that was married to a guy who read poetry for fun."

I laughed before responding, "Well, this guy also has one of those obnoxious raised trucks you can hear from a mile down the road. Seriously, I know whenever he is just 'stopping by' his unit before he even turns into the parking lot."

"What's wrong with having a truck like that? Doesn't it wreak *masculinity*?" she asked playfully.

I scoffed. "No, it wreaks overcompensation."

Lydia snorted out a laugh into her glass of wine. "He can't be that bad. What's his name anyway?"

"Dylan." I swirled my wine. "His last name is Thompson, I think."

"Oh," Lydia said as she nodded slowly, a smile spreading across her face.

"You know him?" I narrowed my eyes on my friend.

"Most people around here do."

"Great, so he gets around too. See? I was right. Heartbreaker musician."

"No, I didn't say that. And he is anything but a heartbreaker." She pressed her lips together pondering her next words. "He's a nice guy. Popular with the ladies, of course—I mean, have you seen him? But he doesn't seem to be the playboy type. Not how I've come to know him. You know Zach's mom, Mindy?" I nodded, remembering Toby's friend's mother from school pick-up. "Well, she has been trying to set him up for years. She used to be friends with—well, never mind. Small town gossip." She waved her hand dismissively, cutting herself off from the story she was about to tell.

I narrowed my eyes on her for a moment, wondering if I even cared enough to pry.

"Well, doesn't he just sound perfect," I said instead, and I didn't even try to hide my sarcasm.

"He's definitely not perfect. No one is." She smiled at me intentionally and then shrugged. "But I like him."

"Wait. Do you *know him* or just know *of* him?"

Lydia smiled. "Both. But my mouth is shut, you need to figure him out for yourself. It'd be no fun if I told you all his secrets."

Summer 12

W HY ARE YOU putting that in the refrigerator?" I asked, licking a cookie dough covered spatula.

"Because that's how you make sure the cookies don't fall flat in the oven," Tate answered, closing the refrigerator and grabbing the dish towel off the counter.

"Yeah, like yours, Mom," Toby chimed in, licking dough off the spoon Tate handed to him. I shot him a lighthearted glare then pressed my forehead to Toby's and rubbed my nose against his.

"Really? I thought it was because I melted the butter instead of using room temperature," I said.

"Well, yes, that is yet another amateur mistake." Tate winked at me as I wiped the last of the dough off the spatula with my finger and let him lick it off.

"What else makes them so good?" I eyed him curiously.

"Peanut butter."

"Peanut butter?"

He kissed my cheek and smiled. "But just a smidge. Peanut butter makes everything taste better."

I leaned back against the counter. "It's really unfortunate I'm such a terrible baker."

"Don't feel too bad, Mom. You make really good cobbler still," Toby said as he hopped off the chair and tossed his spoon in the sink.

"Well, thank you for that reminder, bud." I smiled at Toby and gave his shoulder a gentle squeeze. My fingertips inadvertently brushed against the small lump on his neck and his eyes darted up at me.

"Don't touch it, Mom. Not 'til we know what it is." Toby's eyes were desperate with worry.

My heart sunk into my stomach. "Oh, honey, you don't have to worry about what the lump is. We'll know soon enough." I plastered a reassuring smile on my face even though my heart pounded with concern, and I wished I hadn't touched the lump.

"But what if it's bad? The doctor said it could be cancer and Caden said his grandpa died of cancer. I don't want to give you cancer—I don't want you to die." Toby's eyes were glassy saucers as he pleaded with me.

I pulled him into my arms and cradled his face in my hands, making his face look at me. "We won't know what the lump is until the doctor tells us so until then we don't need to think too much about it, okay?" He nodded; his mouth turned down. "But even if it is cancer, people can't get it from just touching it. That's not how cancer works."

Toby's forehead continued to wrinkle as he nodded. I hated these were words I even had to say. Child and cancer simply do not belong in the same sentence. But somehow, they found their way next to each other that summer.

After we got home from our first camping trip of the summer, Toby was picking at his neck while playing in our backyard and I sat reading in a lounge chair.

Hey, Mom. There's something on my neck, he had said. *Can you look at it?"*

I peered at his tanned neck curiously. It was a lump. About the size of a blueberry just below his hairline.

I think it's a bug bite, I had said. *Does it itch?*

No. Should it itch?

Most bug bites do. Does it hurt?

He had shrugged and continued playing in the backyard, barefoot, tearing across the grass.

After two weeks of what was initially perceived as a bug bite, the lump never healed. It never disappeared under the surface of his skin. It never itched and never hurt. But he'd rub it night after night. I finally made an appointment with his pediatrician, who ordered an ultrasound which determined it was a tumor. I held Toby's hands as his doctor numbed his sweet, small neck and slid a needle into the lump to biopsy the tumor. Tate towered over us—his hands on our shoulders as he whispered a prayer.

Tate and I held our breath the week after the biopsy. I thought about it constantly, but I refused to cry. I refused to worry. I swallowed every tear, not letting fear get the best of me. I didn't want to prepare for cancer until we had to. How could you prepare for it anyway?

"Why do you think God wants me to have cancer?" Toby asked innocently, his eyes bright in the kitchen light, as Tate preheated the oven.

I opened my mouth and closed it, struggling to find the right words even though Tate and I rehearsed how we'd talk about what was going on with his lump late at night when the lights were off, and our heads were on our pillows. Sacred pillow-talk between the two of us always calmed my spirit in ways I couldn't describe.

"God doesn't want you to have cancer, Tobes," Tate filled in for me. "God only wants good things for us."

Toby contemplated for a moment—his young, logical mind trying to make sense of something adults could barely explain. "But if He doesn't want us to get cancer, how come we can?"

I let out a breath. I hated this question because I had asked it so many times myself.

"Because we live in a broken world," Tate answered without pausing as he bent down on a knee to be at Toby's eye level. "It's full of good and bad things. Sometimes bad things happen to good people. Sometimes great things happen to good people.

But whatever happens, it doesn't mean God doesn't love you, and it doesn't mean we should ever stop believing we get to be the good in this world—to fight for the cures, to love other people, and make sure good always conquers evil."

The emotion rose in my throat, and I cleared it away quickly. I refused to cry in front of him—I never wanted Toby to see me worry.

"Like in *Power Rangers*?" Toby asked.

I laughed—a welcomed release in my twisted chest.

"Basically," Tate said matter-of-factly and nodded.

"I could fight some cancer," Toby said, his eyes on Tate. The logic and determination in his small voice made me smile. "Can I be the red one?"

Tate smiled and swallowed hard, his Adam's apple running up and down his throat. "Only if I can be the blue one."

"Deal." Toby leaped into Tate's arms and buried his face in his shoulder. Tate looked at me, tears kissing his eyes, and I forced a shaky smile. I was so thankful he was there to say the right thing—to speak truth without causing worry.

I hoped one day I would learn to do the same.

How ARE LYDIA and Tim liking Newport?" my mother asked as she ladled spaghetti sauce over her noodles. "They've been there, what? A year now?"

"Just under," Tate answered. "They seem to really like it. Lydia's still teaching—said the classroom size is much smaller than up here."

"I bet," my dad agreed. "The district here is just exploding with all the new construction popping up in the area. I mean, it's great for business, I'm sure." He looked expectantly at Tate who nodded and let out a small laugh. "But I wish they really considered the schools when the permits were approved for all these neighborhoods."

"And the infrastructure...the traffic is becoming astronomical no matter what direction you're headed. I mean, construction on I-5 has been nonstop for at least a decade,"

Tate's mother added as my mother passed her the bowl of garlic bread.

"Try three decades," I joked.

"Yeah, and they don't seem even close to finishing," Tate said, adding more spaghetti to his plate.

"You better eat some salad too." I eyed Tate like a child. I hated to nag him, but I loved him enough to remind him he no longer has his twenty-year-old metabolism, and he needed to eat his vegetables. Pasta and red meat didn't agree with him like it used to.

He laughed and reluctantly placed a small helping of Caesar salad on his plate then glared at me playfully.

"I want you around for a long time, mister," I said and kissed him on his cheek while he twirled pasta on his fork. I turned back to my mother. "What were you asking again, Mom?"

My mother laughed and covered her mouth with a napkin. The conversation never died at these family dinners, but it tended to be sporadic and full of tangents and open-ended sentences.

"How are Lydia and Tim liking Newport?" she repeated.

"Oh!" My face brightened. "They love it. The kids loved their new school this year and Tim likes the guys he works with."

"But I heard Lydia is not too fond of him coming home smelling like crab meat," Tate added.

The table erupted in laughter.

"I don't blame her," Tate's mother said. "But I'll bet that's a smell you'll get used to."

"I certainly wouldn't mind it," my dad said. "The smell of crab and salt water will always smell like a trip I want to be on."

I smiled at him, fondly remembering all the years we spent crabbing together.

"Tate, did I ever tell you about the time Tabitha got pinched by a Dungeness?" My father's smile was giddy.

"Dad, no, don't tell him…I was a dumb kid…"

"Mom, don't say dumb," Toby scolded, taking a bite of garlic bread.

"Sorry, Toby. I didn't make a good choice," I agreed and then corrected my phrasing.

"I'll bet that hurt like the dickens," Tate's father added.

"It did," I said, leaning over the table toward him.

"What happened?" Tate asked, wanting the details of the story.

"Well, we had just pulled up a couple dinners worth of crabs and had them in a bucket. After a few hours they stop fighting and slowly start to…" his voice trailed off.

"Die?!" Toby exclaimed, always eager to talk about violence when permitted.

My dad chuckled. "Yes, die." He wiped his mouth with a napkin. "Anyway, I was getting the boiling water ready, and I just hear the loudest, most ear-piercingly, shrill scream coming from Tabitha on the back deck. I thought someone had chopped off her arm. Come to find out, the crab—and it was a biggun—had pinched her little index finger and would not let up. I tell you, I've never heard a scream like that come from *anybody*."

"Thanks, Dad," I grumbled. The table laughed while my cheeks flushed, and I dropped my head to my hands. "In my defense I was like eight years old and I thought the crab was almost dead. I didn't realize the strength in their claws lasted until its heart beat its last."

Tate squeezed my thigh under the table. "I'm glad you made it out alive, Tabby," he said sarcastically, using my least favorite nickname.

"Everybody should be," I teased and exaggeratedly flipped my hair over my shoulder. I eyed a giggling Toby. "Especially you, Toby."

I pointed my finger at him playfully and his mouth dropped into an O.

"I take it you learned your lesson, though?" Tate's mother asked, pushing her glasses back up her nose.

I nodded. "The hard way."

"As usual." Tate added, and I laughed.

"I do not always need to learn the hard way," I said in my own defense. My mom snorted a laugh and covered it with her napkin. My jaw dropped in mock offense.

"You're just stubborn, Tabitha," Tate said with a shrug then laughed and kissed my forehead. "But I wouldn't have you any other way."

I smiled at him, and my phone began to ring on the kitchen counter. I excused myself from the dining room and walked to the kitchen.

The doctor's office number lit up the screen.

The phone felt like a jagged piece of glass in my hand. The specialist promised he'd call as soon as the results were in no matter the time of day or night. I had begged him to after all.

"Hello?" I answered timidly. I stepped in the entryway of the dining room and silently motioned for Tate to join me in the kitchen as I kept the phone pressed to my ear. My mother's eyes were alert when they met mine, but she closed them tightly and nodded with a smile, then asked Toby about playing soccer in the fall to distract the table from the conversation taking place in the kitchen.

"May I speak with a parent of Tobias Jones?"

"This is his mother, Tabitha." I almost stuttered. I felt like I was dreaming.

"Hi Tabitha. This is Dr. Spencer. The results for Tobias's biopsy are in. Is now a good time to chat?"

At my side, Tate slipped his arm around me as I held the phone on speaker between us. We leaned against the counter, bracing ourselves for the worst but desperately hoping for the best.

I nodded my response unable to speak so Tate did so for me.

"Go ahead, Dr. Spencer. We're both here."

The doctor cleared his throat over the line, and I pressed my eyes closed. "The tumor is benign."

I crumbled in relief against Tate's chest. His heart was pounding, and I felt the breath escape his lungs.

"That is a tremendous relief to hear," he said.

"Now we'll still want to have it removed so he'll need to get a scan, but the surgery and recovery will be far less involved than if it were…"

I barely registered the rest of the conversation. Cancer and child don't belong in the same sentence, but I wasn't a fool to believe it couldn't be or that it isn't a harsh reality for so many families.

I peered into the dining room where our sweet, happy boy was dancing in his chair with a joyful disposition and spaghetti smeared on his cheek. I refused to let this world take his joy no matter what lay ahead.

I rested my head on Tate's chest with my arms tightly wrapped around his waist and squeezed out a few tears that landed on his gray shirt before taking a deep breath and composing myself enough to return to the dinner table with the best news we'd heard all summer.

Tate popped sparkling cider, our mothers cried, and we danced on the dining room chairs to celebrate our boy being cancer free.

Life was unpredictable, but Tate was my constant. My pillar of strength. My dance in the rain. My calm in the storm. My everything good in this world.

Six

THE HARSH WIND of autumn whipped past my face as I peered out at the ocean at Moolack Beach. I had parked on the side of Highway 101 and made my way down the lush, steep trail to the wet sand below. I perched on a rock and watched the waves cascade into each other, one after another—crashing over and over.

It looked a lot like how grief feels.

The sky was a light gray and a darker shade of gray mist hovered over the water while white foam marbled throughout the frigid and pounding water. It was hard to tell where the sky ended and the ocean began.

Toby was settling into school just fine and Charlie really took to his daycare teacher, Ms. May. The condo was starting to feel like home and the renovations were finally complete. I'd sit on the balcony no matter how cold it was and do my accounting with the sounds of seagulls swarming the crab dock and sea lions barking in the distance.

It all felt like a dream. Not a bad one necessarily but not really a good one either—just a dream.

Without the distractions of getting the condo renovated, the fog of sadness seemed to return. I didn't know where it came from or how many more waves of grief could crash down on me before I drowned. I started going to that spot on Moolack Beach just outside of Newport when I knew I just needed to sit in my sadness. I'd grab an afternoon coffee and let the sound of the water wash out the sounds of sadness inside my head.

I missed Tate. I missed him with every fiber of my being. A dull ache coursed through my body constantly until I barely had any energy left. He was my lighthouse and now that he was gone, I was stuck bobbing aimlessly in the ocean.

As I sat on the rock, hypnotized by the water, I heard a familiar voice from behind me.

"Shouldn't you be working?" Dylan asked playfully, his hood over his eyes, a disarming smile on his face, and his hands in the pockets of his sweatshirt as he came closer to me.

I turned to the sound of his voice, quickly wiping my wet cheeks with the back of my hand.

"Shouldn't I say the same about you?" I let out a breath, shaking the emotion from my voice as I pulled my knees to my chest.

His smile faded when he saw my tear-streaked face and he swallowed hard as he dipped his head into a nod.

"You do have a job, right? Or do you just own condo rentals and play guitar on the boardwalk?" I smiled genuinely at him but because I had just been crying and thinking about Tate, my words came out sharper than I anticipated.

"I do." He nodded and attempted to ignore my tears. "I work at Coastal Seafood, but my shift ends at two."

I glanced at my watch, noting that I needed to pick up the boys earlier that day because Toby was starting soccer practice. His new friend, Zach, had convinced him to play, and his mother Mindy all but shoved the registration packet in my face at school pick-up.

"Ah, so you work with everyone else in this town?" Coastal Seafood was a seafood supplier that harvested, processed, and distributed everything from fish to Dungeness crab. It was a busy facility just down the street from the condo and I often passed by when I was out for a walk or stopping by the coffee shop before making my trek to Moolack Beach for some alone time.

He nodded and chuckled softly.

"So, that's how you know Tim then?" The epiphany hit me like a wave on the shore.

"Tim Stewart?" His brow furrowed as his mind tried to make the connection. I nodded. "Yeah, I know Tim. How do you know Tim?"

"His wife is my best friend," I answered, pressing my lips into a smile.

He smiled slowly, connecting all the dots. There was so much we didn't know about each other; we never even tried to. Or rather, I never tried to. But our six degrees of separation whittled down to two and I wondered how well Lydia knew Dylan after all.

"They're good people," Dylan said, looking out at the water.

"They are." I nodded. My face felt swollen and my bones tired as I stared out at the ocean too.

"Well, I'm sorry," he said finally, as if remembering how awkward it was to run into me when I was in the middle of a good cry on the beach. "I didn't mean to interrupt your quiet time. I'll move along so you can have some peace."

"Well, it seems to be a pattern of yours," I said with a laugh, not meeting his eyes.

"What do you mean?" He attempted to smile but he looked at me curiously.

"You and interrupting. Doesn't really seem to matter what I'm doing; you show up and interrupt whatever it is." I shrugged and half-smiled, half-laughed.

He smirked inquisitively.

"You don't like me much, do you?"

My eyes darted to him quickly, surprised by the confrontation. I honestly didn't understand why I continued to be so rude to him. Even if I was trying to be funny or playful, my words came out sharp and unapologetic. It was as if my social skills died with Tate.

I didn't understand why Dylan was everywhere even though

he owned the condo above mine and worked just up the street from where I lived. But more than that, I didn't understand why I kind of liked seeing him. It was a love/hate feeling I had never known. A comfort that made me uncomfortable. A familiarity I wasn't ready to know.

"I—It's not that. Really. I'm just going through a lot right now, and I'm sorry if I've taken it out on you. Life is just hard, I guess." Embarrassment sat heavy in my gut and tears filled my eyes until they spilled over. I wiped them away quickly, hoping he didn't notice.

"Life doesn't always have to be hard, Tabitha." He gave me a half smile that made my heart ache. Part of it was his choice of words. The other part was the guilt I felt because it was then, I realized, that I was attracted to him. It was a strange thing to realize when the husband I loved more than anyone in the world had only been gone a year.

I stared at him a moment and let out a shaky breath.

"No, it doesn't have to be. But when you are thirty-seven and newly widowed with two young boys, life just *is* hard."

His expression changed at my statement; his empathetic eyes softened as he continued to look at me. There was a beat of silence before he cleared his throat.

"I'm sorry, I didn't know." He pressed his lips together and let his eyes fall to his feet digging in the sand.

"It's alright. I didn't expect you to know. I didn't exactly lead with it when I met you."

"You didn't lead with much." He chuckled softly. More to himself.

This made me smile. I really had been so standoffish with him.

"Want to tell me about him?" he asked.

"Who? Tate?" I was surprised he asked. Most people wanted to avoid the subject after I said my husband died but there Dylan was, barely an acquaintance, asking about him. The longer Tate was gone, the more I longed to talk about him. I didn't want to forget anything about him but sometimes it felt like everyone around me already had.

"Is that his name?" His smile was small but sincere.

I nodded and smiled softly. "Tate was everything. He was the best dad—and Toby's best friend. He made us laugh so hard tears leaked out of our eyes. He made the best chocolate chip cookies. He would wake up in the middle of the night every night with Charlie to change his diaper before bringing him to me so I could nurse him in bed. He always kissed me goodbye—he never forgot." A sense of love and appreciation washed over me as I smiled, remembering Tate. "He was a good one."

"You must miss him." Dylan continued to watch me as I nodded through my tears, his eyes full of empathy and something that felt like understanding.

"Newport is our fresh start," I offered without prompting.

He nodded, seeming to understand. "It's a good place to be."

I sniffed and wiped my nose with the back of my hand. "I'm sorry I've been so rude to you. You have been nothing but kind to me and didn't deserve the new lady in town constantly ripping your head off." I laughed and he returned it.

"Well, that one night when Charlie wouldn't sleep, I probably deserved it."

"Oh, you really did," I agreed, a genuine laugh bubbling out of me and a tiny part of my grief released into the salty air—a small relief that startled me.

"You haven't been rude, Tabitha," Dylan said finally, and I looked at him curiously. "You've been sad. That comes out in all kinds of ways."

I swallowed the lump that rose in my throat. "It does," I said, looking back out at the gray autumn sky.

"Do you ever just get so angry with how life is turning out you want to scream?" he asked.

I fixed my eyes on him; my expression calm.

"Asks the guy who saw me chuck a broken saw in the dumpster while *screaming*."

"I mean, that was actually pretty impressive," he said as he laughed—a shy and endearing sound.

"*That* was actually pretty embarrassing." I buried my face in my hands and laughed.

"I mean, that saw didn't even stand a chance against you. You tossed it like it was nothing. You're tiny but scrappy, aren't you?" he teased as a smile pulled at one side of his mouth. A warm expression was seated behind his eyes and it caused a rush of comfort and affection to wash over me.

I pressed my lips together and shrugged. "Yeah, well, I have to be scrappy these days."

Dylan nodded, his smile softening with empathy. "It's okay to fall apart every once in a while."

I let out a long sigh. "I have two kids. I don't have the luxury of being able to fall apart." My voice was tired as I said it. I tried to offer a small smile but it was more of a twitch.

Dylan's sad eyes stayed on me as he nodded. It was like he knew without actually knowing, and I wondered why I had a sudden urge to tell him the details.

"You know, my dad was the one that told me when life gets overwhelming, you sometimes just need to drive to the beach and scream," he said, taking a step closer to me.

My brow furrowed with a question.

"No one can hear you scream next to the roar of the ocean," he continued as he looked at me with a half-smile.

I absorbed his statement with a nod as a smile appeared on my face. "So, you're saying if I need to throw a temper tantrum, I should do it at the beach and not the parking lot?"

He shook his head and laughed.

"Try it," he said.

"Try what?" I asked, drawing back slightly.

"Screaming," he answered. "Think of everything about life that is hard, that you wish were different, that you wish you could change. Then just...scream."

"I am not screaming, but thanks for the idea," I scoffed.

"No? Then I'll go," he said as he turned toward the water and let out a roar of a scream muffled by the crashing waves. His arms were outstretched as the ocean breeze billowed past him.

My eyes narrowed on him and my jaw dropped slightly.

"Try it," he said again, his dark and gentle eyes landing on mine.

I studied him a moment before drawing in a deep breath and positioning my shoulders toward the ocean.

I thought of everything that had gone wrong in the last year. Everything I couldn't fix no matter what decision I made. I thought of Tate and how desperately I wanted him back. I thought of how Charlie would never know him. I thought of all the nights I rocked a sobbing Toby to sleep because he missed his dad. I thought of how long it had been since I felt Tate's skin against mine. I thought of how many midnight hours I spent staring at Tate's empty side of the bed while my head lay on a pillowcase wet with tears. I thought of how much I hated what happened to us. I thought of how badly the kids needed their mom back. I thought of how much I wanted *myself* back, because I knew a part of me died with Tate.

I squeezed my tear-filled eyes shut…and I screamed.

It was long and loud, and I felt every emotion rip through my chest. I screamed as I cried until somehow, my scream turned into a laugh.

It was comical really: screaming into the gray and angry ocean next to a man I hardly knew and finding more relief than any therapy session in the last year.

I wiped wet and exhausted tears from my face and shook my head as I looked at Dylan watching me with both sincerity and understanding, a smile pulling at his lips.

"Feels good, doesn't it?" he asked. "Even when nothing else does."

I let out a long sigh and a laugh tumbled with it. I nodded and offered a smile, my cheeks hot with emotion.

"Your dad certainly knew what he was talking about," I said.

Dylan pressed his lips together and nodded.

"Yep, he certainly did," he said.

A silence lingered while we both watched the waves in front of us. Our eyes flitted back to each other and I offered a brief smile before turning back to the water. A strange urge to keep talking wrapped itself around my throat but I swallowed hard and stayed quiet.

"Well, I should leave you to it. Enjoy screaming on the beach," Dylan said finally, taking a small step backward.

I let out a laugh. "Yeah, I gotta get going anyway. Toby starts soccer tonight." I stood wiping the sand off my pants.

He nodded and his mouth curved into a smile that was almost smug—like he already knew I had somewhere else I needed to be.

"See you later, Tabitha."

"Bye, Dylan." I offered a small smile as he turned to make his way down the beach. "Hey, Dylan?" I called after him, stunned at my own desire to make this request. "Do you think you could swing by sometime to teach Toby to play guitar? He's been asking for you. You don't have to stay long, and I'd be happy to pay you."

"No need to pay me." His face broke into a smile, like he had been waiting for me to ask all this time. "You have my number."

He turned again and I watched him walk until he disappeared around the curve of the hillside.

AFTER I PICKED up Charlie from daycare, I drove straight to Toby's school. He was dressed in long-sleeves and athletic tights under his soccer shorts with a black beanie on his head. His green eyes glowed in the cloudy sunlight, and he looked so much like Tate. It was like being teleported into one of Tate's childhood pictures.

"What?" Toby said, noticing my stare as he hopped in the car so I could drive him over to the middle school for practice.

"You mean, 'hello, Mom,'" I said, narrowing my eyes on him.

"Right. Sorry. *Hello*, Mom." He shrugged as he slung the seatbelt over his shoulder. "You were just staring at me funny. You okay?"

I laughed and shook away whatever trance I had been in when I arrived. "I am. How was your day?"

"Good."

"Excited for soccer?"

"Yep." He pressed his lips together in a straight line and

said no more, already trying to play it cool. But as his mother I could see the eagerness and excitement twinkle behind his eyes. Sports were so good for him, even before we lost Tate. It was the perfect way to channel all his energy and, as of late, his grief.

"You still thinking you want to do guitar lessons? Just to see if you like it?" I asked as we pulled into the parking lot of the middle school for practice.

"With Dylan?" His eyes brightened. I seriously didn't know how or why he liked him so quickly. "Yeah, for sure," he answered excitedly while he bounced his knee.

"Okay, then I'll make sure to ask him and we'll get something figured out." I slid out of the minivan and walked to the sliding door to get Charlie out of his car seat.

"Cool, now I'll get to see Dylan all the time."

I scoffed slightly. "Well, we can't expect it *all* the time. Just a lesson here and there probably."

"But I'll get to see him at soccer too," Toby answered definitively.

I pulled Charlie out of his seat and into my arms and furrowed my brow at Toby.

"Soccer?"

"Yeah, Zach said Dylan's our coach."

I stared at him blankly, trying to understand how I missed it when I filled out the soccer registration and received the practice schedule via email.

"Coach Thompson?" Toby looked at me expectantly as I connected the dots. I had completely forgotten his last name, nor did I pay much attention to who his coach was. I just figured I'd meet him at practice—it's not like I knew many people in town yet.

I nodded at Toby pretending I actually remembered, and he ran full speed ahead of me toward the soccer field.

He joined the swarm of eleven and twelve-year-old boys as they ran from goal post to goal post. I walked toward the field with Charlie toddling next to me, his chubby fingers clinging to my hand. As I made my way closer to the crowd of parents, I waved at Lydia who had already arrived. Dylan was standing in front of them passing out the game schedule and double checking the roster.

When I was a few feet away from him, he looked up at me and smiled like he'd been waiting for me to arrive.

"What's your son's name?" he asked playfully as he handed me the calendar, winking subtly.

I rolled my eyes and couldn't help but smile. His charms were really growing on me. "I didn't realize you were Toby's coach."

"I could tell," he said, letting out a soft chuckle.

"I *just* saw you at the beach. Why didn't you tell me?"

"I wanted to surprise you." He shrugged, a smirk pulling at the ends of his lips. "Alright, guys! Bring it in!"

The swarm of adolescent boys edged me and Charlie away from Dylan as he began to lead them through soccer drills. Lydia walked over to me and cleared her throat.

"What was that all about?" she asked, her lips pursed and eyebrows raised.

"What?" I played dumb.

"Chatting it up with the coach." She gave me a playful nudge and I scoffed slightly.

"Nothing. I ran into Dylan at the beach earlier."

"Oh," she said as her face spread into a smile.

"Don't do that." I gave her a knowing stare.

She nodded. "Okay, fine. You're right."

"Why didn't you tell me Dylan was the coach?" I asked, hopeful she wasn't trying to set me up.

"I didn't think I needed to since his name was *written in the email*," she answered playfully.

"The email didn't have his first name on it." I bent down and opened an applesauce pouch for Charlie.

"Minor detail. Besides, I'm pretty sure he's the only Thompson around here other than his dad."

"Really?" I didn't even try to hide my surprise. Thompson seemed like such a common surname.

She eyed me over her travel mug of coffee and shrugged. "It's a small town."

I spent the majority of the practice chasing Charlie as he ran through the field next to where the team was practicing, stopping every time he found a pinecone or an earthworm. He was a constant distraction. Every time I was able to stop and watch Toby practice, I was pleased to find him celebrating and high fiving with new friends. I loved seeing him like that: just a normal kid without a care in the world. When he scored a goal during the scrimmage, Charlie and I spun around in circles and cheered for him, no doubt embarrassing him. I didn't care. It was a normal thing for a mom to do and these days normal felt like a luxury.

I caught eyes with Dylan when I was cheering, and he smiled at me—his jaw was peppered with a five o'clock shadow and the glint in his eyes felt mesmerizing.

I gave him a small smile and blinked my eyes away.

When the scrimmage was over, the boys huddled and did one final cheer before scattering to each of their parents. They all smelled like mud, rain, and pre-pubescent body odor.

"Good job, bud," I said, handing Toby a blue Gatorade.

"Thanks, Mom." He guzzled half the bottle as Dylan approached us.

"Good job, Toby. I didn't realize you were such an awesome soccer player." Dylan said it to Toby, but his eyes met mine briefly.

"Thanks, Coach," he said wiping his mouth with the back of his hand.

"Hey, I was thinking since there isn't soccer on Thursdays, that could be a good night to swing by to teach Toby guitar." Dylan turned to me when he said this, and I drew in a sharp breath. That would mean a lot of Dylan every week.

Toby turned to me with hopeful eyes. I looked between him and Dylan, feeling hesitant.

"Are you sure it's not too much?" I wanted him to say yes but I also wanted him to say no. I worried now that he knew I was a widowed mother, he felt obligated to fulfill his promise to Toby. I didn't want him to think I needed any handouts. After all, he was also Toby's soccer coach. How much was too much?

"It'll be fun." Dylan shrugged, nonchalantly. "We'll just see how it goes. See you Thursday at seven?"

I pressed my lips together and nodded. A part of me was

excited for Toby. The other part of me felt like a charity case.

Seven

"MOM! HURRY! THE sink's exploding!" Toby yelled from the kitchen as I wrapped Charlie in a towel after his bath.

"What?" I hollered, rushing to the kitchen to find water spraying in all directions from the faucet.

Another leaky faucet, but this one happened to be angry.

"Hurry! Turn off the water!" I yelled.

Toby did as he was told as I grabbed a few towels from the hall closet.

"Here. Get your brother dressed for me. And change your shirt, too. Dylan will be here to teach you guitar soon."

I handed Charlie to Toby, who obediently took Charlie to the bedroom and get him dressed in pajamas. I wiped up the flood that rushed through the kitchen and opened the cabinet under the sink to see if I could tighten the faucet somehow. When Tate scheduled to have the cabinets and countertops replaced, I had assumed he also bought new faucets instead of reinstalling the ones from decades past. I assumed wrong. I tinkered with the faucet for a few minutes and was sure I had fixed it without needing to replace it.

My concentration was nearly broken at the sound of a knock at the door. I hollered for Toby to answer it when Charlie waddled into the kitchen in footie pajamas.

"Mama!" he said, holding out a plastic dinosaur. "Rawr!"

"Hey, buddy," I said, smiling as I stood from under the sink to turn on the water to confirm I had solved the problem. As soon as I twisted the knob, water shot directly at my face, making my mascara run and soaking my t-shirt.

"Shit!" I said, turning off the water and wiping my face. "I swear if one more damn thing breaks in this godforsaken place…"

"You'll what?" Dylan asked, walking into the kitchen with a handsome smile that turned immediately into pity when he surveyed the soaking wet kitchen.

For a split second, I had forgotten he had knocked on the door and Toby had answered it. I was so embarrassed and caught off guard at the sight of him.

Charlie squealed and laughed. "Mama's wet!" he said, pointing at me.

I stared at Dylan and I could tell he was biting back a laugh.

My face broke into a smile and I laughed at the absurdity of my flooded kitchen, mascara-streaked face, and wet t-shirt. Dylan's eyes dropped to the floor as his laughter echoed mine and he handed me another towel I had set on the counter.

"Want some help with that?" he asked.

I dabbed my face with the towel and wiped the mascara streaks from my eyes.

"Oh, no. I can handle it. I think I just need to go grab a new faucet. These ones are so old; they're loose and cracking. I really should have just bought one for the kitchen when I replaced the bathroom faucet, but I suppose I was just hoping to stretch the budget as much as possible."

"Want me to watch the boys while you run out and grab one? I'd offer to go get one myself, but I wouldn't want to pick something you don't like." He pressed his lips together in a shy smile as he shoved his hands in his pockets.

"Oh, I can get one tomorrow. I'm sure the hardware store is

closing soon." I waved off the offer.

"They close at nine," he said, glancing at his watch. "It's only seven. Really. I don't mind."

I narrowed my brow and contemplated the offer. "Okay," I said slowly. "Let me just get Charlie down for the night. You and Toby can get started out here if you'd like."

"Guitar won't wake him up?"

"As long as you don't plug it into an amp." I gave him a wry smile and wiped it off my face just as quickly, afraid it would seem like I was flirting.

"Ready, Toby?" he said, playfully socking him in the shoulder.

"Yep! Let's do it."

As they sat on the couch, I disappeared in the bedroom with Charlie to change my shirt and threw my hair into a messy bun on the top of my head. In the boys' bedroom, I rocked Charlie as I texted Lydia quickly.

Me: Is Dylan safe enough to stay at the condo with the boys while I run out to the store?

Lydia: I knew it! What's going on?

I rolled my eyes and continued singing a lullaby to Charlie.

Me: Nothing. I'll tell you tomorrow. He's a decent guy, right? I just need to run and grab a new faucet really quickly.

Lydia: Yes, he's safe. Also, can't wait for you to tell me everything!

I smiled feeling like a schoolgirl with a crush I had no business having as a widowed mother of two. After Charlie drifted to sleep in my arms, I laid him down in his crib and turned on the white noise machine before leaving for the hardware store.

When I returned with a new faucet, Charlie was still sound asleep, and Toby was strumming on Dylan's guitar. I snuck quietly down the hallway and watched Toby captively listen to Dylan as he told him where to place his fingers on the strings.

After setting the faucet on the counter, they both turned their eyes up to look at me.

"Mom, listen. This is A and this is D," he said, changing chords with his fingers and strumming.

"Wow. I'm impressed," I said, moving into the room to sit on the arm of the couch next to him.

Dylan smiled at Toby before looking at me. "He's a natural. But his fingers are going to be sore tomorrow."

Toby set the guitar down and stretched his fingers, examining them. "Do you think we could do this every day?"

Dylan and I laughed. "No, honey, not every day."

"Maybe every week though? Once or twice, if that works," Dylan suggested, looking at me and raising his dark eyebrows.

"Oh, that is more than generous. We would have to pay you if we make this a regular thing."

"You really don't have to. Just don't fire me if I'm late." He winked at me and I swallowed hard. "Might want to get him a smaller guitar though. It'll make it easier to learn."

"Oh, I hadn't even thought of that," I said making a mental note to add one to my cart that evening.

"Mom, can we? Can I get a blue one?" Toby's eyes were eager and excited. For the first time in a long time, his eyes didn't look like he was masking any pain.

"Yeah," I said, letting out a breath. "We'll figure it out. Now you need to brush your teeth and head off to bed. I'll come kiss you in a minute."

Toby thanked Dylan and practically ran into the bathroom to brush his teeth. I ran my hand over my face and looked over at Dylan, giving him a tired smile.

"Thank you for coming over tonight. That meant a lot to Toby," I said, standing and walking to the kitchen.

"No problem. What should we say? Every Thursday, same time?" he asked, following me across the room.

"You really don't have to," I said, pulling open the box for the new faucet.

He shrugged. "I really don't mind."

I swallowed and nodded. I was afraid I was mistaking his kindness for pity. While I carried the death of Tate place to place, I didn't want it to define me or make people treat me differently. I just needed them to know it was a part of me, but not all of me.

"Want help?" he asked, walking around the kitchen counter peninsula.

I let out a tired sigh and smiled at him. I didn't need him to be my knight in shining armor and fix the broken things in my rundown condo. I was perfectly capable of handling it myself.

Just as I shook my head no, Charlie let out a cry from the bedroom.

"You sure?" Dylan's face broke into a smile and I reluctantly excused myself to check on Charlie. He was inconsolable when I reached his crib, and I knew his molars must have started to come in. I rubbed teething gel across his swollen gums and gave him a dose of pain meds, rocking him in the chair perched between Toby's twin bed and Charlie's crib.

Toby was already snoring with his book open across his chest. I turned off his reading light as I consoled Charlie. Toby didn't even flinch at the cries coming from his brother. It always amazed me how soundly children slept once they were no longer babies.

After nearly twenty minutes of comforting and rocking Charlie back to sleep, I had almost forgotten Dylan was still in the condo. A part of me assumed he would have just excused himself.

When I walked into the kitchen, I found him lying under the sink with a wrench and his black t-shirt clinging to his abdominal muscles, the waistband of his boxers exposed.

I stared a beat longer than I should have before blinking my eyes away and stifling a laugh. Dylan had officially turned me into a walking cliché.

He poked his head out. "What's so funny?"

"Nothing," I said with a breath, my face unable to not smile. "Everything. You. The sink. The teething toddler. The snoring pre-teen boy. It's all ridiculous. So, I am laughing." I placed my elbows on the counter as I pressed my palms against my eyes.

His eyes narrowed on me, clearly not understanding my train of thought.

"Well, I'm just about done," he said, ignoring my outburst and tightening one last bolt before standing up next to the sink and turning it on. "Look at that, huh? Brand new faucet."

I peeled my hands away from my face to see his wide, proud smile, and affection for him swept over me briefly.

"Thank you. That was very nice of you."

"No problem," he said, placing the old faucet in the box for the new one.

I took in a breath, feeling completely out of my element but exhausted enough to not care. "Would you like a drink, Dylan?"

He chuckled softly. "I thought you didn't like me very much."

I shrugged. "I thought you were irritating." I smiled playfully, letting the honesty fall from my lips.

He raised his eyebrows and laughed. "Oh, so you don't now?"

"You're my kid's soccer coach and teaching him to play guitar *and* you just replaced my broken faucet," I said as I walked to the refrigerator, pulling out two bottles of beer and opening them. I held one out to him. "Nothing irritating about that. You deserve a beer at the very least."

He took the bottle from me and narrowed his dark eyes on mine. His stare skirted across my face and it looked, once again, like he was amused by me. I couldn't quite understand the look he kept giving me—it was watchful, curious even—but I had grown not to mind it at this point.

"Thank you," he said, clinking his bottle with mine and taking a drink.

"Thank *you*," I repeated letting the quiet linger a moment.

"Toby seems like he's adjusting well to Newport," Dylan said finally.

"He really is. Kids are pretty resilient." I shrugged, wishing I had some of that same resiliency.

"How's he doing with his dad being gone?" Dylan asked. I

was again startled that he brought Tate up, so I stared at him for a long moment. He gave a noncommittal shrug. "Toby mentioned him while you were gone is all. We were talking about great guitar players and he said his dad loved Jimmy Hendrix."

I laughed, lightening the mood. "He did. That's actually his middle name."

"Tate's?"

I shook my head. "No, Tobias Hendrix. Tate begged for it and I just wanted something simple like Michael or James. Tate beat me at Rock, Paper, Scissors after two rounds and *that* is how Toby got his middle name."

"Well, now he has to be a rockstar." Dylan smiled and his eyes were moody yet bright under the pendant lights. "Is that him?" he asked nodding at the last family portrait we had ever taken hanging on the wall in the family room.

The four of us were huddled on our bed, the white duvet cover billowing beneath us; Charlie was only a newborn, and my cheeks were still puffy from pregnancy. But we were happy. All of us.

"Yeah," I said plainly, feeling a rush of nostalgia remembering the day the picture was taken.

"How'd he die?"

"Car accident," I answered plainly.

He nodded, not asking for more.

"Toby looks a lot like him," Dylan said turning back to me and leaning his elbows over the kitchen peninsula. I mirrored him on the other side of the counter.

"Practically twins." I nodded. "Their personalities too."

He smiled and his eyes told me he was truly paying attention, absorbing each word I said.

"Does that make it easier or harder?" The sincerity of his question surprised me. He didn't dance around the subject of Tate like most people. He dove right in, gently though. As if he knew how fragile the discussion could be.

"Both," I answered simply, smiling and feeling far more content than I did emotional.

"I get that." He nodded but didn't pry any further as he

looked down at the beer bottle rotating in his hand.

I cleared my throat to distract myself from my growing attraction to him.

"So, tell me about yourself?" I asked.

"What do you want to know?"

"Well, what else is there? You're a local, you play guitar, you own the condo above me, you work at the crab and fish facility at the Port, you know how to crab, you spend your spare time coaching soccer, and you just replaced my kitchen faucet. I don't know who your friends are or if you're married or where you went to college. I actually don't even know where you live." I shrugged. "You're a bit of mystery."

He smiled and took a sip of his beer. "A mystery that you just listed six truths about."

I laughed. "Come on, give me something to work with. You grew up in Newport?"

He nodded. "Born and raised."

"Where'd you go to college?"

"University of Oregon. Majored in Education. Then moved to Portland for several years before moving home." He answered the unasked questions in succession.

I nodded, absorbing his answers.

"Were you a teacher in Portland?"

He nodded. "High school music teacher." A faint smile touched his lips.

My mouth opened slightly, and I closed it.

"Surprised?"

"A little." I let out a small laugh. "Why aren't you the music teacher here?"

"And take Mrs. Hathaway's job?" He shook his head. "No way. She's been the music teacher at the high school for decades and I don't really want to travel out of the district."

"Well, maybe when she retires." I smiled at my own suggestion. He was musical and athletic, and he strangely fit perfectly in both categories. I could totally picture what kind of teacher he was—patient, hip, passionate, charming. I really thought the hot schoolteacher thing only existed in movies. But apparently, once upon a time, it existed in Portland in the form of Dylan Thompson.

"Maybe." He nodded. "The schedule at the fish place works better for me right now anyway."

"When did you come back to Newport?"

"I moved back two years ago almost." He shrugged, not meeting my eyes. "Family stuff."

I nodded, wanting him to elaborate but not wanting to pry. "And where do you live now? You're always at the resort for someone that says he doesn't live here."

"I live in a house just across the street from the Port."

My mouth fell open and I closed it. "Those houses are huge. How do you afford it?" I shook my head, backtracking. "I'm sorry that's none of my business."

He smiled softly. "Family house."

"Oh, so you moved back in with your parents," I teased.

He laughed softly but it seemed almost sad. I ignored it, worried I was just being self-conscious.

"Why'd you move home?" I asked, thoughtfully.

"It's complicated." He half-smiled and winced slightly.

"Don't you wish life didn't have to be complicated?" I shrugged and didn't press him for details.

Lydia was right. Dylan was a really nice guy. Genuine. Funny. Overcompensatingly caring. Irritatingly handsome. Once again, guilt coursed through my veins as I realized it wasn't the first time I allowed these thoughts to cross my mind.

"Well, it's been really nice to get to know you, Dylan Thompson." I stuck out my hand to shake his. "My apologies for getting us off to a rocky start."

He smiled as he shook my hand. "Apology accepted, Tabitha Jones."

The warmth of his hand as it embraced mine ran up my arm and spread across my chest. The gesture was innocent, but it reminded me how much I missed the feel of Tate's hand in mine.

My eyes drifted from our hands and landed on Dylan's—there was a tenderness and curiosity buried in his eyes as his mouth curved into a gentle smile. My heartbeat sped up as he ran his index finger across my wrist. I pulled my hand away quickly, realizing I was the one not letting go.

A part of me didn't want to. A part of me even longed to fall into his arms and let him hold me. The other part of me smiled and told him we should call it a night.

Summer 11

"ALRIGHT, TOBY!" I cheered as he ran into my arms after his t-ball game. His hat was too big for his head and he stumbled over his feet while he ran, clutching his glove in one hand and a juice box in the other.

"Did you see my home run?" he asked, his eyes wild with excitement and pride.

Tate trailed behind him, laughing. "You hit a double but still, really impressive, bud." He gave a congratulatory pat on his small shoulders.

"But I crossed the finished line. That's a home run, right?" Toby's brow was furrowed as he stared at the grass at his feet while his five-year-old brain tried to make sense of all the rules he had to follow.

"Not a *home* run," Tate answered patiently. "When you hit the ball, it was a double which meant you made it to second base. When you ran to home plate, it's because another batter on your team got you in. That's just called a run."

Toby stared blankly at Tate and sipped his juice box then raised his eyebrows.

Tate laughed. "It's fine, it'll make sense eventually."

"Well, whatever those rules are, you did great. I'm proud of you," I said, bending down to adjust his hat. "Did you have fun?"

"Yep, can I play at the park?"

"Sure." Toby took off running with his other pint-sized teammates and I placed a delicate hand on Tate's arm. "Nice work, Coach."

"Coaching t-ball is not coaching; it is directing a circus." His eyebrows shot up and he took off his ball cap and wiped the sweat off his brow before putting the hat back on backwards so I could easily kiss him.

"Well, I know it means a lot to Toby. He really needs this quality time with you." I cleared my throat and leaned into Tate's side and he nodded solemnly, his back stiffening slightly.

"What?" I pulled back, reading my husband's body language.

"Why do you have to say it like that?"

"Like what?" I asked with an edge in my voice creeping into irritation.

"Like I don't spend time with him." He dropped his hand from around my shoulders, so I turned to face him.

"Tate, you know how busy you've been with work this summer. Even Toby said something."

His eyes didn't leave mine—I could see the frustration behind his green irises. "This happens every summer, Tabitha. Real estate is crazy in the summer, you know that."

"I do know that and I'm proud of how well you've been doing but Toby's getting older, and he notices when you're busy is all. I'm not implying that you're neglectful, just that your son misses you."

"So then why say it?" His tone was tense and frustrated.

I let out a breath. "Because it's nice that you're coaching him. I know he loves it, and it makes him happy. That's it. That's all I meant." I held out my hands.

He rubbed his brow. This was one of his most successful and busy summers in real estate to date. He was overwhelmed. I could tell, even though he wouldn't admit it. When Tate got stressed, it completely occupied his mind. He couldn't leave tasks undone or emails unanswered. It was the nature of the business; it was also consuming.

But he loved it and I championed him through each sale. I also had to remind him this was the last summer before Toby would be off to school and we needed to take advantage of it.

This little burst of insecurity at the baseball field stemmed from stress, not my words or how he was as a father.

"I mean, and it's kind of nice that his coach is *super* hot," I teased playfully, easing the tension from his shoulders. My lips pulled slowly into a frisky smile.

He returned it. "No parenting guilt trips," he said, holding out his pinky to me.

"Never." I wrapped my pinky around his and kissed my thumb before pressing it against his. It was always an unspoken promise between us but sometimes we needed to say it out loud to each other. Being a parent was hard. Being a working adult was hard. Life in general was hard. But Tate and I were the balance the other always needed. The mirror we needed to see ourselves through.

TOBIAS HENDRIX! I *said* no throwing balls in the house! *Look*! Look what you did!" I shouted through my teeth at Toby, my fingers clenched around his arm as I pointed at the broken vase teetering off the counter with shards of glass littering the kitchen floor. "Go! Go to your room! I don't want to look at you right now."

My heart pounded and overwhelming frustrations pulsed through my fingertips.

Toby looked up at me—his green eyes like glassy saucers and his chin quivering—before slumping out of the kitchen and up the stairs with his head down.

Tate emerged from the office at the sound of my yelling. His eyes were calm and patient as he assessed the situation.

"Can you believe this?" I continued to raise my voice. "How many damn times do I have to tell him not to throw balls in the house? That could have been the window or the fireplace or, I don't know, someone's *face*. What the *hell*..." I let out an exasperated and angry groan, my temper boiling to the surface.

Tate just nodded in understanding, taking in my frustration, and simply grabbed the broom and began sweeping. My hands began to shake as I picked up the large pieces of glass and tossed them in the trash. Guilt and regret surged through my veins. I completely lost my temper. Toby was just a boy. It was an accident. I didn't even really like the vase. I was just tired after getting home from work and Tate had been busy with five house closings that week. I wanted to come home and relax but I had a sweet boy that couldn't wait for his dad to finish his paperwork so they could go outside and play catch. I was hardly patient as I cleaned up our dinner dishes; how could I have expected Toby to be patient at only five years old?

I slid my back against the cabinet and crumbled to the floor and began crying. My exhaustion and guilt bubbling over.

"I'm sorry I lost it," I said to Tate as he dumped the glassy contents of the dustpan in the garbage.

He quietly strode over to me and sat on the floor—shoulder to shoulder, his elbows propped on his knees. The rhythm of his breath calmed my heart, the strong and quiet presence of friendship pulling the guilt from my throat.

"You okay?" he asked, his voice steady.

"I think I'm just tired. I need a break. We've been busy." I wiped my wet cheeks with my fingers. "I really overreacted. I'm sorry." I looked at him with pleading eyes.

"Hey, no parenting guilt trips, right?" He held out his pinkie and I wrapped mine around his.

I nodded and let more tears spill down my face. "Right." I looked around at the clean kitchen that was only missing a broken vase. "I hate that I lost my temper—he's just a little kid."

Tate nodded and shrugged. "He can be rowdy, and it can be frustrating." After a long pause, I began to feel Tate's shoulders shake and I turned to look at him. He was laughing.

My mouth dropped open. "What is so funny?"

"He's just a rowdy boy. I'm surprised it's taken this long for him to throw a ball in the house and break something. Me and Justin broke all kinds of things growing up. You would have had our hides." He continued to laugh until tears leaked out of his eyes.

"It's not funny," I said. "I really lost my temper with him, Tate. It was dangerous. Something of more value could have broken. I mean, he could have been cut on the glass," I continued to plead my case even though I knew I had overreacted. Tate's laughter grew until finally my chest released and I began to laugh as well.

"Being a parent is the most exhausting, crazy thing," he said finally.

I shook my head, wiped under my eyes with my fingers, and looked at him feeling so thankful for him. Tate always taught me to laugh at life's mishaps even when I wanted to scream. He had a way of dissolving the frustration built up inside me and helping me release it with laughter.

I rested my head on his shoulder. "Thank you."

"For what?" I wanted to absorb each breath he took and let it calm the raging ocean inside me.

"Just being you. Being so relaxed about everything. I feel like I'd be a terrible mother without you balancing me out."

"That's nonsense. We all lose our shit sometimes." He tilted my chin up to look at him and the smile that spread across my face warmed in my heart.

I nodded and let out a shuddered breath. "Well, I think there's a little boy I need to apologize to."

"He needs to apologize too." He kissed my forehead. "He's old enough to know better."

I smiled and wiped my eyes, before rising and walking over to the staircase. I knew the importance of apologizing to my kids as much as I knew the importance of holding them accountable for their choices. It was an orchestrated song and dance. It needed its balance.

Just like marriage.

Just like life.

"Hey, Toby," I said softly as the door to his room crept open. He was sitting on his bed mindlessly playing with his stuffed animals. He looked up at me with remorseful eyes. I plopped next to him on the bed. "Can I get a hug?"

He nodded and crawled under my arm. His small body tucked next to me, reminding me how small he was and how undeserving he was of my harsh anger just minutes earlier. The shouting words I uttered still echoed in my brain and it made me cringe. Regret as a parent knows how to grab hold of the flesh and sink deep in the skin.

"I'm sorry I yelled at you." I cupped my hands over his face and looked him square in the eye. "Even though I was angry and what you did wasn't okay, I should not have talked to you like that because it wasn't kind and it wasn't loving. Was it?"

He shook his head, his eyes drifting to the floor.

"Do you understand why I got so upset?" He nodded. "Tell me why."

"I broke the rules." The sweet and earnest sorrow in his eyes made me want to cry.

"And what happened when you broke the rules?"

"I broke something." He looked back up at me. "I'm sorry, Mommy."

"I forgive you." I pulled him into my arms, his face smooshed against my shoulder.

"I forgive you, too, Mommy."

I wanted to cry again, and I felt so stupid about it. It was a small mishap—a stupid reason to get angry. Yet, teaching our son to forgive and love through other's mistakes shot a hole in my heart that could only be filled with gratitude. For Toby. For Tate. For the beautiful life we built.

ALRIGHT, SO I'LL pick you up at your office for dinner tonight or do you want to meet there?" Tate asked over the phone the next day as my workday dwindled on.

I drummed my fingers on my desk, feigning irritation.

"You know the answer to that." I hated meeting people at restaurants. I had for years. I hated arriving early and waiting at a half empty table like I was on some terrible online dating app.

I hated arriving second and wandering the restaurant in a sea of unknown faces trying to find one that was familiar and expecting me. It was a stupid sliver of anxiety that surfaced after I had Toby. Embarrassing, really. But I couldn't let go of it and Tate never made me. Even if it was a stark contrast from the independent and unapproachable girl he met back in college.

He laughed over the phone.

"See you at six?" His voice was calm and sexy and made my heart flutter even after all these years. The idea of date night—even something as simple as dinner at Shenanigan's—made my heart beat out of my chest.

As I closed out the files and tabs on my computer before shutting down the monitor. I escaped to the bathroom to freshen up. I touched up my makeup and painted my lips a deep shade of pink before spraying my hair with texture spray to give it a few more hours of life the fluorescent lighting of the office had sucked out of it. I changed out of my blazer and slacks and slipped on a blue maxi dress that hugged my hips and flowed at my feet. I smiled at the wife I'd become. I was officially in my thirties and never felt more beautiful or sexy. Gone were my twenties, flooded with uncertainty and doubt. I let out a satisfied breath as I looked myself over one last time and sprayed perfume on my neck and dabbed some on my wrists.

I couldn't wait to see Tate. I smiled to myself before exiting the restroom and waltzed passed the reception area and through the glass revolving door to where Tate stood waiting at his car, leaned up against the gray metal in khakis and a blue button-up shirt.

He eyed me from across the walkway like it was the first time he laid eyes on me. His eyes stayed glued to me as they slid up and down my body and a smile slowly spread across his face. I slung my bag off my shoulder and wrapped the leather strap around my hand as I pressed my body into his and kissed him without even saying hello.

He practically moaned into my mouth and it made me laugh. We were way overdue for a date night. Tate had been so busy that summer. We missed each other as much as Toby missed spending time with his dad.

When we arrived at the restaurant, we were seated outside on the dock. The salty air whipped through my hair and the sinking sun beat down on our shoulders. The water was calm and glassy, and Mt. Rainier pitched itself into the deep blue sky as if God Himself painted the backdrop for our date. I leaned over the table, a delicate hand on my neck. Tate leaned back in his chair and staired out at the water, no doubt soaking in his love for the Pacific Northwest.

"I can't believe summer is almost over," I said, admiring my wonderful husband.

"And Toby is going to kindergarten." He placed a hand on my arm. His words gave me a shiver.

"Don't say that." I laughed and took a sip of wine. "Isn't it weird that we'll have a kindergartener? I feel like I just had him."

Tate nodded and raised his eyebrows. "It's going by really fast."

"It makes me feel so old when we talk like that."

He laughed and took along pull from his lager. "Like what?"

I shrugged. "When we say things like 'it's going so fast' or when we talk about how old our kid is. I feel like I married you yesterday and yet..." I searched my mind for words.

"It feels like we could have never lived life without each other," he said, finishing my sentence. He smiled and winked at me, and it made my head spin.

"Exactly." I loved how well he understood me. There was always a succinctness in our minds and our hearts. It's why we worked so well. We knew how to love each other. We knew how to forgive each other. But more than anything we knew how to understand each other. I raised my glass of white wine to his beer. "Cheers to another fabulous summer!"

We clinked glasses and the waitress plopped berry cobbler in front of us with a scoop of sweet, creamy vanilla ice cream on top. We thanked her and dug our spoons into the shared dessert. Every bite of cobbler tasted sweeter. Not just this particular one, but since the first night we met. I'd never forget it—I never wanted to.

Tate scooped the last bite of cobbler and ice cream on his spoon and held it up to me before setting it down on the dish between us. "Rock, Paper, Scissors for the last bite?"

I eyed him mischievously. "Best two out of three?"

"You're on."

We squared our shoulders, excited and anxious—like the couple of kids in love we had always been. My paper covered his rock. His scissors cut my paper. Then his rock pounded my scissors.

I released an exaggerated gasp. "You win," I conceded in playful reluctance.

He smiled in a way that would always wreck my heart and make me want him to take me home no matter how many years we spent together.

"Best three out of five?" he said, holding out his hands for another round.

I smiled at him and kissed his irresistible face. He held up the spoon and fed me the last bite, the sweetness of summer lingering on my lips. I didn't care about the last bite of cobbler. He knew it. He just never wanted me to miss out on anything.

That was always Tate. Giving me second chances. Letting me redeem myself when I had completely lost my mind. Forgiving me when I was crazy. And loving me for exactly who I was.

Eight

THE WEEKS TICKED on and Dylan showed up every Thursday, promptly at seven o'clock to teach Toby guitar. I had bought Toby a three-quarters sized guitar— a blue one like he asked—and he practiced every day despite his fingertips splitting and cracking. I was proud of him. My mother always told me music was healing—she played guitar herself—and I definitely saw drops of healing with every strum of Toby's guitar.

Most Thursday nights Dylan stayed after the lesson to hang out with me. I didn't always invite him to stay, and he never asked to, but we'd start talking and couldn't stop. Sometimes I'd grab each of us a beer or sometimes I'd make tea. Sometimes we didn't drink anything—just let our words and laughter dance in the air between us. I missed having an adult around to talk to at the end of a long day and something about him comforted me.

When my parents came to visit one week, they were able to meet Dylan. My mother was charmed by him, which I figured she would be. Dylan was very charming. I had mistaken it for smugness initially. I assumed it was inauthentic, but he was true to himself with every word he said and everything he did. He remained much of a mystery to me despite our frequent chats, so when my parents peppered me with questions after he left, I didn't really have answers.

I laid out what I knew about him and what I wondered about him. I started realizing he let me do most of the talking when we were together. He probably knew the details of my life better than I knew any of his.

"Do you love him?" my mom asked with a playful smile. She was kidding. At least I assumed she was.

I rolled my eyes.

"I do!" Toby said, overhearing from the couch in the family room and I laughed.

My mother eyed me standing in the kitchen, flushed from laughter as she realized how much Toby had taken to him. Her face spread into a smile.

"Mom, Tate has only been gone a year."

"It's been longer than a year," she responded softly. The reminder of how much time was passing stung.

"Dylan is just a friend—one I feel like I need right now," I said definitively. "If not for myself, for the boys...*especially* the boys."

She nodded, agreeing. "Will Dylan be at Toby's birthday party next week?"

"Of course," I said, starting the dishwasher. I couldn't believe Toby was already going to be twelve. It didn't sound right. His dad died when he was ten and his eleventh birthday just two months later didn't feel at all like a celebration. I looked at Toby thoughtfully as he played his video games on the couch, before remembering the time. "Toby. Teeth and bed. And please don't wake up your brother."

He hopped off the couch and padded down the hallway.

My mother watched me closely as my father followed Toby in his bedroom to tuck him in. Even though he was inching closer to his teenage years, he still adored his Papa.

"You seem good, honey." My mother nodded at me; her hands clasped on the counter.

Tears stung the backs of my eyes. "I'm getting there."

AT TOBY'S PARTY, Dylan played with the kids, beating all of them—including Tim and Lydia's boys—at video games and played his guitar with Toby while the room sang the Happy Birthday song. Tate's parents, Terrence and Melanie, were there too. Even Tate's brother, Justin, made it up from San Diego. I was nervous to have them all over. Tate's parents weren't too keen on me moving with the kids to Oregon and they hadn't come to visit yet. But I was glad they came and rented a room in the building next to ours alongside my parents.

We were stuffed like sausages in our small condo but the smile on Toby's face all night made the gathering worth every unsaid heartbreak about the evening.

It wasn't the first year of birthdays we celebrated without Tate, but the air felt different this time. The somberness of the year prior had lifted a little. We all knew how much we missed Tate and wished he were still around. But we didn't feel the need to discuss and cry over every single detail, even though we knew how much he would have loved the chocolate cake and how he would have snapped so many pictures of Charlie eating a cupcake—his chubby fingers covered in chocolate and his face filled with glee.

So much was good about the evening—it was a glimpse of normalcy and I was thankful to feel it.

My parents and in-laws migrated to their rooms by nine o'clock, long after Charlie was passed out in his crib. Lydia helped me clean the kitchen before ushering her husband and boys outside to their car.

When I closed the door after saying goodbye, I turned back down the hallway to find Toby, Justin, and Dylan entranced in a video game.

A sense of misplaced déjà vu washed over me.

Justin was Tate's childless younger brother and always hung around last at every family gathering. We were incredibly close but had drifted over the years since he married Sarah and moved to San Diego. I was excited he flew in for the party and I knew his parents were too. We had only seen him a few times since Tate died. I could see the shock hit him differently each time.

This time in particular, I noticed his eyes watching Dylan the whole night. Studying him. Not in an intimidating way—a curious, almost protective way. It made me feel like he was taking notes and going to tell Tate. A preposterous feeling, I knew, but one that made me feel vulnerable as the night drifted on, and they were the last guests standing—both equally engaged in laughter and competition with Toby.

It made me smile but it also made my heart pound with nerves.

"Toby," I said softly, interrupting the competition. "It's time for bed."

"Do I have to? Even though it's a special occasion?" His eyes pleaded with me.

"Fine. Just five more minutes though. And *only* because it's your birthday."

"Thank you!" He smiled wide and nudged Dylan.

Justin cleared his throat and looked at me with a curiosity in his eyes. My smile twitched and I turned to watch them play— my eyes darting between my brother-in-law and Dylan. I tried to focus on what they were playing, but the buttons they pressed on their controllers made no sense as to how they were making the people move on the screen. Tate always knew how to play video games and they always went over my head. I was thankful for Dylan and Justin to be there to play with Toby at least. I really wished his uncle didn't live so far away.

"Well, I think I'd better get going too. I can't party like I used to." Justin stood and stretched his arms over his head, letting out a short laugh. "Dylan, nice to meet you."

Dylan stood and shook his hand. "You too, Justin."

The interaction wasn't awkward or uncomfortable, but it simply felt so bizarre to me—completely surreal. Even though Dylan was just a friend, I knew my family was curious about the nature of our relationship.

"I'll walk you out, Justin," I said following him to the door. We walked outside and I closed the door behind me, giving us at least a semblance of privacy. "Thank you so much for flying up for this." My voice nearly broke, and I pulled him in for a hug. While he looked nothing like his brother, there was a familiarity in his arms that would always remind me of Tate, if only because nearly every memory I had of Justin had Tate etched in it.

"I'm sorry Sarah couldn't make it," he said apologetically.

I nodded in response as I pulled away. "We miss you guys."

A hint of grief flashed in his dark eyes, but he only nodded before clearing his throat.

"Dylan is a nice guy."

My mouth dropped open. I wanted to explain—water down the complicated nature of how meeting him must have felt— and reassure him he was just a friend.

"You don't have to explain, Tabitha," he said, reading my thoughts. He offered a small smile, shaking his head slightly.

Tears stung the back of my eyes. I still felt the urge to explain our friendship that was slowly forming. If not for Justin or the world but for myself. I knew I was sticking my toes in unknown waters.

"He really is just a friend," I confirmed, as I twisted my wedding ring with my thumb before adding unnecessarily, "You know I'll never stop loving Tate, right?"

"Of course." He shrugged with a sadness on his shoulders. "But it's okay to let go of the life you thought you'd have."

My throat caught on this statement and my eyes welled with tears. There were memories laced in his words. "Even if it's everything I ever wanted?"

He smiled, remembering the same summer. "Even if it's everything you ever wanted."

I drew in a shaky breath and nodded. "Don't be a stranger, okay?"

"Never." He smiled—no doubt pushing back his own emotions—and kissed my forehead. "Love you, sis."

After he walked away, I drew in a few breaths to compose myself before walking back inside and busied myself with loading leftover glasses in the dishwasher and tossing a few rogue napkins in the trash.

"Alright, honey. Off to bed," I said from the kitchen as

'Game Over' flashed across the screen.

Toby set down the controller and turned to Dylan. "See you next week, Dylan!"

"See you next week. Happy birthday," Dylan said as they did the special hand shake they had created weeks ago.

"Love you, Mom," Toby muttered as he hugged me and ran off to bed.

"Love you, too," I called as he disappeared into his room. I turned and smiled at Dylan as he stretched his arms over his head and leaned back on the couch.

"Thank you for coming," I said, walking over to Dylan with a beer.

"Are you kicking me out or asking me to have a drink with you?" He looked at the beer and back at me.

I laughed softly, realizing my contradictory statement and action. I shrugged. "Habit, I guess."

I had grown accustomed to him staying a bit past bedtime. It never moved beyond simple conversation and it didn't mean more than friendship, but I truly enjoyed his company. Being a widow was lonely.

I sat on the opposite end of the couch with my own beer in my hand, letting the quiet evening linger.

"You're a great mom, Tabitha," he said, taking a drink of his beer.

I was slightly taken aback at the unexpected compliment.

"Well, thank you. That was nice of you to say."

He nodded shyly. "You can tell you love them with everything you have."

Tears stung my eyes, but I blinked them away. I was doing my best every day, but most of the time I felt like it wasn't enough. That it would never amount to nearly enough without Tate. Being a single mother was defeating no matter how many people told me I was doing a great job. But Dylan's words hit me differently for some reason that night. They penetrated my skin and landed in my heart instead of ricocheting off my mind.

"Well, sometimes it feels like they're the only thing keeping me going. We were this close to not having them," I said, my index finger and thumb pinching the air.

"Really?" His eyes were full of curiosity.

"Yep. My sweet little miracles. Pregnancy is weird like that. They were both surprises. And in between there was a lot of medical intervention that didn't work. But I guess I'm great at getting pregnant on accident." I let out a small laugh and took a drink of my beer. "Apparently my body hates fertility drugs but loves to surprise us."

My mind lingered on the word 'us' as I stared at the dewy bottle in my hand. I could sense Dylan watching me. I looked up and was met with kind and sympathetic eyes. A faint smile curved on his lips and he nodded. Never digging. Never pushing. Always listening and absorbing the words I unloaded.

"Your parents are great," he said, finally.

"You said that last week." I laughed, welcoming the change in subject.

"Your in-laws too."

I nodded. "Yeah, I love Terrance and Melanie. They gave me a good one," I said, looking up from my beer at Dylan.

Dylan seemed to take in what I just said and let the silence fill the air.

"Is it weird at all? Having in-laws when your husband is…"

"Dead?" I finished for him. It had gotten easier for me to say the word but everyone around me always tip-toed around it. "Yes, it's weird. And no, it's totally normal."

I smiled with raised eyebrows and Dylan laughed.

"No, Tate's parents are great. They always have been. They don't always agree with my choices as of late, but they don't have their son to voice their concerns to, so they try to do it with me. And what I've learned is I'm an intimidating force to argue with." I smiled mischievously over the top of my beer bottle.

Dylan breathed out a laugh. "Well, you scared the hell out of me at first."

"Did I really?"

He nodded and picked at his teeth with his tongue. "Still do most days."

My mouth fell open in mock offense.

"Really?" I asked, not even hiding my surprise.

SIXTEEN *Summers*

"Really."

"How so?" I was curious. I knew I was kind of rude to him when we first met but rude didn't automatically translate to intimidating. Or did it?

"I don't know. The way you carry yourself. There's a strength in you. The way you answer questions without worrying what the other person thinks. Or the way you knew exactly what kind of saw to buy at the hardware store. Or the way you cuss when your kitchen faucet explodes and follow it immediately with an uncontrollable laugh."

I learned that from Tate.

I smiled and pulled my legs on the couch, tucking them under my body so I was facing him. "Those things don't exactly wreak intimidating."

"Maybe not. But chucking a broken saw in a dumpster while yelling and calling me Derek like it's the most painful insult in the world is pretty intimidating," he teased.

I buried my face in my hands as my cheeks went hot. "Oh my gosh, I can't believe I did that." I raised my head, an embarrassed smile on my face. "I'm sorry I called you Derek so many times."

He let out a breath through his smile. "I've been called worse."

"Oh, I bet you have," I teased, taking a sip of my beer and eyeing him out of the corner of my eye.

"Should I be offended by you saying that?" he asked, an astonished smile on his face.

"If you want to be." I shrugged and pulled a loose string from a throw pillow. "But I won't lose any sleep over it."

He ran a hand down his face as he smiled and shook his head. "See? That's exactly what I mean. I can't really figure you out." He shrugged. "Even when I try."

"What you really mean is you were surprised I didn't like you right away, huh? Dylan Thompson is not used to not getting his way with the ladies," I joked.

"No." He shook his head, laughing. "I don't usually get my way with the ladies anyway."

I stared at him and took a drink of my beer, my eyes staying on his. "I don't believe you."

He shrugged. And waited for me to say more and I realized I truly knew nothing about his love life. I never asked—didn't even care to know.

Until now.

I shifted the dewy bottle between my fingers. "Were you ever married?"

"Nah." He shook his head and took a drink.

"Alright, Dylan." I inched closer to him. "Since everyone in town is saying you're such a catch, tell me why you never settled down?"

"I settled down once." His smile was shy, like he was hiding an unexpected secret. He tilted his head side to side, contemplating. "Maybe twice. Once and a half."

I laughed. "What does that even mean?"

"It means I had one long and serious relationship and one that almost reached the same level." He shifted on the couch, sinking deeper into the corner of it.

"But you were never married?"

"No, we never got there."

"And why didn't you ever marry either of them?"

He shrugged. "I don't really believe in marriage."

"Oh." I was completely taken aback by this. Dylan wasn't the first person I knew that felt this way, but he was the first person I had ever grown close enough to that I didn't understand why he wouldn't want to get married. "Why not?"

"I just don't think it's necessary. I think it's a construct of society that never really made sense."

"So, you don't believe in monogamy," I said. My tone was light but internally I was thankful I was realizing this now before we even thought of moving past friendship. I knew then we would *definitely* only be friends. I took a long swig of beer.

"No, I believe in monogamy. I just don't believe in signing a contract to make it exist." He smiled playfully and turned the questioning to me. "Why do *you* believe in marriage?"

I thought for a moment, contemplating my answer.

"See?" he said, the smug look I remembered returning. "You don't even know why you believe in it, just that society tells you to."

I narrowed my eyes on him, playfully indignant to his pessimism. "Who hurt you, Dylan? Honestly," I asked placing a hand under my chin and giving him an icy glare from across the couch.

"No one," he said with a smile and a small shake of his head.

"Oh, please. I can see your tortured injuries from here," I continued to playfully taunt him.

He tilted his head back and let out a laugh that echoed in my chest. I swallowed hard at the feeling, pushing it down and away from my mind.

"So, you'd rather assume I'm damaged goods than tell me why you believe in marriage?" he asked, clearly not wanting to discuss his past relationships.

"Okay, fine," I said finally, sitting up straighter. "My belief in marriage is in my bones. The vows. The promises. The beautiful life you create with someone you love desperately and deeply. I believe it'd be a sad and lonely world without marriage."

"All things you can create without a contract." He raised his smug eyebrows and I suddenly wanted to prove how amazing marriage could be. My mouth dropped open and I closed it just as quickly.

"I believe in marriage because I believe God wants us to find the family that wasn't handed to us at birth. And when we find them, we know we are never meant to be without them again." I hated that I said that. I hated it because I still believed I wasn't supposed to be without Tate and yet, I was. My chin shook for a moment at my own words, and I cleared my throat as my fingers played with the hem of my sweatshirt. "And I had a beautiful marriage. It's hard not to believe in it after being married to someone like Tate."

"Now if all marriages were like yours, I'd imagine more people would believe in them." Dylan nodded and a smile slowly spread across his face. "Do you think you'd ever get married again?"

I paused a moment to contemplate the question, my eyes

not meeting his face.

"I'm sorry, you don't have to answer that if you don't want to," he said softly.

"No, it's okay. I honestly don't know." I rubbed my lips together and gazed at my half empty beer bottle. "Does lightning strike the same place twice?"

He gave me a sad smile and nodded, looking away.

"I think there's still hope for you to find someone to make you believe in marriage." I raised my eyebrows and smiled, backtracking from the last question to the point I just proved. "You're only thirty-four."

"And you're only thirty-seven." He raised his eyebrows at me, and his lips parted into a smile.

His smile was dripping with sincerity, but it was a crass reminder of how much life I had ahead of me; how much life I had left without Tate.

"I'm sorry he passed," he said, reading my mind. His eyes stayed on me; not like he was amused by me but as if he truly cared about the broken pieces of my heart.

"Thank you," I said softly.

"You still have a beautiful life, Tabitha." His voice was low, almost a whisper—the sharp lines of his face softened next to the light of the lamp next to him.

"I know." My voice was small as my eyes landed on his. I forced a smile, so I didn't start to cry.

He reached over the couch and grabbed my hand. His touch was warm, and it sent a shiver down my spine I wasn't prepared for. I squeezed his hand tight, looking away from him briefly before falling back into his gaze. His eyes never left me. They shone bright with empathy and admiration and a glimpse of something else too. Something I feared I wasn't ready for.

"You're amazing, Tabitha." He continued to hold my hand. "You are the strongest woman I've ever met and an even better mother. You should be proud of the life you're creating."

I was speechless after the unexpected compliment I didn't know I needed to hear.

I nodded as he pulled my hand to his mouth and kissed my knuckles twice—sweet and innocent but also unexpectedly intimate. Something inside me melted and I cleared my throat to regain my composure.

It felt wrong that it felt completely right to feel his lips on my skin.

"Would you like to go out with me sometime?" he asked.

I drew in a sharp breath. "Oh, I don't think that's the best idea."

He looked down, rejected, before looking back at me, his eyes hopeful once again. "Just a drink. I won't even pick you up if it's too much pressure."

I studied him a moment. I wanted desperately to say yes, but I feared what it meant if I did.

"Just a drink," he repeated, reading my thoughts.

"Fine," I said. "But you better pick me up. I don't like going to restaurants alone."

He looked at me in surprise. "And here I thought Tabitha Jones wasn't afraid of anything."

"We all have our limits," I said, and we laughed into the rest of the night.

Nine

WHEN DYLAN STOOD on my doorstep two nights later, I slipped out the door, leaving the boys with a babysitter named Lizzie whom I met through Lydia.

"Where's your truck?" I asked against the cold, night air.

He nodded behind him. "But we're walking. Ever been to Seadogs?"

"That turquoise building by the Port?"

He nodded.

I shook my head and smiled as I linked my arm in his, and we made the fifteen-minute walk from my condo to the restaurant. The seagulls continued to caw, and the sea lions never quieted down. I could taste the salt from the air on my lips. Comfortable conversation flowed between us with each step along the dock. The depth and cadence of his voice growing more and more familiar with each word he spoke.

I found our friendship easy to slip into, even though there was still so much I didn't know about him.

When we made it to the bar, it appeared to be a sunken

down log cabin with a deck that sat even lower, strung with twinkling lights glistening on the water's edge. It was quaint and cozy and entirely unimpressive—perfect for my first hesitant date with a friend. Though, I still wasn't entirely sure it was a date. It was just a drink.

"Hey, there, Dylan. What'll it be?" the bartender asked, wiping down the bar. He wore a white apron over his pot belly and his full head of hair was the perfect blend of salt and pepper. "And who's this beautiful young lady?"

"This is Tabitha," Dylan said proudly as we walked over to the nearly empty bar. "She just moved here from Tacoma a few months ago."

The bartender nodded and smiled. "I'm Harry. You two have a seat now and I'll be right with you."

"Nice to meet you, Harry," I said, nodding and took a seat next to Dylan at the bar.

The right side of his mouth curled into a grin and his dark eyes glimmered even though he wore his hat low.

"What do you think?" he asked.

"It's quaint." I smiled, surveying the room.

"Probably the most impressive date you've ever been on, huh?" He leaned in playfully, a comfortable banter always bouncing between us.

I leaned against the bar and rested my chin in the palm of my hand. "It's just a drink." I smirked at him and his head fell into a bashful smile.

When Harry returned, he took our drink orders. While making us each a rum and ginger ale, he asked, "How's your dad, Dylan? I sure miss seeing him around."

Dylan swallowed hard; a look of sadness washed over his face, but he didn't meet my eyes. "You know, same as usual."

Harry placed the drinks on white, paper napkins and gently pushed them toward us. "Well, I sure hope he finds a way to get better. And if not, I really hope you find some peace."

"Thank you," Dylan said and took a swig of his drink before leaning his elbows on the bar and looking at me like the exchange with Harry didn't just happen.

I watched him a moment, almost expectantly, but he didn't

say anything, just offered a small smile. I tilted my head, desperately wanting to know more and take away whatever glimpse of sadness I saw in his eyes.

"What's going on with your dad?"

He twisted his lips. "I don't know if it's something you really should worry about."

"I'm not worried about it, I'm just asking. I've seen you every week for months now and I didn't know I should even be asking how your dad is doing."

He drew in a breath and let it go before looking at me, his brown eyes filling with worry and growing a shade darker. "My dad has Alzheimer's. It's the reason I moved back here."

I saw the devastation in his eyes, and I immediately felt it in my chest.

"I'm so sorry, Dylan. That must be so hard." The side of his mouth twitched into a smile as I reached over and squeezed his arm. "How advanced is it?"

"Well, he thinks I'm his best friend from the Vietnam War and is still writing letters to my mom that left him when I was eight." He met my eyes. "So, not well."

I held his gaze as long as I could, wanting to absorb some of the hurt. How painful loss must have been when it was slowly dripping away, drop by drop. My loss was different. Sudden. Shocking. A tidal wave with no warning. Dylan lived with the knowledge his dad was slipping away; alive but completely unaware of who he was, not even remembering his own son.

"I'm sorry," I said, wrapping my hands around his arm and leaning my head on his shoulder. I didn't say more because I knew there weren't words to say in this situation. He leaned down and kissed the top of my head and I felt affection rush through me. Discovering Dylan's own hurts made me realize just how much I cared for him. I looked up and met his eyes. "I'd love to meet him someday."

He gave me a timid smile and I nodded.

"Do you ever see your mom?" I asked.

He gave his head a small shake, not offering more so I let it go.

"Want to talk about something else?" I asked, clearly

understanding he didn't want to continue the conversation.

"Great idea." His face spread into the smile I had grown to love and washed away any glint of sadness buried beneath.

The rest of the evening was filled with drinks and laughter. An unspeakable bond was forming between us in the most unlikely circumstances. I felt hesitant and afraid every time I felt connected to Dylan. I also felt the sharp, broken pieces in my own heart dulling around the edges, making me feel like healing could be possible.

When we walked out of the bar later that night, Dylan encased my hand in his and kissed the back of it tenderly. I smiled as we walked to the edge of the dock to admire the view of the Yaquina Bay Bridge lit up against the night sky. Dylan leaned his elbows on the railing, and I mirrored him. The wind whipped past my face and the peace of the night washed over the silence between us.

"Why haven't you told me about your dad?" I asked finally.

"It never came up." He shrugged.

I looked at him knowingly. "It could have though. We've talked every week for months now."

"It just never seemed important enough to bring to your attention."

"Dylan, your dad has Alzheimer's and doesn't remember who you are. That's important. Do you just not trust me with that kind of thing?"

He turned to face me. His voice almost breathless against the night air. "You lost your husband, Tabitha. A husband who you love. Unexpectedly. My own problems didn't seem worthy of bringing up."

"That's not a friendship then. People are allowed to be sad about more than one thing, Dylan."

"It's not the same, Tabitha, and you know it." His gaze didn't leave mine and I saw every layer of Dylan I felt like I was missing since I met him.

"We don't have to compare our problems to each other and see who has it worse. It's grief, Dylan. And it's okay to be sad even if someone else is sad too." I grabbed the edge of his coat and pulled him closer to me, willing him to keep his eyes on mine. "It's okay to not be okay," I finished with a shrug and a smile I hoped he found comfort in.

His dark eyes glimmered with a hesitation I was all too familiar with. I could tell the conversation was out of his comfort zone.

"It's weird knowing someone won't get better," he said in a low voice. "There isn't some miracle treatment or cure for Alzheimer's. Once the ball starts rolling down the hill, it can't be stopped or paused or pushed back to the top. I used to pray he would get better—that this disease would disappear." His mouth twitched as he looked out at the water, his elbows resting against the railing of the dock. "But now I just pray he'll remember me one more time. And for long enough that I know he's proud of me."

A chill ran up my arm as I reached out and placed my hand on top of his. The wind blew between us, carrying small pieces of our pain with it.

"I want that for you, too," I said softly. Every word that tumbled out of his mouth about his father was so heavy. I could tell how much he loved him. I could also tell how much he missed him. "I bet somewhere in his broken mind, he is very proud of you. Even if he can't figure out how to say it."

"Thank you for saying that," Dylan said softly as he turned to face me, our fingers woven together and our bodies inching closer.

A smile pulled at the corners of his mouth, and then he ran his fingers through my hair and tilted my chin up with gentle fingers.

"You are very unexpected, Tabitha Jones."

His words made a smile I couldn't contain spread across my face. "I feel the same about you, Dylan Thompson."

He stared at me a moment, wonder glistening in his eyes before he smiled and asked, "Can I kiss you?"

My heart pounded as time froze and I nodded, unable to speak.

He moved in closer, slow at first until his lips danced across mine. The touch ignited something I had feared was there but was suddenly so happy to find: a solace and safety in the surrender of finally kissing Dylan. He gripped my back and pulled me flush against his body as he ran his fingers through my hair and down my neck. I was exhausted with relief when I kissed him. Completely lost in his touch. There was an unleashing of so many emotions, it almost frightened me. I would have gone anywhere and done anything for him.

But in that moment, I also thought of Tate.

Summer 10

TATE, TRY THESE tacos. It is the best thing you will ever taste," his brother, Justin, said with his feet in the sand and takeout containers littering the beach blanket.

"I'm pretty sure every bite of Mexican food we've had this week is the best thing I've ever tasted." Tate laughed and so did I.

Our week stay in San Diego to visit Justin and Sarah was drawing to a close and we had enjoyed every minute of it. We weren't ready to leave. The mild heat, the beaches, the zoo, the hiking, the water parks—everything we could possibly want for a family vacation all within twenty minutes of each other. But the food was by far our favorite.

"That's true," I agreed. "I'm pretty sure this entire week in San Diego has completely ruined us for Mexican food up North."

"Well, yeah, of course. But you see this one is different because it's has this special sauce." Justin took another bite and held up his half-eaten taco. "So good."

"What's the sauce?" Tate asked his brother, but his mouth

was stuffed with fried fish and fresh tortilla hindering him from being able to communicate properly.

"It has a cilantro crema on it," Justin's wife, Sarah, answered turning away from the sandcastle she was sculpting with Toby.

"Isn't that just cilantro and sour cream?" Tate raised an eyebrow skeptically.

"That's like saying aioli is just mayonnaise," I responded, my mouth open in mock offense.

"Aioli *is* mayonnaise," Tate confirmed.

I laughed. This was always an ongoing argument for us. He hated how fancy four-star restaurants would dress up the name of a condiment to make rich folks feel better about having their salmon slathered in mayonnaise.

"It *is?*" Sarah's forehead crumpled in confusion. She clearly hadn't heard this argument yet.

"Eggs and oil whipped into a frenzy," Tate answered, nodding.

I shrugged and looked at Sarah. "Well, he's not wrong. But at least aioli has some garlic and herbs or something in it."

Sarah narrowed her brow, clearly studying the information that just entered in her brain. "I will never look at the Gordon Biersch aioli the same."

"The brewery?" Tate asked. "I didn't realize their burgers were fancy enough for aioli."

"They're not, but the waiter called the chipotle mayonnaise for the burger chipotle *aioli.*" Justin shrugged, letting out a small laugh.

"Yeah, and I said, 'oh fancy, I'll have that'—like an idiot," Sarah said, her face frozen in embarrassment before laughing at herself.

"That's a bad word, Auntie Sarah," Toby said, turning over another bucket of sand. His quick commentary made the four adults laugh and Sarah held a hand to her mouth.

"Sorry, you guys. I'm not used to being around kids," Sarah apologized through a laugh.

"Don't worry about it." I waved off her apology then watched her as she effortlessly played with Toby in the sand.

Justin joined them as soon as he finished his taco, letting

Toby bury his legs in the sand and making him squeal with laughter as Justin emerged as a sand monster.

Justin looked nothing like Tate but they both had an effortless way about them—playful, genuine, kind. Sarah was the same way. It surprised me they decided not to have kids. They would be amazing parents. But I also understood people's reasoning for choosing to have kids or not is entirely personal and absolutely no one else's business. I didn't need to be an aunt and Tate didn't need to be an uncle. We had our boy. And we also had Lydia and Tim's kids. That would more than suffice. The absence of what we thought we'd have as adults did not take away the beauty and importance of what was already there.

As the pair took hold of Toby's hands and frolicked with him in the ocean's waves, Tate and I hung back on the blanket to finish off more tacos and soak up the San Diego sun.

"Could you ever live here?" he asked out of the blue.

"In my dreams maybe." I placed a hand like a visor on my brow and squinted at Tate lying next to me on the blanket.

He nodded but didn't speak.

"Why? Could you?" I asked.

He shrugged. "I don't know. It's just so beautiful here. It'd be like being on vacation year-round."

I turned over on my stomach and let my fingers dance across Tate's chest. "It only feels that way because we *are* on vacation. It doesn't matter where you live though, every place will stop feeling like a vacation eventually."

He looked up at me, his eyes squinting in the sun. "That's very negative of you," he teased.

"Negative? Realistic? Same, same." I shrugged and laughed. "Plus, it's so expensive. Our rent alone would suck up our dreams of a vacation house or early retirement."

"We wouldn't *need* a vacation house."

I laughed. "So, San Diego is the only place you ever want to go then?"

He twisted his lips and studied me—the kind of look that reminded me how much he loved me. How much he respected me. How much I knew we couldn't live without each other.

"Our future would fall apart without you, Tabitha," he said

finally.

I smiled and shook my head, dismissing the compliment. "Are you not happy in Washington?"

"No, I am. I just really like it here. It'd be nice to live near Justin and Sarah, too."

I nodded and swallowed hard as my mind wandered. Tate was a go-getter—always full of dreams and ambitions. It made life exciting. Full. He never wanted to leave a single moment wasted. He filled the space in between the big memories with wonder and romance and laughter. He never wanted to just be. Simply existing—even for a few days—was never an option for him. It sometimes made me wonder if he just wasn't content.

He eyed me curiously, reading my mind. "Don't worry, every day is like being on vacation with you, Tabitha."

I rolled my eyes and laughed. He propped himself up with his elbow and laid on his side, pulling me close to him.

"You don't believe me?"

I looked up at him. "I think you have our roles reversed."

"Not true," he said, shaking his head.

"It is true—*you* are the vacation." I shrugged. "I'm the reality check."

He laughed and it echoed against the sounds of the waves in the distance. The sun setting over the water made the sky luminous and gave Tate's skin an iridescent glow. He turned me over, so I was flat on my back and brushed away the hair that had fallen in my face.

"The sun can't set without the moon," he said so softly it was almost a whisper and leaned down to kiss me.

When he pulled back, I smiled and said, "But the moon can't shine without the sun."

"Which is exactly why we make sense," he said, tapping his finger on my nose.

A small laugh escaped my lungs—one that felt like the definition of contentment.

"I'm better because of you, Tate."

"I'm better because of you, Tabitha."

Ten

"HOW ARE THINGS with Dylan?" Lydia asked. She sat on her couch, while the boys played in the crisp November sun.

Charlie waddled toward me. A sweet excuse to not meet my best friend's stare.

"Fine," I said plainly.

She narrowed her eyes on me. "Do I need to give you some truth juice to get you talking? Because I have plenty of wine in the fridge."

I laughed. "What do you want to know?"

Lydia cleared her throat and moved to the couch next to me. "I want to know why he met your parents...*twice*. I want to know why he was the last one to leave Toby's birthday. I want to know why he told Tim he has a drink with you at your place every week after Toby's guitar lessons. And...I want to know why Harry at Seadogs asked my friend, Trisha, who Dylan's new friend is."

My eyes widened at her line of questioning. "Gosh, this is a small town."

She leaned her chin into her hand and smiled. "Spill the beans or I'm asking Harry."

I laughed genuinely, trying to hide the flush in my cheeks.

"Things are fine with Dylan. I guess." I shrugged and handed Charlie a cup of cheese crackers.

Lydia drummed her fingers along her chin, a smile plastered on her face. Waiting. Expecting the truth I hadn't told her yet.

My hands started shaking as I sat on the couch next her. I felt sick to my stomach, like I was about to confess to a priest at church.

"I kissed him," I said while unexpected tears filled my eyes. I was almost embarrassed to admit it. I was even more embarrassed I was crying.

Lydia laughed softly. "Oh, honey, that's it? I was expecting something far more juicy."

My mouth dropped open slightly and then I closed it before narrowing my eyes on my friend. She returned to the kitchen counter to stir more hazelnut coffee creamer in her mug before turning to sit back down on the couch next to me.

"Was it terrible?" she asked incredulously.

I shook my head and wiped the tears from under my eyes.

"Why are you crying then? I don't understand." She started laughing at me.

"This is serious, Lydia." I returned her laugh through the embarrassing tears falling down my cheeks.

Lydia continued to laugh and then composed herself as Charlie clapped along to the commotion. "You're right. I'm sorry. I'll be serious."

"It was just weird, you know? I didn't expect it to feel...okay to kiss him. I haven't kissed anyone since Tate," I said. "And the last person I kissed besides him was nearly nineteen years ago. That's basically two decades and now I have aged myself. It almost feels like a betrayal. To my marriage. To Tate's family. To our kids. I don't even know how to explain it."

"Tate has been gone for over a year, Tabitha. This is not a betrayal. This is just a part of healing and moving on from the loss."

I sighed, deep and heavy. "What would Tate think?"

"Honestly?"

I nodded.

"Honestly, I think he'd be happy for you."

I scoffed and wiped more tears from my face. "Yeah, right."

"No, really. Tate loved you so much. He always wanted the very best for you. He always wanted you to be safe and loved. There's no way in hell he wanted to leave this world prematurely, and the last thing I think he'd want is for you to be alone. Not if you find somebody that's good for you and you care about. You are allowed to heal and move on. You don't need anyone's permission for that."

"I just still miss him so much." I buried my face in my hands. "I feel like I'm going to do it all wrong. I even thought of Tate while I kissed Dylan."

"Well, it's probably normal to think of Tate. You never fell out of love with him. You lost him." Lydia took a sip of coffee and shrugged as if that were an uncomplicated statement to make.

"That is true." I contemplated this for a moment. "I feel like I will always compare everyone to Tate and I know I'm going to do that to Dylan. That scares me and I don't know why."

"I do," Lydia said leaning in closer. "It's because you don't want anyone to fall short. But you need to realize that whoever you find love with again will probably do just that. He'll probably disappoint you and hurt your feelings too. But you'll do the same. The thing is—" she adjusted her position on the couch, "—you'll need to decide whether or not the good outweighs the bad and whether or not that person is going to partner with you in life through thick and thin. Because as much as you loved Tate, you two weren't perfect all the time either."

I nodded. I knew our marriage wasn't perfect. I knew Tate wasn't perfect either—but it was easier to remember him that way; those were the memories I chose to hang onto.

"I just have so much baggage. I'm such a mess. I'm doing my best, but it never feels like it's completely enough."

"Everyone has baggage, Tabitha. But you get to decide how you carry it and if you want to let someone help you with your suitcases; whether that's Dylan or somebody else."

"So, you're saying I should give Dylan a chance?"

"I don't care what you do." Lydia shrugged. "It's not for me to decide. I don't have to end up shacked up with him. But I do think he is a really good person that loves being around you and your kids."

All these things were true, of course, and it threatened my ability to think clearly. I couldn't figure out how to find the balance between missing someone that's gone and loving someone that's new. My energy was consumed by simply putting one foot in front of the other most days. I had somehow managed to stay on both feet since Tate died. But I let myself believe that was all there was left for me to do.

I smiled slightly and wiped my mascara-streaked tears from my eyes and let out a deep breath before looking at Lydia again. She was staring at her coffee.

"Do you think life gives us more than one great love story?"

Lydia looked up and placed her hand on my arm. "Absolutely. And if you don't, it's because you aren't allowing yourself to be open to it."

LYDIA'S WORDS HUNG in my heart for days after she said them.

A huge part of me believed love for me was done when Tate died. A part of me wanted it to die with him. How could anyone ever compare? How would that be fair and honor the love story I missed and painfully wanted back?

I no longer cried every day without Tate. My new life without him had mostly normalized, but at night, when the boys were asleep and I was alone in a bedroom I had always planned to share with him, I realized my entire memory of him was shattered. I still wanted him in bed next to me but somehow, I had forgotten what his skin felt like. I could barely remember how he smelled. Even the taste of his kisses faded from my memory. I longed for him and cried myself to sleep many nights, but with the current reality of Dylan prancing across my senses, those nights were becoming much less frequent.

I knew Dylan loved the color red over blue. I knew he smelled like soap and aftershave, but he had the faint smell of saltwater if I caught him after work. I knew his favorite music to play on the guitar was sad even when he was happy. I knew what his skin felt like when it was wet from the rain. I knew he thought it was funny I didn't eat chicken, even though I fed it to the crabs I ate for dinner. I knew the sound of his laugh as it echoed inside the walls of my home. I knew his breath smelled like cinnamon and his kiss tasted like rum.

I knew my memory of Tate was fading. And I knew that I was being fine-tuned to remember every fiber of Dylan.

I didn't want to replace Tate. But I didn't want to be done with Dylan either. I had to find a balance of loving someone no longer here and being with someone that showed up every day—wondering if both was even possible.

CAN I TAKE you and the boys out to dinner tonight?"

I smiled into my phone at the prospect of seeing Dylan that day, as I clicked out of a few tabs on my laptop.

"What time?" I asked already knowing I'd say yes.

"I can drive us over to Mo's after soccer."

I frowned and swallowed hard realizing how many mother's heads would turn as I got into his truck.

"Unless you want to drive separate," he said, reading my mind over the phone.

I chuckled uncomfortably.

"Well, I was just thinking about Charlie's car seat. It's such a pain to take it out and switch cars."

"And you wouldn't want Zach's mom to start any more rumors." His voice was smiling over the line and I bit back one of my own.

Zach and Toby had become close friends, so Toby often told him about how often he saw Dylan outside of practice. I had gotten to know Zach's mom, Mindy, from twice weekly practices, and I really enjoyed her. She had a laugh that could be heard across the field and always brought extra granola bars and waters, even if it wasn't Zach's snack day. She was very kind but also incredibly observant. Dylan had placed a hand on my back when we were walking away from the field after practice one day and her eyes zeroed in on it. Before I knew it, she had mentioned it to at least three other moms from the team, including Lydia, who, of course, called me. She told Lydia it looked completely innocent but was also laced with a secret. I laughed nervously when she told me, because Mindy was spot on.

"I don't care what Mindy says. If we start pretending we don't hang out outside of practice and she finds out we actually do, the gossip will get even juicier." Dylan laughed on the other end and it made me smile. "We're just friends, right? Let them talk."

Dylan cleared his throat. "Right."

"So, why don't you just ride over with me in my super cool minivan?"

He laughed. "That works."

I pressed my lips together when I hung up the phone, trying not to get too excited to see him. It had been a couple weeks since our night out together. He had come over for Toby's guitar lessons every Thursday and I saw him at practice, but we hadn't kissed since that night on the dock. I often wondered if maybe it was a fluke; simply two lonely hearts with rum pulsing through their veins.

But I also wondered if it was out of my own hesitation. I longed for him and wanted to avoid him all at the same time, which was practically impossible.

When Dylan got in our van after practice, I could feel Mindy's eyes sear into my back. I turned around to look at her. I smiled and waved, letting her know I knew she saw us. She stood with her hands clasped at her mouth and pressed them into her exaggerated smile. She gossiped like crazy, but I knew the idea of me and Dylan made her excited too. She'd nudge me and encourage me to sneak a look at Dylan during every water break at practice and every timeout during the Saturday games. Then she'd follow it with, "No pressure," and I'd roll my eyes.

She wanted good things for people, even if she embellished

the details.

After a loud and laughter-filled drive to just outside of town, I pulled down a side road flanked with evergreen trees that led to a small strip of stores and restaurants.

Nearly everything in Newport was quaint and Mo's was no exception. Dylan raved about it the whole drive over. The sun was dipping into the ocean, turning the sky a bright orange and the clouds a deep purple. The sky was almost clear—a rare occurrence for the Oregon coast in November.

"I don't know how I feel about clams," Toby said from the backseat as I parked. "Can pescatarians even eat clams, Mom?"

I smiled. "Yes, we can eat clams."

"How has this kid never had clam chowder?" Dylan asked.

I shrugged. "Tate was allergic to clams, so we just didn't eat it much."

"Yeah, he used to say he couldn't kiss Mom if she ate them and 'that would be *terrible*,'" Toby said dramatically, sliding out of the backseat.

I looked over at Dylan when he said this before getting out of the van. His eyes lingered on my face. There was a kindness in them, but also a bit of longing. Toby brought up Tate all the time in front of Dylan. It never seemed to bother him, but I wondered if it felt strange hearing about Tate kissing me. Even though realistically I knew it shouldn't.

I gave him a faint smile and slid out of the vehicle to unbuckle Charlie from his seat. When we started walking toward the small, blue, cottage-like building with 'Mo's' plastered across the front, Charlie reached for Dylan and he picked him up without a second thought.

"I tell you what, Toby. If you really don't like this clam chowder, I will…" He pretended to be thinking hard, "…eat yours for you."

Toby laughed. "I thought you were going to say pay me ten bucks."

"You wish," Dylan said giving him a playful punch in the shoulder and holding open the door to the restaurant.

We walked across the black and white tile floor and Dylan ordered three bread bowls of clam chowder.

"Want dessert too? They have really good cobbler?" he asked.

Tears stung my eyes and I blinked heavy, hoping he didn't notice. I saw Toby's body stiffen. Even the word 'cobbler' felt like a death sentence since Tate died.

"How about brownies?" I said, recovering and squeezing Toby's shoulder.

"Sure," Dylan said, turning to the counter and adding brownies and two chocolate milks to the order.

He paid for the food and carried the full plastic bag out to the picnic tables across the street. The tables sat on a grassy area littered with trees and foliage until they reached the edge of the fenced-off cliff that dropped down to the ocean below.

"What do you think?" he asked, eager for Toby to be satisfied.

Toby practically inhaled the chowder.

"This is really good," he said with his mouth full. "I didn't realize it'd have an edible bowl."

"That's the best part." Dylan smiled and looked at me as I blew on spoonful and fed it to Charlie.

"Thank you. This is really delicious," I said.

"I can't believe you've lived here nearly three months and you're just now having Mo's," Dylan said.

"I blame you—you should've told us sooner." I winked at him as Toby finished the last bite of his bread bowl and Charlie started to toddle off. "Toby, can you walk with your brother?"

He nodded and I admired my boys as they wandered the park; Toby bent over to help examine whatever interesting piece of nature Charlie had discovered.

A silence lingered between Dylan and I as the wind whipped past our faces and the light of the sunset dimmed.

"So, what's wrong with cobbler?" he asked, interrupting the quiet.

"You noticed our reaction then?" I looked at him and then out at the ocean. "I was making cobbler when I asked Tate to go to the store for butter." I turned back to him. "He didn't make it home."

Sadness washed over Dylan's face and he stayed quiet a

moment, absorbing what I told him.

"I'm sorry," he said finally as he laced his hand in mine, squeezing slightly.

His hand was warm—rough in places and soft in others. I leaned into his arm, resting my head on his shoulder for a brief moment.

"Thank you," I said, then turned my head up to look at him. "And thank you for being such a good role model for Toby. I think between guitar and soccer, I've been seeing more glimpses of who he was before Tate died."

"He's a good kid," Dylan said, nodding toward Toby and inching closer to me.

"He is. Thanks." I offered a small smile.

"And you're a great mom," he added.

I smiled and stared at him, feeling incredibly grateful for our friendship but also completely terrified of it.

"I'd like to take you out on a real date sometime," he said, his eyes not leaving mine. "If you want."

"I'd like that." I pressed my lips together, trying to withhold a smile. "Not just a drink?"

"I don't think it can ever be 'just a drink' with you." His face broke into a smile that wrecked my heart.

My hair was loosely blowing in the wind and he tucked a piece behind my ear. His fingers delicately ran down my neck as his watchful eyes admired me. An energy pulsed between us; it felt vaguely familiar yet entirely new. I wanted to pull him closer, but I also didn't want Toby to see. I grabbed Dylan's hand and pulled it down before letting go and shifting away from him slightly.

"I don't want to confuse Toby right now."

Dylan nodded, smiling gently. "Sorry. I wasn't thinking."

"Don't be sorry." I shrugged and smiled as I watched Toby collect seashells with Charlie. "I'm not."

Summer 9

MA'AM? MA'AM, CAN you hear me?"
Fluorescent lights flashed above my head as I heard the distant echo of voices and beeping. Everything sounded far away—like my head was submerged under water. I wondered if I *was* dreaming.

"What's her name?" a woman asked.

"Errr, uh. Tabitha. It's Tabitha Jones," a man answered.

A beep, then two and a rush of metal rolling down a hard, glassy surface. My head pulsed with pain. Every time I managed to open my eyes, I slammed them back shut again. My eyelids felt like cinder blocks and my throat like sand.

"Tabitha. Honey, can you hear me?" The woman's voice was sharp but almost warm, which didn't make sense. I was conscious enough to know that. "Tabitha, squeeze my hand if you can hear me."

I squeezed as hard as I could but only the tips of my fingers moved.

"She's really out of it. Order a CT-SCAN ASAP." Those were the last words I heard before I drifted off into unremarkable slumber.

BEEP…BEEP…BEEP.

I peeled my eyes open and stared at the sterile room. I was wrapped in stiff white sheets with an IV in one arm and a blood pressure monitor on the other. My head hurt but more than anything my stomach was swollen and tender and throbbed with a sharp pain every other minute. I felt shaky and tired. Exhausted and completely depleted, even though I had just woken up from a deep sleep.

I squeezed my eyes shut and opened them again to see if maybe I was dreaming. I needed to make sense of everything around me. I had no idea what had happened. As my eyes scanned the room it was clear I was in a hospital. As the patient.

But why couldn't I remember what happened?

Had I been mugged? Drugged?

I remembered picking Toby up from daycare after work and driving home. He showed me the picture he painted with his fingertips and we danced in the car to a song that made us both laugh.

We were laughing. Yes, I was sure I remembered laughing.

Then voices and lights.

And now, this hospital bed in this sterile room with Tate curled up in the painfully small pleather chair in the corner of the room.

What happened?

I cleared my throat and tried to sit up, but my belly had a stabbing pain pulsing almost constantly. It reminded me of contractions toward the end of labor. It made me shaky and nauseous; I thought I might vomit.

What was happening? I pressed a hand against my stomach and a wave of dizziness washed over me. I laid back down.

Tate opened his eyes at my movement and slid from the chair quicker than my eyes could follow until he was pressed against the side of the bed, holding both of my hands in his.

"Tabitha? It's Tate, babe. Are you awake?"

I nodded, though I don't know how prominent it was because my head ached like my brain wanted to push past my skull.

I saw him push a red button next to me calling for the nurse. My mouth was dry and tacky. I desperately needed a sip of water, almost as much as I needed to understand what happened.

The door clicked open, and I heard the squeak of tennis shoes across the linoleum.

"Is she waking up?" the woman's voice asked Tate.

"Yeah, I think so. She cleared her throat and opened her eyes but didn't say anything." The desperation in Tate's voice made me want to cry. I knew he was worried—terrified, really—and I didn't know why and it caused fear to creep up the back of my neck.

"Tabitha, it's your nurse, Megan. Can you hear me, honey?" Her voice was kind and too young to call me 'honey,' but it made me want to smile.

"I can hear you," I croaked out and cleared my throat. I blinked heavy, surveying the room again, feeling less dizzy this time. "Wh—what happened?"

Tate kissed my knuckles and breathed a sigh of relief I could feel trickle down my arm. I closed my eyes my eyelids were so, so heavy.

"You were in a car accident, Tabitha," the nurse's voice said.

I shot up; the pain absorbed by adrenaline.

"Where's Toby?" I cried out, as my eyes darted around the room, desperately searching for him like he might be there.

"He's at your mom and dad's house. He was completely fine. The accident wasn't all that bad but…" Tate answered, and his voice trailed off. He cleared his throat.

The concern for my child made my senses grow sharper. "But what? What happened? Why am I in a hospital bed with no recollection of what happened?"

My eyes darted from the nurse's deep blue eyes to Tate's green, concerned ones. Both sets held answers but they both seemed hesitant to reveal too much. The nurse began taking my vitals—checking my breathing, my heartrate, my blood pressure, asking about my pain level.

"What *happened?*" I asked as desperately and forcefully as I could without being completely uncouth.

The nurse dropped her medical façade for a moment and sat on the bed like she was my best friend and swallowed hard. "We think you passed out before your car left the road and landed in a ditch. You hit your head pretty bad and have a possible concussion that we'll need to monitor for some time."

I closed my eyes and nodded. A pang of guilt shot across my chest.

How irresponsible of me.

"Why would I pass out? I was just coming home from work. What's wrong with me?" My eyes shifted between the nurse and Tate.

She looked at Tate empathetically. Tears were pooled in the corners of his eyes, but none fell. She cleared her throat and turned back to me. "Well, your husband thought maybe you were pregnant, but we ruled that out and, in the process, discovered you had an ovarian cyst rupture while you were driving."

The air escaped my lungs and I sat back and stared at her before being able to look at Tate. His eyes were wandering, and he continued to kiss my knuckles.

"I—" I cleared my throat. "I've never had that happen."

She nodded. "It's common with women but not always consistent. And extremely painful."

"But I was fine all day at work."

"It doesn't really cause pain until it ruptures and for whatever reason it happened while you were driving. The first responders seemed to believe you were trying to pull over before you passed out and ran into the ditch. Those last few moments you might not remember though because you did hit your head in the process and have a bit of a concussion."

I swallowed hard. "But I'm not pregnant?"

The nurse shook her head gently, like she knew how hard we were trying. I was sure Tate had told her about the clomiphene. "No. But you do have a lot of fluid in your uterus from the rupture so your belly will feel swollen and tender for a couple of weeks. The doctor says to just keep taking ibuprofen and rest." She shrugged. "You'll be able to resume normal activity whenever you feel up to it."

I nodded blankly, staring into the abyss of the late-night hospital room.

"If you need anything else tonight, hit the call button, but my guess is the doctor will discharge you tomorrow morning so you can recover in the comfort of your own home." She smiled genuinely, like an old friend, before walking out of the room, leaving me with Tate.

He pulled my hand to his heart and rubbed my shoulder. I'd never seen him so shaken before. He was always so calm and confident. But not in that moment. He was shaking slightly, and dark circles under his eyes deepened every time he blinked away his tears. He looked like he was going to fall completely apart— a wavering worry consumed the steadiness I had always known. I was afraid he was going to break if he spoke a single word.

I kept my face plain as I stared at him and watched his shaky lips kiss my hand.

"Tate," I said finally. He looked at me with bloodshot and tired eyes. "I'm sorry I'm not pregnant again."

My chin quivered and he shook his head. "Tabitha. I don't care that you're not pregnant. That is the last thing I'm thinking about right now."

No longer able to keep my emotions in check, my face broke into tears and he pulled me into his chest.

It was the fifth attempt with clomiphene. The fifth failed attempt. It made no sense it wasn't working. It made no sense a cyst ruptured and drove me off the road either.

What's wrong with me?

"I'm so sorry. You're sure Toby is okay?" I asked through tears spilling down my face faster than I could catch them.

He pulled back and wiped the tears on my cheeks with his thumb. "Not a scratch, babe. They think you only hit your head because you were unconscious." He stared at our intertwined fingers for a moment. "I honestly don't know how you slowed down and got to the side of the road. Because it could've—" He cleared the emotion from his throat. "It could've been worse.

And I'm just so thankful I didn't lose you."

I tried to hold back the tears, to swallow them, but my chest heaved and my face gave me away. "Why do I keep letting you down, Tate? Why?"

"Tabitha, no. No, you aren't letting me down. That's not it." His hands and lips and tears were in my hair as I cried into the sterile hospital room. "I only care about you and Toby at the end of the day." He held my face in his hands. "I want you at the end of every single day of my life, no matter the circumstances. No matter what hurt comes along with that. It's you, Tabitha. Always and forever."

I nodded and closed my eyes on the tears waiting on the rim of my eyelids and they fell like rain down my wet cheeks.

"Sixth times the charm, then?" I asked finally.

He smiled into my hair before kissing me on my forehead. "Let's just get you home and rest for a while."

"A long while?" I asked, wondering what this would mean for us having more kids in the future and if we'd have to take more drastic steps for it to happen.

"As long as we need."

Eleven

I ARRIVED AT DYLAN'S house on the night of our date five minutes early. As excited as I was, I think my early arrival stemmed more from me not wanting to allow myself to back out. I was incredibly nervous. Not because it was Dylan but because I hadn't been on a first date in nearly twenty years. Tate and I got together when we were so young, he was really all I knew of dating at all.

I told Dylan I'd meet him at his house so Toby wouldn't see who I had dressed up for. As much as he loved Dylan, I still felt the need to keep a boundary around us until I was positive I knew where this was headed. I dressed in dark denim jeans with black heels and a white blouse that hung off my shoulder underneath a long, tan peacoat. My hair was curled in long waves and I put on lipstick for the first time in what felt like ages.

My heart pounded with each step toward his yellow front door. His house was as massive and beautiful as I pictured when he told me where it was located. It was perched directly across the street from the Port, draped in cedar shingles, faded by the salty air, with white colonial windows, and decorated with string lights wrapped around the porch. It was Newport from every angle and it made me smile.

I stood on the doorstep, my nerves growing as I waited for the yellow front door to open. The door swung open gently and revealed Dylan, standing there with an ease and shy confidence I had grown to adore. He wore dark jeans and a button-up shirt, his face clean-shaven and his ball cap was missing, revealing thick black hair I only got glimpses of during our late-night chats at the condo. His face spread into a speechless smile, revealing his right dimple as his eyes danced over my face and my attire.

I couldn't help but smile as my nerves washed away and were replaced with anticipation.

"You look beautiful." He annunciated each syllable playfully as he grabbed my hand and kissed it, pulling me inside and away from the frigid November air.

"Thank you," I said, swallowing hard and hugging him as he kissed my cheek. He smelled fresh and clean with hints of aftershave—a scent that was becoming more and more comfortable and familiar. "You clean up nicely, too."

He let out an almost embarrassed laugh and I returned it. We were no doubt noticing how infrequently we dressed to impress each other. I was usually dressed in jeans or even sweatpants when he came for guitar lessons. He was either in joggers for soccer practice or utility pants and a raincoat for work.

"Come on in," he said. "Want to have a drink before we head out?"

"Sure. Your house is amazing," I said surveying the old wood floors and dark paneling on the walls. It was classic and quaint on the outside, but it screamed 1960 on the inside. It was clean and tidy but was most definitely missing a woman's touch.

"Thanks," he said. "It's really my dad's house and his parents' house before that."

I smiled and nodded. "I didn't realize people still do that—keep houses in the family, I mean."

"Well, you do when you have that view," he said, nodding

to the back wall of windows that led to a wrap-around porch with a perfect view of the bay and the bridge lit up in the evening light. It was breathtaking and nearly identical to the view my condo had. His home was located incredibly close to mine, I probably could have walked there, confirming why it was always so easy for him to drop in at my place. "I just don't know how much longer I want to hang on to it."

"Really?" I asked, taking the glass of wine from his hand. "You don't want to keep it in the family?"

"It's not huge but it's more than I need." He shrugged and held up his glass. "Cheers."

I clinked glasses with him and took a sip of my wine, eyeing him over the glass. My face broke into another smile. I couldn't help it. There was just something about him. He was confident and charming, yet comfortable—like I'd known him for years. But my body still danced with nerves and anticipation—a thrill I hadn't felt in far too long.

"What's the plan for this evening?" I asked.

"I think we'll head up to Otter Rock to visit one of the wineries." He stood beside me next to the window, a hand on the small of my back. "But before we go, there's someone I'd like you to meet."

MY HEART BEAT faster as we pulled into the memory care facility for Dylan's father. I was honored to meet his dad. I knew how much Dylan cared about him even while he was slipping away one memory at a time. I also was nervous, knowing how big of a deal this was. Dylan kept the deterioration of his dad's condition private—not a secret—but he rarely spoke of the painful details, and I knew he had never brought a friend to see him since his memory had worsened.

"Anything I should know before we head inside?" I asked tentatively.

Dylan smiled at my nervousness. "If he calls me Gerald, just go with it. That's his best friend from the Vietnam War. And if he mentions Isabelle. That's my mom. She left us when I was little, and I haven't heard from her since." He glanced over at me as I nodded through the information. "But just be yourself. He'll love it even if he has no idea what's going on."

We walked into the facility hand-in-hand, and we signed in at the nurse's station at the front. It smelled as sterile as a hospital but with the faint scent of potpourri. It was an oddly sad smell, but the hope in Dylan's eyes made me thankful he trusted me enough to be there.

"How does he seem today, Lois?" Dylan asked the nurse sitting at the station.

"Last night was rough but the day nurse said he's had a better day today." She flipped through a file folder and placed it in a cabinet.

"Asking for my mom at all?"

"Of course." She gave Dylan a sad smile and he nodded. She turned to me. "Well, are you going to introduce me to your friend or not?"

"Oh, I'm Tabitha," I said, giving a brief, apologetic wave.

"Nice to meet you, Tabitha. I sure hope you're keeping this boy out of trouble." She gave a hearty laugh that made her sound much older than she looked.

He smiled mischievously. A smile I didn't recognize.

"Trouble?" I narrowed my eyes on him. "Uh-oh. Is there something I should be worried about?" I asked the nurse as I nudged Dylan's side.

"I have known this boy since he was in diapers. He was a prankster all through middle school. He did that thing…what did you call it?" She snapped her fingers in the air like she was trying to snatch the word.

"Lawn hopping," Dylan said through a breath of a smile.

"Lawn hopping!" She pointed at him. "Stole every last bird house, flamingo, and lawn ornament out of Ms. Johnson's yard and put them at whoever's house he was pranking that night. It was hysterical because no one could figure out who was doing it until Ms. Johnson caught him red-handed. I thought for sure she was going to beat his hide raw."

"You little thief," I teased as I laughed and shook my head at him.

A flush ran up his neck. This was such a stark contrast to who he seemed to be now. Soccer coach, guitar teacher, laborer, handyman. Friend. The mystery about him was continuously getting pulled away and it always left me wanting to know more.

"He didn't quite straighten out until high school when Coach Davis made him agree to a strict honor code if he wanted to stay on the football team."

"Is that right?" I leaned over the counter, placing my chin on my hand, enjoying each secret about Dylan tumbling from her lips.

"Oh yes." She nodded, also clearly loving filling me in on Dylan's childhood. "First string quarterback all three years of high school, and he got a scholarship to play at Oregon. They even retired his jersey at the high school. Still hanging in the gym."

"Impressive," I said.

I couldn't keep from smiling. It was like talking to one of Dylan's relatives, and she was showing me all his old baby photos. It was intriguing and enchanting. As much as I'd loved getting to know him the last few months, I realized how much I still didn't know about him. And how much I still wanted to learn.

"I'm surprised he never told you. He used to brag about it all the time." The nurse crossed her arms and pursed her lips, a smug grin pulling at the corners of her mouth.

"I'll bet he did," I said, playfully eyeing Dylan, and he let out a shy laugh.

"Alright. Thank you, Lois, for that walk down memory lane but I should really go see my dad," he replied gently rapping his knuckles against the reception desk.

"It was nice to meet you, Lois."

She nodded and waved at us as we padded down the brown-carpeted hallway to Dylan's father's room.

A soft glow emitted from the doorway, and it smelled like peppermint and chicken noodle soup inside. The bed was tautly made, and a small man sat in an armchair in the corner of the room next to the window.

"Hey, Dad." Dylan's words led with such trepidation, I

could tell he wasn't sure what version of his dad he was going to get.

"Hi, son." His father's voice was sad as he nodded a hello.

"I brought a friend. This is Tabitha," he said, still holding my hand and he brushed his thumb across my wrist. "Tabitha, this is my dad, Robert."

"Hi Robert. It's nice to meet you."

"Well, hello," the man in the chair said to me. It came out like a question. He glanced around the room, suddenly confused as to how he got there.

He was small and slight, with hair thinning on the top of his head, dark gray on the sides. He had Dylan's eyes but that was all that seemed to link them to each other. He looked at Dylan again and a beat of recognition flashed across his eyes. Like he was thrilled to unexpectedly see an old friend.

"Gerald!" he said, flapping his hands around Dylan's back as he leaned out of the chair to hug his son. "It's so good to see you! What has it been? Five? Ten years?"

Dylan swallowed hard, and I felt emotion rise in my throat.

"I've definitely missed you," Dylan said, sitting next to him and patting his knee. It was heartbreaking to hear him speak words that were so honest but not understood on the other end.

"Who's this?" He looked at me, not remembering just being introduced.

"Tabitha." Dylan smiled patiently.

"It's nice to meet you," I said again and sat in the third chair in the room.

"You, too." He nodded and leaned toward Dylan. "She's a beauty. Where'd you find her?"

I laughed.

"She can hear you," Dylan said, raising his eyebrows.

"Oops." Robert held up a hand to his mouth and began to laugh hysterically before looking at me again. "I'm sorry. I'm not so good with the ladies. I'm not sure how Isabelle puts up with me."

I smiled empathetically and my eyes flitted toward Dylan. His gaze told me everything I needed to know. This was hard. To be in the presence of someone he loved dearly that was very much living but completely gone cognitively. It broke my heart for him, and it reminded me loss comes in different forms for everyone. I wondered if it would have been easier or harder to lose Tate slowly. I felt almost certain it didn't matter: loss was loss.

The conversation went in relentless circles until we stood to leave. I leaned in and hugged Robert then walked to the edge of the room while Dylan said goodbye. Robert had a moment of recognition and loudly whispered in his son's ear, "She's beautiful, son."

I couldn't be sure, but I thought I saw a glimmer of a tear in Dylan's eye that was gone just as quickly as I saw it. He patted his father on the back and turned to meet me by the door.

It wasn't a romantic start to our date, but it was as intimate as it could have possibly been.

WE DROVE NORTH to a winery in Otter Rock. It was perched on the edge of the beach; the night was black, and the roar of the ocean echoed in the wind.

My nerves had melted away, and I was truly content to be sitting at a wooden cocktail table with Dylan, sipping too many kinds of wine and pairing each with different kinds of cheese, fruit, and chocolates. Our hands were constantly tangled together; there was rarely a moment we weren't touching. But he still hadn't kissed me again. I worried he sensed my own hesitation all those weeks ago on the dock and the remnants that remained now.

But our eyes stayed locked on each other so much of the night, I knew his feelings must have been growing as strong as mine. It surprised me how much I wanted him to kiss me again—longed for it even.

After our final tasting, we walked out of the restaurant and sat on a bench on the patio underneath a heater, offering only a small amount of relief from the chill of the November evening. I was wrapped under his arm and once again I realized how familiar everything about him had become—his smell, his touch, the cadence of his breath, and the way his voice sounded against the waves crashing in the distance—everything about him I had begun to find comfort in since meeting him. Slowly but steadily.

"I'm glad I met your dad," I said finally.

He dipped his head and smiled at me. "Me too. I think he liked you."

"Really?" My eyes narrowed. It was an hour of fictionalized conversation that revolved around Gerald and Isabelle.

"It might be hard for you to tell but…" he turned and met my eyes, "I could tell."

My lips curled into a smile. It was a huge compliment and a relief I didn't know I wanted.

"I care about you, Tabitha," he said. His eyes stayed on me—they held a depth I was just barely getting to know but desperately wanted more of. An uncontainable smile spread across my face and my heart beat harder in my chest. I don't know if it was meeting his dad or the amount of wine I drank, but I finally felt the courage to completely stop ignoring the direction this was headed.

"I care about you, too."

He brushed my hair from my face and ran his fingers through it, then, holding me by the nape of my neck, pulled my face toward his until his lips barely brushed against mine. His thumb ran along my jaw and I leaned in completely and kissed him as my body moved closer to his. A jolt of energy shot through me—my stomach, my back, my chest, my limbs—until I was positive my entire being was entangled with everything Dylan was. We kissed until my lips were tender and I wondered how we had held back all this time. I wondered how we could hold back anymore.

I didn't know it was possible to feel the sincerity in how Dylan kissed me and the tenderness in how he looked at me again. I was still afraid. But I also knew I'd be just as afraid without him.

Summer 8

I LOVED THAT MARRIAGES were laced with secrets. At least ours was. Not big ones. But private ones. The inside jokes no one would understand. The pinky promises. The words spoken in the darkness while our heads rested on pillows. Hurts only we knew we felt. Expressions only we could read.

Tate always knew when I thought something was funny even if it didn't make me laugh. He knew when I was stressed because of how it was etched across my forehead. He knew when I was irritated because he said he could see it rise in my chest.

"You alright?" he whispered in my ear as we stood on the edge of the white tent lit up by candlelight and filled with reception tables draped in white linens and hydrangeas. Tate's brother, Justin, was getting married. *Finally,* according to their mother. The wedding was whimsical and enchanting, the aisle was lush with flowers and ribbon while his bride, Sarah, dressed in silk, practically danced to him standing under the arbor in a white suit and tie. Lanterns hung in the trees of the venue giving the entire summer evening a warm glow that felt both idealistic and romantic. I had been up since six o'clock that morning, setting up centerpieces and decorating the aisle with my mother while Sarah and her bridesmaids were pampered by hair stylists and makeup artists in the crisp air conditioning, worrying about nothing more than nerves and whether or not they had lipstick on their teeth.

I drew in a sharp breath and closed my phone, pressing my lips into a tense smile. "Yeah, fine. Just tired—been a long day."

He placed his hand on my lower back. The warmth from his fingers bringing me both comfort and calling me out as they gently coaxed me to speak.

"Let's just let this be Justin and Sarah's day." I turned to face him and forced a smile, not wanting to say the words I'd just read out loud. I knew it'd make me cry.

He nodded as Toby toddled over to us with a juice box and a ridiculously adorable suit that matched his Uncle Justin. His two-year old belly hung out underneath the vest and the gel in his hair made him look like he belonged in a magazine. It also made him look so much older than the toddler he was.

"Daddy!" Toby said with a small and innocent voice that made my heart swell, and I shoveled away the tears rising in my chest. Tate scooped Toby in his arms and kissed his chubby cheek.

I stared at them in a daze, feeling both content and sad. I didn't know why the clomiphene didn't work this month. I didn't understand why it didn't work three months ago either. Even though Toby was still a toddler, I could see glimpses of him as a boy and I desperately wanted to give him a sibling before he was too old, even though I didn't know what too old was or if there was such thing.

Toby squirmed out of Tate's arms and launched himself into his grandpa's leg. I continued to watch silently as Tate's parents showed him how to blow bubbles into the dusk of night while music echoed in the warm August air.

Tate slid his hand down my hand and intertwined his fingers in mine.

"Dance with me?" he suggested, pulling my reluctant and

rigid body onto the dance floor.

We swayed to the music silently, a smile plastered on my face. I kept swallowing, pushing, begging my frustration to not surface. Not yet. No one needed an upset sister-in-law on their special day.

"You're tense." His voice was barely above a whisper as his lips brushed against my ear.

"I'm fine, Tate." I was short with my words, not wanting to unleash the beast of emotion raging inside me.

He pulled my face in his hands and looked at me, still twirling me around the dance floor. His green eyes were smoldering. Desperate. Kind. Full of every hurt and desire I had ever known.

"Tabby," he said knowingly.

"I hate when you call me that."

"I know." He let out a laugh. "Did it distract you enough to tell me what upset you? Because you've been floating around all day and night like a proud sister sprinkling fairy dust on my brother's wedding, and I know you just read something on your phone to make all that disappear."

I swallowed. Not because I was sad but because I felt guilty. Selfish. Ungrateful. What kind of friend was I to not be happy for my best friend?

"Lydia's pregnant," I said finally.

Tate closed his eyes and nodded, absorbing my complicated feelings without me even having to tell him. Tears rolled down my cheeks. I wanted nothing but good and wonderful things for my friend. Truly. I couldn't wait to throw her a baby shower and visit her in the hospital with a brand-new baby wrapped in a blanket with skin smelling like heaven. I wanted all those things for her. But I wanted them for myself too, and it wasn't happening easily this time around.

"I'm so happy for them," I continued through tears. "But I just don't understand why I'm not pregnant."

"We'll never have an answer to these things, Tabitha. No matter how hard we try to, but I don't think worrying about it helps. You've only tried clomiphene twice—it'll happen someday."

He was so positive. So sure. His words carried a certainty and his eyes a hope I knew I'd never destroy.

"But we didn't even have to try with Toby. Now it's been over a year of trying a second time and I'm just worried something is wrong. Toby needs a little brother or sister soon. I mean, he's almost three."

Tate smiled; his perfect lips accentuated by the candlelight. "You mean he's *not even* three. He's still so young—we can't stress about it."

I nodded and laid my head on his chest, listening to his heart beat underneath his three-piece suit. "Am I a terrible person?"

He chuckled softly. "For what?"

"For being equally jealous and happy for Lydia and Tim."

He laid a delicate and nurturing hand on the back of my head, holding me up both physically and emotionally.

"We're allowed to feel more than one thing at a time. What we feel isn't always mutually exclusive."

I nodded as a tear slipped out of my eye and landed on his white pocket square. His chest held many of my tears over the years. Most of them I never had to explain.

There was something sacred about being fully known by someone and being fully loved anyway.

Twelve

THERE WAS A Christmas bizarre at Toby's school the week after Thanksgiving. I didn't want to go. I just wanted the holiday season to tumble in and out as quickly as a storm on the coast.

I used to love Christmas, but with Tate gone I had to force myself to enjoy any part of it. I hoped that eventually I'd learn to love it in different ways. I made the cookies and strung lights on the tree. I played the music and hung the stockings, debating whether or not I should put up Tate's again. I ultimately decided to hang it up. He was still such a part of our traditions even though he wasn't there to share it with us.

I hung the ornaments I begged Tate to throw out for years because they were hideous, multi-colored, glitter-shedders that didn't match any of my coordinated, glass ones. I bought the eggnog I hated but he loved. I watched his favorite Christmas movies as if they were my own childhood favorites. His traditions had somehow become my traditions, and I knew I'd feel even more out of place if I didn't incorporate them somehow. Even if it was a painful reminder of his absence.

It wasn't hurting as bad this year which almost made it worse. I didn't want the memory of him to fade any more than it already had.

Dylan had become a beautiful distraction. I sometimes wondered if that was all he was. Was he a placeholder filling the space between grief and loss? Or was he somebody more?

Most days it felt like something more—a second chance for another love of my life. But I still missed Tate all the time. I longed for him and wanted him back every single day. I didn't know how to give my heart to someone else when I still felt like it belonged to Tate at the same time. I didn't really even know if it was possible.

When Toby asked if Dylan would come with us to the bizarre at the school after one of his guitar lessons, I had felt relieved he had a male role model to consistently show up for him, even though I knew I'd enjoy Dylan's company as well.

When Dylan knocked on the door the night of the bizarre, Toby answered it and Charlie tore down the hallway on his short legs to greet him while I put the last dish in the dishwasher before closing it.

"Daddy!" Charlie shrieked and ran into Dylan's arms as he picked him up.

I stood on the edge of the kitchen. The blood drained from my face, my chin on the floor. I was astonished. I couldn't believe what Charlie said. Dylan walked in with Charlie in his arms and smiled sheepishly. He seemed embarrassed but he also seemed nervous—which he never was.

"You guys ready to head out?" he said, scratching his forehead and breaking the tension of the moment, while my face was still frozen in shock.

"Uh, yeah. Yeah," I said, shaking my head and grabbing my purse off the counter.

Toby was standing in the hallway looking dazed and confused. His brow was furrowed as he looked at me and then at Dylan. We never told him we had gone on a date. He hardly even realized Dylan stayed late after guitar lessons. To Toby, Dylan was simply his soccer coach, musical hero, and video game competition. We had been careful. But kids are intuitive.

Even one-and-a-half-year-olds.

"Ready Toby?" I asked as nonchalantly as I could.

He looked at me longer, his brow still furrowed, before nodding and heading out the front door. The car ride was silent except for Charlie's babbling and the Christmas music humming from the speakers. I snuck a few looks at Toby behind me, but he continued to stare out the window. Dylan kept his eyes on the road, but his lips twitched when I glanced at him.

What an awkward start to our evening. We needed to talk about it. But I didn't know when or even how to broach the subject.

When we arrived at the school, a palpable distance stood between me and Dylan. I don't know if he sensed my hesitation or if my youngest child calling him 'Daddy' caused him to want to retreat, but regardless, he didn't let his knuckles brush against mine while we walked in the parking lot nor did he put his hand on my lower back when we walked into the building.

I found myself missing his touch, even if I completely understood his avoidance.

At the sight of gingerbread houses, handmade ornaments and gifts, baked goods, and hot chocolate, Toby's introspective demeanor seemed to evaporate, as did the tension between Dylan and me.

We found a table on the outskirts of the gymnasium and posted up with our gingerbread house supplies to begin the decorating competition. Toby focused on intricately placing gumdrops on the roofline of his house to mimic Christmas lights and Charlie mostly ate sprinkles and licked his fingers while I decorated his house for him. Dylan made eye contact with me and gave me a small, almost bashful smile over the top of the chimney made of gingerbread sitting between us.

I held on to his stare as long as I could, my smile growing while an entire conversation played out with our eyes. So much of who Dylan was felt right in my life and with the boys. But coming out and making it official seemed like a horribly stupid idea until we were both sure what we wanted from each other. He bit back his lip like he was trying not to laugh and popped a few cinnamon candies in his mouth before giving me one. His finger touched my lip for only a brief second, and it sent a shock down my spine. The cinnamon flavored candy reminded me of what his kisses tasted like at the end of the dock while standing under the stars. My cheeks flushed and I tried and failed to not smile.

His perfect smile grew wide. He knew what he was doing to me. I cleared my throat and looked between Charlie's gingerbread house I had halfway decorated and Toby's gingerbread house as he was lining the windows with icing.

"That's looking great, Toby," I said, wiping Charlie's frosting covered face with a baby wipe.

"Thanks." Toby nodded, not losing focus as he flanked two miniature candy canes on either side of the house's front door. "Dad loved making these."

I smiled and kissed the top of his head. He was barely shorter than me. When Tate died, he was under my chin. "He sure did."

Toby's ears turned bright red, which usually happened before he started crying. I squeezed his shoulder, not wanting to say anything more, knowing he didn't want to start crying in front of half his school.

I looked at Dylan, his watchful gaze was laced with empathy and uncertainty. He'd come to realize that just letting Toby talk about his dad didn't always need to have a response attached to it. Sometimes the silver lining didn't need to be mentioned. More often than not, how proud his dad would be or how much his dad would have loved to be there didn't need to be said either. Sometimes, we just needed to say his name and let the memory of him stay alive as long as possible without anyone trying to make us feel better. Sitting in the pain and feeling it was just as much a part of the healing as anything else.

Dylan placed a knowing hand on my back, and I stiffened; I knew how many pairs of eyes would be seeing the gesture. The gymnasium was packed with everyone from town, not just the school. When he moved his hand away from my back, I could still feel the warmth from his fingertips and a part of me wanted to not care what anyone thought—to be all in all at once. But there were too many layers between us for that to happen.

"Sorry. I can't help it," he whispered in my ear so soft, it was almost undetectable. His lips brushed against my hair and I could smell the cinnamon on his breath. I smiled and turned away, pretending he didn't say anything, but I felt heat rise in my chest and up my neck.

"What do you think, Mom?" Toby asked, holding up a baker's bag of frosting. His house was a glorious mess of gumdrops, candy canes, and frosting.

"I think it's perfect," I said rotating the gingerbread house, getting frosting on my fingers.

"I don't know, it probably could use more frosting," Dylan teased, making Toby laugh. I smiled at them and licked the frosting off my fingers.

"Well, isn't it just so great to see the happy couple out together?" Zach's mom, Mindy, walked up behind us, smiling wide and raising her eyebrows at me.

"Oh, we're not…" I said, looking at Dylan and then back at Mindy. My eyes briefly glanced at Toby. He was definitely paying attention.

Crap.

Dylan pressed his lips together and raised his eyebrows, while Mindy took a step back, her mouth forming into a circle.

"Oh, I see. Whoopsie." Her hands fidgeted against her legs. "Well, Toby your gingerbread house looks great. Did you see Zach's yet?"

"No, where's your table?" Toby said, scanning the gymnasium.

"Right over there." Mindy pointed to the corner of the gymnasium and Toby took off to find his friend and compare houses.

"I'm so sorry," she said, holding a hand to her chest. "I wasn't even thinking about Toby being right there."

"We're not together." I smiled and crossed my arms defiantly as Mindy's eyes drifted to Dylan taking a squirming and restless Charlie out of the stroller.

"I see." She nodded and pressed her lips together, withholding a smile. "Well, it's good to see you guys here then, I guess."

"It's good to see you too," I said, a polite smile plastered on my face.

"Is Trey here?" Dylan asked, breaking the awkward tension with his nonchalant question. Trey was Mindy's husband. He went to high school with Dylan. Like with most people in this small town, they went way back.

"Yes, over there with Tim and Lydia." She pointed to them across the gym, next to the hot chocolate station.

"I'm going to say hi really quick," he said more to me than Mindy.

"Want me to take Charlie?" I asked, holding out my arms but Charlie clung to Dylan's jacket.

"Nah, it's fine, I got him."

I drew in a breath as he walked away with my son and I sensed Mindy's eyes on me like lasers. I looked at her and smiled, hoping it masked everything I was truly feeling.

"You're together though, right?" Her eyes were wide, and her tone made it seem like the answer was obvious.

I smiled and rolled my eyes.

"Right?" She was desperate for confirmation.

"No." I laughed out my answer.

"I mean but the way he looks at you and touches you and picks up Charlie like he's his da—"

"Stop." I cut her off as abruptly as the laugh stopped in my chest. I didn't want to hear her say the last word. Not after Charlie called him that earlier. I smiled to soften my tone. "We're just friends."

But I knew she didn't believe me.

AFTER TUCKING THE over-sugared boys in bed, I walked Dylan out to his truck.

"Thank you for coming, Dylan," I said, crossing my arms to protect myself from the frigid December air whipping between us and the awkward tension that had formed throughout the night. "It meant a lot to Toby."

"My pleasure." He smiled and rocked back on his heels, his

hands in his pockets itching to grab me, words on his tongue he wanted to say but didn't.

"What is it?" I asked plainly, knowing he must want to talk about what Charlie said and everything else that followed this evening.

"So, are we not together for everyone else's sake or are we just not together?"

I laughed, diffusing the tension. I guess he didn't want to talk about Charlie calling him 'Daddy.' He pulled his hands out of his pockets and grabbed mine, lacing his fingers in my hands.

"Tabitha." He pulled me closer, his eyes searching my face.

"Dylan." The pounding of my heart grew stronger, and I knew this could be the conversation that would make us officially cross over into complicated territory. I didn't know what to say. I also didn't want to answer. I knew if I made me and Dylan real, it meant Tate and I were no longer. It would mean he was really gone. A harsh reality a part of me still couldn't face.

He leaned in and kissed my forehead.

"Is that a yes or a no?" he continued to press gently.

I drew in a slow breath. "Do we have to label it right now?"

His eyes bounced off the pavement and landed on me. "No, I guess we don't."

His words told me it was okay, but his eyes told me he wanted a different answer.

"I like what we have. I like where it's going." I shrugged into his arms, wrapping my arms around his waist while his hands rubbed my back. "I just want to keep what we have between us right now."

He nodded, conceding to whatever I wanted. He placed his hands on the small of my back pulling me against him. I rested my head against his chest, breathing in his scent and hearing his heartbeat. The very sound made a lump rise in my throat and I swallowed it down. He pulled me away gently, his fingers dancing through my hair as he tilted my face toward his. I hoped he didn't see the tears trying to escape the corners of my eyes as he leaned in and kissed me.

The wind was knocked out of my chest as his lips met mine.

His kiss pulsed through my body. I didn't want it to end. I didn't want to let go. I wanted to linger in his arms, my lips on his. I wanted to feel his heartbeat against mine for as long as I could. It was a moment I wanted to last forever. If only because I knew how quickly forever could be taken from me.

Thirteen

D YLAN WILL BE here soon for guitar. Finish your homework before he gets here. Okay, Toby?" I said while wiping down the counters in the kitchen after dinner as Charlie played in the Tupperware drawer.

Toby tapped his pencil aimlessly, his cheek smashed against a hand, and his eyebrows cinched together.

"Toby?" I asked softly, trying to get his attention. "You alright?"

"I hate math," he said, his posture unmoving. I knew this wasn't true. I knew we were tapping into the realm of teenage angst. I also sensed something else was brewing in his mind.

"Want help?" I offered, making my way around the kitchen peninsula to where he sat at the kitchen table. He dropped his pencil, pushed the paper toward me aggressively, and threw his arms across his chest. I looked down at the worksheet full of algebra problems that were no different than the test he aced last week.

"Hey," I said softly, tilting his defiant chin toward me. "What's going on?"

I sat down next to him, waiting for him to answer me.

"I can't do these problems. They're too hard." He wouldn't meet my eyes and I knew no matter how much he didn't want to admit it, the problems that were too hard weren't written on the paper.

"You miss him today?" I asked, reaching my hands over to clasp his arm. He still wouldn't look at me even as his chin shook, and he nodded his head. I swallowed my emotions. "I miss him, too."

"Do *you*?" His tone was accusatory, and his eyes shot to mine like lasers. "Because when Dylan's around it doesn't seem like you do."

I was immediately taken aback. His words sent a rush of guilt across my chest and up my throat. I had to swallow it down. I knew Toby was right: when Dylan was around the pain dulled around the edges and didn't return the same way it used to feel when he left. I cleared my throat and decided to skirt around the subject.

"I thought you liked having Dylan come over to teach you guitar."

Toby shrugged as two tears ran down his cheek. I reached out and wiped them away with my thumb and pulled him into my arms as my own eyes began to well with tears.

"Hey, bud. If it's too much, you don't have to keep taking lessons with him. If you need a break, that's okay."

Toby let out a cry into my shoulder and I held him and rocked him, letting him cry harder and harder into my shoulder. My emotions mirrored his, and I realized we had been doing so well for so long, that we had hit our limit; something inside of us was snapping. Breaking. We talked about Tate all of the time, but we hadn't sat in our hurt like this in what felt like a very long time. I hadn't even felt the need to go to Moolack Beach for a good cry in weeks. But the grief hit Toby out of the blue and ricocheted off of me. I knew this had far less to do with Dylan than it did to do with Tate.

Charlie was oblivious to the depth of the conversation and tears at the kitchen table. He was also oblivious to the grief—he'd never know any different and the knowledge of that wrecked me. He continued to throw Tupperware on the floor in the kitchen when there was a knock at the door.

I knew it was Dylan.

"We'll just cancel for tonight, okay?" I said, wiping my own tears away and Toby nodded.

I answered the door with swollen eyes and tear-streaked cheeks. Dylan's bright eyes switched to worry at the sight of my emotions written all over my face.

"Hey." My voice came out far more tired than I expected. "Tonight's not a good night."

"Everything okay?" Dylan searched my face.

"I'm sorry, I should have called you sooner, but it just happened." I drew in a sharp breath. "He's just really missing Tate tonight. I miss him too. The holidays have been hard on us."

"I understand." His expression was solemn as he dipped his head into a nod. "I'm sorry."

He grabbed my hands and pulled me closer, clearly wanting to comfort me, but I pulled away from him gently. I didn't want to risk Toby seeing and further complicate his emotions tonight. He was already aware of far too much. He missed his dad with his entire twelve-year-old being and he didn't need to accidentally catch his mother wrapped in another man's arms.

"Can I call you later?" I asked, my eyes pleaded with him to understand.

"Of course." He gave me a brief hug and kissed the top of my head.

It made me want to cry even harder, but I blinked away the tears. I desperately wanted him to stay, but I knew I needed to be there for Toby and not use Dylan as a distraction from what we were going through. It was a strange conundrum trying to decide if letting myself fall in love was the right thing for my boys—even stranger that I felt like it was actually within grasp.

I closed the door as he walked away and turned to Toby, who was now sitting on the couch. His legs were tucked under him and his eyes were sad and tired. I sat next to him, letting the silence between us fill the space. Charlie marched in and handed Toby a rogue plastic lid from the drawer.

Toby let out a small laugh through his nose and I smiled at him.

"Want to talk about Dad?"

Toby shrugged and chewed the inside of his cheek, before glancing at the fireplace. "Why'd you hang up Dad's stocking?"

I shrugged and let out breath. "I guess I just don't know how not to yet."

"Is that going to be Dylan's stocking?" He glanced at me out of the corner of his eye.

My head jerked back in surprise. "Why would you ask that? Of course Dad's stocking isn't Dylan's."

He fiddled with the edge of a throw pillow and turned to meet my eyes. "Why did Charlie call Dylan 'Daddy'?"

Tears stung my eyes at the question. The answer was simple and complicated; tender yet terrible.

"Because Dylan spends a lot of time with us, so Charlie's just gotten used to him. It's kind of like how you accidentally called Mrs. Richardson 'Mom' in kindergarten." I let out a soft chuckle, knowing I was downplaying the magnitude of how it felt to hear Charlie say it about Dylan.

Toby returned the laugh and then thought for a moment.

"But it's different though, isn't it?" he asked.

"It is." I nodded seriously. "Charlie never really got to know Dad. He doesn't even remember him. He loved him while he was a baby but—" I shook my head, unable to keep the tears from spilling down my face, "—he'll never know Dad the way you and I do."

Toby wiped the tears on his cheeks with the back of his hand. "That just seems really unfair, Mom."

"It *is* really unfair." My eyes were swollen, and my chest ached. I kept swallowing to keep from sobbing. "I never wanted this for us. But it's up to me and you to teach Charlie about Dad. Tell him all the funny things he said. How he always found the best hiding places in hide-and-seek and played the music too loud in the van. Or how he'd moonwalk in the kitchen after he made the best chocolate chip cookies."

I tapped my forehead to Toby's, giving him a sad smile.

"I don't want to forget him."

I wrapped my arms around him tighter, grief spilling out of my eyes and down my face. "Me neither."

"And I don't want Dylan to replace him."

I pulled away and cupped my hands around his cheeks, my questioning eyes searching his. "What makes you say that?"

Toby shrugged. "Because of what Charlie said. And how much he's around. I don't want to have to call him Dad."

I smiled gently and shook my head. "You will never have to call Dylan Dad. He will never replace Dad. He's just a good friend to us."

Toby nodded and chewed on the inside of his cheek, contemplating my statement.

"Do you not like when Dylan is around?" I asked, narrowing my eyes and wondering if perhaps everything was too much too soon.

"No, I do." He nodded as his mouth turned into a frown. "I think Dylan likes us a lot. It's nice having him around. I just don't like that Dad's not."

I pulled him in for another hug as Charlie tumbled onto my lap. "Me neither, buddy. Me neither."

I knew exactly how he felt. It was complicated and twisted—the battle between of half-full and half-empty; the silver lining that didn't change the harsh reality.

Summer 7

"NOPE, NOPE, NOPE. Absolutely not." I stood in the half-packed kitchen in our small Craftsman house downtown, staring at Tate carrying two out of ten boxes of his memorabilia we kept buried in our one-car garage.

As many amazing memories as that small house held, I was thrilled to be leaving. A two bedroom, eleven hundred square foot home built at the turn of the twentieth century with a toddler made me realize that families actually can outgrow a house. In fact, the house can seem to explode at the seams. We probably could have made it work, but Tate loved to hang on to everything. And everything didn't fit in that wooden box perched next to the freeway.

I was so ready to say goodbye to it. Start over and move on with our wonderful life in a bigger house, in a better neighborhood on the North end of town, that was in a better school boundary, and didn't back up to the freeway. The constant whooshing sound in our backyard stopped bothering me about a year after we moved in, but I was sure I'd never get used to the sound of car accidents. The sharp crash of metal scraping against metal, tumbling violently across the cement. The tiny hairs on my arms would stand on end and a sharp chill would ripple like a wave down my back while my heart pounded inside my chest.

It terrified me every time.

I was happy to say goodbye to that.

"What?" An astonished smile pulled at Tate's perfectly crooked mouth. "You know how important this stuff is to me."

"Important?" I raised my eyebrows and placed my hands on my hips. "Oh, honey, we have different definitions of important, don't we?"

Tate set the boxes on the floor and studied them before looking back at me. "What do you mean?"

"I mean, those boxes have been taking up space and collecting dust in the tiny little garage of our tiny little house for the last four years of our marriage."

"And now we're heading to a much larger house with plenty of extra space—even an extra bedroom."

"That we hope to fill with a child one day," I reminded him.

"Yeah, one day. But until then it can be the museum of Tate Jones with artifacts and memorabilia dating back to the late eighties."

I practically ignored him and continued wrapping plates in bubble wrap and placed them delicately in the open box in front of me. "You have not even looked at any of it since we got married."

"So? Doesn't mean I didn't want to, but now with the new, bigger house there will be plenty of opportunities to take a walk down memory lane." His smile was convincing, but I had no desire to hang on to every one of his yearbooks from grade school to high school, dozens and dozens of trophies from t-ball to varsity track, and t-shirts and jerseys that hadn't seen the light of day in over a decade and probably smelled like mildew.

I paused my packing and stared at his desperate and handsome face. He was so sentimental. I always loved it. Or rather, I loved the *idea* of it. In actuality, being sentimental felt a lot like clutter. And I hated clutter.

SIXTEEN *Summers*

He raised his eyebrows and pressed his lips together in an imploring smile, making me laugh.

"No," I said finally.

"Tabby…"

"Ugh, you brought out the 'Tabby,' now you definitely aren't bringing those to the new house." I walked over and kissed his cheek while he stuck out his lip in a dramatic pout. "Ask your parents. Your mom might want to hang on to it."

"Can't. Dad said me and Justin can't put any more of our crap in their attic."

"Well, that's saying something if your own parents won't hang on to it."

He glared at me playfully.

"Storage unit?" I suggested. "Because seriously, babe, ten boxes are too much to hang on to."

"But it's everything, Tabitha. Every trophy holds a memory, every shirt reminds me of a different season, and every journal captures my entire soul from a different year in my life."

"Alright, Whitman," I teased him.

He wasn't just sentimental, he held on to the pieces of his life like lyrics hang onto the melody of a song. I just held onto Tate. He was my song, and I would've listened to him every moment for the rest of my life if I could. I cared about every part of him—both past and present.

But he wasn't bringing those damn boxes to the next house.

I let out a sigh and gazed into his eyes like I was ready to relent. "Rock, paper, scissors?"

His eyes brightened and he assumed a position, his hands poised in front of him, ready.

"Best three out of five?"

"Two out of three. We've got stuff to do." I held out my palm and my fist hovered over it.

His rock pounded my scissors. My rock pounded his scissors. My paper covered his rock. It happened quickly, in succession as if we practiced the whole bit.

I gave him a smug smile and raised my eyebrows quickly. "Get a storage unit."

His shoulders sagged and he let out a small chuckle that

172

made me bite my lip. I slid my arms around his waist, my fingers curving over every muscle on his back, and I pulled him into me, resting my head on his chest.

He was all the memorabilia I needed. All the memories. All the sentiment.

Just Tate.

He ran his fingers through my hair and pulled my head back gently to look at him. His lips were curved into a moody and playful smile and his eyes smoldered inside his dark eyelashes. He leaned down to press his lips to mine. It was the kind of kiss that started slow, and melted into my entire body, making my heart hammer in my chest and my knees give out.

We ended up in a sweaty and naked heap on the kitchen floor in our half-packed kitchen. The heat of the August afternoon air in our unairconditioned house made my back practically stick to the linoleum beneath us. It was messy and spontaneous, yet full of passion and mischief. There was nothing glamorous about it and yet, it felt like the most romantic place for it to happen.

Tate did that to me. Every time. No matter how many years we spent together. He was all the romance I'd ever need.

"You win," he said, tracing a finger down the side of my face that sent a shiver down my spine and warmed in my heart.

Fourteen

"AM I MOVING on too fast?" I asked Lydia against the wind at the beach. We sat huddled on a blanket, as we watched our boys fly kites with Tim in the crisp January sun.

Everything between me and Dylan was a steady progression. It was easy and complicated all at once. I was walking in the wake of a tragedy, picking up the pieces I could and finding new pieces of heartache along the way.

"Tate's been gone almost a year and a half, Tabitha." Her eyes were sad and empathetic as she peered over at me. "I don't think anybody would think you can't start moving on. But it doesn't really matter what anyone else says. What do you think? Do you feel like it's going too fast?"

I shook my head slightly. "Not really."

"Did you sleep with him and not tell me?" She studied my face before I even responded.

"No," I answered, letting out a soft chuckle.

"So then I guess I'm wondering where you're coming from?"

"I don't know," I said looking out at the waves and then back at Lydia. "Most of the time it feels right. But most of the time I still think about Tate and miss him. So, I feel like I'm constantly wondering what he would be thinking of me right now. I knew him so well. Completely. Every life decision since he died, I know what he'd be saying. Even moving to Newport, I knew he'd be saying, 'You're crazy but I know you'll make it work!' or more likely, 'Tabby, what took you so long to go find an adventure?' But with Dylan I just don't know exactly what Tate would think."

"Oh God, you hated when he called you Tabby," Lydia said, pulling her windblown hair back with a twist of her hand.

I laughed. "I did. God, I had forgotten how much that irritated me. And he'd always say it when he was trying to get me to talk about something I didn't want to or conceding to whatever I wanted."

Lydia smiled thoughtfully. "He usually did concede to whatever you wanted."

I swallowed hard and nodded. "Except when he bought a condo in Newport without telling me."

"Well, aren't you glad he did? It's been working out rather well from where I'm sitting." She nudged me.

I kept my eyes on the boys running in the sand in the distance with Tim. It was working out. I was still able to work from home, though I felt like I needed to find a local position somewhere in Newport to keep me grounded here. Dylan continued to spend a lot of time with our family. Between guitar lessons, events around town, and casual dinners at home, I was surprised he hadn't run off yet. He was single, childless, and incredibly handsome, but he still came around, stayed late, and found ways to effortlessly fit himself in my life knowing it was more challenging for me to fit in his.

"Charlie still calls him Daddy," I confessed, my tone unmoving.

Lydia raised her eyebrow, then shrugged. "Not surprised."

I twisted my wedding ring on my finger and thought for a moment before asking what had truly been on my mind.

"What do you think Tate would think of Dylan?"

"Tate would have liked him." She shrugged.

My eyes narrowed on her. "But how do you know?" I asked almost desperately.

"In case you've forgotten, I knew Tate. He was my friend too." Tim approached them with Charlie in his arms while the older boys continued to fly their kites. She nodded toward him. "Tim knew Tate too."

"Uh-oh. What'd I do?" Tim's face spread into a guilty smile as he set Charlie down next to the sand toys. He picked up a green shovel and aimlessly started digging.

"Tabitha wants to know what Tate would think of Dylan."

"Way to segue into that one, Lydia." I rolled my eyes.

"Oh please, you know Tim knows all sides of this story."

I drew in a breath at the reality that always sat in front of me, but I tried so hard not to think about. Not only was Tim married to my best friend, he was friends with Tate, and was also friends with Dylan. Had been since even before Tate died.

"I don't know if I want to get in the middle of all this," Tim said, plopping next to his wife on the blanket.

"I'm not asking for your opinion on Tabitha and Dylan, just what you think Tate would have thought about Dylan...in general," Lydia said, trying to convince him to answer.

Tim dipped his head and then peered up at the ocean. "Dylan's a good guy, Tabitha. I don't think you need to worry about what Tate would think and just start thinking about what's best for you and the boys. No one can tell you what to do—you're the one that has to live the rest of your life. It's your choice. Outside opinions are only going to muzzle your line of reasoning." He shrugged.

Lydia and I looked at him, slightly dumbfounded.

"Well, there you have it," Lydia said, scratching the back of her neck and letting out a laugh.

"What? Was that harsh?" Tim asked, oblivious to the truth bomb he just dropped.

I shook my head and smiled. "No, it was just..." I searched my mind for the right word, "...honest."

"CAN YOU MEET me in the lobby of your complex?" Mindy asked over the phone.

It was an unusual proposition coming from Mindy. She had called after the boys and I arrived back at the condo from our day at the beach. Charlie had fallen asleep on the way home and was snoozing in his crib while Toby played on his tablet.

"Maybe?" I drew it out like a slow question, less out of hesitation and more out of figuring out logistics.

"What do you mean 'maybe'?" Her voice was laced with excitement and I was oddly curious what this gossip queen wanted from me and why I needed to go to the lobby.

I laughed. "It's just that Charlie is sleeping, and I don't want to wake him."

"The lobby is one hundred yards from your condo and Toby is twelve. I was watching other people's babies at that age. He can handle it." She laughed as she said this and for some strange reason it eased my hesitation. It was weird to think how much older twelve sounded than ten. It was even weirder to realize the amount of life he had to live in two short years.

I let out a breath. "Fine. Be there in five."

"Toby, keep an ear out for your brother. I'm running down to the lobby really quick," I said grabbing my keys and walking toward the door.

"For real?" he asked, pulling off his headphones.

"For real. And keep your headphones off."

When I arrived in the lobby, I smiled at Cynthia at the front desk. She was the weekend receptionist. Gabby was the weekday one. I'd grown to know both of them as most permanent residents do, collecting mail daily, replacing lost key cards, and buying bait from The Bait Shop. Living in the condo, I often forgot I was living at a resort because it was anything but luxurious. It was quaint and sleepy but also charming and enchanting. Tate promised we would make so many memories here. Five short months later, we definitely had.

Mindy was standing at the bottom of the short staircase that led to the abandoned restaurant with an obnoxious smile on her face and her husband, Trey, standing next to her.

"Are you ready?" she asked excitedly.

"I hope so." I couldn't help but laugh. We had gotten to know each other through our boys and events around town, but we weren't all that close.

"Follow me," she said as she and Trey walked up the stairs. The wall of windows with a view of the bay were covered in plastic and blue painter's tape. The tile along the bar was demolished. The floors were covered in paper. And it smelled like a fresh coat of white paint.

"You didn't," I said, connecting the dots.

"We did!" she squealed clapping her hands together. "The old Waterfront Grille is now Carter's Catch!"

Trey nodded next to his wife proudly. "She's excited. Can you tell?" He smiled at me.

"Wow! Congratulations, Mr. and Mrs. Carter. That's amazing!" I smiled and admired the construction zone that would soon be their restaurant.

"Can't you picture it? Subway tile along the bar here and we'll refinish the floors and get beams for the ceiling that match. I was thinking tables with concrete tops with brightly colored chairs. Like aqua maybe? Or yellow? I can't decide. And the bar will be concrete too. The pendants I picked out are black and we'll have ten strung down the length of it, I think." She admired the room. "Can you picture it?"

"Absolutely." I nodded. "I can't wait to eat here and see it all finished."

"We were thinking we'll keep the menu simple: clam chowder, Dungeness crab, fresh fish. A total dream for a pescatarian like yourself," Trey said, in a way that made me envision the dazzling businessman he was. It was almost like they were trying to sell the restaurant to me. For a moment I wanted to tell them the life insurance I received after Tate died was not as much as they thought.

"Perfect," I said instead and smiled genuinely at them. "When will you open?"

"April!" she squealed and clapped her hands again, obviously overwhelmed with excitement. This time Trey laughed along with me.

"There's one thing we wanted to ask you..." his voice trailed off.

I raised my eyebrows. "What's that?"

"We need someone to do the bookkeeping and payroll." Trey stuffed his hands in his pockets. "Would you be interested?"

I was slightly taken aback. I had only recently mentioned to Lydia that I think I needed to find something more local. As much as I loved working from home for my old company in Washington, it felt like a tether to a life I was no longer living.

I swallowed and nodded. "That's incredibly generous of you to offer. Are you sure?"

"Of course, we're sure!" Mindy grabbed my hand. "What do you think?"

"I mean...possibly," I said hesitantly. "I'd have to consider the logistics of it and see if it's feasible for my family."

"Absolutely!" Her nod was so enthusiastic, it was practically a bounce. "Just think. You would literally live where you work. You could still work from the condo but there will be an office here too, of course." Her eyes were wide when she looked at Trey, who held out a blue folder to me.

I opened it and my eyes quickly scanned the salary, the benefit package, and the hours. I drew in a breath, knowing the numbers were close enough to what I was already making that it could work, but I also felt a hesitation wrap around my chest.

Mindy and Trey watched me expectantly.

"If you have any questions or need to negotiate any of the details, let us know. We'd really like to make this work," Trey said.

I nodded and looked back up to them. "I just need to discuss it with—" I stopped short. I almost said Tate and it felt like a punch to my gut. I cleared my throat. "Can I think about it for a bit? Get back to you tomorrow?"

"Of course," Mindy said. "Trey, grab the champagne."

He grabbed the single bottle and three plastic cups from the remaining fridge under the bar, popped the bottle, and poured each of us a glass.

"To *hopefully* welcoming you to the team," he said with a

small smile. I took the champagne from him and clinked my plastic cup with theirs.

"Thank you." I smiled as I sipped the bubbly, sweet beverage.

"Oh, this is going to be so fun! I mean, if you accept the offer." Mindy couldn't contain herself. "Dylan will be so happy to hear it."

I started coughing and choked on the champagne—the embarrassing kind that stung my nose and made my eyes water. "I'm sorry? Why would you bring up Dylan?"

"Because he mentioned your name to Trey when he went out for drinks with him and Tim."

"Oh." I nodded slowly. "Right. I forgot you two are friends," I said, more to Tim.

"He just adores you," Mindy said, with an exaggerated smile.

"Mindy," Trey said with a warning. His expression read like he had been sworn to secrecy. He smiled sheepishly at me.

I tried and failed not to smile. As much as I wanted to keep what Dylan and I had under wraps, it was comforting to know his feelings were genuine and I wasn't some dirty little secret he made out with from time to time out of convenience.

Though, honestly, pursuing me was anything but convenient for him. I was constantly with my kids. Every night out with him was met with a time limit and a rush to get home to the sitter. Our goodbyes were laced with desperation and my lips always ached for one last kiss that was never enough. I was the epitome of inconvenient, and yet, his commitment to being consistent with me and the kids never faltered. It made me incredibly thankful to hear he actually cared for me, even coming off of a gushing Mindy's lips.

"It's fine." I waved off the concerns. "Dylan is a good friend."

"Yeah, sure." Mindy rolled her eyes playfully. "It's just nice to see him with someone great. He needs someone to mend his broken heart after what happened with Felicity in Portland."

I narrowed my eyes on her. Dylan never told me the details of their relationship, stating that it simply didn't work out. He moved on with Heather for years afterward but said that didn't work out either. He didn't believe in marriage, so I just assumed that was a part of it. He didn't elaborate and I didn't pry. A part of me wanted to know, the other part of me worried it would taint the view I had of him.

Trey exchanged a look with his wife.

"What? Was I not supposed to mention her? I figured you already knew considering all the time the two of y'all spend together."

I nodded and shrugged, playing off the awkward secrets being revealed and pretending like it was just water under the bridge. "Don't worry about it. Like I said, we're friends."

I continued to downplay our relationship. I didn't know how to claim him. I didn't know how to say the words in my head, let alone out loud, even though a huge part of me wanted to. A part of me, though it only whispered in my head rather than yelled, still felt like I belonged to someone else.

"Right." Mindy pursed her mauve-colored lips, withholding another smile. She turned to Trey and then back to me. "Well, this is going to be great. We're really excited to have you work with us."

"Me too," I said, though I barely had time to process it. "I think this will be a good thing for me."

I walked around the empty space, envisioning Mindy's plans for the remodel and remembering what it was the last time I was there. It was outdated with chipped and water-ringed wooden tables, blue walls, and outdated tile. My eyes zeroed in on the window where Tate and I sat eating crab cakes and discussing cabinet colors for the condo he had just purchased. The condo I now called home. I stood in the barren, empty restaurant in the midst of a makeover, and it was another illustration of how much my world had transformed without my permission, even if it was still becoming something else that was just as beautiful.

Fifteen

THE NEXT DAY I opened the door to my condo to see Dylan standing on the concrete slab with a dozen pink roses in one hand, a paper bag I knew contained fish and chips from Clearwater, and a smug smile on his face. My eyes narrowed on the flowers then back to his irresistibly kissable face.

"Why do you have flowers?" I asked, curiously.

He walked over the threshold and kissed my neck as his full hands wrapped around my waist. "Because I hear congratulations are in order."

"For?" I drew out the vowel longer than necessary.

"Accepting the position at Trey and Mindy's new restaurant," he answered, moving his lips from my neck and kissing my mouth.

I closed the door and nodded with a small smile.

"I didn't even tell you about it yet," I said following him down the long hallway to the kitchen. I had just called Trey that morning after sleeping on the offer the night before. It was almost as impulsive as uprooting my family to Newport but every time I did something like that, I could hear Tate telling me how brave I was.

"Well, of course Trey texted me this morning right after you said yes," he said as he set the takeout containers on the counter and pulled forks out of the drawer on the right. He was so comfortable. Completely at home. He knew where everything was and I watched him cautiously, feeling entirely overwhelmed with how well he eased his way around my home and my life.

"Right, of course," I said, swallowing hard, watching him effortlessly maneuver around my kitchen.

He squeezed the lemon over my fish then paused as he opened the tartar sauce container. "What? Are you having second thoughts about the job?"

I shook my eyes away from his hands, carefully preparing my food for me: a fresh squeeze of lemon, tartar sauce, and garlic fries for me. Ketchup, hot sauce, and sweet potato fries for him. I didn't tell him my order, but he knew it. And I knew his. I didn't remember reaching this point in our relationship, but somehow we had, and my heart pounded simply looking at the food and flowers laid out on the counter between us. I looked up at his eyes.

"No, no of course not. I just—" I eyed at him curiously. "Why didn't you tell me you mentioned my name to them?"

He shrugged. "I guess it was just in passing over a few drinks. Trey didn't even tell me he was going to ask you until last night after he already had."

"Oh, okay." I bit the inside of my cheek and pulled the brown container of food toward me and mindlessly dipped a garlic fry in his ketchup.

Dylan leaned his elbows over the counter and watched me carefully for a moment. I could feel his eyes searching my face. "What's wrong?"

I pressed my eyes closed. I loved he could read me so well and I hated it just as much. No one knew me like Tate did, but I could physically feel Dylan chipping away at the stone hedge around my heart and it terrified me.

"Nothing."

"Tabitha." He reached over and touched my hand and I

slipped it away quickly. Even what I felt in his touch startled me.

A chill ran up my spine and it felt so out of place. I didn't even know how to articulate it. I stared at the countertop for an uncomfortable amount of time before speaking.

"I'm scared," I said, my voice just above a whisper.

Without saying anything, he walked around the kitchen peninsula and wrapped me in his arms.

"Why? What happened?" he asked, holding me against his chest. His embrace was welcomed but I felt the inherent need to push him away. And I did so gently as I looked up at him before I responded.

"You happened. And you scare me."

His eyes landed on the floor as he dipped his head and swallowed hard, no doubt searching for a response. He looked back up at me with a question in his eyes. A doubt I knew I couldn't clear from his mind.

"Okay," he said timidly and took a small step back.

I ran a hand over my forehead. "Okay? That's all you can say?"

"I don't know what else to say." He shrugged. "You didn't even tell me about Mindy and Trey offering you the position with their restaurant last night and when I show up to celebrate like a good friend should, you're acting like you don't even want me here. I feel like sometimes I'm the only one trying." He threw up his hands. "And now you just said I scare you. I don't know what to do with that, Tabitha."

I tilted my head back with each statement, recognizing the truth, the honesty, and all the ways he saw me clearly. I swallowed hard before I spoke.

"I guess I'm just hoping you'll convince me not to be afraid. To promise me it's going to be okay. That you and I and whatever *this* is will be okay." I shrugged, emotion tugging at my voice. I looked away, feeling suddenly embarrassed.

"I can't promise you that," Dylan said finally.

I closed my eyes and let out a breath. It was the response I expected, but not the one I wanted to hear.

"Not yet anyway. We are—" He searched for words for a moment. "Hell, Tabitha, I don't even know what we are but I'm still trying. I show up for you, yet you always brush aside whatever we've become and now you're telling me I scare you even though I am constantly waiting patiently in the wings for you."

My eyes felt swollen with tears, but I didn't want to cry—I *chose* not to cry.

"Do you at least hear what I'm saying?" Dylan asked, trying to break through my silence.

I nodded. We stared at each other a minute. Neither of us knowing what to say. Neither of us able to cleanse the awkward tension cloaked in the room.

"I like where this is going—"

He let out a frustrated sigh and his hand fell to the cold countertop, interrupting my train of thought.

"What?" I asked, my voice clipped and irritated.

"You keep saying that, Tabitha—that you like where this is going. Why can't you just be clear? Is this even remotely what you want? Do you want this to move past where we are? Because, honestly, I don't want to waste your time and I certainly don't want to invest mine into someone that doesn't want me to be a part of her family."

The air left my lungs.

"I'm allowed to take things slow, Dylan. I've only known you for five months."

He raised his eyebrows and nodded. "And we've gotten very close in five months."

My head jerked back, and I placed my hands on my hips. "So now we're moving too fast? Which is it? Tell me, please."

He paused and looked at me carefully. "I just want to know where I stand with you. I want to know that I'm not a placeholder. That there is something in me that you see yourself being with in the long run."

"I do, Dylan," I began, my voice softer than before. "I do see you being a part of my family's life. I am incredibly grateful for how you treat my boys and what you mean to them. There are so many things I like about you. I like how kind you are to my kids. I like how easy it is to be around you. I like the way my hand fits in yours and how content my heart feels when I'm around you. I do want you around for a very long time. But me wanting that is what terrifies me. When Tate died, I never thought I'd be with anyone else. Ever. And now that it seems like it might happen…" I shook my head as my voice trailed off, unable to articulate how exactly it made me feel. I wiped a rogue tear from under my eye and looked square at Dylan. "And I'm sorry that isn't exactly what you want to hear, but I don't have room to sugar coat anything in my life right now."

"I am not asking you to sugar coat anything, Tabitha. But I care about you so much it actually hurts sometimes. And I just want to feel like you want me as much as I want you."

My chest felt like it was caving in and my voice shook. "I don't know if I can say that yet."

He looked at me a long moment. An entire sixty seconds passing until finally, he let out a breath and nodded.

"Alright." He grabbed his keys off the counter, leaving his food behind. "I guess I'll just leave you to the rest of your day then. Congrats on the new job."

I nodded, unsure of how to convince him to stay and wondering if I even wanted him to. I followed him to the front door, and he turned around before opening it, his fingers fidgeting with his keys.

"Dylan…" I said, grabbing his hand and wrapping my arms around him. I pressed my head against his chest and breathed in his comforting scent. His heart thrummed against my ear. "Don't be mad at me, please," I whispered.

A breath escaped his mouth that walked the line between a scoff and a laugh. His hand cradled my hair and his mouth pressed against the top of my head. "I'm not mad."

"You are."

He pulled back and looked at me. "Mad and confused are two different things," he said as he kissed my forehead and slipped out the front door.

I WAS IN over my head. I knew it.

Nobody wanted to stay in limbo forever no matter how fun

the dance was. I didn't know if Dylan was growing tired of my complacency or simply tired of me. I worried the thrill of chasing the grieving widow was wearing thin. I worried. But my heart knew better.

"Go out with me tonight?" I asked him over the phone a few days later.

I could feel him smile over the phone before he cleared his throat. "Will you pick me up? I don't like going to restaurants alone," he teased, his voice deep and less guarded than a few days before.

I laughed and felt the tension slack between us. "Well, what if I don't take you to a restaurant?"

"Where are you going to take me, Tabitha?" he asked curiously.

"Don't worry about it. It's a surprise. I'll pick you up at seven."

"Sounds good," Dylan answered.

When we hung up the phone, something released in my chest. The weight pressing worry on my heart had lifted. Dylan and I would be okay. We were just still discovering each other's worlds and figuring out how they fit together.

As my workday evaporated into daycare and school pickup, I grew more excited to see Dylan. As much as I was terrified of what we were turning into, I wasn't ready for it to end. I hated every word he said to me at my kitchen counter earlier that week, but I also listened to him. Heard him. I realized Tate made life all about me all the years we were together, but that was the exception not the rule. I couldn't expect the same from Dylan. He had his own feelings. His own goals. His own life he needed to live, and I still needed to decide if I wanted to be a part of it.

"Alright, pizza is on the counter. Bedtime for Charlie is at seven and Tate can stay up 'til eight-thirty."

"You mean Toby?" Lizzie, our babysitter, said. She eyed me curiously as she set plates on the kitchen table next to glasses of milk.

"Huh?" I asked, but the blood had already rushed down my face and landed in the pit of my stomach.

"You mean Toby. You said Tate," Lizzie answered, nervously snapping her fingers painted with black nail polish at her side. She smiled timidly as I stared at her before shaking my head.

I couldn't remember the last time I called Toby Tate. I used to do it all the time. It had stopped after Tate died but now that Toby was almost a teenager, he reminded me more and more of him. I was surprised I hadn't done it sooner.

"Right." I swallowed. "Sorry, Toby looks a lot like my late husband."

She rubbed her pink lip glossed lips together and nodded.

"I'm sorry about their dad," she blurted and looked immediately like she wanted to eat her words off the floor. "Sorry, I said that. That was rude when you're about to go out on a date."

"No, it's fine. Don't worry about it." I smiled reassuringly. "And thank you, Lizzie. We miss him very much." I placed a hand on her arm as I grabbed my purse. "Call me if you need anything. I won't be more than twenty minutes away."

My phone buzzed in my purse as I kissed both boys goodbye and stepped out the front door. As I slid into the driver's seat, I pulled out my phone to read my missed messages. One missed call and two unread texts from Dylan.

Can you call me?
I have to cancel tonight.

My stomach fell to the floor in disappointment. I called him right away and he answered on the second ring.

"Hey, I'm so sorry. I need to cancel—"

"I know, I saw your texts. Is everything okay?" I worried it was our conversation just a few days ago. I worried he'd hit his limit. I worried this was the end. And the more I worried, the more I realized how much I cared.

"No," he said, clearing his throat. "My dad had a really rough day. Lois called to see if I could come by and see if I can settle him down." He let out a breath over the receiver and then a rough laugh escaped his throat. "Or, I guess, see if *Gerald* can settle him down."

I smiled but my heart broke when he said it. It was so complicated. It was so convoluted. It was everything I didn't want for him, but I wasn't sure how to help him through it.

"I'm so sorry, Dylan," I said empathetically. "I just—I wish there was something I could do..."

He sighed audibly over the phone. "Me too. But hey, I'll make it up to you. Tomorrow?"

"You don't need to make it up to me, Dylan." I smiled at the promise of another date but drew myself back into the moment. "Call me after you leave? Doesn't matter what time."

"Yeah," he said, his voice deep and steady over the line. "Yeah, I'll call you."

When I hung up the phone, I stared at my lit phone screen until it turned black. I contemplated going back inside my condo. Instead, I put my car in drive and drove to the memory care facility.

I arrived before Dylan. The parking lot was nearly empty, except for the facility bus they used for field trips and a few of the staff cars. Dylan's truck hadn't arrived yet.

When I walked through the glass doors, I spotted Lois right away, and she stood from the reception chair immediately with a relieved smile on her face.

"Tabitha. It is so good to see you. Is Dylan with you?"

"I think he's on his way," I said, glancing down the hallway as I signed the guest sign-in sheet. "Do you think it'd be okay if I went and saw Robert without him, or should I wait?"

Lois opened her mouth and closed it. "I honestly have no idea. It has been one of those rare, hard days for Robert. He is confused about everything from what we're feeding him to why there's a toothbrush in his bathroom. He, uh—" Lois looked at the floor sadly. "He is just not himself anymore."

My heart broke for Robert. For the people who cared for him. But mostly, it broke for Dylan.

I nodded, unsure if I should have even come.

Lois let out a deep sigh. "It's worth a shot." She nodded toward Robert's room. "Head on back."

I walked across the brown carpet, slowly and hesitantly.

When I reached Robert's room, the door was open and only the light from his bedside table shone. I knocked softly on the open door and poked my head inside.

"Robert, are you awake?"

"Who's there?" a panicked voice said from the bed.

"It's me. Tabitha. Dylan's friend," I said softly, knowing he wouldn't remember but hoping the familiarity of his son's name would somehow comfort him.

He nodded with his brow furrowed and stared at the window. The blinds were drawn closed.

"Would you like me to open the blinds?" I asked. "So you can see outside?"

His eyes darted toward me and back at the window in a panic and he nodded. "Yes. Yes, I don't like not knowing where I am."

I opened the blinds to reveal the dark evening sky and a rose bush lit up by an outdoor lantern hanging outside the window.

"There. Is that better?"

He pulled the sheets closer to his chest. "Yes." He nodded curtly. "I hate those blinds. Isabelle always hated vertical blinds. She said they were tacky."

I smiled at the memory of his ex-wife regardless of how gruff his voice sounded. "Well, I agree with Isabelle."

He chuckled and it came out with an unexpected cough. "What was your name again?"

"Tabitha," I said softly, offering a smile.

"Tabitha," he repeated and nodded like it seemed familiar.

"Mind if I sit, Robert?" I asked and he looked at me in surprise.

"No, of course not. I'm sorry I don't have anything to offer you to drink." He fiddled with the edge of the blanket.

"I don't need anything but to sit and have a conversation with you. Does that sound okay?"

His head bobbed nervously. "Not sure what you want to talk to an old man like me about, but I don't mind the company, I guess."

He stared down at his shaky hands clasped on the blue quilt draped over his frail body. He looked at me with sad eyes that reminded me so much of Dylan; I wanted to reach out and hug him.

"I don't mind the company either." I smiled and rested my hand on his and he squeezed it tightly. He looked at me briefly and then at the door as Dylan walked in.

Dylan looked between me and his father, his eyes wide with confusion and surprise.

"Hey, Dad," he said slowly with a half-smile. He looked at me out of the corner of his eye. His eyes were heartbroken but layered with gratitude. "How's it going?"

"Gerald! It's good to see you, old friend. Looky here, this is my friend, Tabitha." He leaned away from me and held a hand to his mouth as if he was telling Dylan a secret I couldn't hear. "She likes my company."

A broken laugh escaped his throat and it made Dylan smile wider than I'd seen in a week.

"She's good company," Dylan said, looking intently at me, as he pulled up a chair on the other side of the bed.

"She is. I'll bet she knows Isabelle—man, the two of them would have a ball together. Don't you think? She even looks a bit like her."

Dylan laughed and looked between me and his dad. "Wasn't she a brunette?"

Robert waved off the comparison. "A brunette yes with golden skin that reminded me of caramel. Smelled sweet like candy too. She said it was coconut. But her eyes—they were a clear blue, lined in dark lashes that made me feel like I was getting hypnotized by a crystal ball." He looked back at me. "You've got those eyes."

Dylan nodded slowly, his lips slowly turning upward.

"Knock, knock," Lois said, holding a tray of plastic cups and a pitcher of water. "Just thought y'all might be thirsty." She set the tray down next to Robert's bed and turned to me and whispered in my ear, "This is a complete one-eighty from a few hours ago."

I smiled at her and as she walked back past the bed, she squeezed Dylan's shoulder. He rested a knowing hand on hers while looking at me before she walked out of the room. His eyes held both adoration and appreciation for me, and he didn't look away until his father spoke.

"Tabitha, can I ask you something?" Robert asked, his eyebrows raised.

"Of course," I said, peeling my eyes from Dylan's as I leaned toward Robert, anticipating what he wanted to say.

"If you weren't with my good pal, Gerald, here, who would you be with? I'll bet you have a line of men waiting for you."

Dylan jerked his head back. "I'm not sure that's an appropriate question to ask right now, Robert."

He waved off the concern. "Ah, it's just a question. Because, let me tell ya, this girl right here has options," he said, pointing a playful finger at me.

I wanted to laugh. I wanted to cry. I wanted to give the right answer even if Dylan's father wouldn't remember it the next day.

Robert turned back to me, "Well? Who's runner up for you?"

I looked between Robert and Dylan and my eyes stayed on him. "I don't think there is a runner-up."

Dylan held my stare and swallowed hard before looking back at his father.

Robert gave me a knowing smile and winked. "But there are second chances."

I felt like a club slammed against my chest. I shot my eyes at Dylan and he was looking at me with an expression I couldn't read but wanted to desperately understand. It was the strangest thing for a halfway lucid man to say to the widow dating his son whom he couldn't remember. But it was also entirely accurate no matter how much I struggled to make this relationship my reality.

I stared at Dylan as long as I could, wanting to cry but choosing not to. He finally smiled and the conversation continued to spiral in every direction until Robert finally closed his eyes and drifted to sleep.

I shut off the lamp and kissed his cold, damp forehead. "Goodnight, Robert," I whispered before slipping out of the room while Dylan said his goodbyes.

I walked to the empty reception area and stared at old pictures of Newport blown up in black and white hanging on the walls next to an emerald green sofa.

"Have a goodnight, Lois," Dylan said behind me and I turned to face them. Lois was walking from the opposite hallway with two manilla folders held against her chest.

"Same to you both." Lois smiled at Dylan, but her eyes landed on me. I returned the smile and gave a small wave.

That night could have been a complete disaster in more ways than one, but it wasn't. I still worried I had completely overstepped but the way Dylan rested his hand on my lower back as we exited the building told me I was right where I needed to be.

"Thank you for coming," he said when we made it to my van in the parking lot. I rested my back against the driver's door.

"I'm sorry I didn't tell you I'd be here." I fiddled with my keys, hoping he was actually thankful.

"It couldn't have gone better." He looked at his feet then back at me. "My dad really likes you."

"Really?"

He let out a laugh. "I mean, he remembers your name so that's saying something."

I playfully flipped my hair over my shoulder. "Glad I made a good impression."

He drew his body closer, his hands on my waist as he bent down and nudged his nose against mine and it made me smile.

"I'm sorry about the other day," I said, wrapping my arms around him and pulling him flush against me.

He nodded slowly, accepting my apology.

"I really do care about you, Dylan," I continued. "I just— have no clue what I'm doing."

He tucked my hair behind my ear as he listened to me. "No one knows what they're doing. Even when we pretend. There is nothing about this that will be entirely predictable."

I didn't know if it was the depth of the evening or the forgiveness in the way he pulled me in for a kiss, but I felt a resolve from our argument a week earlier. He broke away from my mouth and rested a finger on my lips.

"Second chances aren't so bad, I guess," he said softly.

My head jerked back slightly at his statement and I closed my eyes to hide my reaction, pressing my forehead to his lips.

"What's the matter?" he asked, pulling away.

"Nothing." I kept my voice tight.

"No," he began slowly. "That was something. What did I say to make you stiffen up like that?"

I let out a long, exhausted breath.

"It's too complicated to understand."

"Well, if you don't even try to explain it, how will I ever know what bothered you?"

I held my gaze on his and cleared my throat, fearing I was going to hurt his feelings. I wondered if he'd ever fully understand how hard life had been since Tate died.

"Second chances are great in theory, but…" My voice trailed off. I didn't know how to articulate my feelings without coming across as brash and insensitive. "Life has just been hard without Tate. I guess. I don't know," I finished quickly.

Dylan nodded slowly and chewed at the inside of his cheek while taking a small step back. "I am trying really hard to be there for you, Tabitha; to give you space and make this work. Why do you keep making it difficult?"

"Because it is difficult," I answered quickly, my voice soft against the wind. "Look, I'm trying. I know I can't expect you to wait forever but some things I just can't rush no matter how good it *seems*. A part of me agrees with you entirely: second chances really aren't so bad. But there is still a part of me that wishes I never needed one."

Emotion clipped at my throat, and I looked at him hoping he would have the right words to say but his expression told me he didn't. Sadness washed over his face; a desperation spiked with rejection glazing over his eyes. He pulled me into his arms. We stood there in the middle of the dark, empty parking lot, our arms wrapped around each other with doubt encircling us but something a little bit stronger still trying to break through.

SIXTEEN *Summers*

Summer 6

I STARED AT THE babysitter's checklist I had just scrawled on a piece of paper that was now delicately placed on the countertop. I let out a deep and shuddered breath.

Leaving Toby was hard even though I knew it was good for me to take a break.

Post-partum depression was a strange thing. I longed for a break from the exhaustion, the bottles, the baby food, and the nap schedule. Every day meshed together: the rush of the morning, daycare drop-off, eight hours of crunching numbers, daycare pick-up, dinner, then—hopefully—bed. I missed feeling like myself. I missed *being* myself. I knew Tate did too.

Motherhood was hard and nothing like I expected it would be. We lost so much of each other after having Toby, and we were desperately trying to find each other again—to get the 'us' we always knew back. Whenever we did have an opportunity to escape back into each other, a pang of guilt would shoot across my stomach and I wondered constantly if I was doing it all wrong—or maybe just feeling everything wrong.

Motherhood is a trip.

Tate came up behind me and kissed me gently on the side of my head before placing a hand on mine, making me release the pen that was itching to add another item on the list.

"Taylor's been babysitting for us for months. She knows the routine." His voice was soft and calm, like he was dealing with a hostage situation.

"Mm-hmm." I twisted my lips and drummed my fingers on the counter. "Should we really go out tonight though? Toby did come home from daycare with a runny nose yesterday and if—"

"And if she can't get him to sleep, she'll call us, and we'll head home. Plus, you know you don't want to miss singing karaoke for Tim's birthday." His lips pulled into a playfully arrogant smile and he put a hand to his chest. "Plus, I've been practicing all week, and I know you don't want to miss my performance."

I laughed and felt the release of anxiety escape from my chest.

"But then again, if I don't go, you won't have the second best performance," I teased and gave him a wry smile as I flipped my hair over my shoulder.

His eyes watched me a moment before he kissed me deeply, shooting heat down my spine. "You're not as good as you think, Tabitha," he whispered, and I laughed before giving him a smug smile.

"I think you've forgotten who you married."

AFTER A COUPLE of beers and two hours of ridiculous singing, I felt my nerves dissipate and the old version of myself returning. The one that was carefree and fun; that sang karaoke with Tate and created an unofficial ranking of everyone's performances with our best friends, Lydia and Tim.

Nights out were good for my mental health; they were just hard to come by and even harder to convince myself I needed them. When I weaned off my antidepressants I was prescribed after Toby was born, it was almost immediately replaced with motherhood anxiety. I was thankful to have Lydia walking alongside me—Caden was only a few months younger than Toby—but she seemed to be handling the transition better than I did. I envied her some but mostly appreciated the fact she didn't hold my struggles against me. I sometimes wondered, if Tate and I had actually been ready and trying to have a baby, would my transition into motherhood have been smoother?

When I had found myself completely exhausted and vomiting every morning the previous January, I knew my birth control had failed. It wasn't what we were expecting. We had only been married a little over a year and had barely dipped our toes in our careers. When two lines bled across the indicator window on the pregnancy test, Tate was thrilled, practically dancing in the bathroom doorway.

I, on the other hand, was terrified. At least at first, but as time crept on and my belly grew, I settled into the idea of being a mom. I couldn't wait for it. Longed for it. But post-partum depression fell over me like an avalanche as soon as he was born. I was buried in it and I wondered if I'd ever see the light again.

Tate was the main reason I had made it this far. But Lydia was a close second.

"Oh my God, I don't know how I'm supposed to stay up past ten tonight." Lydia laughed and held open her eyes with her fingers.

"Caden still not sleeping through the night?" I asked, sipping my beer.

"No, not even close. He thinks it's a terrible idea and I am. So. Tired. I honestly don't think I can have another drink unless it's coffee," she joked, half-serious. "You're so lucky Toby at least sleeps at night."

I nodded with my eyebrows raised. "That I am. I'm still exhausted even though I'm not up all night. If I were you, I would be long gone by now." I forced out a small laugh. "And Tate would be scattering my ashes telling people I died of motherhood."

Lydia's mouth dropped opened before laughing. "That's morbid, Tabitha."

"What is?" Tim asked, returning to the table with Tate.

197

I swatted away the concern. "Oh, nothing. I just said if Toby didn't sleep, I might have died from exhaustion. I don't know how Lydia does it."

"She's a saint," Tim said, kissing his wife on the cheek.

My eyes wandered over them, feeling both admiration and regret for not being able to push through like Lydia.

Maybe next time.

Tate's eyes fell on me as he moved closer and wrapped a knowing arm around my waist.

"No use in talking about death and dying when you beautiful women are still bringing life into the world," he said, flashing a charming smile at both of us.

Lydia swallowed hard and turned her drink on the table playing with the dripping condensation. "You know that's actually something Tim and I *have* been talking more about lately."

"Really?" I drew back in surprise.

Tim nodded. "After Caden was born, we finally drew up a will and had it notarized and everything."

"You did?" An astonished smile danced across my face.

"That's probably a good idea," Tate said. "Honestly, we've been so busy with…everything going on, that I've just kept the thought in the back of my mind."

I swallowed. Depression was a greedy distraction.

"But you two know you'd get our kids, right?" I asked seriously and Lydia laughed.

"Of course, we know that. And you two would get Caden." She shrugged. "That's always been something we've discussed but now it's all on paper and official. It protects Caden if he were to lose us both but really protects Tim and I if one of us were to die before the other."

My eyes bulged. "I don't even want to think about that kind of thing," I said, wanting to brush this conversation far, far away from my anxious mind but I could sense Tate absorbing each word and wanting to elaborate on the details of death and loss.

"Here's a question," Tim said taking a swig of his beer, "if one of you were to die, would you want the other one to marry someone else?"

"Well, that's a miserable thing to think about," I said. As practical as I was, I didn't want to think about dying, let alone talk about it with my husband and best friends. I wasn't ready to die. I wasn't ready for any of us to die.

"I would want Tabitha to find someone," Tate said so quickly and without flinching I was almost offended. I dropped my hands from my beer to the table and my jaw dropped as I peered at him.

"Really?"

"Really. I wouldn't want you to be alone. Not if you didn't want to be."

I swallowed hard and looked at Tim and Lydia, hoping to see their expressions confirm this was preposterous. They simultaneously nodded and shrugged like that was the agreement both of them had come to as well.

"Really?" I repeated but now directed it at our friends.

"What? Do you want Tate to be alone if you die?" Lydia asked.

"No," I said slowly. "I guess it's just hard to imagine being so—I don't know—*whatever* about it."

"It's not about being 'whatever' about it. Of course, we would expect the other person to be incredible," Tim said, "but I just wouldn't want Lydia to have to worry about whether or not I approve of her finding someone after I'm gone."

I turned to Tate. "But I don't want to be with anyone but you, Tate. I honestly can't even picture that."

"But I would never want you to be alone." He kissed my forehead gently. "Not because you couldn't be, but just because life is better when you have a partner."

My eyes narrowed on his. "Are you trying to get rid of me?"

He laughed. "No, not at all. You just love big—you always have. I know you. Loving others makes you happy. I can't imagine you not sharing that with someone."

"But it would be so hard to love someone that isn't you," I argued.

Tate smiled softly and kissed the side of my head.

"If I die and you find someone great—then I think you deserve to be happy." He shrugged as if this was just a boring topic to discuss nonchalantly.

"And I will be there to remind you to quit wallowing in your self-pity and move on," Lydia said, clinking her glass with mine.

"Thank you, Lydia," I said sarcastically as I reluctantly clinked glasses with her. "Well, too bad for you, Tate. I don't want you to have anyone but me."

The table roared in laughter and Tate leaned in to kiss me.

"You're the only love I'll ever need, Tabitha."

Sixteen

S INCE MOVING TO Newport, I hadn't spent a single
night without my kids. The year before that, I rarely let
them stay over anywhere either. Death destroyed my sense
of security. I hardly wanted to be without them for longer
than the hours of the workday let alone overnight, even when I
was completely exhausted.

For months after Tate died, I would wait anxiously until I
could see them again—the sight of them breathing, laughing,
and their hearts beating would be my only relief from the
anxiety pulsing through my veins.

Therapy helped this issue. So did time.

A full month into the renovations with the restaurant, I had
my feet in two ponds. I was tying up loose ends at my old
position in Washington and diving headfirst into Mindy and
Trey's new adventure. Their books were a mess. The money was
there but the balance was nowhere to be found. It took me
hours, pining over receipts and permits to button up the
numbers side of the restaurant and get the books under control.

I was exhausted and overwhelmed with work. My mother

201

called me and quickly realized just how dire my need for a break was, and I met them in Portland the next Friday so she and my dad could take the boys for the weekend.

They were ecstatic. We hadn't been to their house since Christmas time and before that was before we even moved to Newport. Time had become a confusing warp of reality. It felt like we had lived in Newport forever. It also felt like no time had passed at all.

After I made the two-hour drive back to town, I crashed on the couch, every ounce of exhaustion consuming my body and I slept until I heard a soft knock at my front door.

I groaned and rolled off the couch, stumbling down the hallway to open my door.

The sight of Dylan was a surprise and a relief that made me smile. The expectant way he stood. The curve of his smile. The glint in his eyes. His familiar scent as it blew past me. Everything about him.

My eyes were still sleepy, my body barely awake from my afternoon siesta, but I didn't care. I pulled him inside and let him wrap his arms around me. His hands ran through my hair and cradled my face. The touch of our lips ignited a fire that warmed in my belly and spread throughout my entire body as he pressed me against the wall. His hands slid around my waist and under my shirt and trailed the skin on my lower back. My hands slipped under his shirt in response and my fingers danced across the curve of every muscle. His skin was warm but it made me shiver with anticipation.

We had never been alone. Not completely. And certainly never for very long. But now that we were, I couldn't see anything but him. He let out a soft moan in my mouth and my body pulsed with desire. We hadn't talked about this moment, but it was clearly something we both had been waiting for.

"I thought I got to take you out tonight," he whispered into my ear through our kisses.

"You're early," I said, not breaking away from his lips, thankful we had hours before we had to leave.

"No, I'm not."

"What time is it?" I pulled back, confused—the temperature

of the moment dropping.

"Seven," he said, continuing to kiss me.

My body froze as I looked up at him. "I slept for *three hours?*"

His mouth slowly pulled into a smile. His dark eyes sparkled as they examined my reaction.

"You must have been tired." He laughed softly into my mouth and kissed me again.

"Dylan, I'm so sorry." I covered my face with my hands. "I thought I had only laid down for an hour."

He shrugged and smiled. "I don't care. You probably needed the sleep."

"Well, obviously." I ran a hand through my mussed-up hair. "We're going to be so late."

"It doesn't matter. Our friends can wait," he said plainly. We were meeting Lydia, Tim, Mindy, and Trey at Seadogs for karaoke night. Tim insisted. "I just want to spend time with you. It doesn't matter where we are."

I looked at him with regret. "I even had an outfit picked out."

"But I like the one you have on." He stood back and admired my black leggings and t-shirt.

I scoffed, unable to hide my blush.

"I didn't realize karaoke with our friends warranted picking out an outfit." He smiled mischievously, and I took note of his use of the word 'our.'

At some point, we became a '*we*' and the friends we hung out with and time we spent together became '*ours*.' I didn't really know how it happened, but I stopped fighting it. It felt right.

"It does when you haven't worn real pants in days." I planted a kiss on his lips.

"Real pants are overrated," he murmured as he kissed my neck and gripped my waist.

"I mean, it's not like Harry enforces a dress code. Maybe I should just stay in my sweats," I quipped. "I mean pirates aren't particularly known for being well-dressed."

He narrowed his eyes with a smile that was no doubt withholding a laugh. "You know 'sea dogs' refers to sailors not pirates, right?"

I cocked my head to the side, a dumbfounded expression on my face. "Are you sure? I could've sworn they were pirates."

Dylan laughed and buried his face in my neck.

"I love you," he said through his laugh. It was muffled by my hair and his lips against my skin, but distinct. I knew he said it.

My head snapped back and my mouth dropped open. I searched his face with wide eyes. He looked just as surprised to hear those three little words. I knew instantly he didn't mean to say it. It slipped. A complete accident.

His eyes dropped from mine and he furrowed his brow and cleared his throat. "I mean—"

"No, no," I said quickly. "It's okay. We can—I mean, you don't need to explain…People says things sometimes when they're…" I continued to stumble over my words as he opened his mouth to respond. I didn't know if he was going to confirm or object and I wasn't ready to find out. "Give me fifteen minutes," I said in a hurry and turned to go to my bedroom.

"Hey," Dylan said softly as he pulled me back to him by my arm. He gazed down at me; his eyes intense yet vulnerable. My breathing was shallow with nerves. He searched my face for a moment.

I felt so safe. Completely wanted. Loved even. But I was also terrified. I swallowed hard as an embarrassing urge to cry climbed up my throat.

He licked his lips then pressed them together and nodded like he understood what I was feeling even though I said nothing.

"Take your time," he whispered as he kissed my forehead, his confident demeanor returning.

I didn't know if he was referring to the time it would take for me to get ready or the time it would take for me to admit I loved him too, so I simply nodded and walked to my room to change.

After I freshened up, I stood at the dresser in my room with shaking hands. I replayed Dylan's words and how he said them over and over. I knew he didn't mean to say it, but it felt so good to hear it. The way it rolled off his tongue and into my ears and warmed in my chest. So much about Dylan was easy when everything else about my life was still so hard.

I opened my jewelry box on top of my dresser and pulled out a pair of earrings. As I put the second one in my left ear while looking in the mirror, I froze.

My wedding band glimmered on my hand. I had never taken it off. It felt like it was permanently adhered to my left ring finger after sixteen years. I never really thought to take it off because I never remembered it was on. The ring was simple and unobtrusive. Everything Tate allowed me to be even if he was always the life of the party. I swallowed hard as I peered down at my shaking hand and twisted the diamond around with my thumb. I slipped it off with my right hand, placed it at the bottom of the jewelry box, and closed my eyes hard.

Don't be mad at me, Tate.

A deep part of me knew he wouldn't be, but an even deeper part of me still felt like I belonged to him no matter how certain his absence was.

I drew in a shaky breath, feeling at peace with my decision but also terrified. I hadn't completely healed from his death, and I knew I may never completely, but things were getting easier. And this somehow felt like the right step. It was probably something I should have done a while ago.

I walked into the living room where Dylan was leaned back on the couch flipping through his phone, patiently waiting. His eyes turned toward me and lit up instantly. He always looked at me like I was his dream. A gaze where desire and admiration met. It made my heartrate speed up.

"Shall we?" I said, approaching him. My words broke the trance and he blinked, regaining his composure.

"Yeah, sure." He slipped his phone into his pocket and smiled under his blush before looking me in the eye again. It was funny to think I ever thought of him as smug. The shyness in his smile I had mistaken for conceit, and the forwardness in his demeanor I had mistaken for arrogance. He had slowly become one of the kindest, most genuine souls I'd ever known, and yet I still felt like I was waiting for the other shoe to drop.

WHEN WE WALKED into Seadogs hand in hand, Harry smiled at us from behind the bar while Tim's rendition of an old country song pierced through the speakers.

Mindy spotted us first. She smiled and waved so enthusiastically her curls bounced on her head. After we greeted our friends and ordered drinks, Tim passed us the binder filled with laminated pages of hundreds and hundreds of karaoke songs to choose from.

I pretended to study it, but I already knew what'd I'd sing—everybody has a karaoke song—even though I hadn't sung karaoke in years.

Karaoke was Tate's favorite. He was terrible at it but that, in combination with his enthusiasm, was what made his performances great. He and Tim would always sing a duet after a few beers. Lydia and I have pictures and pictures of their many performances dating back to college. It oddly felt like a monumental deal to be out singing karaoke with friends. I was so distracted by spending some long-awaited child-free time with Dylan, I hadn't even wondered how I'd feel doing something Tate and I used to do all the time with some of the same people we used to do it with.

I was happier than I'd been in a long time, but it did make me miss Tate. Not the kind of longing that would have made me crumble to the ground. The good kind that let every sweet memory linger in every particle around me so I could deeply appreciate who he was and what we had.

As the night dwindled on—each of us taking ridiculous turns on the microphone—the laughter echoed even louder than our off-key singing.

"It's so good to see you happy." Lydia leaned into me at the table.

I smiled as my eyes watched Dylan make his way over to the table after his turn singing. A shy, flirtatious smile spread across his face and he wrapped his arm around me and kissed my cheek. I downplayed our relationship over and over, but our friends weren't stupid. They knew. They saw our connection first-hand. It was a relief to feel like I belonged in a couple setting again, even if I had no idea how permanent Dylan was. The only thing I knew for sure was, in life, I was guaranteed nothing.

"Gosh, this place reminds me of college," Lydia said, laughing and finishing off her rum and soda.

"Really?" I said, looking around.

"Chummy's downtown? Don't you think?"

I surveyed the room, noting the wood paneling, linoleum floors, and sporadic bar art littering the walls. I saw no resemblance to the dark college bar with multi-colored rope lights under the bar top.

"I think you're reminded of a feeling not a place."

She laughed—a drunken, euphoric giggle that made me smile. "Well, yeah. That's what I meant."

"Honey, every karaoke bar reminds you of the other," Tim interjected, taking a long pull from his beer.

Dylan shrugged. "Well, once the sound of terrible singing rings through a room, it's hard not to associate them all together."

The table laughed and nodded in agreement.

"We used to karaoke all the time," Tim said. He puffed out his chest in mock-arrogance. "I was always the best."

"Really?" Mindy was surprised. "I always think of karaoke as more of a once-in-a-while type of thing."

"No way." Tim shook his head. "We did it almost weekly for years since college—even after kids—until..."

His voice trailed off and I knew what he was going to say. The whole table did. An awkward hush washed over all of us, and Dylan placed a reassuring hand on my back. I smiled at his touch and at the memory of Tate.

I cleared my throat to clear the awkward tension.

"It's okay, Tim," I said. "We can talk about him. Tate always did put your performances to shame anyway." I eyed him playfully over my drink and he laughed. It came out shaky and forced, but as he comprehended my words it became a genuine and joyful roar of laughter.

"That is not true, Tabitha, and you know it. Tate was terrible at singing. He only got the reaction he did from the crowd because of his dance moves." Tim continued to laugh. It wasn't unusual to talk about Tate with Tim but for the first time in a long while the conversation wasn't heavy which was a complete relief.

"Best moon-walker this side of the Mississippi," Lydia added, rotating her drink on the table.

"I wish I got to see that," Trey said, smiling genuinely and placing his arm around his wife.

"Seriously, Tabitha," Mindy said, leaning her elbows on the table, her smile as eager as ever. "I would have loved to have known him."

I nodded and smiled softly. I could sense Dylan's quietness as he absorbed the table reminiscing about my late husband. I turned my eyes to Dylan's, and he was looking at me intently with an expression I couldn't quite read, but it made my heart flutter.

"He was a good one to know," Tim said finally, and I agreed.

WHEN WE WALKED back to the condo after saying goodbye to our friends, I interlocked my fingers with Dylan's and pulled his arm into my body. His fingers squeezed my hand tightly and he lifted it up to kiss my knuckles.

"You took off your wedding ring." His voice was steady, but a glint of excitement was etched in his simple curiosity.

"I did," I answered, staring at the dock below us as we began walking in the direction of my condo.

I waited for him to say something more, but he didn't. He didn't question it. Not when it was on my finger and not after it was off. He just let it be a part of me the same way he let Tate be a part of me.

"Is it weird for you to hear about Tate?" I asked as the salty, night air whipped past our faces.

He shook his head slightly. "Weird isn't the word I'd use."

"What word would you use?" I tilted my head as I looked up at him.

"Sad." He shrugged. "It's hard for me to think about everything you went through—what it must have been like when he died and what that did to you. I wish I had been there for you…"

My eyes filled with tears and I nodded.

"I think about Toby and how much I know he misses him, and I think about Charlie never getting to know him. It doesn't make sense he died," he continued as he gave me a small, half-smile. When his eyes met mine, I couldn't quite read him. "I sometimes wish he didn't die, and I wish I could just take away that hard and dark part of your life. But then there's a side of me that knows I wouldn't have ever come to know you like I have if he were still alive."

I nodded in understanding because I did, in fact, completely understand. The battle within his mind was one I had inside my own heart. I missed Tate with every fiber of my being, and I still longed to get to know all the corners of Dylan's heart.

Tate was like a song I hadn't heard in years but still knew every lyric once the melody played. I couldn't escape him. I didn't want to. I wanted to remember every part of him, even the parts that had already faded.

But I also knew I needed to learn how to love two people. Or at least be okay I already did.

"Thank you," I said after we made it through my front door.

"For what?" he asked as we walked through the condo and out to the balcony to admire the view. He leaned his back against the rail and pulled me into him, face-to-face. I was so close I could smell the cinnamon on his breath and the aftershave on his cheek.

"For everything you've been to me and the boys." I smiled up at him, his eyes not leaving mine. "I'm really happy I met you."

"I'm more than happy I met you." He brushed his finger down my cheek, giving me a welcomed tremble down my spine. His eyes were warm and his gaze was penetrating as he looked down at me. "I meant what I said earlier."

The air escaped my lungs. I couldn't move. I couldn't breathe. I couldn't think.

"I'm in love with you, Tabitha," he said, his voice deep and smooth in the night air.

My heart pounded as he looked down at me. The world fell silent. Time stopped moving. For a moment, it was just me and Dylan. I was at a loss for words. I opened my mouth. I wanted to say it back. I knew I loved him too. I just didn't know if I was completely ready to tell him or what it would mean if I did.

Tears pooled along my lashes and I offered a small smile as my heart pounded in my chest. He slid his thumb over my lips and tilted my face toward his as he leaned down to kiss me softly.

"I wasn't ready for you," I whispered as my body curved perfectly under his arms.

"And I feel like I've spent my entire life waiting for you," he said, his breath in my hair, his lips on my skin.

I molded my body closer to his as I intertwined my fingers behind his neck pulling him down to kiss me. The kiss felt like a tidal wave slamming into the shore. I felt a burning only he could satiate. I couldn't get close enough to him. His hands ran under the hem of my shirt and up my back before he pulled back softly.

"Is this okay?" he asked, his desire and willingness to love me carefully made my soul melt into his hands.

I nodded and allowed myself to be completely wrapped in the moment.

I felt every emotion, every movement, every touch as he slid my coat over my shoulders and slowly pulled my top over my head. He paused as his eyes slid up and down my body with a desperate confidence. My heart continued to pound. My cheeks were hot and a strong desire sat deep in my belly.

He led me back inside, our lips only parting as I pulled his shirt over his head and let my fingers dance across his chest. I moved in a frenzied rush, but he slowed me down with every kiss, holding on to each moment as he thoughtfully pressed his fingers against my body. His lips lingered on my neck, and he raked his fingers through my hair as his hands slowly savored every touch of my skin. A moan escaped my lips and I held on to him tightly, letting my hands explore the curve of every muscle on his body. When he laid my bare back against the couch, he propped himself over me, the broad shape of his shoulders accentuated by the moonlight. A fire burned inside me; desire rushed through my veins.

"Are you still sure?" he whispered, his eyes holding an intensity that reached the depth of my soul.

"Yes. More than anything," I whispered into the night air as I pulled the length of his body closer to me.

He moved over me with an ease and a confidence as he explored every part of my body, as if every inch of my skin was his to discover. His touch on my bare skin sent electricity down my spine as his body overtook mine and completely consumed me.

It felt reckless and wild, yet safe and tender. It was everything I had imagined and feared.

And when it was over, I felt like I wanted to do it for the rest of my life.

I placed my palm on his chest and rested my chin on the back of my hand as his fingertips danced down my back. He looked at me with the same watchful admiration that used to make me think he was amused by me, but now, I could tell, was simply because he loved me.

He was *in love* with me. And I was in love with him.

I swallowed hard, wanting to be all in. Wanting to confess my love. Wanting to feel free. Wanting to not worry about what came next.

But still, I wanted to bridge the gaps between us.

"Why haven't you told me what happened with Felicity?" I asked, filling the silence.

He narrowed his eyes in surprise at the mention of her name, and I could see a brief flash of pain behind his eyes.

"I did tell you about Felicity."

"You told me it didn't work out, but you never said why. And everyone in town keeps implying it was a bigger deal than you're trying to make me believe."

"I mean, it was a really bad breakup but she was simply

someone I loved and lost. I don't really think it's necessary to tell the details." He shrugged.

I raised an eyebrow. "But I've loved and lost and told you all the details."

He sighed. "It's a different kind of loss though, Tabitha. It doesn't seem fair to burden you with it."

"It's not a burden to tell me. If she was an important part of your life for so many years and now she's not, I'd like to know about it. Especially if it means you and I are going to stay together."

"Is that an ultimatum?" He eyed me playfully and smiled.

"No…" I smiled but answered seriously. "But I need to proceed with caution with all of my relationships. You don't have to tell me everything, just enough so I understand."

Dylan nodded, ready to concede. He cleared his throat, but his voice remained deep and sleepy. "Felicity was my high school girlfriend. We were the complete cliché. I was the captain of the football team in a small town, and she was the cheerleader. We went away to college together, and then moved to Portland and lived there for another five years. When I went to her office to pick her up for a date on the night I planned to propose, something just felt off. I knew it but I just mistook it for nerves." He cleared his throat again and he paused, his mind lingering in the memory. "Long story, short: she was pregnant with her boss's baby and she didn't want to marry me."

My mouth fell open.

He nodded and raised his eyebrows. "Quite the predicament. Especially since her dad is still the high school football coach around here."

"No way! Coach Davis?"

He nodded. "Why do you think I coach soccer instead?"

I laughed as my mind settled into the layers of this complicated small-town drama.

"I'm so sorry. She was your once then?"

"My what?" His forehead furrowed in confusion.

"You told me you almost settled down once and a half when we first met. She was your once then?"

"I forgot about that." He chuckled softly. "Yeah, she was."

"And your half was Heather?"

His mouth turned downward into a frown and he nodded. "Heather was a nice person. Bit of a free bird. I thought we were serious. She thought we were fluid."

I cringed. "Some rebound."

Dylan laughed. "Then two years ago, I came back to Newport to be with my dad."

"And there's been no one since?"

He shrugged. "No one important enough to mention. But honestly no one seems that important since I met you."

I tried not to smile but my lips parted, and my cheeks flushed like a schoolgirl with a crush. A crush I was sure was love. "I'm sorry you went through all that."

"You don't look very sorry," he said, running a finger down my smiling cheek and raising his eyebrows at me.

"I can't help but smile around you right now." I laughed then settled myself and gave him the most serious look I could muster. "But really, I am sorry."

He shrugged. "It could be worse."

My cheek twitched and I nodded, understanding why he hadn't told me the details. It could be worse. I had experienced the worst, and I was still living through it—in limbo between loving my dead husband and falling in love with someone new.

"So, you didn't always not believe in marriage."

He half-smiled and bit his lip. "Yeah, I guess not," he confessed reluctantly.

"We all have someone that ruins us for something else, don't we?"

He nodded, completely understanding my sentiment.

"Thank you for telling me," I said, my voice small. "And thank you for being so patient with me these last few months."

"You're worth it." He smiled and brushed my hair from my face. "I really do love you."

Tears filled my eyes, and I knew what life was handing me was far too precious for me to be hesitant with. I knew I couldn't hold back anymore.

"I love you too," I said and a rush of relief coursed through me.

A relief I could also see reflected in Dylan's eyes.

Summer 5

O H MY, TABITHA! Look at that belly. It is just swollen to perfection," my mother said hugging my pregnant stomach before wrapping her arms around my shoulders. "Isn't it, Carlisle?"

My father smiled and nodded—a man of few words with a glistening tear in his eye.

"You look beautiful, Tabitha."

I swallowed an unexpected and hormonal lump in my throat. "Thanks, Dad. Can't believe I only have two months left and then I'm a mom. Doesn't seem real, does it?"

My mother smiled wide; her blue eyes bright in the August sun streaming through the trees on their back patio. The air smelled like charcoal from the grill; a tablecloth covering the wooden picnic table was scattered with citronella candles, yellow roses, and chips and dip.

"Where would you like me to put this, Jenny?" Tate asked, giving my mother a side hug and holding the cobbler in his other arm.

"Let me take that for you. I'll get it warming in the oven

while I grab the potato salad." She graciously took the dish from Tate while he turned to my father.

"Good to see you, Carlisle. It smells delicious."

My father smiled proudly. "I'm grilling the salmon I got from your brother. I'll tell you, there is nothing like fresh salmon this time of year, is there?"

"That's awesome. I didn't realize Justin had given you some," I said scooping a tortilla chip in salsa, knowing the heartburn that would hit in an hour would make me regret it.

"He's had a lucky salmon season, that's for sure," Tate said, placing a hand on my shoulder and massaging it in a way that made me want him to rub my feet. I plopped down on the picnic table.

"You alright, honey?" my dad asked.

"Hmm?" I turned my eyes toward him and raised my eyebrows. "Oh, yes. I'm fine. I'm just so tired now. I feel like women were only supposed to be pregnant seven months because I am *done*."

"Yeah, the last two months are Eve's fault. If she hadn't eaten that gosh-darn apple," my mother said, plopping the potato salad covered in plastic wrap on the table.

I let out an exasperated and very pregnant sigh that almost sounded like a laugh. "I think you're right. Every day I come home from work, my feet are so swollen—and I sit at a desk all day."

"I remember your mom just collapsing on the couch every evening when she was pregnant with you." My dad let out a soft chuckle as he flipped the salmon. The sizzle of the grill emitted a scent that made my stomach growl.

"I'm going to really have to push through these last two months because it is *rough*."

"What's rough?"

I turned to the upbeat voice from the man standing in the doorway of the French doors.

"Justin!" I exclaimed as I waddled from my perch at the table. "I didn't know you were coming tonight!"

"What's up, brother," Tate said, pulling in his younger brother and slapping his back.

"Are you crying?" Justin asked, looking at me as I meandered over for a hug myself.

I wiped my eyes and laughed. "I guess so. Pregnancy does that to me, I suppose."

"Is everything okay?" he looked at me, concern flashing across his face.

"Yes, gosh, I'm so embarrassed," I said, wiping my eyes. "I'm just hopped up on hormones and exhaustion." I smiled and gazed fondly at my husband's brother and closest friend. My baby's uncle I knew he'd grow to love. "I just didn't know you were coming, and I'm happy to see you."

Justin shrugged sheepishly and gave a boyish and endearing smile. "Yeah, well, I miss far too many of these family dinners."

"Can I get you a beer, Justin?" my dad asked.

"That'd be great. Thank you," he responded.

"Tate?"

Tate looked at me to get permission and I nodded my okay—I could handle the yeasty smell of beer on his breath for tonight. Something told me I might even crave it.

"Sure," Tate answered as my mother busied herself with placing a salad on the table with a tin bucket of plastic cutlery.

"Are my parents going to make it tonight? They didn't answer the phone when I called," Justin asked.

"No, they are off on Orcas Island this evening—met some friends from years back, I guess," my mother answered before wringing her hands and eyeing the table scape. "Can I get y'all anything else?"

"No, Mom. I think we're okay. Just relax." My mother was the best host no matter how small the gathering, but there were so many times I just wanted her to sit back, relax, and enjoy the company she was serving so well.

She nodded and held a finger in the air. "I'm going to grab the garlic bread."

Once she retreated inside, my father pulled the salmon off the grill and onto a serving platter while my mother returned with a basket of garlic bread in one hand and paper plates in the other.

The five of us sat at the table, dishing our plates and I felt so incredibly lucky to have the family we did. My parents loved Tate and I, and Tate's parents loved us just as much. I also adored having the brother I always wanted, become such a seamless part of my family.

I rubbed my belly between each bite and wondered exactly who this little boy would be. Would he look like me? Blonde and blue-eyed? Or would he look like his dad? A dusty brunette with green eyes and an irresistible smile? Or maybe his Uncle Justin with the same dusty brown hair but eyes so dark they were almost black? I didn't know. I didn't care. I was just overwhelmed with how beautiful life was falling into place after such a short time had passed since college. Tate and I were lucky. I knew it and so did he.

After the food was devoured and the plates were cleared, Tate meandered inside with my parents to help clean up and get the cobbler ready while I sat at the table with Justin, him nursing a beer and me turning my water glass gingerly between my fingers.

"I'm glad you made it tonight," I said, truly meaning it and hoping he understood how much we wanted him around—how much Tate *needed* him around.

He nodded solemnly. "I'm doing my best, Tabitha."

"I never said you weren't, Justin. But your brother misses you." I shrugged. "I miss you too. We don't see you as much as we used to."

I could see him swallow. I had a history of making him uncomfortable—always asking the questions that danced in everyone's head but no one asked.

"Well, you know." He shrugged. His brow furrowed for a moment before he forced it to release, and he smiled at me. "Amelia was complicated."

"Was?" I asked, unsure of where he stood with his on and off again girlfriend.

"Was," he said plainly, staring down at his dewy bottle before taking a swig.

"I'm sorry," I said. "Is it really over this time though?"

He drew in a sharp breath and looked at me with a question in his eyes. "How do you do that?"

"Do what?"

"Get me talking about things I want to leave alone."

I let out a small laugh. "You haven't told me anything."

"Yeah, but I want to." He twisted his lips like he had a dark secret and not the details of his recent breakup.

"Then tell me. Because, honestly, it wasn't terribly hard to figure out." I shrugged and took a long drink of water.

"Why not?"

"Because you've missed family dinners for months. And they always seem to correlate when you're with Amelia because I have a feeling she doesn't want to meet the family." I smiled at him, knowingly. Amelia was beautiful. Complicated. And entirely untraditional, which would have been fine for Justin except he wanted the tradition—the white picket fence, the wedding bells. All of what me and Tate had, he wanted. But he fell in love with someone that was the complete opposite. It was hard for them to find a compromise.

"But she met you…"

"She did." I nodded.

"And? What'd you think?"

"I really liked her. But what I think of her doesn't matter—how you feel about her does. Whatever you're wanting or looking for in a partner is important to me and your brother because it's important to you." I leaned back, letting the air fill my lungs. "I would learn to love whoever you do."

"Really?" He seemed confused.

"Of course. I love you, Justin. When I married Tate, you became my family—I'll always be on your side."

His eyebrows pinched together, and his eyes looked sad. "Even if I don't ever want to settle down and get married?"

I swallowed an empathetic cry. "The breakup was that bad?"

He nodded. "I mean, she's amazing. Fierce. Clever. Complicated. Incredible." He shook his head and pressed the heels of his hands into his eyes. "And just impossible."

"Did she cheat on you?" I asked sincerely.

He looked at me blankly and stared back at his almost empty beer bottle, not saying another word.

I reached out and placed my hand on his—his big sister he

wasn't born with but would always have.

"Hey," I said, pulling him out of his trance and letting his attention drift back from his dark and scarred memories with Amelia to sitting at the picnic table in my parents' backyard with his pregnant sister-in-law. "It's okay to let this one go."

"Even if it was everything I thought I wanted?"

I leaned in. "Even if it's everything you thought you wanted. Life never turns out exactly how we plan for it to."

"Says the happily married woman pregnant with her first baby," he said sardonically.

I laughed. "Well, you know as good as anyone this baby was *not* planned."

He smiled and nodded before clearing his throat.

"I really did love her."

"I know," I said, feeling the need to elaborate but not entirely understanding every word I wanted to say. "We all have something that ruins us for something else. But I think it's probably okay to look and see what's next, even if it's not what we planned for."

He nodded and finished off his beer as Tate and my parents escaped the house with warm cobbler and cold vanilla ice cream in hand.

Seventeen

MINDY WALKED IN the small office off the kitchen of the under-construction restaurant. Carter's Catch was on track to open in exactly six weeks, and I was still making sure Mindy and Trey were staying within budget and handling all the new-hire paperwork for the servers and line-chefs that were due to start training in two weeks. Opening a restaurant—while whimsical in theory—was exhausting, time-consuming, and stressful. Mindy wore every emotion on her face as she leaned on the desk next to where I was sitting at the computer, punching in the last few numbers from vendor receipts.

She let out an audible sigh, and I looked up at her hesitantly, wondering why she didn't just come right out and say what was wrong.

"What happened?" I asked.

She sighed again. "The tile guy canceled." She threw her hands up and then slapped them down on her thighs. "Not rescheduled. *Canceled.* And every other tile installer I've called can't get out here until late next month which would mean pushing back the opening at worst or having tile installed the week before opening at best. And I'll be honest, tile installation cannot happen while we're perfecting the menu with Izzy and Gabriel." She pressed two fingers between her eyebrows and closed her eyes.

"So, you decided on Izzy and Gabriel then?" I asked, making sure I was keeping track of who exactly was on payroll.

Mindy eyed me. "Don't change the subject."

I shook my head and chuckled softly. "You're right. Okay. What are our options then?"

She shrugged. "I have already called everyone in town."

"What about someone in Lincoln City?"

"I checked."

"Corvallis?"

She shook her head. "I think we really need to consider pushing back the opening. We won't even be able to get our final inspection from the Department of Health in time."

"Could Trey do it? It's only subway tile. That's really easy to work with."

She scoffed. "No, Trey is a lot of things, but handy is not one of them. He can barely screw in a light bulb."

I snorted. "Let me do it."

"Handle the date change?"

I let out a laugh. "No, the tile."

"I'm sorry?" Mindy looked at me confused, just as an exasperated Trey walked in the office.

"Well, if we can't get the tile done then we can't get the faucets or bar equipment installed either which could push us back a couple more weeks." He ran his hand across his face. "Can't catch a break."

I smiled and Mindy continued to look at me.

"Can you really install it?" she asked.

I shrugged. "Yeah. I mean, it will take me a while because of the size of the bar but I did the backsplash in the condo and Tate and I did the backsplash at our house in Washington."

"Tabitha, that would be a huge help," Trey said earnestly. "Are you sure it's not too much trouble? What with handling the books and all?"

"Well, you might need to cut your accountant some slack for the next week or so, but I'd be happy to do it. I want this restaurant to open on time and for it to go as smoothly as possible also. My job is on the line here too." I gave him a slow, reassuring smile and Trey gave me an overbearing hug, making me laugh. Mindy stood by clapping her hands and bouncing up and down.

"Oh, my gosh. I'm so glad we hired you. Aren't you so glad, Trey?"

He nodded. "Can we help you with it at all?"

"Honestly?"

Mindy and Trey nodded in unison.

"Can you pick up the boys from daycare and school?"

BY DAY THREE of tiling the restaurant bar, Dylan promised to meet me after his shift so we could finish it together. While the tiling project was easy, it was also tedious, and Mindy wanted the tile to stretch around the bar and also have the backsplash reach the ceiling. I was thankful Mindy had at least opted for an easy to install stainless steel backsplash to match the counters in the kitchen so I wouldn't have to also tile that area. The results of her design looked beautiful—modern and industrial, yet classic and charming—but it was taking forever for me to finish my task.

When I heard footsteps coming up the small staircase leading to the restaurant, I prayed it was Dylan. If he were here to start grouting, I could finish tiling.

"I can't believe this used to be the old Waterfront Grille. What a transformation!" The voice was deep and billowy, but I recognized it from Friday night football games and the few times I met him around town: Coach Davis.

I stood, wiping the mortar on the front of my pants, leaving my fingertips crusty and dry.

"You've met Tabitha Jones, right?" Mindy said, gesturing toward me.

"Coach Davis. Hi. It's good to see you," I said, holding out my dirty hand before thinking better of it and pulling it back. "Sorry. I'm filthy, otherwise I'd shake your hand."

"No worries. And please, call me Jim."

I nodded.

"Tabitha has just been a complete lifesaver with this whole process. I can't imagine how we'd be on track without her."

"Is that so? Very impressive." He nodded, smiling wide with approval. "You know this used to be my parent's restaurant?"

"Oh, I didn't know that," I said, politely intrigued by this information.

"They started the Waterfront Grill decades ago. Hung onto it for a bit before selling it to someone else since neither me or my sister wanted to take over. Then it just kind of floundered, as I'm sure you heard. It's nice to see it's getting some new life put in it."

He smiled and scanned the room. It was still covered in plastic and paper covered the floors, but light fixtures had been replaced, the walls painted, the floors redone, and the kitchen overhauled.

"I told Jim he could come by and check it out, seeing his family has so much history here." Mindy's smile was sweet and proud. She had worked so hard to transform the old space into something new and beautiful. I was thankful to be a part of it.

I opened my mouth to speak again but my attention was pulled from behind me.

"Sorry about that, Trevor had to go to the bathroom." A woman with long, brown hair walked in with a young boy, maybe four or five, holding on to her hand.

Mindy made eye-contact with me—her eyes were wide, and she plastered a smile on her face.

I narrowed my eyes on hers, confused.

"Tabitha this is my daughter, Felicity, and her son, Trevor. She, too, has a lot of memories in this place," Coach Davis said.

Surprise lurched in my throat, and I swallowed it down and smiled. I was irritated Mindy hadn't given me a heads up. I was even more irritated I was covered in mortar and tile dust, my hair in a sweaty bun, no makeup on my face, and I was meeting Dylan's ex for the first time. I hated meeting exes. The very idea of it was uncomfortable no matter how the encounter was framed. She was tall and slender in an outfit that was both stylish and sophisticated. Even her son was dressed to Christmas-card perfection. She was effortlessly beautiful—not at all how I pictured her. Not at all how I *wanted* to picture her, at least. An arrogance danced around her though. Like she expected everyone to know who she was. I partly hated that I actually did.

"Nice to meet you, Felicity," I said politely.

"Nice to meet you too," she said, tossing her hair over her shoulder.

"And this is my son, Trevor." She gushed at him and nudged him slightly.

"Nice to meet you," the boy said in a small voice. His eyes were bright and round, his hair combed and styled to the side. He looked so much like his mother. But he had brown eyes and for a brief moment, I thought he looked a lot like Dylan.

My heart raced and I cleared my throat, trying to clear away the thought.

"Nice to meet you too, Trevor." I smiled at him and leaned down to his level. "I'd shake your hand but..." I waved my fingers between us, "I'm a little bit messy."

Trevor giggled and covered his mouth with his free hand as Dylan walked in behind him. I had forgotten he was on his way. He was as shocked as I was to see Felicity. Probably more so. *Definitely* more so.

His head physically jerked back at the sight of her, and I could see him swallow hard as a blotchy flush of anger crept up his neck.

I wanted to grab his hand and squeeze it letting him know I understood how awkward the whole encounter was. I also wanted to wring Mindy's neck after everyone left.

Felicity whisked around and her eyes lit up when she saw Dylan. I felt suddenly protective of him as my heart continued to pound in my chest.

"Dylan!" she exclaimed and pulled him in for an overbearing hug. Her hair draped over his face as he hesitantly placed his hands on her back. She held onto him for a moment longer than was socially acceptable, and Dylan looked over at me.

I smiled because I didn't know what else to do.

"Good to see you," he said with his lips pressed into a straight line. "Coach Davis. Mindy." He nodded at each of them before walking over to me and kissing me on the cheek. I flushed slightly and my eyes landed on Felicity, who was studying us.

"Oh." She raised her eyebrows, looking between me and Dylan. "You. And you, then. Okay." She nodded, obviously flustered, eyeing me in my ripped and mortar covered jeans. "I didn't realize you were…"

Dylan nodded and half-smiled at me without saying anything.

"I see." Felicity cleared her throat finally, regaining her composure. "And you remember Trevor."

Remember?

Felicity gestured to her child like he was a prized possession, not the love child that tore their relationship apart.

"Hey, buddy. Getting big these days. Almost taller than me." He playfully socked Trevor in the shoulder and Trevor laughed. I smiled at the interaction; I loved how good Dylan was with kids. All while wondering: *what if?*

"Anyway, I was just showing the Davises the progress on the restaurant." Mindy broke the awkward silence lingering between us.

"I'll bet Grandpa and Grandma Davis would have loved it," Dylan said, crossing his arms—not in defiance but because I could tell he didn't know what to do with his hands. His statement cut through my heart. It was kind and it was true. But it was also a reminder of the lifetime of history he had with Felicity. I may have had his present, but we had no history—not yet.

Felicity smiled at him and held his gaze as long as she could until he looked away from her and at me. His loathing expression was full of apologies.

I almost felt like laughing.

"It really is lovely, Mindy. You should be proud," Felicity

said, gracefully spinning around the room.

"Thank you," Mindy said, smiling awkwardly.

"Well, I'll let you guys get back to looking around. I've got to finish up the tile—don't want the mortar to dry out," I said, thankful I had a righteous excuse to escape the conversation.

"Oh, yes, absolutely. It was so nice to meet you, Tabitha." Felicity's words were completely polite and kind, but her eyes followed me with an emotion I could only describe as jealousy.

I nodded and turned back to the bar, finding relief and my breath next to the mortar and trowel. I continued to tile the front side of the bar diligently while Dylan continued to exchange pleasantries with Felicity and her father. I pretended not to hear her say she wanted to catch up with him. I pretended I didn't hear him say sure. I pretended not to hear Coach Davis say how much they missed him.

I pretended but Dylan knew I had heard it all.

When they left, he wordlessly knelt behind me and slipped his arms around my waist.

"If you make this tile turn out crooked..." I scolded him through a smile, and he nuzzled his face into my neck, kissing it softly.

"I'm sorry," he mumbled.

I turned around; my fingers caked in mortar. "Dylan, you don't need to be sorry. I didn't know she was coming any more than you did."

He nodded and his eyes, heavy with guilt, fell to the floor. I eyed him suspiciously.

"Wait. You did know?"

"I knew she was in town. I didn't know she'd be at the restaurant right now," he relented.

"I see." I turned and adjusted the tile I had just placed on the bar. "How'd you know she was in town?"

He picked at his teeth with his tongue, contemplative. "She had texted me."

My mouth opened slightly, and I narrowed my eyes on him. "Why would she text you? After what she did to you and after all these years? That doesn't make sense." I shook my head, thinking the idea was preposterous.

He shrugged. "We have a complicated history."

I rolled my eyes. "It's not that complicated." I kept working. "Why didn't you tell me she texted you?"

"I didn't think it was important. I didn't respond to it."

I stared at him for a moment before nodding and turning back to the tile. I didn't know how it made me feel. I didn't have time for drama, even less time for omissions turning into secrets.

He watched me place three subway tiles on the bar before speaking again.

"I should've told you."

I nodded and started scraping the mortar on the side of the bar to continue tiling without saying anything.

It didn't necessarily upset me he didn't tell me she texted him. It didn't necessarily bother me to meet her out of the blue even though it was awkward. I was bothered because, for the first time, I realized he truly used to belong to someone else. Someone that wasn't taken from this world but actively chose to leave his life. Someone he was ready to sign on to forever with, but she chose to walk away.

She could linger in and out as much as this small town allowed. He'd never have to worry about running into Tate at the grocery store or at a friend's new business. But I never knew when I'd run into Felicity. She was gone but not completely. There were traces of her in Dylan's life and the very grain of this town I would never know.

I paused and looked at him. He was dutifully mixing grout in a slow rhythm before starting to grout the other end of the bar.

"Is it hard to see her?" I asked.

He turned his eyes toward me.

"To see Felicity? No." He shook his head. "She likes to pretend what she did wasn't so bad—that it's all water under the bridge, so that can be irritating. But it's not hard. I don't miss her. I just don't like her all that much anymore." He gave me a small, shy smile and raised his eyebrows at me.

I studied him a moment. "Is it hard to see Trevor?"

"It's kind of weird. But she picked the life she's living and likes it. She's a good mom from what I hear, too." He shrugged and continued to grout.

"He looks a bit like you."

He glanced at me out of the corner of his eye and continued to push grout into the cracks between each tile.

"You've thought that, too, haven't you?"

He pressed his lips together before meeting my eye. "I'm not the only person in the world with brown eyes, Tabitha."

I swallowed and offered a small smile. "But have you—have you asked her? I mean, since the breakup?"

"Of course, I asked her. And of course, she said, no, Trevor is not mine." He continued to work, not meeting my eye right away. I clearly hit a nerve.

I nodded in understanding and we continued to tile until our hands were caked in mortar and our knees ached. After I laid the last tile piece in the top corner, I collected the supplies and stood up while Dylan kept working. When he finally finished grouting the tile, he was standing there, a small smile on his face—the one I had come to know and love.

"Hey," he said, brushing my cheek with his messy hand. "You know I'm all yours, right?"

I smiled. "I'm not jealous, Dylan."

"You're not?"

"I'm not twelve-years-old." I laughed.

"Not even a little?"

"You want me to be jealous?"

"A little bit." His face mocked offense and I found it incredibly endearing.

I glanced at my watch. "Okay. Go get cleaned up. Mindy and Trey are watching the kids until nine tonight. I'll meet you at your place and show you how jealous I am."

He stepped closer until his lips brushed against my ear, making my pulse quicken.

"Why don't you come get cleaned up with me?" His lips spread into a seductive smile and his eyes glinted at a night I could hardly wait for.

Eighteen

ON THE DRIVE over to Dylan's, I unlocked my phone and called Mindy to check on the boys.

She picked up on the third ring.

"Hello!" she said in sing-song voice. I could hear Charlie giggling in the background.

"Hello." I smiled over the line. It was such a comfort to find a solid village of people I loved and trusted my boys with. "It sounds like you guys are having fun."

"Yes! Charlie is dressed like a superhero and is wrestling with Trey. He thinks it's hilarious." Mindy laughed. "Gosh, he's so precious. I miss when Zach was two—it's such a fun age!"

"Fun and busy," I said, as I turned out on the main road. "Well, the tile is done. We just have to seal the grout tomorrow, which won't take nearly as long and then it's all set for the bar equipment to be installed. I'll send you a picture."

Mindy squealed. "I'm so excited! I can't believe you got it all done. You're a miracle worker."

"Well, it definitely went faster today with Dylan helping." A brief silence hung over the line. "I'm actually going to Dylan's before I pick the boys up, is that okay? Or do you need me to pick them up now?"

"Oh, no, that's fine. We're about to order pizza and the big boys are playing video games now that they've finished their homework. Plus, I owe you."

"For what?"

"For tiling the bar at the restaurant—that really relieved a huge burden for us."

"Oh, right," I said, letting out a quick breath. "It really isn't a problem. I want the restaurant to succeed just as much as you."

"I appreciate that, Tabitha. You have been a tremendous help—Trey and I really owe you." She paused awkwardly. "And I'm really sorry about this afternoon with Felicity. I should have warned you."

Her voice was earnest and sincerely apologetic.

"It's fine, Mindy. Awkward, yes. But I was going to run into her eventually, I'm sure." I cleared my throat. "She and Dylan haven't been together for a very long time. And if it weren't for the ancient, small town gossip creeping to the surface, it would have been even less awkward."

She laughed. "Right. Yes, you're *absolutely* right."

"I'll pick the boys up by nine," I said, turning into Dylan's neighborhood. "Does that work?"

"Sure thing. They'll be dressed in PJs ready to go!"

After I hung up the phone, my fingers itched to call her back. I wanted to ask if anyone ever thought Trevor was actually Dylan's child. If anyone in town would know the rumors, it would be Mindy. I convinced myself not to. It not only would be a betrayal to Dylan, but if it wasn't a rumor already, it would be once the idea crossed Mindy's mind. Plus, Dylan was adamant he already had that conversation with Felicity.

I needed to let it go.

Still, the boy's big, round, brown eyes haunted my memories—they were eerily similar to Dylan's. The more I thought about it, the more I realized, he also had Dylan's dimple. I shook the thoughts from my head, wondering if I was projecting.

But I couldn't help but continue to think, *what if?*

What if Trevor really was Dylan's?

Would it change how I felt about him?

Absolutely not.

But what would that mean for Dylan?

That I didn't have an answer to.

When I pulled up to Dylan's house, the front porch light was on and a warm glow emitted from the living room windows. I knocked twice and opened the door simultaneously, while announcing my presence.

"Hey," he said, standing near the doorway, having clearly arrived just before me.

The sight of him made me forget every single question that raced through my mind on the drive over.

The way his dirty t-shirt fit snugly against his broad shoulders as he slipped off his jacket. The way he wore his hat backwards and let his lips curve into a half-smile when he looked at me. The way his dark gaze was piercing and mesmerizing all at the same time. The way my heart beat faster every time he was near me. The way we were finally completely alone for the first time in a long time.

He hung his jacket in the closet and turned to take mine from my hands. My eyes were all over him, burning through his clothes and mortar and sweat from hours and hours of labor all day.

"Are you checking me out?" he asked with a playful expression as he turned his back to the closet and faced me.

I bit my lip to keep from smiling and nodded slowly.

He stepped closer and I wondered if he could hear my heart beating as he brushed his hand through my hair until his fingers were entangled in the loose waves hanging down my back. He pulled gently, tilting my face to meet his. He looked at me with such intensity; I was as nervous as I was excited. I couldn't look away even as my hands began to tremble with anticipation.

He did that to me somehow. He was kind and gentle but completely disarming. Every weapon I used to defend my heart fell to my feet in his presence.

His hands ran down my back and slipped around my waist

as he pulled me against him. Our breath caught on each other's until our lips touched, and we kissed each other with a fury of heat and desire.

"You're filthy, Tabitha," he whispered as his thumb brushed against the dried mortar on my cheek.

I let out a laugh as he nibbled my neck.

"So are you," I practically moaned as I slipped off his hat and tossed it to the ground so I could push my fingers through his hair.

"We should probably do something about that," he agreed. The deep and moody expression in his eyes made my pulse quicken.

I nodded and swallowed hard, completely stunted for words.

He picked me up with one swift motion and I wrapped my legs around him as he carried me to the bathroom, an uninhibited laugh escaping my lips.

While the water in the shower ran, he set me on the counter and slowly slid his hands up my back. My arms were delicately draped over his shoulders as his lips hovered over my skin, begging me to kiss him. My hands moved to cradle his face, drawing him closer until our lips met. The kiss was slow and enticing. His mouth moved over mine and traced along my jaw before sliding down my neck as his hands wandered over my skin and stripped the clothes off my body. Heat surged through my veins; my legs began to tremble. His lips and hands were everywhere—pushing, pulling, begging. I gripped his hair as his lips sunk into the hollow of my neck and I let out a shuddered breath. My back arched as he gripped my hips and I pulled his mouth back to mine, my teeth catching his bottom lip. Our breathing grew heavy with every push and pull of our lips until we were both panting as we kissed and touched and teased.

Dylan kept pulling back.

Pausing.

Staring.

Admiring.

Raking his eyes over my body and savoring every part of me.

SIXTEEN *Summers*

His stare practically invaded my soul. He ran his thumb across my bottom lip and wrapped his fingers around my neck. My head tilted back at his touch, and I released a euphoric breath of a laugh.

"You're beautiful," he whispered as his mouth brushed against mine. I closed the distance between our lips, letting us sink into each other.

I could have kissed him forever.

He kissed me like I was made for him.

He kissed me like I was his only source of oxygen. As if he couldn't breathe without me.

He kissed me like there was nothing left in this world for him but me.

My hands ran down his back, my body aching for him. I couldn't get close enough. I was desperate. It was more than wanting—it was *needing*.

Dylan drew back just inches from my face and took a deep breath, letting it go slowly as his eyes stayed intensely fixed on mine. His fingers trailed along my thighs up to my waist until they were splayed across my rib cage—my heart beating wildly against the palm of his hand. He lifted me to him and I wrapped my legs around his waist as we moved from the counter to the shower. Steam from the water filled our lungs and made our skin slick as our hands explored each other.

I threw my head back and let out a small moan as his teeth nipped at my collarbone. He continued to kiss my neck and shoulder and chest causing a chill to run down my spine, but it was no match for the heat from his skin as it touched mine.

Time slowed down under the rush of the water. Dylan carefully ran a sudsy wash cloth over every inch of my body, looking up at me as he did so and stopping only to let his lips linger across my skin.

I could barely breathe when he touched me.

Barely think.

I slipped under the stream of water, taking the wash cloth from him and returning the favor with deft and gentle hands moving over him. I absorbed every curve and plane of his body. Every look and every touch made me feel weak with want. I ached for him. Like a starving lover, hungering after only him.

I stood next to him, curving the washcloth over his shoulder and kissing his bare, wet skin beneath. His hands ran up my arms and along my neck until they cradled my face and he stared down at me with so much love and passion, I was completely overwhelmed.

"I love you, Tabitha," he whispered as his hand moved from my neck to the swell of my chest and down to my waist. I pulled him closer as his thumb pressed into my hip bone.

"I love you, too," I said with a breathless surrender.

My back was flush against the tile of the shower wall as his body met mine. There was nothing to hold on to but him. Nothing else I wanted.

A heat pulsed between us.

A magnetic passion pulled me to him.

I didn't want to escape him.

I wanted to be consumed by him.

I wrapped myself around him as he filled the hollow ache inside me.

There was a hunger in his eyes but it was deeper than that. There was want but there was also tenderness. A desire but also true, unshakeable love. The kind of love that didn't leave me wanting. The kind of love that wrapped itself around me until I couldn't run from it. I didn't want to. It was the kind of love that made me feel free. And more than anything, it was the kind of love that reminded me there was still a beautiful life waiting for me to live.

DRESSED IN A white t-shirt and gray sweatpants, with his hair still dewy from the shower, Dylan walked around the corner from the kitchen, holding a bottle of red wine and two glasses. His dimple highlighted his charming and satisfied smile and was framed by his perfectly kissable stubble.

I curled onto his couch and admired him as he closed the distance between us and leaned down to kiss me. I hummed into his lips as he lingered another moment before pressing them against mine one more time.

I found him heartbreakingly handsome and was still surprised to find myself falling in so deep.

"I think you earned yourself a drink over these last few days." He set the glasses down on the wooden coffee table while the wood burning fireplace crackled next to the couch. My body sank deep into the cushions. As satisfied as our shower made me feel, my bones ached and my back hurt from days of laying tile.

"Thank you," I said, taking the glass from him, opening and closing my free hand. "My fingers are so stiff. I feel like an old lady."

"You're practically geriatric," he teased, making me laugh. He sat down and I curved my body under his arm. He leaned down to kiss the top of my head, letting his lips remain in my hair, breathing in the scent of me.

I let out a deep sigh of contentment. "Thank you for helping me today. The last leg of a project is always the hardest to complete. It was nice to just get it done quickly."

"Anytime." He nodded and took a sip of wine, rotating the glass on his knee. "Are you excited for the restaurant to open?"

"Of course." I smiled up at him. "It definitely makes me feel like a permanent resident. I might need to start house hunting."

"But I thought you loved the condo?"

"I do," I agreed. "But it is so small, and the boys are growing. It might be nice to have more space. I mean, I'm a minimalist but I do miss the space to tuck away my crap like at my old house."

He nodded, nervously looking at his feet propped on the coffee table and then back at me. "Have you ever considered moving in with me?"

I swallowed. I had thought about it. But I also hadn't thought about it realistically.

"I—" I sat up and turned to face him, pausing as I tried to find the right words. "This is your dad's house though. I don't want to take over."

"Technically, it's my dad's house, but realistically it will be mine. Dad isn't ever going to be well enough to come home."

He shrugged and chewed on the inside of his cheek as he looked at me.

It made me sad for him. He regularly visited his dad, and his father still didn't remember him, and it was getting worse every day. The fleeting moments of recognition came less and less frequent until his father had forgotten how to read. He'd stumble over finding words when simply saying a sentence. He sometimes even forgot his own name. The nurses at the memory care facility helped him bathe and brushed his teeth. His memory was gone but now his overall health was deteriorating rapidly in just a matter of months. Dylan didn't know how much longer he had with his dad, but the hope of recovery didn't exist. That he at least knew for sure. He also knew he'd never get to properly say goodbye. Not in a way where he'd get a lucid moment from his father. Alzheimer's was a thief of so many things.

I held Dylan's stare a moment—seeing the pain behind his eyes but also the earnest request for me to move in, wondering if he knew what he was asking.

"What about my kids?" I asked with a breath through a smile.

"Well, they'd definitely have to find their own place," he teased and laughed, breaking the tension.

"Stop," I said, throwing a pillow at him. "You know what I mean. Two kids are a lot to take on. Having a preteen and a toddler is not simple or easy or clean. There's not a lot of quiet when you add kids to the mix."

"But I want all that, Tabitha." He pulled my legs over his lap and gently rubbed my feet. "I want your complicated, hard, and messy. I'm not signing on with easy—that would be far too boring. I just want you. And your two wonderful boys are just a part of the package."

My eyes smiled as I looked at him; I was thankful he didn't see my children as baggage. "But I haven't really even told Toby we're together."

He tilted his chin down and gave me a knowing stare.

"I mean, I think he knows," I relented, "and I think he's okay with it, but I just can't make choices that spring more change on him right now. At least not until he's fully on board and understanding what we've become."

"Okay, that's fair. But when you tell him and he's on board, would you consider it?"

"Dylan," I said, setting my glass of wine on the table and my feet on the floor. "There are a lot of things we still haven't discussed yet."

"Like?"

"Like, what would I do with my condo? Do you want to have kids? Do you ever see yourself getting married now? Those types of things."

He swallowed and nodded. "Whatever you want. Yes. And only if it's you."

My heart skipped a beat as he answered my questions and I smiled at him while shaking my head in disbelief.

"Dylan." I tilted my head as my eyes begged him to be serious even though I knew he absolutely was.

"Tabitha." The right side of his mouth curled into a flirtatious smile, lighting a fire in my soul while also setting off warning bells in my mind.

I had always dreamed of having one great love story in my life. I had that. While I didn't believe I'd necessarily be alone for the rest of my life, I was much more cautious as I proceeded—there was more at stake. When I fell in love with Tate at twenty-one, I literally had nothing to lose. Sometimes I still felt like that girl was still inside me somewhere, ready to jump headfirst into love. The mid-thirties woman in me wanted to pump the breaks no matter how right everything felt.

"You really mean all that?" I asked finally.

He pulled me to him in one swift, strong movement by my waist.

"I mean all of it."

He was so close; I could almost taste his kisses while the rustic smell of his aftershave danced between us. He kissed my forehead, then my nose, then my mouth, then my chin before tracing his lips on my neck. I wrapped my arms around him and kissed him back, pulling him tighter against me. I was ready to surrender and say yes to everything. But the bigger part of me kept whispering, *not quite yet.*

I pressed my hands against his chest, halting his kisses as I stared at him with a question. "Like, more kids or the ones I already have?"

"More, if that's what you want too." He kissed me again. And then pulled back and smiled seductively. "We could start now."

"Hold on." I half-laughed and pushed him away before standing with my hands on my hips. I knew he was joking—a sexy little jest before he had his way with me for the second time that evening but when I heard it, it felt so irresponsible and out of place. "Can we be serious for just a little bit longer?"

My eyes pleaded with his as he sat on the couch, his face a mixture of surprise and confusion.

"I am being serious. Tabitha, I love you more than I ever thought it was possible to love anyone. I want you to move in with the boys. I want to have babies with you. I want every part of your life to be forever intertwined with mine."

Tears filled my eyes. It was everything anyone would want to hear from someone they loved. I cleared the emotion begging to crawl out of my throat.

"But do you want to get married?" I asked earnestly, my forehead etched with lines of uncertainty. "Not now, obviously. But down the road. Do you see that happening?"

Breath escaped his lips softly and he smiled. "If that's what you want. Yes, more than anything."

"But is that what *you* want though?"

"Tabitha, what's wrong?" He stood and pulled me to him, his arms encasing my shoulders as he kissed the top of my head.

"Nothing." I shrugged in his embrace. "I just think we've been so 'here and now' for the last six months I'm worried we're not completely on the same page. If we're talking moving in together, shouldn't we have a plan? Shouldn't we have talked about our future? You know how important marriage is to me, and I know it's not something you believe in anymore." I paused and took a breath. "I just worry we're setting both of ourselves up for heartache. And I don't want to do that to you. But more than that, I don't want to do that to myself or my boys. Not again."

He listened to me intently, I could see each word be absorbed by his mind and etched across his forehead. He tucked a loose strand of hair behind my ear.

"I think…" he began slowly, "I wasn't expecting you. And you've changed everything for me. You've healed places I didn't know were hurting and filled voids I didn't know were empty. I don't know what the future holds exactly, but I know you're in it."

"But I have to think about it. At least a little bit, Dylan. If not for myself, but for my boys."

He nodded.

"And sometimes, I just feel like there's so much we don't even know about each other." I looked up at him seriously and his eyes found mine.

"Is this because of seeing Felicity today?"

I shook my head and pressed my eyes closed. "No, not just Felicity. But today felt like a reminder of things you've been through before me. People that might creep back into your life when I don't suspect it."

"Don't you trust me?" His words tumbled out sharply and I knew I had offended him.

"Yes," I said, hesitantly. I was so embarrassed for what I was about to say but I knew if we were really going to plan a lifetime together, it had to come out. "But her son looks a lot like you, Dylan. A lot."

"He's not mine." His voice was clipped as he turned and walked away from me.

"He has your eyes and your right dimple. And I saw how you looked at him, it was like *what-could-have-been* flashed across your face in an instant."

"Please leave it alone, Tabitha," he said, his voice angry around the edges.

"Why? Because it still hurts? Because it still bothers you?" The aggression in my voice grew as I desperately tried to get Dylan to be completely transparent with me about his past.

He squeezed the bridge of his nose with two fingers and closed his eyes.

"Yes," he said finally as he stood and retreated to the kitchen before turning to face me. "Yes, it still hurts. Sometimes things happen in our past that still hurt when we think about them. When we remember what we wanted, what we thought we had, and what life gave us instead. It can still hurt. You of all people should understand that."

"Why don't you want to talk about it?" I stood and followed him.

"Because it's painful for me!" he said as he whipped around.

"Like I don't know pain." I held my ground.

"It's different, Tabitha."

"It doesn't matter. You can't keep burying it."

"Yeah, well, neither can you." Dylan's eyes seared into me as he paused across the room, his arms bracing the counter.

"What's that supposed to mean?"

"It means I want a future with you but you keep diverting the conversation. You keep telling me you aren't ready or you're not sure. I don't know what else you want from me."

I swallowed hard. I wanted to fix the pain passing over his face, but I also didn't want to skirt around the subject.

"I'm sorry," I said shaking my head. "But us being completely honest with each other is the only way we *can* have a future together. If things don't work out with Felicity's current husband and she ever comes after you, wanting a paternity test, and you *are* his father, it could really change things for you...*us*." I held my hands up in exasperation and sat down on the couch.

He turned slowly and looked at me for a long moment with a blank expression before sitting next to me again and letting out a long breath. Awkward silence filled the space between us.

"You read my expression right," he said finally. His voice was almost muffled by the salty breeze coming through the back door and I turned to look at him. "I do think about what could have been with Trevor."

I pressed my eyes closed as fear crept up my neck and I waited for him to continue.

"And you're right. There is still a lot we don't know about each other. I should have told you the full story of what happened with me and Felicity."

I raised my eyebrows and let my jaw drop. "So, the long-story-short version wasn't what happened?"

"It was." He nodded, his lips forming a straight line. "But the details were just…messier."

I swallowed and nodded for him to continue.

"I knew something was off the night I picked Felicity up to propose but I ignored it and proposed anyway. She said yes and told me she was pregnant a week later even though she had already known for weeks. She didn't want to get married until after the baby was born but during her pregnancy, everything felt weird—like we were growing apart when we should have been coming together. After Trevor was born, I was so ecstatic to be a dad—never felt more proud. He even looked like me, everyone said so. But Felicity kept drifting from me. I blamed it on everything from hormones to post-partum depression. It wasn't until Trevor was three-and-a-half months old that she confessed to having a two-year long affair with her boss. She said Trevor wasn't mine, and I wanted a paternity test."

I grabbed my wine off the table and took a long swig, entranced in his tragic telling of the biggest heartbreak of his life.

He bit his lip hard, and I could see the hurt laced along his lashes. "I went to every appointment, every ultrasound. I recorded the sound of his heartbeat on my phone, you know? I watched him be born and changed his diapers in the middle of the night before Felicity fed him. I was his dad…" he clicked his tongue across his teeth. "Until we got the results, and I wasn't."

My solemn expression stayed frozen on my face. "And that was it?"

He nodded with a shrug. "She moved in with Phil the next week with Trevor, and they lived happily ever after."

I clasped my hands at my mouth. "That is horrible. I'm really sorry."

"Yeah, me too. So, as I'm sure you can imagine, when I see Trevor, I remember when I thought he was mine."

I reached and grabbed his hand not knowing what to say but understanding the magnitude of hurt Felicity caused him. "I hate that she did that to you."

He nodded, twisting his lips. "Yeah, but you know what, she's a good mom. Phil's an okay guy. Trevor seems happy." He shrugged, letting it go for probably the millionth time.

I couldn't help it—the tears spilled down my face. The pieces of Dylan were falling into place—who he was, what made him the way he had become. It didn't matter that we still had so much to learn about each other—it mattered that I still wanted to know every last detail.

Summer 4

C AN YOU *PLEASE* remember to put your shoes away," I said to Tate while pulling in a breath through my nose.

"Only if you remember to stop putting my water glasses in the dishwasher before I'm done with them." He smirked at me.

He was adorably irritating.

A year into our marriage, we were fully fledged in discovering each other's quirks. As it turns out, there were many. And not the precious, new love kind. These were the quirks we had to come to terms with living with forever—the constant annoyances that built over time.

"Only if you remember to put the toilet seat down," I retorted.

"Only if you stop chewing gum."

My jaw dropped. "That bothers you?"

He rolled his head to look at me standing in the kitchen. "I can hear you from the couch."

I laughed and my cheeks flushed as I pulled the spearmint gum from my mouth and plopped it in the trash.

"Fine," I said triumphantly. "Now go put your shoes away."

Tate laughed as he stood and approached me with sparkling eyes and an irresistible smile before planting a kiss on my lips. His skin was warm and his body solid as he pressed me up against the counter. His fingers raked through my hair and he kissed me deeply. My veins surged with desire, and I suddenly didn't care about his shoes or the toilet seat. He pulled away seductively, cradling my face and looking into my eyes, satisfaction pulling at his smile.

"Where *is* my water glass, Tabitha?" he accused me playfully.

My laugh echoed in the kitchen as he turned to walk away victoriously.

"You're seriously just going to tease me like that?" I stood alone in the kitchen, wanting him to finish what he started.

"As a matter of fact, yes, I am." He smiled smugly then called over his shoulder as he walked around the corner. "I've got a hot date to get ready for."

I couldn't stop smiling all while thinking, *two can play that game.* I walked into the bathroom, pulling my sweatshirt over my head and my sweatpants dropped to the floor, revealing matching lacey undergarments that hung tightly against every curve. Tate's eyes followed me through the mirror while he shaved his face. His top two buttons undone and a longing in his eyes.

I tossed my hair over my shoulder and gave him a coy smile before standing at the closet pretending to pick out my outfit for our much-anticipated date night in Seattle. His warm hands slid over my hips pulling me back toward him as he kissed my neck and let his lips linger down to my shoulder.

I hummed into his touch, turning around and pulling him closer, barely able to pull my mouth away from his. But I did and I brushed my finger against his lips and smiled before looking up at him.

"Sorry," I teased. "I've got a hot date to get ready for."

He groaned. His eyes were hungry and desperate. I loved desperate Tate. It reminded me of Tate from when we first met—always watching me, longing for me, and fighting for my affections.

As much as I wanted him in that moment, I also wanted to win the little game he started. He loved to seduce me, but we both knew who the bigger tease was. My stubborn streak always made it easier to hold out, even as I squirmed in the passenger seat next to him, wishing he'd pull over like a hormonal teenager on a date with the high school heart throb.

A passionate tension pulled between us the entire drive to Seattle—a hungry desire that made me wonder if we shouldn't have played this game. We'd done it before: teased each other until we each broke. The build of passion over a few hours somehow made the collision stronger.

As we neared the city, I could see the Seattle skyline sat perched next to the water, lit up against the summer evening sky. Tate pulled off four exits too early and flipped on to the freeway going the opposite direction.

"Where are you going?" I eyed him over the console. "Isn't our reservation in fifteen minutes?"

He smiled, the corners of his eyes glimmering in the sun setting in the distance. "Maybe."

I narrowed my eyes on him—I usually asked too many questions for him to actually be able to surprise me, but this time I literally had no idea what to expect.

"Where are we going then?" I probed while my heart smiled.

He loosened his tie from around his neck and slid it out of the collar in one fluid motion before tossing it on my lap.

"Blindfold yourself."

I swallowed hard and smirked at him out of the corner of my mouth. "Are you being kinky?"

He laughed. "I'm being *romantic*, Tabitha. Put it on."

I watched him a moment as the car sped down the freeway before reluctantly wrapping his black tie over my eyes and pulling it tightly behind my head.

"Can you see?" he asked.

"No."

"Yes, you can," his voice said with a smile. "Pull it down."

"I cannot, Tate. I swear."

He was silent a moment and I could feel his eyes inspecting me.

"Don't spoil it, Tabitha."

I smiled at his excitement. "I won't. I promise."

We drove for another thirty minutes before the car stopped and Tate turned off the ignition. After getting out of the car, he shuffled to the passenger side and opened my door. He grabbed my hand—his hold strong against my delicate fingers—and pulled me to a standing position.

The pavement under my feet felt familiar, the scent of hydrangeas drifted through my nose, and the sound of the thundering freeway in the distance was one I knew from every day before and after work.

"Tate, are we back home?" I asked, my eyes still covered.

He let out a sharp breath and laughed. "Why is it so hard to surprise you?"

I shrugged and reached for the tie. "Can I take my blindfold off?"

"No, not yet," he said excitedly as he pulled my hand away from the tie and guided me to what I assumed was the side of the house. The cobblestones made my heels rock and shift as I stepped over them into our small back yard. The scent of hydrangeas, roses, and lemon grass grew stronger as we turned the corner and stepped into the yard. My heels sunk in the grass, and I clung to Tate to keep my balance. His arms were warm and strong around my waist and he smelled like citrus and his leathery aftershave.

"Okay," he said so soft it was almost a whisper. His fingers unlaced the tie from the back of my head and the blindfold fell from my face.

I gasped at the site of our backyard. String lights were strung from the deck to the fence, making the grass sparkle below. Candles and vases of white roses bordered the yard, framing what looked to be a makeshift dance floor similar to the one at our wedding. There was even a speaker with an iPod plugged into it while all our wedding songs played. A tent was pitched in the corner of the yard and was littered with pillows, blankets, a bottle of champagne, a charcuterie board, and, of course, homemade cobbler.

Tears stung my eyes at the thoughtfulness—at how beautiful the scene in our quaint yard backing up to the freeway was.

"I figured a fancy dinner in Seattle was a little too predictable for our one-year anniversary," Tate said with his hands in his pockets and a boyishly charming smile dancing across his face. I stared at him for a long moment before speaking. I was truly surprised. In that moment, Tate was irresistible. He was breathtaking. He was my everything.

"Shall we dance?" He held out his hand to me. I kicked off my heels and let him pull me against his body, and we danced barefoot in the grass to each of our favorite wedding songs.

"Did I surprise you?" he whispered into my ear.

I raised my head from his chest as we swayed under the string lights and nodded. "Completely surprised. How did you pull this off?"

He shrugged. "I've got connections."

I laughed and rolled my eyes thinking of Lydia and Tim. "We have great friends."

"Yeah, that too." His green eyes sparkled at me under the string lights. "Want some cobbler? I made it myself."

I bit my lip and let him guide me to the tent. I sat against the plush pillows as he popped open the champagne and poured two glasses. We ate the now cold cobbler straight from the pan sans vanilla ice cream, and I couldn't think of a better way to spend our first anniversary.

He wrapped his hand around my waist and pulled me tightly against his body before kissing me desperately. There was always an insatiable hunger between us. An uncompromising promise. An unmistakable love.

"I love you, Tabitha," he said, brushing my hair from my face and tilting my chin toward him.

"Always will." The smile on my face pulled from my heart and I felt so content. So loved. So happy to be with him for the rest of our lives.

Nineteen

"ARE YOU AND Dylan boyfriend and girlfriend?"

I choked on my glass of water at the sound of my twelve-year-old's question. I kept coughing and drinking, trying to gain my composure. When the tickle finally smoothed out, I set my water glass down and stared at him over my plate of lasagna.

"What makes you ask that?" I cleared my throat.

Toby shrugged. "Because you act like boyfriend and girlfriend. You know, except the kissing part."

I let out a small laugh and then contemplated my words for a moment. "What would you think if we were...boyfriend and girlfriend?"

He nodded through taking a bite of lasagna. "I think that'd be pretty cool."

"Really? Why's that?" If there was one thing I had learned about being a mother of a pre-teen, it was once they started talking, don't let them stop. Otherwise, I'd never know the truth.

"I like Dylan. He's cool." He shrugged. "You're happy when

he's around."

Children—no matter the age—are so intuitive.

I smiled at him, while Charlie sang his ABCs and smashed lasagna in his face with a small fork he still couldn't quite use properly.

"Well, there's actually something I've been wanting to tell you."

He nodded and looked at me expectantly while ripping off a piece of garlic bread and placing it in his mouth.

"I have been wanting to tell you that yes, me and Dylan are...boyfriend and girlfriend." I half-smiled as I waited for his reaction.

Toby bit his lips at they spread into a smile and he nodded. "Cool, Mom."

"'Cool, Mom?'" I repeated, eyeing him curiously. This wasn't necessarily what I was expecting, though I couldn't think of a better reaction.

"Yeah, Dylan's awesome, and I want you to be happy." He shrugged again and turned to his buzzing phone on the table. Tears stung my eyes. The conversation had come and gone just like that.

Just like that?

Just. Like. That.

I watched him check the texts on his phone and smiled, feeling both relief and indescribable love. Most days I felt like the boys and I got the short end of the stick when Tate died. But what I had learned was sticks can grow.

"I love you, Toby."

He looked up at me briefly, a small flush dancing across his pubescent cheeks. "Love you too, Mom."

I TOLD TOBY," I said plainly, sitting in my office chair at the restaurant.

Dylan raised his eyebrows and smiled. "And?"

"It was fine." I shrugged and smiled, almost astounded. "He actually brought it up. Guessed. Which I know neither of us are surprised by that."

"How could anyone be?" he said, as he brushed my hair back and leaned down to kiss me. It started soft and gentle then steadily progressed until heat rushed through my body. What I would have given for him to slam my office door closed, swipe the folders and papers on the floor, and hoist me up on the desk. I let out a breath, pushing the fantasy out of my mind.

I rose from my chair and closed the door behind him anyway. He eyed me mischievously as he pulled me back into his arms.

I cleared my throat. "We can't. Gabby is just down the stairs."

Dylan grabbed my forearms and flipped me against the door, pressing his body against mine and kissing me furiously, his hands running up and down the sides of my body. I groaned into his mouth. I had never felt this wild or free. At least not since Tate.

I thought we were for sure going to have sex on my desk anyway until a jiggle of the door handle and a knock on the door made us both laugh.

"Hello? Tabitha, why's the door locked?" Trey asked.

I opened the door, and the look of surprise was almost immediately replaced with a knowing smile when Trey saw me and Dylan. I couldn't even attempt to hide my blush.

"Hi Trey," Dylan said, his voice smooth and calming. I tried not to laugh.

Trey cleared his throat—clearly uncomfortable—his toes remaining on the edge of the entry to the office. "Sorry for interrupting. Uh, I have the employee paperwork for Izzy. She dropped it by just now." He reached out and set the papers on the desk barely crossing the threshold. "Right. Well, carry on, then."

We all burst out laughing.

"Just come in," I said to Trey, feeling incredibly thankful he was friends with Dylan. Also, really embarrassed about the situation playing out in my boss's mind.

"You sure?" He scanned the room cautiously.

"Yes, Dylan has to head back to work anyway. He was just

on his lunchbreak."

"You're right, I better get going," he responded and kissed me on the cheek.

"I see," Trey said, a mischievous grin splayed on his face.

"Good to see you, man. Beers on me tomorrow?" Dylan suggested, as he grabbed his coat and walked through the door.

"Yeah, sure." Trey smirked and then turned his attention to me after Dylan made his way down the stairs and out of the building. "Are you really going to marry him?"

My mouth dropped open, playfully. "Trey! Where did you get an idea like that?" I fully expected to hear Mindy's name dance across his lips.

"Dylan," he said plainly, looking at me intently with his eyebrows raised.

A chill ran down my arms and I leaned in like a teenager wanting to hear the latest gossip. "Really?"

He laughed. "Really, Tabitha. You scare the shit out of him most of the time, but he really loves you."

I bit down on the hang nail on my thumb and chewed on it while I realized this was actually happening. Not only was I in love with Dylan but the idea and proclamation of the longevity of our relationship was being scattered around town.

It was surreal, even if it was right. It felt like I was being given the chance to live a whole different life after my last life was destroyed. Tears rimmed my eyes and I smiled, blinking them away and trying to look professional.

"Like *really* loves you," Trey added, and I nodded. He turned sharply toward the doorway and gestured to the restaurant beyond. "But anyway, things are looking like they're still on schedule for the grand opening next month. Many thanks to you and your handiwork."

I brushed away the compliment and cleared my throat. "I can't wait."

HEY, STRANGER. I miss you." Lydia was standing in the doorway of my office a few hours after Trey left, and I finished up the paperwork for the day.

I smiled at her.

"You mean since last week?" I asked, partly teasing.

"Ha-ha. Yes, since last week. You used to call and text almost every day and now I only get a few times a week. Between Mindy and Dylan, I'm feeling a little jealous." She held a hand to her heart, pretending to be offended.

"After all these years, Lydia, you know I could never replace you." I smiled and hugged her.

We still did talk often but definitely not in the same frequency as last year. In recent months, I realized just how much I used Lydia as a crutch—a lifeline there at my beck and call. Every time I cried. Anytime I worried.

She was still ever present in the goings-on surrounding my life even if my calls and texts didn't frequent her phone as often as they did last year. I called her after I met Felicity and after I visited Dylan's dad. She knew about all of my deepest conversations with Dylan. Our friendship was more of a sisterhood: a loyal love between two women constantly loving and supporting each other.

She handed me a coffee as she smirked at me. "Now, does Dylan have to die for me to get attention again?"

I eyed her playfully and started laughing. It was such an odd sensation to laugh about Tate's death, but I knew the laughter was rooted in absurdity not cruelty.

"I don't think you can handle another man of mine dying. I will lose my mind." I laughed again and sipped the hot Americano through the lid. "You really aren't appreciating the reprieve he's offered?"

She waved off my statement. "Gosh, I'm teasing. You know I'm happy for you." She shrugged and her lips spread into a small smile. "I just got used to knowing your daily everything. But now, I know you're daily everything is filled with Dylan making promises and plans with my best friend. I think I can be okay with that." She eyed me over the top of her coffee cup. "Well, on one condition…"

"What's that?" I raised my eyebrows.

"I get to be maid of honor."

"I will *not* be having that kind of wedding again." I laughed, remembering the matching periwinkle dresses and white votive candles littering the church sanctuary while I sauntered up the aisle with my father as he gave me away to Tate with a glistening tear in his eye.

It was a fairytale wedding, despite every mishap. Two ambitious twenty-three-year-olds, anxious and excited to start a lifetime of love and unknowns.

"Really? I thought the two of you were really talking about getting married?" Lydia's question pulled me out of my thoughts as she eyed me over her coffee cup.

"Yeah. We've talked about it a little bit...*in the future.*" I turned and placed a file in the cabinet behind me and turned off my monitor. "But even then, I don't see myself doing a big wedding again. It was so stressful. Plus, you and I both know the wedding doesn't make the marriage. Especially after everything that happened at mine." I raised my eyebrows at her.

"True." She laughed, no doubt remembering every mishap of mine and Tate's wedding. "Well, I'm really happy things are working out for you here."

I smiled. "Thanks, Lydia."

"I mean it. When you said you were going to move closer to me, I was hopeful it would work out and you'd never leave, and we'd never have to live far away from each other again, but I honestly didn't imagine life falling into place like this for you."

I drew in a breath, contemplating her words and what my life had beautifully become even if it was entirely unexpected, unplanned, and not even remotely what I wanted in the first place. I stood up and linked my arm with hers before walking out of the office.

"Life will never fall completely into place. It's just about how gracefully we let it fall," I said.

She smiled and leaned her head on my shoulder.

"Now let's go pull up those crab nets."

WHEN WE MADE it to the crab dock, the boys were

wrangled in their lifejackets next to Dylan and Tim with white buckets, pulling up the nets and measuring the crabs to make sure they were to size for harvesting.

"Got any good ones?" Lydia called to all the men in our life.

"My trap caught the most!" Eli said with a triumphant smile.

"But mine had the biggest one," Caden retorted, putting his little brother in his place.

"Boys…" Tim warned softly. "All the traps pulled up more crabs than we need tonight."

I silently greeted Toby by messing with his hair as he smiled at me sheepishly. Standing there, eye-to-eye, I couldn't believe how tall he was getting. He was officially taller than me. At twelve. Time was a thief. Dylan stood next to him holding Charlie in his arms. I leaned in and kissed Charlie on the cheek before giving Dylan a brief kiss.

"Thank you for picking the boys up for me today," I said, wishing I could linger on his lips a little longer but also fully aware of respecting the threshold of embarrassment for Toby.

"Daddy!" Charlie exclaimed, and we laughed nervously.

I saw Caden nudge Toby, and he shrugged in response. Charlie didn't stop calling Dylan 'Daddy' no matter how many times we corrected him. Toby swore it didn't bother him—he was getting older and understanding the complications of adult relationships more every day. He understood but I knew it didn't make it less weird. At least not yet.

Once we tossed the undersized crabs back into the steely gray ocean water, we collapsed our traps, tied up our ropes, and headed back to the condo with two buckets full of soon-to-be crimson-colored crustaceans for dinner.

The large pot of water boiled behind me and Lydia as we stood at the counter, pulling out the butter, hot sauce, and fixings for a salad. The air smelled like the best parts of the sea mixed with the warmth and richness of butter. The big boys were kicking a soccer ball back and forth on the grassy area below the balcony while Tim and Dylan sat in Adirondack chairs on the balcony drinking beers. Charlie was contently perched in Dylan's lap as he pointed at every passing seagull and giggled at the sealions barking in the distance.

It almost felt too good to be true. I never imagined Charlie calling anyone but Tate 'dad.' I never imagined him having anyone outside of myself and my family as his safe place. I never imagined another man coming into my life and fitting perfectly.

"He's good with Charlie," Lydia said, placing another saucepan of butter on the stove to melt, breaking me away from my thoughts.

"Mm-hmm." I nodded and placed the last of the tomato I had been slicing in the salad bowl before wringing my hands on a dish towel, my eyes not leaving Dylan and Charlie outside.

"Well, you sound less than enthused." Lydia snorted out a small laugh through her nose.

I shook my head. "I am—I mean, I am *more* than enthused. I feel very lucky honestly." I turned around, leaning the small of my back on the counter. "It's just crazy. If you told me a year ago this would be happening; that I'd be boiling fresh crab I just caught with my kids, boyfriend, and best friend in Newport, I would have never believed you. I don't even think I wanted this to be a possibility last year."

She turned off the burner under the melted butter and faced me, joy glimmering across her face. "Well, you know what they say: time is a thief but it's also the best thing for a broken heart."

Tears welled behind my eyes and the emotion drew lines across my forehead. I took a deep breath and let it out.

Lydia's eyes went wide. "What'd I say? I'm so sorry, I didn't mean—I just—"

"No, no." I waved off her backtracking apology and wiped the rogue tear off my cheek. "I guess there are times I feel like my heart is still broken and I don't know how it will ever be whole again. Even with Dylan. I mean, he's incredible—everything I could have hoped for, it's just—"

"Do you feel like your settling?" she asked in a hushed voice.

"No! No, not at all. It's the opposite. I sometimes think: what if Dylan and I knew each other first? I wonder if we would have ended up together a long time ago. And then I feel guilty because I loved Tate and he was so good to me and we had a beautiful life, and I wouldn't have those memories or this place." I gestured to the room, biting back tears as the confession tumbled from my lips. "I wouldn't have my boys. Like, what kind of person am I to wonder what life would've been like without my late husband and kids?"

"A normal one!" She slapped my shoulder playfully. "You cannot beat yourself up about wondering something like that. You are in love with Dylan. Did tragedy lead you both to each other? Yes. And that was really hard on a lot of people. You and him in particular. It's only natural to wish you could erase the pain and hurt from someone you love. But I think you just have to remember that isn't your story. And that isn't his story either. You both are different because of what you went through. You live differently. You love differently. You forgive differently. Now..." she grabbed my shoulders and pulled me to look at her squarely, "I'm not entirely sure but it really sounds like you could use a glass of wine."

I laughed and nodded while she pulled the sauvignon blanc out of the refrigerator and poured each of us a glass.

"I do love him, Lydia," I said softly, taking the glass as I watched Dylan playing Giddy-Up, Horsey with Charlie on the balcony. Dylan's smile lit up my heart and the giggles coming out of Charlie made my heart sing.

"Oh, honey. I know that. I'm pretty sure everyone knows that."

I bit my lip and smiled as Charlie ran through the balcony door with Dylan and Tim trailing behind him with empty beer bottles, completely engrossed in whatever discussion they were having outside.

Charlie leapt into my arms as I bent down and scooped him up, giving him a tight squeeze and quick spin.

"You hungry?" I asked, kissing his scrumptious, chubby toddler cheeks.

"Yespweeze," he replied with his face still squished against my lips.

"What about you guys?" I asked Dylan and Tim.

They nodded enthusiastically while Lydia pulled the biscuits out of the oven and turned off the stove. We dumped the boiling crab pot and dosed them with cold water while Dylan and Tim set the table and hollered for the big boys to head back inside and wash up for dinner.

"Thanks for cooking, Mom and Ms. Tabitha," Caden said, breaking into a crab leg and pulling out the good meat before dousing it in melted butter after everyone was seated.

"Thank you boys for catching it," I said, adding hot sauce to my dipping butter.

The chatter around the table continued to fill the space through the cracking of shells and mouthfuls of butter and crabmeat.

"We should do this every Thursday," Toby said finally.

"Eat crab?" Dylan asked, wiping his buttery lips with a napkin.

"Family dinner." He shrugged. "It could be crab; could be pizza. Doesn't matter. We used to do that when my Dad was alive. We'd have family dinners on Sundays with Nana and Papa Morgan, Grandma and Grampa Jones, and Uncle Justin and Aunt Sarah before, you know, everything."

I smiled at Toby and Dylan curled his fingers over my knee under the table. I turned to look at Dylan and his stare told me he not only wanted a lifetime of family dinners with me; he was ready for it.

Summer 3

TABITHA, THERE'S A problem with the flowers." My mother stood at the edge of my childhood bedroom with her hands clasped in front of her and a flush creeping up her neck. Her eyes were wide and horrified while Lydia glued on my second false lash. The howling wind outside rattled the window.

I squinted at my mother. "What kind of problem can white roses cause?"

"Well," she began slowly. "They're all fake."

Lydia dropped her hand and the false lash hung off the tip of my own lashes and fell to my cheek. "You're kidding? What kind of florist even has fake flowers?"

"A cheap one." I shrugged. "I knew we should have picked them up yesterday."

"Well, we can't use the fake ones—it's tacky," my mother said, clearly stressed. The flowers were the most important element of the décor—she was putting together the centerpieces after all.

"Obviously." I drew in a breath and bounced my foot

nervously.

"Crap, what are you going to do?" Lydia asked, pulling the messed-up lash off my face.

"Honestly, let's just skip it. Who cares about flowers? We still have candles and table settings on the table. It won't look terrible."

I truly didn't care; I was just anxious to see Tate and get the grand showcase of our love for each other over with so we could drink wine and dance into the night.

Our heads darted to the window in unison as the wind continued to blow furiously outside, pounding at the siding and rattling the windows like it was angry at the house.

"But what about the bridesmaids when we walk down the aisle? What are we supposed to do with our hands?" Lydia's eyes bulged out of her head.

"I don't know what to do with my hands while I'm walking either," Leslie, one of my other bridesmaids, added, while sipping a bottle of water.

"Fold them in front of your waist like you're holding a delicate flower." I laughed. "I don't care, just don't trip. And eat something please. I can see your hand shaking."

"My dress won't zip if I eat any of that—" She gestured to the table of snacks and hors d'oeuvres. "And I'm pretty sure you want clothed bridesmaids."

I laughed again, the tension from the fake flower fiasco evaporating from my chest.

"I think Lydia and Leslie are right. It will look awkward without them carrying flowers." My mother looked around the room, ignoring my conversation with Leslie. "You know what, I'll figure it out. Y'all just finish getting ready." She paused at the doorway and turned back to me; her eyes rimmed with tears. "You look really lovely, Tabitha."

I smiled and whispered over the catch in my throat, "Please don't make me cry."

My mother nodded with a small smile and walked away.

Lydia let out a breath. "It will all be okay, don't worry. Okay? Your mom is so crafty, she will make it look fantastic."

"I'm not worried." I pressed my lips into a small smile.

"Now, please, help me glue this damn eyelash back on."

Lydia laughed while she dotted white glue on the edge of the false lash line. "How are you so calm today? I was a nut when Tim and I got married last fall."

"I know. I was there."

She snorted out a laugh and shook her head.

"I just want to marry Tate." I let out a breath. "I don't care what the day looks like."

It was true. The church, the flowers, the candles littering the white tablecloths in the field flanking the dance floor, the DJ—none of it really mattered to me. I appreciated every part of it, but I knew the wedding was more for everyone else than it was for us. At least that's what my mother told me. It would never be perfect—even though I knew a part of her wanted it to be—but the only thing that really mattered was me and Tate promising each other forever. The wine, dancing, and fancy dresses were simply a bonus. I wasn't worried about tacky fake flowers or the unexpected summer storm raging outside.

The lights flickered. Lydia and Leslie's eyes shot a concerned look at me.

My mouth dropped open. "We should probably hurry and finish curling our hair."

BY THE TIME my hair was curled and pinned to perfection and false eyelashes securely flanked my blue eyes, the rain still hadn't made an appearance with the raging wind to the relief of my bridesmaids. They helped me into the car to drive us to the church; my giant dress billowed in the backseat of my car—a sea of chiffon and lace.

"You ready?" Lydia asked, her lips a deep mauve color and her eyes bright against her dark eyelashes as she held open my door.

I smiled at her. "You have no idea."

My dad patted my arm at the entrance to the sanctuary. His chin quivered and his eyes gleamed with tears.

"It's okay, Dad," I whispered.

He smiled and blinked tears away. "I'm happy for you, Tabitha. He's a good one," he said softly as we stepped down the aisle, our cadence slow while mine and Tate's song rang throughout the church walls.

The moment I saw Tate standing at the end of the aisle, his hands nervously held in front of his three-piece suit, I felt a peace wash over me. His green eyes sparkled, and his face smiled the same way it did on our first date, and I realized how desperately I wanted to see his smile every day for the rest of my days. Tate was the love of my life. He loved me in every way I hoped. In every way I was promised. In every way I could have ever dreamed.

I glided down the aisle holding a bouquet of wildflowers my mother picked off the side of the road, not even paying attention to the guests on either side of me. All I saw was Tate. The way he pressed his lips together trying not to smile. The way he fidgeted on his feet anxiously and pressed his thumb against his palm until he could hold my hands in front of the pastor after my dad gave me away.

When I held his hands in mine, I was tremendously thankful I'd get to hold them forever. I knew they were the hands that would hold our babies and wipe my tears. I knew his hands would bring me coffee in the morning and rub my feet at night. They were the hands I would get to hold for eternity, and I couldn't wait to say yes to forever.

When we finally kissed for the first time as husband and wife, a loud thud behind me made us turn to see Leslie stumbling off the stage, dizzy and lightheaded from not eating all day. I turned back to Tate, his eyes wide and concerned, and I kissed him again.

"She'll be fine," I whispered into his mouth while gasps echoed across our witnesses. "She just needs a sandwich."

Tate laughed and so did I. He leaned down to kiss me one more time as we heard a boom in the distance, and the sanctuary went nearly pitch black except for the votive candles scattered down the aisle. Our guests' phones began to slowly light up the room.

I looked at him, a surprised smile plastered on my face.

"Good thing there's a lot of candles on the tables." He smiled and shrugged and I leaned my head against his chest.

THE WIND WAS dying down, and the rain didn't fall but the power wasn't expected to return for another three hours. The DJ was frantic, desperately calling around to find a generator for his equipment. Tim didn't hesitate to drive his truck into the field. He pulled up next to the dance floor, opened the doors, and played music through the car speakers.

We ate dinner as quickly as we could before it could get cold, and the toasts were practically yelled into the crowd while the sun began to set. By the time we cut the cake—which was actually berry cobbler—the vanilla ice cream was half-melted, making it the soupiest of cobblers, more or less resembling a milkshake.

"I don't know, Tabitha, this might be the best cobbler we've ever had," he said, licking the syrupy berries off his lips.

"I wonder if there will ever be a cobbler you don't like." I smiled at him playfully and kissed him, tasting the sweetness of vanilla lingering on his lips. I pulled him away from his dessert and my body curved into his arms. We swayed on the candle lit dance floor, the music from Tim's truck vibrating deep into the night.

"This might be one of the craziest weddings I've ever been to," Tate whispered in my ear.

It didn't matter to me that the flowers were fake or that Leslie almost fainted (she was perfectly fine after a sandwich she should have eaten in the first place). It didn't matter to me the power went out for the reception. It didn't matter our DJ ended up being an iPod plugged into Tim's truck. It didn't matter we had melted ice cream for dessert. It didn't matter because I knew I was Mrs. Jones, and I couldn't wait to live our life together.

"I don't know what you're talking about, Tate." I looked up at him while the stars sparkled in the sky above us even as clouds rolled in. "This is the best wedding I've ever been to."

His lips curved into a smile.

"I love you, Tabitha."

I leaned in to kiss him as the sky cracked and the rain began to pour.

"Always will."

Twenty

I WOKE UP THE next morning desperate for Tate.

The curve of his smile. The depth of his voice. The weight of his arms when they were wrapped around me.

God, I missed him.

Most days I missed him in a way that still left me at peace with my life now: the life I was beginning with Dylan—our future brimming just around the corner. Other days I was just wrecked—my heart shattered and my bones aching for one last hug from Tate.

This was one of those days.

I felt like I couldn't function. I needed to be alone and be sad.

I managed to get Toby to school and Charlie to daycare before calling Mindy to let her know I was going to be working from home today.

"What do you mean? You only live two hundred yards away. I need you at the restaurant. We open in three weeks!" I could hear the panic rise in Mindy's voice. She was always a ball of jitters and excitement but her nerves about the impending restaurant opening pinged louder over every syllable. I would have laughed if I wasn't so exhausted from the wave of grief that hit me that morning.

"I know, and I'm just not feeling well today, and I don't want to get anyone sick before the opening because we both know that would be a disaster," I lied.

She paused then cleared her throat. "Okay, you're right. But I swear, if I call you, you better answer or else!"

I let out a small but genuine laugh. Mindy was the least threatening person on this planet.

"I'm serious, Tabitha. I am about to have a heart attack."

"I can tell. Why don't you have a mimosa and take a walk—clear your mind, talk to Jesus."

She chuckled over the line. "I wish I could drink on the job."

"Isn't that the beauty of being in the restaurant business?" I smiled to myself.

She let out an audible breath over the phone. "Okay, fine. Feel better. I'll let you rest."

I hung up the line and nodded, satisfied with myself for talking my boss off the ledge, and I drove over to Moolack Beach.

I made my way down the steep, familiar slope to the dry, cold sand and sat on my usual rock overlooking the ocean. There was so much peace in this space. So much quiet—the waves muffled every other noise, even the ones existing in my own mind. I knew it was okay to miss Tate. It was okay to want him back. And it was still okay to love Dylan.

I knew a part of that must have been so hard for Dylan—Tate was constantly brought up in conversation. By myself, Toby, Lydia, Tim, even Caden and Eli. It was like he was this invisible person that still hovered over my life and Dylan never knew him. Nor would he ever get to. But he always listened and nodded and let us all reminisce about the first man I ever loved, realizing he was the second.

A part of me wanted to give him more credit, the other part of me understood this was simply a part of the deal—and he had to take it or leave it.

My phone rang and I looked down at it. It was Dylan. I ignored it. I wasn't done with the quiet yet. I looked back at the ocean, mesmerized by the crash of each wave and every ripple left in the sand. The ripples reminded me of what every wave of grief does to the soul. The water crashed down on the delicate and movable sand, pushing it, molding it, and leaving its mark before abandoning it completely, and then returning unexpectedly. It also reminded me how temporary the wave can be—even when it leaves a deep crevice in the sand, it will settle and flatten eventually.

I let the minutes pass until they turned into hours. I let myself feel the depth of my grief. I sat on the rock, stuck in my sadness, knowing the wave would pull away. And I held on to the promise that the ripple it left behind would smooth out.

Eventually.

"There you are. Mindy said you were sick, and I wanted to check on you."

I turned to the familiar and smooth voice behind me. It made me smile through my sadness.

"Mindy sending out search parties now?"

"Something like that." Dylan laughed and sat next to me, kissing the side of my forehead and wrapping an arm around me. "No, she called me and said you were sick, so I went to check on you on my lunchbreak and you weren't home. Since you didn't answer my call, I got a little worried."

I smiled. It was sweet he worried, even though it was unnecessary.

"So, you knew you'd find me here," I said plainly.

He nodded and shrugged. He knew this was the place I went when I needed to be quiet with my thoughts.

"So, you also knew I was probably okay." It wasn't a question, and I eyed him knowingly.

"You know I don't like seeing you sad." He brushed my windblown hair behind my ear and cradled my face like a broken picture frame.

"Then maybe you shouldn't have come." My words were harsher than I intended.

He jerked his head back slightly, like he forgot about this

side of me. The one that tried to be funny but came out rude instead. The stressed, exhausted, grieving widow with a sharp tongue.

"You okay?" he asked softly.

"I'm just sad." I smiled weakly and looked back at the ocean.

"Want to scream it out?" he asked.

"No," I answered quickly.

"Did I do something wrong?" I could tell he wanted to make things right. He had seen so many months of me healing, I know he wasn't expecting me to turn down a corner and get lost in an alley of sorrow.

"Did you kill my husband?" I ask tiredly, not even trying to hide my sarcastic tone.

He dipped his head between his shoulders and looked out at the ocean, his brow furrowed. I struck a nerve, I knew it. It was always written all over his face.

"I'm sorry," I said. "I just miss him today. I miss him a lot and I don't know why."

He was silent, rubbing my shoulder and pulling me closer. I could feel nervous energy pulse through his hands and his breathing sped up. I pressed my eyes closed. I didn't want to hear what he was thinking or how I hurt his feelings. Not right then. I needed this moment to stay mine. And Tate's.

"What can I do?" He wasn't asking to ignore the reality of my feelings or place a bandage on my wounds, but I was too exhausted to give him the opportunity to fix it.

"I don't need comfort right now, Dylan." I shook my head and picked at my fingers in my lap. "Right now, I just need to be alone and sad and miss my husband."

He recoiled slightly at the last word and tried to recover quickly. I felt guilty for a split second, but I didn't take it back or apologize. I didn't want to. I didn't feel like it was even necessary. Because the word still felt so true. Tate was still my husband in my mind—he always would be. I twisted my finger over my empty ring finger, feeling both the absence of the gold band and the absence of someone I would never hear say my name again.

"I get that, Tabitha. I'm not trying to minimize any of it. I just want to be here for you. And sometimes when I try to do that, you switch and bite my head off."

"I said I was sorry," I snapped back.

"Right," he said hesitantly. "But you know if you want to talk about Tate, I'll listen. I want to hear every part of your life—the good and the bad. I want to always be there for you but sometimes you make it hard when you treat me like an irritation plaguing your time with Tate." He shrugged. "I guess I just feel like an outsider. Like you'll never let me all the way in—like all of you isn't for me."

His honesty exhausted my senses.

"And you've been so transparent this whole time?" I stared at him a beat, before letting out a breath. "If you're inviting me in your life—and my boys—you're inviting Tate too. It feels pretty clear you don't actually want that."

"What do you mean? Of course, I want that. It's not about you being sad about Tate, it's about you pushing me away when it comes to him. Not all the time. But enough times it feels like Tate is always going to be standing between us."

I narrowed my eyes on him, not wanting to hear his side.

"But he isn't ever going away, Dylan. He was and is still an important part of my life. I'm going to talk about him. I'm going to cry about him. I'm going to miss him. And sometimes I'm going to need time alone when I'm feeling this way. He didn't leave me and choose somebody else. I *lost* him. He *died*. There's a difference."

My voice broke and tears slipped down my cheeks. I shuddered into Dylan's arms as he pulled me in, tucking my head under his chin.

"I get that. Or at least I'm trying to but I'm just trying to make sure that somewhere in the pieces he left, there's room for me. I can't compete with him." I looked up at him as he spoke. His brown eyes were sorrowful and uncertain. He couldn't help but be honest—I couldn't help but not want to hear it.

"No one asked you to." I pulled away completely. "But if that's how you see this then I think you've got me all wrong—maybe we never had it right."

"So, I have to find a way to be okay with you not letting me all the way in and to let your memory of Tate always stand between us?" His words were desperate and pleading against the crash of the waves in front of us.

"I guess." I didn't meet his eyes. I couldn't—I knew it'd make me cry again.

"And I can't say how hard that can be for me sometimes?"

I shrugged. "I can't force you to be okay with my life. It's complicated and confusing, I get that."

I could feel his eyes on me, drifting over my face, begging me to look at him but I wouldn't.

"I love you, Tabitha. More than I ever thought possible," he said finally, "but I don't know how to be the runner up in your life."

My head snapped toward Dylan and my mouth dropped open as I scoffed. I was shocked by his statement. I couldn't believe he was feeling this way. I couldn't believe he had the audacity to voice it. He never let on it was bothering him this much. He was always so supportive, but apparently he was keeping the struggle in his mind hidden from me.

"You're not the runner up, Dylan. It's not a competition. He's *dead*. And I'll admit most days I still want him here but not because I don't want *you* here." I gained my composure for a moment to keep from crying. My breath was shaky as it entered and left my lungs. "I want you just as bad. You are everything I prayed for after he died. I couldn't ask for a better person to step into our family. I know Tate would feel the same way."

"But you mention him in your decision-making process all the time, and when you're having a rough day without him you push me away. And it reminds me you're still in love with him. If he hadn't died, you'd still be with him. And I think a part of you still wants that and not me. I don't know…" he shook his head in defeat, "…but it makes me feel like I don't know where I fit in your life."

My chin quivered and I nodded. I knew what he was saying. I knew *exactly* what he was saying. I felt shocked by how well Dylan knew me. He knew what I was feeling. He knew what I was thinking. But knowing didn't make the reality less hard. And

I could tell he had been struggling with this reality much longer than I knew.

"You're right," I said finally. My words were somber. "If he were still alive, I would still be with him. I wouldn't have been left to pick up the pieces for my broken-hearted kid that just wants to see his dad one more time. Or explain to my other kid how amazing his dad he will never know was." I let out an exhausted and emotional sigh. "Of *course*, a part of me still wants that."

Guilt and regret washed over his face. "Tabitha, I'm sorry. I shouldn't have said that—I know you've been through a lot, I just—"

"No, I don't think you do know," I interjected, wiping tears off my cheeks with the back of my hand. My face had turned to stone. "After all this time, it would seem you still don't understand. If you invite me into your life, you're inviting Tate too. It's clear you don't want that."

He was silent and dipped his head between his shoulders.

"I'm sorry," he said and reached over and grabbed my hand. "I love you, Tabitha."

I swallowed. I loved him. But I felt the inherent need to protect myself.

"I think you should go."

His eyes met mine and his hand reached out and held my face. "No, please. Don't be angry with me."

"I need you to leave." It came out like a plea as my eyes welled with tears.

Something inside me snapped. The other shoe finally dropped, and it didn't seem to even fit in the first place. Maybe it never had. I closed my eyes hard, and two tears escaped down my cheeks. He wiped them away with his thumb still holding my face in his hands. For a moment, I was afraid he was going to kiss me. A part of me wanted him to. If he kissed me, I could forget I was angry. If he kissed me, I could pretend, if only for a moment, we hadn't had this argument.

"I'll go." He nodded finally. "If that's really what you want, I'll go." He kissed my forehead and I wondered if it was the last time I'd feel his lips on my skin. "I'll call you later," he said.

"Don't," I said sharply as I shook my head. "Please don't call me."

He looked like I kicked him in the stomach. "Tabitha, don't do this."

"We need some time apart, Dylan. I think we both know that. We were too much too soon," I said, not meeting his eyes as I stared out at the dark and angry ocean in front of me.

I could feel his eyes searching my face, begging me to say something else. To change my mind. To fall into his arms and say everything was going to be okay.

I refused to relent. I refused because I knew the best kinds of love aren't clouded, they're pure. And only space and time away from Dylan would give me the clarity I needed to know whether or not this was that kind of love.

Summer 2

I STARED AT TATE as he laid in the lounge chair sitting in the white sand, completely engrossed in a book. The sun made the ocean glisten and I realized I had never seen the Pacific Ocean that bright of a blue. It shone like a treasured jewel in the midst of the sea.

"Cabo was a good choice," I said, disrupting his reading.

He looked up at me and smiled. His skin was two shades darker from our week in Mexico to celebrate college graduation. I was always so jealous at how easily his skin turned a beautiful shade of light brown. Lydia and Tim were frolicking in the waves with margaritas in hand, and chips and fresh guacamole sat on the table between Tate and me.

"I really had to twist your arm to join us on this trip, didn't I?" He was being sarcastic.

While I did worry about the cost of the all-inclusive resort since we were so fresh out of college—not to mention a part of me felt too young to go on a couple's trip with Lydia and Tim— I knew Tate was right: life wasn't going to slow down after college, and we needed to commemorate our accomplishments.

Especially since Tate just passed his test for his real estate license.

Tate spent the previous year pulling me out of my practicality and I learned to love life a different way because of him. He was a lover of all things: people, the Earth, words written on pages, pictures on paintings, but most of all, me. We fell hard and fast for each other over the previous year, and I didn't regret a single moment.

"You can take me anywhere, Tate Jones." I winked at him, grabbing his book and tossing it in the sand before crawling on his chair to kiss him.

"How dare you disrespect Walt Whitman like that?" he teased me.

I laughed, playful and melodic, as he wrapped his hands around my waist and kissed me back.

"I have something special planned for us tonight. Just me and you," he said, pulling back and tucking my hair behind my ear.

"Should I be nervous?" I eyed him coyly—he was always the braver more adventurous one.

"No, you should be excited." His mouth curled into a smile, slow and seductive and it made my heartbeat speed up. "But first...shots all around," he said as the waiter showed up with four shots of tequila and a bowl of limes. Lydia and Tim walked unsteadily through the sand to our spot on the beach.

Tim took the tray and distributed each shot glass, complete with salt and limes.

"I think I'm going to smell like tequila for a week after we get home," Lydia quipped, and I laughed.

"Please. You and Tim drank more than this on St. Patrick's Day last spring," Tate teased, and Tim ran an embarrassed hand down his face.

"Alright, alright," Tim said, reeling his best friend in. "Being that it is our last full day in Cabo, I'd like to propose a toast." He playfully cleared his throat. "To trading in Tipsy Tuesdays for five o'clock shadows and college t-shirts for a suit and tie."

We laughed and clinked glasses before shooting back the pungent liquid and sucking on our limes. I shivered after taking my shot then looked at each of them with gratefulness. We were wild college friends that had just crossed the threshold into adulthood. Our summer was going to be filled with internships and interviews, early bedtimes and six o'clock alarms. A far contrast from our lives over the last four years.

This trip was the end of many things, but I also knew it was the beginning of so much more.

READY?" I ASKED when I emerged from the hotel bathroom in a strapless maxi dress that danced around my tanned legs with each movement.

Tate stood with his back leaned against the wall, a hand in his pocket and the other typing a text message on his phone when his eyes turned up toward me. He looked surprised for a brief moment. He slipped his phone back in his pocket and his face broke into a smile. He pulled me in for a deep kiss and butterflies hatched in my chest.

I wondered how long we had before our reservation.

When he told me to dress up, I was partly relieved we wouldn't be skydiving or doing anything crazy, but nerves still pinged at my fingertips. As he led me down the long hallway to the elevator, I fidgeted with the side of my dress and Tate reached for my hand.

"Why are you nervous?" He looked at me like he already knew.

My eyes turned up to his. I wasn't surprised he noticed I was nervous, but I was surprised I didn't have an answer.

"I don't know." I let out an embarrassed laugh and he kissed my forehead.

He laced his fingers in mine as we made our way out of the hotel to the warm night air and down a small wooden path that led to the beach. A white blanket was laid out on the sand with chocolate covered strawberries, champagne, and two glasses— no doubt set up by Lydia and Tim. I turned to Tate and smiled wide.

"Are you going to ask me to marry you?" I eyed him as the

sun set behind his broad shoulders.

"Tabitha!" Tate laughed and covered his face with his hand. "You're impossible to surprise."

I giggled into the night air. I couldn't believe I called him on the cliché laid out before me on a white sandy beach at sunset in Mexico. It really was beautiful, but it was also obvious. I found myself constantly teasing him for his sensitive, poetic side, even though I found it completely endearing.

"This is a pretty obvious surprise." I smiled wryly and grabbed his hands.

"Well, then no, I'm not going to ask you to marry me," he responded defiantly and pulled me in for a kiss.

"Really?" I couldn't help but smile.

"Really." He narrowed his eyes on me, brushing a wild strand of hair out of my eyes, a seductive smile pulling at his lips. "But I will drink champagne with you until the sun sinks into the Earth."

He was always such a romantic, and I knew he wanted to marry me. We had discussed it many times. I just didn't know when. We always said we wanted to wait until after graduation and after we were both employed. Now that both those boxes were checked, I felt like I was just waiting and waiting, and I had a really hard time keeping my mouth shut when I thought the moment had arrived. I also knew how perfect he wanted it to be, and I felt a pit of guilt sink in my stomach out of fear I had spoiled the whole thing.

"Fine," I said, sitting on the blanket and crossing my ankles while he poured champagne and handed me a glass.

"To new beginnings," he said, his eyes smiling at me as the bubbles in the glass popped above the rim. "And a lifetime of trying to surprise you."

I smiled and sipped my champagne before laying my head on his chest. "Did my big mouth ruin it?" Regret laced my words.

He let out a small laugh. "You didn't ruin anything."

"You sure?" I plastered a smile on my face and looked up at him. "I feel like I ruined it. I'll still say yes—I'll even act surprised."

He laughed and placed his hand on my cheek, turning my face toward his. "I'm going to marry you one day, Tabitha. But when I ask you, you won't see it coming."

AFTER A NIGHT of champagne and making love under the light of the stars, we marched our tanned and jubilant faces onto to the airplane back to Seattle.

The week of too much sun and tequila caused me to fall asleep mid-flight and I didn't wake until the plane jerked with turbulence. I blinked heavy and stretched my neck, tipping it side to side.

"For the happy couple," the flight attendant said placing two plastic cups of cheap champagne on the pull-out tray in front of Tate.

"Oh, we didn't order this," I said groggily, holding up the plastic cup to return it to her.

Then I saw it as it glimmered on my finger under the lights of the dimly lit airplane. My mouth dropped open, and the flight attendant flashed a knowing smile before walking away.

I looked at Tate, he was smiling proudly while love danced in his eyes. He loved me so much. He was always so sure about me. His intentions were always crystal clear and his love for me was pure.

"I told you, you'd be surprised." He encased my hand in his, adjusting the ring he placed on my left hand in my sleep with his fingers. "I want to love you forever, Tabitha. Will you marry me?"

Tears spilled onto my cheeks as I nodded and said, "Yes!"

I pressed my lips against his while Lydia and Tim silently cheered from across the aisle. I pulled back and looked at him quizzically.

"But you didn't get on one knee," I teased, and he let out a small laugh.

"Now that would be too much of a cliché for you now, wouldn't it?" He leaned in to kiss me again and my fingers shook with excitement and nerves.

The flight attendant got on the intercom and announced our engagement, to which the entire plane of two hundred strangers roared with a congratulatory cheer.

My cheeks flushed and I let out an embarrassed laugh through my tears.

"Nope. Still the cheesiest cliché." I shook my head. "But I expected nothing less from you."

Twenty-One

"OM, IS DYLAN coming over for dinner tonight?"
I looked up from the cucumber I was chopping on the kitchen counter.

I cleared my throat. "Uh, what makes you ask that?"

"Because it's Thursday and he always comes over for dinner." Toby shrugged standing on the other side of the peninsula. His expression was expectant, and I didn't want to tell him Dylan and I had a fight. I didn't want him to know we hadn't spoken in days. I didn't want anything to seem amiss.

"Oh, right. Well, Dylan can't make it tonight. He had to go visit his dad in the memory care facility he lives at." I slid the chopped cucumbers into my hand with the knife and dropped them into the salad bowl. I let out a sharp breath, feeling equal parts terrible I lied and equal parts sure that's where Dylan actually was tonight. If Dylan wasn't with us or his friends, he was usually with his dad.

Toby's mouth formed a circle and he nodded.

"Mom?" he asked.

"Yes, honey?"

"Do you think Dylan's dad will get better?"

I set the spoons I was using to toss the salad down gently on the edge of the bowl. I shook my head. "No. I don't think he will."

Toby searched the counter for words to say. "That must really suck."

I swallowed, timidly approaching the direction of this conversation.

"Like, his dad's alive but not who he used to be." He looked up from the quartz stone between us with sad eyes. "I'm glad that never happened to Dad."

I nodded. "Me too."

He chewed the side of his cheek as his eyes wandered the room before looking back at me. "It's hard seeing Dylan sad."

Air entered my lungs quickly, and my throat caught unable to find the right words to say. I cleared the hesitation from my throat.

"Does Dylan talk to you about his dad?" I asked curiously.

"Sometimes," Toby said with a shrug. "When I ask him questions. He's not always sad about it. But today he was."

I choked on my throat and disguised it with a cough. "He did? When did you see him?"

"At school. He was dropping off something for summer league soccer sign-ups. At least that's what he said. But he looked sad and when he hugged me, he hugged me for longer than he normally does. Kind of how Dad did when he was worried about my lump."

My eyes filled with tears, and I blinked hard and fast, willing them away. "He did?"

Toby looked at the countertop again, contemplating his interpretations of Dylan's emotions.

"Yeah, I guess it makes sense he wants to see his dad tonight and not us." He shrugged and walked away, and I felt the walls in my chest crumble.

I stared at my phone on the counter and held my thumb over Dylan's name. It had been days since we spoke, days since we saw each other. It was so unlike us. Regretful sorrow filled my chest, realizing there was an 'us' I had painstakingly tried to water down for months. I never stopped to wonder how it made Dylan feel every time I mislabeled us.

Regret coursed through my veins.

As my thumb hovered over our text thread, I impulsively pressed the keyboard when my phone rang simultaneously.

Justin.

It was an odd relief to hear from Tate's brother in that very moment.

"Hey!" I answered.

"Hey, Tabitha. How's it going?"

"Good," I lied. "I'm so glad you called."

"Really? Why's that?" he said with a soft chuckle.

I drew in a breath and paused. I didn't have the right answer. "I don't know. I just miss you, I guess. It's been a long six months since we've seen you."

"I know, I feel terrible." He cleared his throat. "Sarah and I were thinking maybe you and the boys could visit this summer. Stay at our place? We'll take care of the airfare."

"Oh, you don't have to pay." I waved off his suggestion through the phone. "But yes, please. I could really use some good Mexican food and San Diego beaches."

He laughed and it sounded so much like Tate, it made my stomach twist with longing.

"Things going okay in Newport?"

"Yeah. I'm working for a new, up and coming restaurant as the bookkeeper so that's exciting. Charlie is loving daycare and already knows all his letters. And Toby—my goodness—he is just growing like a weed and guess what. His voice started *squeaking* this week. Justin, I am not ready for it." I smiled as I updated my brother-in-law.

"Ah, Tate would have loved to be there to tease him, I'm sure." Justin laughed again and I returned it. My chest began to swell, and my hands shook as I dumped shrimp in the skillet warming on the stove.

I smiled out of the side of my mouth. "Yeah, he really would have."

"I've been missing him a lot lately. Since his birthday a few weeks ago."

The blood drained from my face. I felt the exact same and for some reason, struggled to articulate that to Dylan.

"Important dates are definitely hard," I agreed, as my chin shook.

"We um…" his voice trailed off. "Well, we found out Sarah is pregnant on his birthday."

Justin was waiting for me to congratulate him, but I opened my mouth and no words came out, leaving a deafening pause on the line.

"Tabitha, are you there? Look, I know it's a shock since we said we didn't want kids but—"

"I'm here." My voice cracked and I let myself cry. "I am so happy for you both. Oh, congratulations, Justin. This is huge. Your brother…" I shook my head, composing my words and my thoughts. "Your brother would have been so excited."

I heard Justin's voice break and he cleared it away. "Yeah, a Thanksgiving baby. Guess we'll have a whole new reason to be thankful." As he said the words, I could see him so vividly in his San Diego bungalow. Standing on the patio next to his artificial grass, nervously rubbing his fingers together, terrified of what was to come but knowing he had to be brave because that was what Tate would have wanted.

"Yes, we will," I agreed as I smiled into the saucepan, stirring the shrimp. "There are still always reasons to be thankful. God, I am so happy for you both. I cannot wait."

"Life's really changing quickly, isn't it?" As he said it, I could see his face. The same expression Tate would give but with an entirely different color palette.

"Too quickly." My throat caught and I cleared away the emotion. "How's Sarah feeling?

"Wait, wait, wait. I heard that, Tabitha. What's the matter?"

"Nothing." I froze, wondering what gave me away.

"You started crying…"

"I'm just happy for you guys. I cry when I'm happy."

"No, that was a different kind of cry—I heard it," Justin pressed.

I gave a small, exhausted laugh into the phone,

remembering how well Justin and I knew each other.

"What happened?"

I shrugged, defeated from trying to explain my emotions. "Life is just really hard sometimes. I miss your brother. I miss..." my voice trailed off as my confession skipped over my tongue.

Justin waited patiently for me to continue and when I didn't, he asked, "Did something happen with Dylan?"

I cleared my throat.

"I never told you we were together."

"I know but Toby did. What happened?" His voice was so calm and steady. It reminded me again of Tate, and I felt like crying even harder.

As I realized how much Toby had probably told his uncle, embarrassment wrapped around my throat as I contemplated how to explain the stupid fight Dylan and I had on the beach.

"It's just really hard to miss Tate and love someone new. That's all." I swallowed. "It blew up and now we're taking a break."

"Who asked for the break?"

"Me."

I could see him nodding in my mind.

"Tabitha, it's okay to move on. It's okay to let someone mess up as they try to figure out what it's like to be with someone who's grieving." He scoffed. "Hell, Sarah has trouble with it sometimes and we've been together for ten years. And my brother died, not my spouse."

His words penetrated my skin. I hated them even though I needed to hear them.

"What did Toby say about Dylan?"

"Oh, he loves him. He said he's really good at video games." He laughed then cleared his throat hesitantly. "He also said your happy around him and Charlie calls him Daddy."

Guilt rang in my ears as they lit on fire, but I stayed quiet.

"It's okay to move on, Tabitha," Justin practically whispered.

"I know. It's just...nothing is how Tate and I pictured it for our family."

"Well, someone once said to me, it's okay to let go of things in life. Create something else."

"Even if it was everything I wanted?" I smiled into the phone to keep from crying.

"Even if."

Twenty-Two

I T HAD BEEN two weeks since I saw Dylan. The longest period of time since I'd known him. He was everywhere since that first day on the dock. Three seasons and a lifetime ago. Now he was nowhere.

It felt good to take a break.

Kind of.

I felt like I could breathe easy, but I also felt like I was gasping for air. I wanted to hear his voice and lay in his arms. I wanted to watch him play guitar with Toby and hear Charlie call him Daddy. That alone made my stomach sink with regret. Dylan was so good to us. He was also good *for* us.

I needed to apologize. But I also didn't want to. I wanted to let the time tick by because I needed to be sure. I needed to clear my head and make sure pursuing a future with Dylan was what was best for my family and not a temporary fix that filled a lonely void.

As my fingers tapped mindlessly on my desktop calendar, I stared at the date highlighted for the restaurant opening, wondering if Dylan would be there.

"One week until the opening!" Mindy shrieked, as she frantically walked through my office door, startling me out of my thoughts. Trey followed closely behind, his brow sweating, and he wiped it with the back of his hand.

"Really? I wasn't aware," I teased her, focusing again on inputting numbers in a spreadsheet on the computer.

"Hey, can Mindy stay with you the next few days?" Trey asked and Mindy playfully slapped his arm. "Seriously. She's driving me insane. Do you see this sweat?" He pointed at his brow. "I have done nothing labor-intensive to deserve this sweat."

Mindy put her hands on her hips. "It is not my fault the linens did not get to the cleaners on-time, or that there was a miscommunication with the seafood supplier. Not to mention the gluten-free breadcrumbs were on *back order*." Her mouth fell open and her eyes bulged out of their sockets.

"Heaven forbid we don't have gluten-free crab cakes on opening night." Trey rolled his eyes.

I coughed out a laugh and shook it off just as quickly while clicking out of my tabs on the computer. "I mean, she's right, Trey, it's important for restaurants to be sensitive to folks with food allergies and sensitivities." I gave a weak smile.

"Spoken like a true pescatarian." His eyes narrowed on me playfully and Mindy finally laughed.

"Well, I have a lot to do. You good, Tabitha? Feeling ready?" she asked, the intensity in her voice taken down a notch.

"As ready as I'll ever be."

"Great. Because I'm really going to need another set of eyes for the night and quite possibly an extra pair of hands. Do you mind? I really want you to enjoy the night but if you could just help me make sure staff is where they need to be, and the chefs are following proper protocol? Or just if anything seems amiss?" Her eyebrows grazed the ceiling.

"Sure thing, Mindy." My voice was calm as I realized just how hands-on she expected me to be Opening Night.

"You are the best! Didn't I tell you she was the best, Trey?" She squeezed his arm and squealed as she tore out of the office.

Trey ran an exasperated hand down his face.

"I love her but she's…" he paused to let out a breath and find the right word.

"Passionate?" I suggested as I collected my phone and keys on the desk and turned off the monitor.

"Very passionate." Trey pointed at me thoughtfully and smirked. "Really, though. Thank you for everything. When Mindy talked me into opening a restaurant, I thought I was crazy. I wanted to back out several times. She's got a lot of ideas and…"

"Passion?" I suggested with a smile.

He laughed. "Yes, a lot of passion but there is a lot of energy that comes with it. And you've talked her off a ledge a few times through all this. We definitely needed your calm presence in the building."

"Well, pleasure's all mine." I nodded and reached for my purse before standing and heading for the office door.

"You know, Dylan's been asking about you." His words stopped me in my tracks, and I turned around to find him standing there with his hands out like he just dropped a hot potato on the floor. "I just tell him you're good—working hard." He shrugged and his fingers nervously rubbed against each other. I knew he didn't want to get involved. I also knew he cared about his friend. "Look, Tabitha, I've been friends with him since we were kids, and I don't want to get into the middle of whatever it is—"

"How is he?" I interrupted, not letting my emotions creep across my face.

Trey let out a long breath and half-smiled, half-cringed. "Like I said, I don't want to get in the middle of it, but it might be good to call him."

I chewed on the side of my cheek while my mind chewed on the words he just said.

"But is he okay?" I asked, clarifying.

"Describe 'okay.' I mean, he really loves you, Tabitha. He's pretty wrecked about whatever happened between the two of you."

I looked down and twisted my left ring finger, still permanently indented from the years it was cloaked in a gold band that told the world I belonged to someone. Tears stung my eyes as I realized I still did.

A tear fell when I realized it was two people.

I wiped it away quickly.

"I have to go." I flashed a brief smile and walked out of the restaurant into the lobby where Gabby smiled and waved me over. A stack of mail and a small box towered next to her.

"Tabitha! Wait. I have your mail for you. You got a package today, so they left everything with me. I hope that's fine," Gabby said.

"Oh," I said, blinking back my tears—a last stitch effort to compose myself. "Thank you."

I reached over the reception desk and took the mail from her, unintentionally avoiding her eyes.

"Are you alright, Tabitha? Your hands are shaking." Gabby studied me a moment. It was bizarre. We weren't what I'd consider friends, but she saw me so regularly, she could see something simmering below my surface.

I nodded and cleared my throat from any remnants of emotion. At least I tried to.

"I'm fine. Thanks. Too much coffee today." I smiled and darted out of the main building and over to our condo.

I stared at the small brown box in my hand. It was meticulously taped and addressed to me in wispy, cursive penmanship. It reminded me of a doctor's handwriting—ancient and distinguished but really sloppy. The return address read: Scott Storage.

I stopped halfway to the condo in the middle of the parking lot.

I had completely forgotten.

Tate had a storage unit he rented out to store all his memorabilia from his childhood and college. All the things he acquired before he was Tate and Tabitha. I wanted him to get rid of it—thought he was a bit of a hoarder. But he loved each photograph and trophy like it was the actual memory. We compromised and rented a storage unit. He never visited but just knowing his precious things from his childhood were safely locked away behind a rolling orange door made him happy.

SIXTEEN *Summers*

A couple months after he died, I received late payment notices for the unit. Tate had always paid for it, so I had completely forgotten about it. With his death fresh in my heart, I just couldn't bear to go through one more thing of his and decide what to get rid of and what to hold on to. His closet was hard enough. I had decided to pay for the unit through the following summer.

When I received a bill just before moving to Newport, I knew it wasn't a good time to open more wounds. I paid for another year and made the drive to the new life we were living.

Except this time, I asked for a key and planned to visit sometime this year to finally sort through my husband's life. I didn't realize it would take them over eight months to actually get one to me.

Still standing in the parking lot, I tore the box open and held a small, brass key with a blue plastic key chain in the palm of my hand. The key to the very last pieces of my husband on Earth. I was in a time-warp. It was precious, yet terrifying. I knew what I'd find in there—dirty cardboard boxes filled with yearbooks and letterman jackets, along with rusty trophies from t-ball through senior year of high school. I knew his graduation tassels and report cards sat in a Nike shoebox and his baby shoes were in a white filing box next to his favorite teddy bear and all his journals.

I also knew it was time to unpack the rest of his life.

I DROPPED THE kids at my parents' house the next morning after making the five-hour drive. Mindy was upset I took the day off without her approval, but I didn't care. She knew I'd be back in time for the opening.

This was more important anyway. There were always going to be pieces of me tethered to Tate. But if I was truly going to move on and heal from this loss, I had to examine every single piece that was left.

I slid open storage unit number 207 and stared at the remnants and artifacts left of my dead husband. Each item in the old and dusty storage unit held such precious value to Tate. I needed to see what—if anything—was left for me to hold on to.

The unit was just as I suspected: littered with dusty, brown cardboard boxes. They lined the back wall sporadically like he'd dumped them in a hurry. I spotted the Nike box right away. I smiled remembering telling Tate to not take too long when he went to drop off the truck load. The unit was far too big for the number of boxes inside—which was both a relief and a heartbreak. Why hadn't I just let him keep all this at the house? Why were ten boxes of memories too many for me to let him hold onto?

I sobbed into the dusk of night, feeling selfish for worrying about the clutter when I should have just loved him for everything he was.

I pressed my palms to my eyes and squeezed out the last of my tears before diving into the boxes. The contents were just as I suspected—yearbooks, letterman jackets, baby pictures, poetry books. I tucked the baby pictures in my 'keep' box, along with his baby shoes. I also made a box for his parents and his brother to go through. They probably wanted to keep the high school memories more than I did.

The boxes were easy to sort through and I was far less emotional than I thought they'd be. An odd sensation washed over me. It was like I could smell him in the room. The distinct smell of his cologne intermingled with his sweat and the tart sting of citrus. It danced all around me. A part of me felt like he was there with me—laughing when I read the inscriptions in his yearbooks and running my fingers over the pictures of his precious baby face. Looking at every baby picture made me realize just how much he looked not only like Toby but Charlie too. My tears spilled over his graduation tassels because I remembered standing next to him at college graduation as we turned to each other and shifted our tassels from right to left, laughing like the ridiculous couple in love we had been.

We had a lifetime of memories between us, even though it was cut short to just sixteen years.

I oddly felt Dylan in the room too. Or maybe he just

lingered in the back of my mind. He didn't feel out of place though—it just felt like he was waiting. Waiting for me to hold on to the pieces I needed to keep going and let go of the ones that needed to be released so I could move forward.

The last box was littered with journals from high school through college. I sat and read through each one. The single bulb glowing above me was the only light I had, but I had no intention of calling it a night until it was finished. There were entries that made me laugh, reminding me exactly what his voice sounded like. Others that didn't sound quite like Tate at all, but I savored every last page and decided to keep the journals for the boys.

When I got to the bottom of the box, I found a sealed white envelope that had yellowed with time, sitting on the bottom of the box. I picked it up and traced my fingers along the familiar handwriting that used to write in my birthday cards and leave love notes on the coffee maker.

It read:

The letter I never gave to Tabitha.

My heart lurched in my throat and pounded so loud I could hear it in my ears.

My hands shook as I gently opened the envelope—feeling both eager for and terrified of its contents. There weren't secrets between Tate and I, so I was curious to find the letter dated from the first summer we met. Tears stung my eyes as I read the last unknown words Tate would ever say to me.

Hello Tabitha,

If you're reading this, it probably means I had the guts to slip it on your desk in class without you looking. It probably also means you didn't show up tonight and now I am most likely sitting in my apartment eating ramen noodles and listening to Jimmy Hendrix, thinking about you and who you're with.

You're a dream, Tabitha Morgan. Has anyone ever said that to you? When I saw you sitting in the front row of class last semester, I knew—I knew you were someone special. Someone that deserved a beautiful life until her heart beat its last.

Is it weird to think that at 21?

Probably.

When I saw you today while you sat on the concrete bench on top of Terrell Library, I knew I had to talk to you. I hoped this time you'd actually talk to me too.

I told you about the poetry book I was reading, and you told me you only read textbooks. It made me laugh. You hardly gave me the time of day. But there was something in your eyes that felt promising. Like you are actually going to show up at the Lentil Festival tonight and have the best cobbler you've ever tasted.

Anyway, I hope I see you tonight. I hope I see you every night for the rest of your life. You make me believe in love at first sight.

You are beautiful and I'm sure I could love you forever.

And if forever isn't in the cards for us, I believe there will not be a single day that goes by that you are not wholly and relentlessly loved. I hope you give me the chance to be that one. If not, I hope the next guy knows how lucky he truly is.

I also hope this letter doesn't embarrass me years from now. But like I said, Tabitha Morgan, you are a dream.

Tate

Summer 1

WHAT ARE YOU reading?"
The voice came from behind me. It was deep and
smooth, laced with curiosity. I sat on the concrete
bench that rimmed the tower of windows on the roof
of Holland & Terrell Library in the center of campus.

"Excuse me?" I shielded my eyes from the August sun as I
tried to look at him.

"I've never seen someone so engrossed in a book before, so
I figured I should add it to my reading list." He closed his book
and walked over to where I was sitting.

My eyes followed him, and my brow furrowed as I held up
my financial accounting textbook so he could see the cover. I
watched his eyes read the black and white lettering and his lips
pulled into a grin before he looked at me.

I laughed.

"Bet you're going to put this at the top of your reading list
now, aren't you?" I gave him a wry smile.

"It's syllabus week." He scoffed. "Why are you studying?"

"Why are you?" I retorted and nodded at the book under his

arm.

"Maya Angelou." He held up the book and shrugged. "I like poetry."

I wanted to laugh but I just smiled and narrowed my eyes on him. "What kind?"

"All of it. Angelou, Whitman, Poe." He shrugged, listing the classics I didn't realize people read for fun.

"Edgar Allan Poe?" I questioned.

"Yeah. You've heard of him?"

I rolled my eyes. "In seventh grade required reading."

His serious face broke into another smile. "What'd you think?"

"A little dark, to be honest."

"Everybody's a little dark sometimes."

I paused in the conversation to study him. I couldn't imagine that this bright-eyed and playful spirit with joy spilling out of his smile in gym shorts reading poetry could ever be dark.

I cleared my throat.

"Let me guess. English major? Philosophy?" I cocked my head to the side. He definitely struck me as someone going to college simply for the experience only to be left with four years of debt and a throw away degree.

He laughed and sat next to me. "Business Administration."

"So, you're taking some sort of poetry elective then?" I had nothing against poetry, but he looked more like he walked out of football practice in his crimson basketball shorts and white t-shirt, not open mic poetry night at The Daily Grind on Main Street.

He chuckled softly and looked down at his feet and shrugged. "I like reading—I'll read anything. Poetry is my favorite when I'm in between books." He turned his eyes toward me. "What do you like to read?"

"Textbooks." I raised my eyebrows.

He laughed at me and I realized how much the sound of it made me smile. "You can't only read textbooks—you've got to read something that doesn't just change your mind but changes your heart."

I looked him over. *Who is this guy?*

"I don't have time for anything else."

"But it's syllabus week—you should have plenty of time for a good book." He squinted as he looked at me, his dark eyelashes dancing around his emerald eyes. He was far more charming than I expected. He was laid back but forward, and it intrigued me. Of all the college pickup lines I had heard the previous three years, chatting me up about poetry and books was quite original. Something also told me it was authentic.

"Well, I actually have an assignment due Thursday," I said smugly. "I guess we don't all have easy syllabus weeks."

I closed my textbook and slipped it in my bag, indicating I was getting ready to leave but really, I just needed to escape this conversation so I could finish my assignment and go out with Lydia that night like I promised.

"Professor Stevens?" He didn't move from his spot on the bench. He was laid back and squinting, his eyes earnestly watching me like he desperately wanted to get to know every small and boring detail of my life.

"How'd you know?"

"Because he's the only professor in the business school that assigns anything the first week. I had him for a finance class last semester."

I nodded slowly. The sincerity in his eyes as he looked at me made me blush, and I didn't know why.

"Right. Well, I better get going." I slung my bag over my shoulder.

"What are you doing tonight?" he asked, standing up quickly from the bench.

"I'm not telling you." I scoffed and smiled.

"Why not?"

"Because I don't know you—I don't even know your name."

"Tate Jones." He held out his hand and I shook it reluctantly.

"Okay." I stared at him and blinked heavy. "But you don't even know my name or anything about me that would make you care about what I'm up to tonight, Tate."

"That's not true." He shook his head, smiling boyishly.

I crossed my arms as disbelief washed over my face. "Really?"

"I know you bite your nails when you read. I know your eyes smile even when your face frowns. I know you'd rather study for an assignment due in two days than stroll Greek row on Tipsy Tuesday." I laughed through my nose and rolled my eyes. "I know you're a senior and majoring in accounting. I know you choose to sit in the front row in all your classes." My eyes widened in alarm, wondering how much this poetry buff named Tate knew about me. "Well, at least the classes I have with you." He smiled. "And you only raise your hand to answer a question if somebody already got it wrong." He twitched his fingers nervously. "And I know you're beautiful and I'd really like to spend some time with you tonight."

As the shock began to wear off, my face pulled into a smile. He was desperate enough that I found him adorable.

"I didn't realize I had a stalker," I said haughtily.

A playfully irresistible smile spread across his face. "The best ones never get caught."

I laughed genuinely at this. He seemed a little obsessed with me. It was strange but I also loved it.

I cleared my throat.

"Well, my name is Tabitha Morgan, but I have a feeling you already knew that."

His smile grew wider as his eyes lingered over my face. "Meet me at the Lentil Festival tonight?"

"I don't like lentils," I said defiantly while I studied his face.

"What about cobbler?"

"What about it?"

"Do you like it? There's a stand at the festival that has the best berry cobbler. They serve it warm so the vanilla ice cream melts over the top."

My mouth watered. That did sound good. And his eagerness to spend time with me—while completely unexpected—was also entirely flattering.

"I'll think about it."

His smile grew wider, his green eyes hopeful. "See you at seven? We can meet in front of The Daily Grind."

"We'll see," I said nonchalantly, knowing full-well I'd be there and walked away.

TATE WAS LEANING up against a brick wall outside of The Daily Grind when he saw me approaching him and his face lit up.

"You made it."

"I did," I said, looping my thumbs in the belt loops on my jean shorts and rocking back on my heels. "Even ditched my roommate to be here so that cobbler better knock my socks off."

Tate laughed and reached for my hand, pulling me into the crowd of locals and college kids. Music pulsed down the side street lined with vendors, selling everything from jewelry and candles to lentil hummus and lentil soup.

"I didn't realize there were so many ways to eat lentils." I eyed the sample cup of lentil chili Tate handed me curiously.

"Just try it." He smiled as he scooped the warm soup onto his spoon and fed it to me.

It was salty with a kick of cayenne, but still had the distinct dry texture of lentils making my tongue click against the roof of my mouth.

"You don't like it." He laughed, licking the remnants off the spoon.

"I like regular chili," I confirmed with an exaggerated and apologetic smile.

"I'll win you over eventually, Tabitha. Just wait until we find the cobbler stand." His fingers brushed against mine as he took the sample cup from me and finished it himself.

My heart sped up at his touch. He had a way about him that was as irresistible as it was comfortable. We walked through the street, vendor to vendor, laughing and chatting like we had known each other for years until we found the cobbler stand. He ordered two warm berry cobblers with vanilla ice cream and watched me earnestly as I took my first bite.

The tartness of the berries was perfectly balanced by the

sweetness of the ice cream and highlighted by the crunch of the baked crumble. I could taste the brown sugar and butter melting on my tongue.

"It's delicious," I said finally, and Tate gave me a triumphant nod as we meandered down the street.

"Tastes like summer feels, right?"

I laughed. "God, you really are a poetry nut, aren't you?"

He licked ice cream off his lip and shrugged. I could see him blush under the streetlight hovering over the bench we sat down at.

"Is that a bad thing?"

I turned sideways on the bench to face him as I scraped the last of my cobbler on a spoon.

"It's actually adorable," I said flirtatiously.

He stretched his arms over the bench as he leaned back. "I knew I'd win you over eventually, Tabitha."

I tried not to smile. I was surprised at how much I liked him so quickly, but even more so at how unexpected the whole evening was.

"Tell me something," he said, setting his cobbler down and giving me his full attention.

"About what?"

"You." A smirk pulled at one side of my mouth.

"Like what?"

"Anything." He shrugged. "Everything. What's your favorite color?"

"Yellow."

He raised his eyebrows and nodded.

"What's yours?"

"Blue."

"Typical," I teased. "When's your birthday?"

"March 13th. Yours?"

"January 27th."

"What's your favorite subject?"

"Math. Yours?"

"Same."

"I don't believe you."

"Why?" He chuckled softly.

"Because you read poetry." I raised an eyebrow.

"You're never going to let me live that down, are you?"

I searched for words for a moment. "I just have never dated a guy that's into poetry before. It's different. It's kind of nice."

"So, we're dating?" He looked at me expectantly, a smile creeping across his mouth.

I paused for a moment.

"Not yet." I bit my lip, trying not to smile. He nodded with a smile charming enough to make me want to kiss him.

"You'll get used to it."

"What? Dating you?" I asked.

He tipped his head back and laughed. "No, Tabitha, the poetry."

I bit my lip harder, completely unable to keep from smiling. I wondered how he was so sure and how I was so instantly charmed.

"Question," I said meeting his gaze. "Why me?"

"What do you mean?"

"I mean, you picked me out of sea of college girls. Hunted me down at the library and knew everything from my name to what I look like when I read. And then somehow convinced me to ditch my roommate and go to the Lentil Festival of all places with you. So, why me?"

"I don't think things like that have an answer, do you? I mean, when I first saw you last semester I, of course, thought you were beautiful and then as class went on, I realized you were smart. Confident. Poised." He shrugged. "I don't know. I just wanted to get to know you."

I narrowed my eyes on him, absorbing the compliments but feeling skeptical. "Then what took you so long to talk to me?"

He laughed. "You scare me a little bit."

My mouth fell open and then I laughed. "Why?"

"I don't know. I tried to say hi to you once at the start of class and you just smiled and opened your laptop and started typing. Completely ignored me."

"I did not."

"You did." He pressed his lips together and nodded in confirmation.

"Well, I'm sorry. I didn't mean to be rude to you." I cringed slightly.

"You weren't rude—just focused." His lips curved as his eyes lingered in the memory. "You drew me in. And I knew somehow, someway I'd have to find the opportunity to talk to you."

I nodded, taking in his answer to my complicated question.

"Well, I'm glad you finally did," I said as I brushed my fingers against his arm. "Even if I still don't understand your obsession with me."

"Obsession? Ouch!" He held a hand to his chest as he laughed through his words. "You really think I'm crazy, don't you?"

"Well, what else am I supposed to think about you?" I teased.

"Just that I really like you, I guess." Our fingers were woven together now, and he drew in a breath. "I don't know but there is something about you, Tabitha."

"What do you mean?" I narrowed my curious eyes on him.

"I don't know, just something that makes me believe you're going to be very happy with me."

"You seem so sure of yourself," I said as I let him hold my hand and pull me closer. I'd never known someone to be as romantic as he was. I still felt skeptical even though he seemed so genuine and kind. Everything I ever dreamed of on paper.

He shrugged. "Hey, maybe it won't be me. But whoever it is will be the luckiest guy in the world."

His words were seared into my heart in that moment, and the kiss that followed danced in my memories in all the years that followed.

Twenty-Three

I DIDN'T LEAVE a single piece of myself at Tate's storage unit. I didn't leave a single piece of him there either. I swept out the corners and signed the cancellation contract with the most conviction I'd had in months. I missed our life together, but I knew it no longer existed. I held on to the pieces I could, knowing I'd take so much with me. But knowing there was so much I had to let go.

I thought of all our beautiful years with each other—every summer a highlight reel of our marriage. Our summers together weren't just a glimpse of our time together but so much of why I became who I was and how I approached the world around me.

I grew up with Tate. He was my witness, but he was also my guide. And I knew I would miss him forever.

The letter was safely tucked in my nightstand and I knew I'd never let myself get rid of it. They were his last words to me. Even if they were written in the very beginning.

I had sixteen beautiful summers with Tate—a part of me knew our years together helped build me. He loved me completely, carried the hurts that were too heavy for me, made me laugh when I was far too serious, and forgave me when I was rude and rigid. I learned how to love because of Tate, but in his absence, I learned how to persevere.

A WEEK AFTER clearing out the storage unit, I perfected my lipstick and hair before kissing the boys and leaving them with a sitter before heading into the much-anticipated Opening Night of Carter's Catch. I was excited and honored to be a part of the team that made it possible. Mindy's vision flourished in the outdated space—it was now clad with rejuvenated hardwoods, subway tile with black grout, industrial lighting, cozy dining tables lit with candles, an incredible view of the Yaquina Bay bridge, and delicious food.

I met Mindy and Trey an hour before opening and we stood in a circle with Izzy and Gabriel, outlining the game plan. The crab cakes were ready to be doused and fried in hot oil, the salads needed minimal prep from Tina, Rob, and Maddie, and the delectable chowder was simmering on low heat waiting to be consumed by guests.

Mindy was dressed in a black jumpsuit and Trey in a black suit making them both look sophisticated and professional. Trey hid his nerves well, but Mindy's bounced through each eyelash.

"Everything will be fine," I said, calmly grabbing her hand making sure Trey was listening. "One, the restaurant looks phenomenal so consider half the battle won. And two, there is enough food in the kitchen to feed the entire city of Newport." I leaned in like I was telling a dirty secret. "And Izzy and Gabriel are damn good cooks."

Mindy laughed and squeezed Trey's arm.

"Relax. Enjoy the night. This is your creation, and it is exquisite." I smiled holding Mindy's hands tighter.

"Oh, my Lord, can we give her raise, Trey?"

He laughed. "Thank you for everything, Tabitha. You're truly a lifesaver."

The rest of the night played out like most opening nights

do. I found myself mingling throughout each table, making sure everyone was satisfied with each dish and every act of service. Each smile and congratulations dulled Mindy's anxiety to the point where I could visibly see the stress gone, and she was finally enjoying the night.

The restaurant itself was beautiful—mostly candlelit and updated in a rustic yet modern theme. I loved how much I loved it, but mostly I loved I was a part of it.

As the night went on, the opening night pressure floated away. The crowd dwindled to the point only Lydia and Tim remained, prompting a final toast for a successful opening.

We stood around the bar with the staff and popped one final bottle of champagne, pouring some in everyone's glass. The night was perfect. Except for one thing.

I wished Dylan came.

I knew how upset he was after our morning at the beach three weeks prior, but I had hoped he would just get over it and forgive me for every harsh word, and I'd forgive him for every doubt he was feeling. I hoped we would find a way to work it out, no matter how much I knew we had complications to wade through.

I didn't think when I told him not to call me, he actually wouldn't call me. He was only respecting my wishes and giving me the space I had asked for. I couldn't even truly be angry. But as time passed, I only wanted the space I asked for to be filled with him.

I knew I was allowed to miss him. I just wasn't anticipating it would be this much.

As I tossed the last of my champagne back, I rose to the sound of a voice I longed for during the last three weeks but never admitted to wanting to hear.

"Is it too late for a drink?" Dylan asked, standing at the top of the stairs.

I wanted to cry. But I didn't. Our eyes locked as the world disappeared. I cared only about Dylan and by the look on his face, I could tell he cared only about me.

"Yeah, sure." Trey smiled and asked the bartender to pour a round of whiskey shots.

My eyes didn't leave Dylan's. I hadn't looked at him in weeks and yet, it felt like a lifetime ago. I missed him terribly. I wanted every part of him. I didn't want to wait any longer.

His eyes were desperate and remorseful. I couldn't shake mine from his. They were like magnets drawing me to him.

"So, how about that drink?" Trey asked, breaking the trance between Dylan and me, as he handed us each a glass.

I shook my head out of a daze and smiled, taking the shot glass from Trey. We clinked glasses with our friends and Dylan congratulated them on the opening of their restaurant. Our friends attempted to steer the conversation into simple small talk and poured another round of whiskey, ignoring the elephant in the room, when Dylan gently grabbed my elbow.

"Can we talk outside for a bit?" he whispered in my ear.

"Please," I agreed, nodding subtly.

We made our way out to the dock behind the restaurant and lobby, our gaze landing on the light from the bridge glistening across the water of the bay. We stood there quietly, our arms draped over the railing of the dock, not speaking a single word to each other. The only sound between us was the gentle crash of the waves against the rocky bay shore and the sealions barking in the distance.

There were so many things we should have said—so many things we still needed to figure out. But I didn't care. Being in his presence made me realize how much I regretted the distance I wedged between us. I knew what a last kiss felt like. I never wanted one with Dylan. I turned to face him and wrapped my arms around his shoulders, as I pressed my lips against his without thinking.

He tasted like cinnamon and whiskey and apologies and I knew I was never going to let him go. His arms pulled me tighter, and I could feel his heart beating across my chest. I melted into his arms. I could barely breathe. I was completely lost in his kiss, though it felt exactly like coming home.

When he finally grabbed my arms and pulled me away gently, he smiled the same amused smile I'd grown to love, and it made my heart beat even faster.

I gazed into his eyes for a moment before breaking the

silence.

"I'm sorry," I said softly in the wind.

"I'm sorry, too."

His eyes stayed on mine and he smiled, but the silence lingered.

"The boys miss you," I said hesitantly.

He dipped his head down.

"A lot," I said and cleared the emotion clogging my vocal cords. "They love you, Dylan. Both of them."

My eyes pleaded with him.

He looked up at me finally.

"But do you love me?" he asked.

I stared into his deep, brown eyes studying everything I had come to know and everything I still needed to find out.

"I think you've known the answer to that for a while now."

"I think I've wanted to know the answer to that, Tabitha. But it ends up feeling like I'm reaching and never knowing for sure."

I nodded in understanding.

"I think that as complicated as my life has been, you've never drifted—it never scared you away. And I'm not exactly sure why but I think it has to do with you truly caring about me." I smiled at him as emotion swirled in my chest. "And me truly caring about you."

He nodded and looked up and down at the space between us.

"It has been so hard to not see the boys," he confessed.

My chin quivered and I steadied it with a smile.

"As much as I miss you. I miss them too, and I don't know how to respect your boundaries and still be a part of their life." He paused. "Of *your* life."

I took a step closer and clasped my hands on his coat and pulled him to me. "I am thankful you respected my boundaries even when there has been a part of me wishing you would have ignored them. But if you hadn't, I wouldn't have realized how much I miss you and how much I want you in our lives even if it's a mess."

"Do you mean that?" he asked, lacing his fingers through

my hair and gently taking hold of the back of my neck.

I nodded. "I should have apologized sooner. I shouldn't have said the things I did. But grieving is really hard, even when you start healing. And most of the time, healing feels really scary too." I drew in a shaky breath and he ran his thumb across my cheek as he listened quietly. "I'm always going to miss Tate and I'm always going to love him. But these last few weeks without you reminded me I'm always going to love you, too. And I don't want to give up on us, and I don't want you to feel like you come second to anybody…even my grief. So, I want you to know I'm ready for you. Because I know what losing someone forever feels like, and I never want to lose you…I *can't* lose you."

There were far too many uncertain things in life. Dylan was not one of them. He stared at me a moment, soaking in my confession and my apology.

"I love you, Dylan," I said, unapologetically and without fear.

"I love you too, Tabitha." He pressed his lips against mine and kissed me hard, his hands in my hair and mine tightly wrapped around his waist as the salty wind blew around us.

I pulled away gently to speak.

"I think we still have a lot to figure out, but I do love you, Dylan." I looked down and then back at his eyes. "I really am so sorry for how angry I was at the beach."

He absorbed my apology and nodded. "I might have deserved it."

I shook my head slightly with a small smile. "I don't think you deserved it. I think we are still just learning so many things about each other and—"

He shook his head and cut me off. "Let's not make excuses. Let's just let it be. We love each other and we had a fight. When two people love each other, they fight." His perfect lips spread into a smile before he leaned down and kissed me again.

"Can we just start over?" I asked.

He shook his head. "No," he said as he dragged his thumb from my cheek down to my chin. "I don't want to start over. I don't want to forget a single piece of you. Every memory. Every kiss. Every late night laughing on your couch. You are my favorite person in the entire world and I don't want to give any part of us up."

I nodded and smiled as tears kissed my eyes.

I pulled him close, not wanting to break away. His hands ran along my spine and tickled the back of my neck. My body was neatly pressed against his, a solid heartbeat drumming between us.

He looked down at me intently.

"You are very unexpected, Tabitha Jones."

I smiled and savored the same words he said to me on the night of our first kiss.

I ran my finger down his cheek and along his jaw. "So are you."

He stared deeply into my eyes in a way I couldn't escape from. There was an unexpected truth and belonging I wanted from him and knew I was destined for.

"I love you, Tabitha," he said like he couldn't repeat it enough. "I've been waiting for what we have for years even if I didn't realize it. And I'm ready to be all in. Just say when."

His lips curved into a smile that wrecked my heart before I leaned in and kissed his lips. I pulled back to stare into the eyes that loved me in ways I was always promised to be loved.

It wasn't the story I planned, but I knew he was going to be a part of the life Tate would want me to live without him. Not everything happened to me for a clear and explicable reason. But whatever did happen fell like a domino, knocking the rest of my life back into place.

Sometimes it looked chaotic.

Sometimes it looked like crashing.

Sometimes it looked like falling.

But falling isn't always a bad thing.

I molded my body into his arms, releasing every fear and doubt.

"When."

Five Years Later

Dear Tate,

I *miss you.*

I'll never stop missing you. I've come to realize that more and more after every passing year.

What I wouldn't give to have you back in our lives. To hold your hand one last time. To hear the sound of your laugh echo in the kitchen. To hear you sing off-key in a crowded room. To watch you play catch with Charlie—he's the most adorable seven-year-old now. And Toby looks more and more like you, especially now that he's just as tall. Even his voice sounds just like yours. It wrecks me sometimes but I'm mostly thankful for the reminder. He's turning into such a great young man, which makes me feel grateful but also incredibly sad you aren't here to witness it.

I'm married now.

His name is Dylan, and he is wonderful, and he loves us so well. We eloped on the beach three years ago and we have a two-year-old daughter named Grace. She was a surprise, of course. She has blonde curls and her dad's eyes. Your boys are so sweet and protective of their sister. You'd be very proud.

I wish you could meet Dylan. I know you'd like him. Your brother and your parents do. It was a strange blend at first but somehow, we found our footing. I know you'd love the way he loves me but more than that, I know you'd love how much he loves your boys. Charlie still calls him Dad and he has become Toby's best friend. He dances with my daughter in the kitchen and makes us berry cobbler every summer because he doesn't want us to forget you. It was a painful memory, and he helped us make it beautiful again.

He didn't replace you. He couldn't have. And he didn't love us back together either. But he loved us as we glued our broken pieces back together, and created a beautiful life again.

Since you've been gone, I have learned where there is tragedy, there is also hope. Where there is brokenness, there is also healing. And the pain we feel is just a reminder that there is still more life in us to live.

I love you forever, Tate.
Always will.

Tabitha

I signed the letter and folded it delicately before placing it in my pocket and hopping off the rock at Moolack Beach. I let out a deep breath and stared out at the waves as they glided across the sand, smoothing out the ripples and tickling the toes of my three children and the second love of my life.

Dylan looked up and smiled at me as he swung Grace in a circle, while Toby tossed a football to Charlie. Their laughter echoed across the sand and their faces were bright and full of wonder and life.

"We're okay, Tate," I whispered into the wind. "We'll miss you forever. But we're okay."

Tate's Berry Cobbler

Ingredients:

5-6 cups of assorted berries
2 Tbsp granulated sugar
½ Tbsp orange zest
Juice of half a lemon (about 1 Tbsp)
1 tsp baking powder
1 tsp salt
2 cups all-purpose flour
1 cup unsalted butter, softened
1 ½ cups brown sugar
2 tsp vanilla extract

Directions:

Preheat oven to 375 degrees.

1. In a large mixing bowl, coat the assorted berries with granulated sugar.
2. Add the orange zest and lemon juice to the berries, mixing gently, then add to a 9x13 pan.
3. In a small mixing bowl combine the baking powder, salt, and flour, then set aside.
4. In a medium mixing bowl combine the softened butter, brown sugar, and vanilla extract.
5. Add the flour mixture to the brown sugar mixture—the consistency will be crumbly.
6. Pour the crumbles on top of the berry mixture in the pan.
7. Bake at 375 degrees for 40 minutes or until the topping is golden brown. Serve with vanilla ice cream.

Enjoy the taste of summer!

SIXTEEN *Summers*

312

Acknowledgements

First, I must thank you, my dear and wonderful husband, for giving me the idea for this book even though we drank far too much wine that night and you don't remember. You'll always be my favorite love affair. Thank you for believing in me and giving me all the content—you are all the romance I need.

To my incredible, amazing, funny kids—Isaiah, Maci, Emmie—one day you'll be old enough to read these stories. And until then I will always be grateful for all the grace you've shown me during my writing binges. The delivered pizza and "snack" dinners always sounded like a treat to you three, but little did you know it was my desperate attempt to keep you fed while I kept putting words on the pages. You three are my sweet little witnesses. My breaths of fresh air. My hope at the end of a tired day. You keep me going even when I've run out of patience. I love being your Mama.

Big thank you to my mom, Riley, Kelsey, Trish, and Amy for always reading my first drafts. You get the very worst versions of my stories but still ask for them on the next go-round. I love you, girls. Thank you for being a part of my tribe.

To my editor, Annie Hilen, sorry I suck at commas. Thank you for always being so honest and thorough. Your help and input are always needed. Don't ever leave me.

Thank you to my amazing friends with crazy beautiful writing skills, Katie and Trish, for helping me write the synopsis on the back of this book. I hate doing it. You're good at it. I love you for dealing with all two-hundred-seventy-eight texts I sent you about it in succession. Friends forever—no backing out now.

And last, but certainly not least, to my readers: I don't know how you found me or this book, but I'm glad you're here. Thank you for giving my stories a shot. I hope you love them. And I hope you stick with me for the long haul. Because this is only the beginning.

XO,

Caitlin

About the Author

Caitlin Moss is also the author of THE CRACKS BETWEEN US. She lives in the Pacific Northwest with her husband, three children, and goldendoodle. She loves connecting with her readers on social media.

For more visit caitlinmossauthor.com.

Made in the USA
Columbia, SC
26 September 2021